CHANGES
TRILOGY

PHIL FORD

authorHOUSE®

AuthorHouse™
1663 Liberty Drive
Bloomington, IN 47403
www.authorhouse.com
Phone: 1-800-839-8640

Published by AuthorHouse 7/1/2014

ISBN: 978-1-4969-1988-5 (sc)
ISBN: 978-1-4969-1987-8 (e)

Library of Congress Control Number: 2014911279

CONTENTS

BOOK ONE

CHANGES

CHAPTER 1

That's when Alex saw them.

They were clearly visible through the partially open, finger-like ceiling that made Trinity Caves a nonthreatening cave dive. Eight adult hammerhead sharks were circling above.

The dive had just begun; all of the divers still had nearly full air tanks. They were quite safe for the time being, since each of the hammerheads in view was much too large to enter the confines of the cave from either end or through the slight openings of the ceiling.

At the moment Alex had come to this conclusion, a dive slate had been passed down the line from Angela who, at the head of the line, was also aware of the unwanted guests. Alex saw from the message on the slate that she had decided the same thing. The slate read, "Alex, at least eight—let's wait them out and then abort the dive."

Each person in the line of anxious divers read the slate, and each, in turn, calmly followed the instructions. Alex returned the slate to Angela with his own message: "I agree. Each diver, record your current psi. Angela, review and return slate in ten minutes."

It had been Alex's desire to open their shop with a specialty reputation as the one shop on Grand Cayman noted for catering to the experienced diver. Locations, equipment, training, and packages were designed around the diver with a long history in diving who wanted to team up with other divers of like backgrounds. They would still offer one-day boat dives for the less-experienced diver, but they would keep the weeklong charters reserved for those with fifty dives or more behind them.

It seemed to be a winning idea. Within thirty days of the Ore Verde Dive Company's grand opening party, they were booked solid two months in advance. It was a time of great excitement, with new experiences and new successes. The dive tours kept them busy throughout the week. On a few of the dives, those with large groups of fairly new divers, Alex; his wife, Angela; and their teenage son, Tony, would team together. Such was the case with today's dive group.

Today was starting out as one of the better days. The sun was swelling in the midmorning sky, being gently released by the horizon. The ocean caressed the sides of the boat with a welcoming rhythm, and the day's group of divers were eager to see the sights of this, their first deep wall dive.

Angela, a master scuba diver herself, stood on the main deck of the dive boat and addressed the group. "This dive is planned for a gradual descent down the buoy line to a depth of about seventy feet, followed by an easygoing cruise to a short set of caves known as Trinity Caves. These caves have a partially open ceiling that starts at a depth of about ninety feet and descends to about a hundred and twenty. When we come out of the caves, we will be at a depth of a hundred and twenty feet. The Cayman Trench then juts beneath you to a depth of twenty-six thousand feet. A spectacularly beautiful reef wall resides just outside the cave's exit, waiting there to thrill us all.

"After we exit the cave, the group should slowly begin to ascend along the wall to about sixty feet, taking about eight to ten minutes. Based on your remaining air supply, some of you can investigate the neighborhood just beneath the boat until your air gauge has reached 800 psi. At that time, you should slowly ascend to a depth of twelve feet for your three-minute decompression safety stop. Following the stop, go to the ladder at the rear of the boat to end the dive and climb from the water."

With this profile in mind, and considering that there were ten divers on the dive, each with less than thirty dives experienced, Angela, Tony, and Alex decided to team up to guide this one. Having done this many times in the past, they agreed that Angela would lead the dive, with

Tony staying in the middle of the pack, and Alex taking up the rear, keeping the group together and preventing stragglers.

"Let's do it." Tony was the first into the water, giant-stepping off the rear of the boat. With his BC—or buoyancy compensator—vest partially inflated, he stayed at the surface and waited for the rest of the group, to keep them together before their descent. When all the divers were in the water, Angela and Tony slowly made their way down the anchor line at the front of the boat.

Alex then instructed Mark, the boat captain of the *Strongbow*, "Keep a sharp eye out for the first divers to surface. It's happened before—one or two divers won't monitor their air supply and they're gonna need to get out of the water quickly."

"Right, boss," replied Mark.

Alex then giant-stepped off the back of the *Strongbow* and begin to follow his group of wet-suited visitors to what many have called "inner space."

At seventy feet precisely, the little group had gathered in a forward-moving line, with Angela in the lead, going toward the entrance of Trinity Caves. The three linked caves stretched out a short distance of nearly forty feet, with a tame descent of just a few degrees for the first two caves and a forty-five degree drop at the entrance to the third. Angela entered the caves, with the first of the divers following close behind.

As Alex came to the mouth of the first cave, he noticed the line of divers had slowed considerably. By the time he reached the midpoint of the first cave, the line had stopped. Often the sights will cause a group of divers to bunch up, so Alex was not initially concerned. But he hadn't expected what he was seeing now.

Alex watched the eight hammers, and it seemed to him they were much too patient. He thought, "If we stay in the caves and don't cause any disturbance, they should lose interest and leave." Alex was quite wrong.

Ten minutes later, the slate reappeared, with each diver's current psi. This was not good. The fear the divers were experiencing was causing them to burn more air. A couple of the divers' numbers were just below

1200 psi. Each diver had started with 3000 psi. Alex had started with 5000 psi. He wore a specially designed two-tank system, but each of the rest was equipped with a one-tank system.

As the minutes passed, concern started to affect Alex—not only for this group of divers but for his wife and son. His anxiety mounted. Alex passed the slate back through the line with a brief message, "How much air? Pass this back immediately."

The slate went through the group and back in only a couple of minutes. Half of the group was at 800 psi. The rest were very close. Both Angela and Tony had nearly 1500 psi. With their diving experience, they worked hard to control their breathing. Alex's air was now at 3800 psi, but he could not effectively buddy-breathe with a group this size, especially in these close quarters. Alex felt he had no choice. He had to do something now.

Slowly, carefully, Alex made his way beneath the line of divers on the underside of the cave pathway. When he arrived at the front, guarded by Angela, Alex saw two more of the fierce creatures. Ten in all.

Alex slated a message to Angela; she shook her head, *no.*

Alex added one brief word to the message, "Tony."

Angela looked directly into Alex's eyes. Her cool blues now took on a hint of sharp steel, further colored with frozen sadness. She slowly nodded yes and placed her hand gently on the side of Alex's face. They each removed their regulators and gently kissed.

Angela showed Alex's message on the slate to each of the divers as she made her way to the more shallow entrance of the caves. The message? It was simple: "I'll get their attention, and you take this group to the boat as fast as you can!"

How does one get the attention of a group of hammerheads? Alex was only aware of one way: blood, and plenty of it. His plan was quite to the point. He would take his dive knife and cut a gash in the meaty portion of his left forearm, causing his blood to flow freely into the water. He would then leave through the exit of the lower cave, the third, at a depth of 120 feet, to draw the attention of the primordial cold-blooded bastards; he would take them as deep as he could. This would allow the remaining divers—Angela, Tony, and the others—to escape from the shallow end of the caves. It would be quite clear to Angela when the moment had arrived for her to lead the group to the surface. The hammerheads' disappearance from her view toward the deeper water would be her signal.

She'd had time to get to the shallow end of the line. Now, it was Alex's turn.

With great trepidation, he took out his knife and made a painful slash against the underside of his left forearm. At that moment, he left the partial confines of the lower cave and began to wave his arm through the water—getting a much quicker response than he'd expected from all ten of the hammers.

Alex dove for the deeper water as quickly as he could. His ear canals responded immediately with sharp needles of pain. He equalized as best he could; his depth was now at 185 feet, with the sharks nipping at his heels. Alex had to keep them busy for at least ten minutes to allow the group to get to safety.

What this really meant was that Alex had to stay alive for at least ten minutes.

At 205 feet, Alex saw a deep indentation in the side of the wall. He moved his back against the wall and held his knife away from his body, out in front of him. There they were. The plan had worked. So far Alex had been able to hold the attention of all ten, with only slight encounters with their slashing teeth. Several cuts made by the aggressive sharks quickly appeared on his right arm from defensively holding the knife. Alex worked hard and kept these enforcers of death at bay for more than fifteen minutes. Now he resigned himself to the fact that he was facing the final moments of his plan and of his life.

His air supply was at 500 psi. The deeper water and the increased activity Alex exerted were causing him to burn up his air rapidly. His physical condition was not good. The self-inflicted cut on his arm was taking its toll. Alex became light-headed and felt as if he were passing out.

So, this was to be it. Angela and Tony were safe, he thought, but he would not be able to hold them again. Alex was surprised this sadness was the strongest emotion he felt—not fear of death or of his persistent would-be devourers. He thought only of Angela and Tony.

Alex and Angela McPherson had been married for sixteen years, and it had proven to be much more successful than anyone had expected. At the time they planned to marry, marriages had been falling by the wayside from divorce; but they had discussed it and determined it was a chance worth taking. They were quite analytical at that time—Angela still was—and having just completed their college final exams, they had been ready for a new adventure. As everyone knows, marriage is a true adventure.

They had first met when Alex had arrived to the Indiana University campus. He'd been scouted to start his freshman year on the school's football team and was there on a full scholarship. Angela was working in the administration office as part of her work/study program to help pay for her education. Having just completed her undergraduate program with a double major in electrical and mechanical engineering, she was poised to enter the graduate program in engineering.

She'd sat at the registration desk with a helpful, but somewhat distracted, look on her face. It was not one of her wildest dreams to play counselor to a rowdy group of jocks. General studies and easy courses were the primary choice of the guys in this room. The jocks were there for one purpose—to play the sport that brought them there and waste as little time as possible on classes they felt would be of no consequence to their future. Alex was more than a surprise to her—Alex became a puzzle, and puzzles, he found out later, were the most exciting thing Angela could ever contemplate.

He loved football and still held the strongest regard for the sport; in fact, he had played extremely hard for all of his junior and senior high school years with only one goal in mind—a college scholarship. Without a full scholarship, Alex doubted his financial ability to enter any college. Alex's home life as he grew up had been filled with much love and admiration among his family members, but they had been humble in their financial abilities.

Alex stood tall directly in front of Angela's table, but words failed him. He looked into the face of this girl patiently waiting for him to tell her his name, so she could process what she called the "basket-weaving schedule." At that moment, Alex could swear he saw the moon in her deep blue eyes.

He thought of the words of an old song and felt his lips move, "Raven hair and ruby lips."

"Excuse me?" Angela replied.

"Uh, I was just, uh ..." Alex stammered.

"Let me have your name. I believe I have the perfect schedule already planned for you," she stated in a matter-of-fact, assuming tone.

"My name ...?" he stammered on. "Name ... my name is Alexander McPherson, Alex."

"Well, Alexander McPherson, if you will just sign here, you may call it a day." Angela said this as she placed the paper in front of him and held out a pen.

Trying to accommodate any request this beautiful woman would make of him, Alex took the pen and aimed it for the dotted line she so delicately indicated with her long, slender finger. Then he noticed something other than the contour of her neck.

"There must be some mistake," he said, sounding quite confused.

"After meeting you and sharing this enriching moment of conversation, I doubt there is any mistake. This schedule will allow you to play whatever sport you are here for and not spend any unwanted time reading or writing."

That statement shook Alex back to reality. "Reading or writing?"

Angela apologized then. "I'm sorry. I did not mean to sound demeaning. It's been a long day."

"There's no need for you to apologize to me, but if I intend to graduate with a degree in marine biology," he said as he looked at the page she was offering him, "I might need more than Intro to Preliminary Business Math, don't you think?"

"Excuse me—Marine Biology? What did you say your name was?"

Alex repeated his name, and Angela quickly went through the card file in front of her, searching through the stack of 4 x 6 information cards. She'd then begun to speak with a more enlightened tone. "Alexander McPherson. You are here for a Marine Bio degree."

Alex had been glad when she'd confirmed this for him. For a moment he had begun to think the instant failure in all brain activity when he'd first seen this lovely lady was about to become a permanent dilemma.

"You're here not only on a football scholarship but a partial assistance grant from the Bellamy Foundation of Educational Achievers."

"You know, you seem to have a lot of information about me on that card; don't you think it only fair you tell me your name? At least then I'd have some information about you."

From the moment Angela told him her name, Alex was determined to convince her that life with him would be a good gamble. They dated through the next four years, and following graduation they were married.

By the end of the next year, Angela was ready to deliver their son, Anthony. They rarely called him Anthony—it was always Tony—but by naming him Anthony, they joined in on the name game of the year by having all of their names begin with the same letter of the alphabet.

Tony turned out to be a fantastic addition to their original gamble. But from time to time as he grew toward his current age of fifteen, Alex and Angela had felt the gamble was close to a losing hand. Angela being quite analytical and Alex being somewhat impatient, sometimes the childhood antics had a way of taking their toll. Alex thought the turning point had come when Tony was twelve. Alex and Angela were concerned about Tony's apparent lack of understanding and respect for the surrounding world—minor issues for an individual living in a world populated to the brim. Alex's work took him out of town often, and Angela's kept her busy into the evening on many occasions. They felt they had to work to provide for the three of them, but they also had to make a special effort to instill a sense of responsibility within their growing son's heart and mind. They were spending more time correcting him than enlightening him. Their original goal for parenting had been to enlighten their child about the things they had already learned, to give him a running start on life.

Alex found a program that began just before Tony's thirteenth birthday, which claimed great success in just this type of situation.

Tony attended a summer program at a respected military school near their home. When their boy returned at the end of the summer, he was the same son they had sent off just three months prior, but with a difference—they saw in him the beginning of consciousness. For the two years following that quite-important summer, Tony had energetically sought knowledge and understanding of the world around him in the same way as his mother had.

Struggling to stay conscious, jabbing at the aggressive hammers, Alex remembered one side of a conversation he'd overheard Angela having with a friend of hers a couple of years back. This was a friend she knew from high school, whom Alex had not met.

"Yes, I'm married and have a child—a son, Tony. I wish you could meet Alex. You'd like him. He earned a degree in marine biology from IU, but there's not much call for that type of career in Indiana. What's he like? Well, he's six one, the most stoic hazel eyes, with salt-and-pepper hair where a solid deep brown used to be. He played college ball, has a black belt in jiu-jitsu from before we met, and still keeps in great shape. Yeah, great! Alex has the kind of build that is obviously strong, but not muscle bound. You know, the kind of body you like to cuddle up next to on a cozy night and also feel safe standing behind in a skirmish. We were kidding around the other day while he was exercising, and I climbed onto his back while he was doing his second set of push-ups, expecting to hold him to the floor. He kept doing the push-ups with me on his back. Man, did that do things to me! I lay on his back while he continued to do those power push-ups and started kissing him on the back of the neck. I got his attention—yeah, great!"

With these memories fresh in his mind and his back flattened against the sea wall, Alex began to pass out. At the same time, he thought he began to hallucinate. He felt something grab his ankle and began pulling him quickly into the depths of the trench. His dive-computer depth gauge showed a reading of 285 feet when Alex McPherson died—or, at least, he thought he died.

CHAPTER 2

"Oh, man."

Alex awoke feeling more pain throughout his body than he could ever remember having. But when he realized it was pain, he began laughing, because he knew he was alive. He wasn't sure how, and that didn't matter to him. What mattered was that he was alive.

Becoming clearer headed, he began to look around him, expecting to see a hospital room, with nurses and a collection of beeping and bleeping equipment. He was very wrong—there was not a nurse in sight. More to the point, there was not a single person in sight. He found he was lying on a wet rock ledge at the edge of a still pool of clear salt water. His equipment was placed neatly along the wall of this damp cavern. The air tanks caught his attention immediately. They were crushed, imploded, as if collapsed from excess pressure. But if that were true, why wasn't he crushed as well?

Next to his equipment was something else; a small piece of equipment that was not his. Alex stood slowly and stumbled over to the wall where his gear was lying. He sat next to the jumbled collection. The strange piece of equipment was a small box that reminded him of a small, opened laptop computer, right down to the six-inch by ten-inch view screen located in the center of the fold-up top. He touched it, and the screen illuminated.

As it did, these words appeared: "You are awake; good. I am sure you are full of questions. We have left this device for your edification.

All you need do is ask questions, and the information stored in this device will answer."

Was he dead, or not? Alex began to think he could still be hallucinating and possibly about to die. "Am I dead?" he asked the box.

"Absolutely not! We would not have allowed that to occur."

"Well, if I'm not dead, then how is it that I am alive?" He remembered clearly his recent hopeless situation.

"We will describe the circumstances surrounding your being brought here. That most certainly will answer many of your questions in short order. Does this meet with your approval?"

"Yes, I'd like that," replied Alex; he had a screwed-up grin on his face.

"To start with, we were aware of you and your group entering the three caves. We were also aware of the menacing team of predators moving decidedly in your group's direction. We continued to watch apprehensively. We saw your group staying in the caves and the predators not leaving the area. We were about to launch a diversion of the predator's favorite foods. Then we saw you make what was the most extreme sacrifice we have witnessed from your species."

"From my *species*?"

"Yes. We … are a different species. May I continue?"

"Go on," responded Alex, feeling a bit reproached.

"We were sure that what you had done surely saved the lives of your fellow visitors and most certainly erased your hope of escaping the predators, even if we attempted our planned diversion. Overcoming our fear of being discovered, we quickly arranged for one of the deep-sea creatures—I believe your species has named this creature a giant squid—to retrieve you from your soon-to-be-lost battle. The squid wrapped around your legs and pulled you quickly into the depths. As we had hoped, the predators soon became weary of their chase as the speed and depth of your savior increased."

"Just how deep was I taken?"

"To elude the predators, you were taken to a depth you would call six hundred feet. Obviously, your equipment was crushed, and logically, your body was also badly damaged. You were brought to our research area, where we began to repair your physical damage as quickly as possible. From the point you were first contacted by our mutual friend, the squid, to the moment you were in our research area was only a span of two of your minutes. Still, your body received a great deal of internal damage. What you did was selfless; a sacrifice of your life for the lives of others. We were determined to save your life. What we had to do to save your life will change your life forever."

"I don't understand." Alex stood and began to slowly walk around the cave, carrying the communicator with him. As he walked, Alex felt the movement of his body providing different sensations than he was used to. "Why does my body feel different? Is this a result of your saving my life? I suppose I should not complain; after all, I am alive."

"Quite true. The physical differences you are experiencing are a result of the changes we have made to your body. Appearance has not changed; skin tone is slightly darker, more like the sun tan—isn't that what your people call the temporary coloration difference as a result of extended periods of exposure to sunlight? Other than that, there is no visible difference. The difference rests in your cellular structure. The pressure of the depths you were brought into crushed many of your cells. The repair we instituted caused alterations in your genetic mapping to not only replace those cells that were destroyed but also to create additional cells. By this altered genetic mapping, fat cells, inert cells, unused space between cells, and many other unessential gaps between the most productive cells in your original physiological genetic mapping were replaced with productive cellular structures."

"And this is why I feel the way I do?"

"In part; but the unusual feelings you are experiencing will pass in time. You will become quite acclimated to your new body. Some of the additional differences you are feeling are due to a second change we had to implement. The changing of your cellular mapping caused your body to have an immediate need for a higher concentration of oxygen than before. You see, your body is now tremendously more efficient. It is stronger and more resistant to damage. The cells in your brain were also affected by our tampering, thus leaving you with a greater ability to learn and, we hope, other positive effects. The increased efficiency of your body's cellular structure, as mentioned, caused a greater immediate need for oxygen. We did not foresee this before we began reviving you. We saw you nearly die again. Our scientists realized the problem and installed an organic oxygen concentrator into the bronchial passages just above the entry path to your lungs. It is this procedure that has you feeling the most ill effects. It was a major process for you to undergo so quickly after the increasing of the density of your cellular structure, and that increased density made the procedure more difficult to perform."

"How long has it been since you saved me?"

"You have been here for six of your days."

"Six days! My family must think I'm dead. I've got to get back to them."

"We understand and agree, but we must finish our explanation first. You have been enhanced, if you will, to be able to withstand great depths within the sea. Your body has, by our estimations, the ability to go to any depth with no ill effects during or after. Your organic oxygen concentrator will function effectively as long as you live, self-adjusting to provide your body with the proper percentage of oxygen to perform effectively. A problem still existed with your inability to extract air from the sea. We had several options here, but we felt we had already altered your body to such a degree—without your permission—both in the name of science and as a reward for your heroism. So, our offer to you is an external device that has been fashioned to look like the breathing device you call a regulator, which you use with your diving equipment. It can be worn around your neck by its attached tubing when you are diving and do not need it. It can be employed at any time. What this device does is instantaneously extract the air from the water through a special diaphragm utilizing an enhanced process of osmosis. It then allows you to exhale through it in a normal fashion without fail. We have rated the effectiveness of this device, as with your new physical structure, as having no limitation related to the depth of the seas of this planet. You will find the enhanced regulator near your damaged equipment."

With that, Alex walked to the stack of badly crushed equipment; he was trying to imagine the pressure that had caused such destruction.

He found the enhanced regulator. It appeared as they had described it, looking much like a complex, two-stage regulator, with a loose-fitting length of bungee cord about twenty inches long. The e-reg was made of a material that resembled chrome.

"Is this made of chrome?"

"No. The material is one of our own creations. Chrome, at any thickness, would never stand up to the pressures this material can withstand."

"Why would you give me such a device? You've already saved my life in a manner I could never have imagined."

"We have several reasons. The ones important to you would be the following: currently you are in a suboceanic cave we have filled with a healthy mixture of nitrogen and oxygen. This cave rests at a depth of twelve hundred feet. Even with your new depth resistance, you would not have enough air to survive your return home. Our method of retrieving you would not work in reverse. The second reason we believe would be of interest to you is that with this device you will have the ability to visit the depths and investigate new undersea environments. I believe that is a reason you chose to be a scuba diver, as you call it. To satisfy this desire of yours is another way of us rewarding you for your heroic behavior in saving the lives of others."

"What about the other reasons you were mentioning?"

"Our other reasons are best withheld at this time. Do not concern yourself."

"If I'm not dreaming all of this, you're telling me I can take this e-reg and leave this cave, a cave that is at a depth of twelve hundred feet, and without difficulty can return to the surface or stay at this depth to look around for as long as I wish."

"That is correct."

Alex walked around for a few moments, concentrating on the unusual information a seemingly well-programmed computer was feeding him. Alex wasn't sure of the scope these changes created, but if he were in fact alive, and they were telling him the truth, what it did mean was that he could go home.

"I must be honest. I don't know if I can believe all of this, but I do want to thank you for my life. I would like to go home now, if I may?"

"You are not being held here and may leave at any time. Just a general statement about your changed cellular structure. There are going to be other differences resulting from the changes. We're not completely aware of all you will discover, and we have done all we know to ensure none of what you may discover will in any way be harmful to you or those around you—but even that is uncertain. Your mind and body have been molecularly compressed and thus enhanced. New strengths and a more broadened awareness are bound to exist. That will be for you to discover. And here is a last statement from us: we have intentionally communicated with you in this manner and not introduced ourselves to further protect our species. You will no longer be in contact with us after you have left the confines of this cave, and we will not contact you. We have tried to show appreciation for your actions and have tried to equip you sufficiently for the tasks that lie ahead. We wish you well. You can now take the e-reg, and if you enter the portal to your left below the surface, you will go back to the open sea directly beneath the area of the three caves. Your new strength will provide you with the ability to reach shore with no difficulty.

You must use your discretion in what and to whom you tell anything about your time with us. Some would call you insane, and some would attempt to dissect you to determine what was changed and how it was done. Do you understand?"

"I think I do. I am all too familiar with the level of acceptance that exists within most of mankind. Again, I want to thank you—whoever you are."

"You are welcome. Farewell."

Alex placed the e-reg in his mouth, put on his fins from the stack of equipment near the wall, and giant-stepped into the water. He found immediately that the changes had allowed his eyes to adjust to the water almost without pause. He could see as clearly under the water as he had above the surface. Alex saw the portal and entered the opening. The end of the tunnel was only eight feet in front of him. Cautiously, he went to the surface.

CHAPTER 3

During the six-mile swim, Alex thought back to the beginning of their Cayman adventure. They had sold all they had to follow a dream—a dream of taking their threesome of a family to a new way of life. It was something they had wanted to do for a long time, but until an unexpected gift of fate came their way, they had had no real way to make the change.

"I have a certified letter for Angela McPherson. Would you sign here?" The postman then turned and left the front door of their Fort Wayne, Indiana, home.

Angela walked into the kitchen while opening the letter. "Alex," she yelled from the kitchen. "You are not going to believe this."

Coming down from the second floor, Alex saw Angela standing in the kitchen holding the opened letter. "What's up?"

"Remember my relatives from Switzerland? I've talked about them a few times."

"Sure. They were doctors or something."

"One is a surgeon and one is in family practice. They've decided to give away their savings before they retire. It says here that they have already paid for their home and have private pension plans set up so there's enough to meet their needs for the rest of their lives."

"You're kidding?"

"No, dear; I'm not. They want their family to have an opportunity to enjoy their lives while they can, rather than waiting until an inheritance is distributed from their will. There's a check for five million dollars in here!"

Alex remembered their discussions following the receipt of the check. They had called the Switzerland relatives and had a long conversation with them to make sure this was what they wanted to do. It was.

Next, Alex, Angela, and Tony had gone to dinner to discuss their plan for moving to Grand Cayman. They would cash in all of their stocks, sell their cars and the house, take those monies and the early inheritance, and start a new life in the sun.

The McPherson's spent their first week setting up arrangements for their new home. After viewing a couple of very nicely appointed homes, they had chosen a site that seemed to fit all of their desires. This home was located on the north side of the island, in the Rum Point area. They came to learn it had recently been the island home of a rock star whose band gathered no moss. The band had felt the island was becoming too crowded and placed the house for sale so they could move to a less traveled place. With one trip to the bank, Alex and Angela closed the deal on their new home.

The house and grounds were stupendous! A three-story design was nested within a grove of palm trees tall enough to crest the top of the roofline. With the four thousand square feet and the open-air design, this home offered a beautiful presentation that would have been gorgeous anywhere, but being located on the beach of this elite area gave it an elegance not often matched. The four-car garage offered a side access for the auto-entry doors, causing the house to loom even larger than it was. Four bedrooms, each with its own private bathroom, were located on the second floor, and the open-style kitchen with its central island-based range was on the main floor. One exit from the kitchen led to a formal dining room, with a large bay window that looked from the rear of the house over a spectacular ocean view. The other kitchen exit led to the large family room. This was where the television and stereo were located. Down a short hall from the family room rested the formal living room, accessed from the foyer, which sported a large two-door entryway with doors that were ten feet high from edge to edge. None of the walls were wallpapered and very few were painted anything other than a flat white. This delighted Angela to no end, for this was another area she excelled in—interior design.

The top floor of this island domain caught the interest of both Angela and Alex most dramatically. This floor was a full fifteen hundred square feet and was divided between a master bedroom suite, an exercise room and, on the end opposite from the master bedroom, a room already wired as a private media room.

The master bedroom had its entry to the front of the house from a suspended landing accessed by a spiral staircase starting from the family room. This slowly turned one full turn as it reached the third floor, bypassing the second floor altogether. The second floor was accessed by the straight stairway going up from the foyer.

The master suite possessed a king-size canopied four-poster bed and two end tables, one on either side of the hand-carved headboard. To the left of the bed, the pathway turned slightly to find a large whirlpool tub against a wall of windows that looked out to the ocean. The sunlight from the wall of windows caused the room to seem endless.

Additional power, antennas, and satellite receptacles, allowing for nearly unlimited equipment, facilitated the media room. Two of the walls faced the ocean. Each had large windows built into a sliding glass-style opening to a balcony, which cornered the outside of the house with an access stairway to the roof area where the antenna array was located. It wasn't until much later that they would realize the true benefits of this area.

The newly constructed private dock reached from the beachfront behind their Rum Bay home out to where the depth was twenty feet. This stretched the dock to about twenty yards in length. The water alongside the dock was shallow enough to wade for the first ten yards and began to deepen from that point. Alex and Angela had a gazebo built on the dock at the ten-yard point, widening the dock to accommodate the structure. This sitting area was perfect to relax with a Mudslide and a pint of English cider and listen to the water while basking in the Rum Bay breeze.

The memories swelled within Alex as he journeyed home.

CHAPTER 4

After making it to shore, Alex was surprised at how strong he still felt following such a long swim. As he considered the unknowns and whatever they had done to his body, Alex was quite certain endurance was one of the gifts he now had. Swimming in from the Trinity Caves location where just six days prior he had encountered the ten ferocious hammerheads, Alex came up in Rum Bay, very close to where his home was located. A short thirty-minute jog brought him to the back doorstep of his home. There was no movement outside of the house, and the inside of the house seemed quite dark.

Alex was concerned to see what kind of mood he was going to find Angela and Tony in, thinking they had lost their father and husband just six days prior in the diving incident. He saw no easy way to do it; he felt he just had to knock on the door and greet whoever answered. After only a few moments, Angela came to the door. The next several minutes were filled with emotional cries, hugs, kisses, half questions, and half sentences—all coming from Angela.

Tony, Angela shared, had gone to spend some time with friends for the afternoon. Angela explained to Alex that Tony had taken it quite hard but he had not yet broken down and shown his true emotions about it. Spending time with his friends seemed to help him keep his mind off the believed death of his father.

It was nearly an hour after Alex had knocked on the door before he was able to start describing to Angela what had taken place. Angela sat quietly for about fifteen minutes before she began to question nearly everything Alex had said. She was wondering if he could possibly have hit his head somewhere and lost consciousness. This might be memory loss, or a hallucination. Maybe it was the effects of the depths he no doubt suffered while trying to elude the sharks. Alex assured her that he was feeling fine and he had not hallucinated any of this, but he still wasn't sure how much of it even *he* believed. Not needing any of the damaged equipment, Alex had left it all behind. The only piece of equipment he'd carried with him was still around his neck, and that was the e-reg.

Angela, being very analytical, had determined tests needed to be run—blood tests, skin tests, tissue samples—and Alex needed to be admitted to the hospital after being gone so long to make sure that he was, in fact, fine. Alex strongly discouraged the idea, remembering what the unknowns had told him about how the human medical staff might react to what they found.

He explained this to Angela, who said, "If what you are telling me is true, Alex, then I agree, we cannot turn you over to a group of doctors and allow them to run tests on you. But we must run tests; we must discover what happened to you."

There was nothing but logic in that, Alex fully agreed. Angela pointed out that she had friends in the States, friends who worked in private laboratories. "We can take the blood samples, do the tissue samples, pack them in ice, and ship them priority mail to the labs in the States, stating we want the results returned to us privately and not to anyone else. We don't need to tell them it is you. We won't tell them anything about it, just say to complete full scans on these particular samples and tell us what they find."

The reunion Alex had with Tony was just as warm as it had been with Angela. Tony truly loved his father, and the thought of losing him had been unbearable. Tony hadn't lost faith in his father being found alive. He had clung to hope that by some miracle Alex was going to come back to them.

The next couple of days were fairly busy, even though they tried hard to relax. Tony went back to work and started back into the life he'd had prior to the dive, now ten days ago. Angela and Alex went about gathering the supplies to do the tissue and blood samples. Angela found it very difficult to take a tissue sample. She was amazed at how dense Alex's skin had become, further validating the statements Alex had made regarding his discussion with the unknowns. If the molecular structure were denser, it was going to be much more difficult to pierce the skin. Alex had to take both samples himself. With all of Angela's strength, she was unable to pierce his skin with either a needle for the blood sample or with a scalpel to scrape his skin for the tissue sample. They had determined that Alex's strength had increased, because he was able to obtain each of these without any trouble.

Packed appropriately on dry ice, the samples were on their way to a northern Indiana laboratory where Angela's friend worked. Prior to sending the package, of course, Angela had called these friends and advised them which tests they would like to have run and that they should forward the information back to Angela as soon as the results were available.

Two weeks had passed when Angela received a lab report from the States. There was a brief note included with the listing of the lab values from Angela's former coworker. The note apologized for the results. It was the lab tech's opinion that although the samples were apparently taken from a living creature, none of the values made any sense. They were so indiscernible it was impossible to detect what animal the sample had come from. The lab tech concluded that the samples had in some way been contaminated, which would have surely altered the results. This could be the only explanation.

Weeks went by like bites of warm popcorn. Two months had passed before Angela and Alex began to plan their next steps. Angela had enjoyed decorating their new home, and Alex, too, was quite pleased with the results. It had been quite an adjustment for this Midwest born and bred citizen to become accustomed to the cotton-candy pink color of the stucco exterior. But the whole island was like that, so, when in Rome …

Tony was still working part time in the island Pizza Hut in Georgetown. It was more of a social step than a desire for money. It had worked well, introducing him to new friends and providing him a greater understanding of the island in a brief couple of months.

Angela and Alex stopped at the Light House restaurant just a few miles from their home as they headed toward Georgetown. While enjoying a delicious lunch of thick-cut white fish and chips, they discussed their future and what steps they must take toward that goal.

"I know it sounds normal to go to the islands and open a dive shop, but it also sounds intriguing and just plain fun." Alex was like a kid with a new toy—he was so full of excitement and energy about the plan. "We have plenty of money to do whatever we want. It just sounds to me like something that will allow us to get productive, yet it'll be quite different from any of our jobs in the past."

"You're right about that!" There was laughter in Angela's voice. "I'll always be an engineer no matter what I do, and you'll always be … you'll always be … What did you do?"

"I worked on the mainland, no water to be seen. It'll take a lot of work to get ready for such a venture, and that will be part of the experience. We'll have to …" Alex was quite right. They had plenty of preparation to do before they could succeed at opening the type of dive shop they both wanted!

They also discussed they would put aside for now the events surrounding the hammerheads, the unknowns, the e-reg, and everything else relating to the changes with Alex. They didn't know what else to do at this point, so they worked on going on with their lives.

Since they wanted to offer boat diving for the experienced diver, Alex and Angela were in for months of learning themselves. Both Angela and Alex were experienced divers, but neither of them possessed certifications beyond the Advanced Level. They needed to become Master Scuba certified. On top of that, they needed to learn more about boats and about the waters around the island.

To achieve all of this, the two of them approached the managers of the island's best known diving company. After some discussion, and a sizable fee up front, they enlisted the services of those qualified to teach them what they needed to learn. They signed on board a boat called the *Disco* as its crew. For the next three months, they would work as crew for the *Disco*'s captain while he instructed them toward their Master Scuba certification and, in addition, their boat captain's licenses.

The captain of the *Disco* was a young man who had lived on Cayman for the past three years and hailed originally from western Canada. At six feet tall, 175 pounds, and blond with sharp blue eyes, this young man captivated the lady divers who rode the *Disco* to their dive sites. Captain Dan Trottier, a good looking kid of twenty-five, had a great wealth of knowledge that far exceeded his years. Dan already had one experienced crew member, Mark Dennison, who had left his home in Devon, England, ten years earlier and had been traveling the tropics, and a few other exotic locales, ever since.

Dan and Mark were both experienced divers. Dan was an instructor of divers and boat captains by experience and certification. Mark had far more experience than Dan but had never taken the time to acquire certification for either. Since Mark shared the same certification as Angela and Alex, he thought it was time to become officially certified along with them. It could only help his future.

Their times together started with Angela and Alex doing the basics of carrying tanks to and from the boat, driving the bus that was used to bring the divers from their hotels to the boat docks, and performing any other gofer aspect the captain saw necessary to the project's success. It was the only way to truly learn, and they would go home with large smiles on their faces. You see, while they were responsible for a lot of the legwork, they were also able to go diving every day they worked.

To ride the boat to each of the sites was an adventure in itself. For the first few weeks, Dan concentrated on the scuba aspects of their training and left the boat training untouched. Gentle rides were the norm. Going to the south, east, or west of the island gave the boat little trouble and seemed to caress the hull into the right position for smooth travel. The north side of the island, beyond the breakers, was another story.

The unabashed swells of the far north side of the island provided six to ten foot swells of mounting water on a normal day. Alex could remember the days before he had gotten his sea legs all too well, especially the first day.

"Alex, I want you to—" Dan began to speak and then stopped; there was a smirk on his face. "Are you feeling okay, Alex?"

Alex began with a controlled tone of voice, trying to sound as normal as possible, "Excuse me, but where would be a good place for me to throw up?"

Dan nearly laughed. "Usually, people don't have time to ask. Right this way," he said, as he led Alex to the leeward side of the boat. After that first day on the north side of the island, Alex never experienced seasickness again. He had continued to gain a great respect for the sea and its powers. Each day on the boats and on the dives, Alex felt his strength growing. His movements were becoming more fluid and effortless.

Two months into their training, Mark, Angela, and Alex had earned their Master Scuba certifications and were well on the way to having enough boat hours in to apply for their boat captain's licenses. The diving was fantastic! Almost without fail, when they dived a site they had dived the week before and the week before that, they would still see something new about the location. They led the charter divers from the boat to the depth decided before the dive and began acting as wet-suit tour guides as well as watch guards. Many of the divers that chartered with this company were fairly new or at least only did such dives one week out of the year. The crew would combine caution, safety, and discovery to enhance each diver's experience to the max!

During their training time, they took groups of divers to sites all around Grand Cayman. On the west side of the island, they visited a site known locally as Orange Canyon. This spot was always aglow with vibrant orange elephant-ear sponges. The reef started at about forty-five feet, with the edge of the wall adorned with sea plumes and lavender sea fans as the wall dropped into the deep. The sea life was excellent at this site, and the divers were all seen with their waterproof fish ID charts out, pointing at the different species all gathered in the area.

Not far from Orange Canyon was one of Angela's favorite spots for interaction with the sea life. Tarpon Alley was not only filled with large schools of giant silvery tarpon, but the area also drew stingray and the largest grouper she had ever seen. The tops of the walls in the Alley were at sixty feet and made an excellent dive for the inexperienced divers. If there were more experienced divers, they would take them over the wall and do a wall dive, descending to about one hundred and twenty feet and then slowly ascending as the divers gracefully sailed by the multicolored inhabitants of the cracks and crevices in the wall. When they reached the sixty-foot top again, it was usually the appropriate time to gather the group and make for the boat.

Mark and Dan's employers also offered a two-day trip, in which the group would leave early on the morning of day one and take a seventy-mile boat ride to Little Cayman. They would arrive just before noon and settle in at a small beachfront hotel. After checking in, Alex and Angela would get a light lunch at noon and then spend the hour after that just walking along the beach or in some way enjoying themselves while they let their lunch digest. At about 2:00 p.m., they would get aboard their dive boat and take a short ride to Bloody Bay Wall. This spot, despite the name that remained from its pirate history, was one of the best dive spots in all of Cayman. The reef wall started very shallow, about fifteen feet, and then dropped off to depths not yet measured. Bright orange and lavender tube sponges were spread all along the wall. The barracuda that lived along the wall grew to as much as six feet in length and were as pleasant to be around as your next-door neighbor. When the divers were there—and Alex and Angela went on several occasions—they would see giant sea turtles and a few resident spotted moray eels. The huge parrotfish were the most fun, though. You could play a sort of water ballet with them during the entire dive, if you chose to.

When Angela and Alex took this two-day trip, they would do a two-tank afternoon boat dive and then offer a one-tank boat night dive on the same spot of Bloody Bay Wall. Because of doing the night dive on the same spot, they were familiar with the layout and would have fewer chances of trouble with the less experienced divers. After a good night's sleep, they would be back on the boat. By 9:00 a.m., they would begin a deep wall dive along the Bloody Bay Wall for a two-tank dive. Following this set of dives, they would steer the boat back to Grand Cayman and have a picnic lunch on the boat as they traversed the seventy mile space between the two islands.

Another favorite spot for night dives was just off the seven-mile beach area on Grand Cayman. The location was the resting place of the wreck of the *Ore Verde*. She was sitting in about fifty feet of water, and the depth was just right to take a nice long night dive without wasting too much air on deepwater movements. Alex always enjoyed this night dive for two reasons. First, he loved wreck diving and the stories behind the ship. The other reason was that this wreck was home to some of the largest lobsters he had ever seen. They would measure three to three and a half feet in length and were beautifully multicolored when you shone your dive light on their shells. You wouldn't see these guys on this wreck in the daytime. They only come out at night.

With much research and even more discussion with the local government, we selected a location for the new dive shop and boat dock. There was a spot along Seven Mile Beach, just north of the Holiday Inn, where a new hotel, The Georgetown, had just opened. It sat directly along the shoreline that faced the location of *Ore Verde*. Alex and Angela had shared several discussions with the new hotel owners, and these had gone well. Including a contracted discount to their guests, the hotel leased them the property on the beach that they needed to build a small, low-profile, crisp-looking hut to house the dive shop. The deal also included access to a long dock directly from the shop to board and dock the dive boats Alex and Angela would place into service with their newly started company.

They needed a name for their new business, and after a long and interesting evening at the Hog Sty Pub, with Angela trying to keep Dan, Mark, and Alex from getting into too much trouble, the four of them decided.

"It's settled then," Alex nearly yelled. He had to yell—the Hog Sty was the kind of pub where detailed and meaningful conversation was impossible. "We'll call our new company the Ore Verde Dive Company."

They had decided on this particular name for a couple of reasons. The first one was a personal thought that since they could do this because they had received the large inheritance from their Swiss relatives, it would be an appropriate title. You see (in case you don't speak Spanish), *Ore Verde* translates to Green Gold—or, in their case, currency or money. The second reason, more obvious to those who would use the services of the company in the future, was the location of the company so near the wreck of the *Ore Verde* herself.

The wreck of the *Ore Verde* had a colorful history regarding the origin of her name and the cause of her being a dive site now rather than a working boat. It was told on the island that the captain was going broke shipping supplies from Jamaica to the Caymans until he got the idea that he should be shipping a more lucrative cargo. Legal cargo was not working for him, so he sought to ship an illegal bounty, "green gold"—*ganga*—or, as it's called in Spanish, *Ore Verde*. One of the problems of shipping an illegal cargo is the quality of crew you have available, and to complicate matters all the more, the captain himself was not a smart man. With these two problems working on the same boat, the captain offered the crew all the ganga they could smoke as their pay for crewing the boat. Unable seamen, thinking behind a cloud of smoke from the green gold, and now being chased by the coast guard, did what any men of their caliber and abilities would do. They jumped ship and allowed the boat to run rough into the reef head, ripping her open and sinking her before her captain knew which end was up and leaving him with all ends wet.

Another conversation the new entrepreneurs had that evening at the Hog Sty concerned the naming of the boats. The guys were enjoying pints of cider, while Angela was slowly sipping an icy Mudslide. Alex leaned over to Pete, the proprietor of this fine establishment, and asked the brand names of the cider he served.

"Strongbow and Blackthorn are the two I serve here," replied Pete proudly.

In tones and accents reminiscent of the old pirates, Mark, Dan, and Alex began to say the names of the ciders at about the same time, "Strongbow and Blackthorn, Strongbow and Blackthorn."

Angela interrupted them, saying, "It sounds like we've decided on the names for our boats. *Strongbow* and *Blackthorn* will be the first boats of the Ore Verde Dive Company."

The agreement was so enthusiastic that they toasted with several fresh pints of English cider and marveled at the sound of the names for the balance of the evening. They also toasted the teaming up of their new friends, Mark and Dan, with the Ore Verde Dive Company, as its first two boat captains. Tony, who was not at the Hog Sty since he was still a bit too young, had already asked if he could join the company when it opened and crew for the summer months. Alex and Angela felt it would be wonderful to have him working with them, but it was more wonderful to have him actually *want* to join them in this new venture. This parenthood thing still had its ups.

CHAPTER 5

I t had been months since the encounter with the hammerheads. Life had been quite normal around the island for the three McPhersons. They had resumed their diving expeditions and had kept the dive company going as planned. This included the purchasing of their new boats.

They had settled on the Fairline Boats manufacturing company, which had its display port located in Chichester, England. Chichester is on the southeast coast of England, just west of Brighton.

After calling and making appointments with the sales staff of Fairline, the McPhersons transferred to a jet out of Miami via the Grand Cayman airport. The flight was pleasant; Alex slept most of the way, as he usually did. They landed south of London at Gatwick Airport. The intent was to miss the hassle attached to London's Heathrow Airport. After landing and going through customs, they rented a car and began their drive to Chichester.

It was a fine drive, and having lived in Cayman for the last several months really helped. Since England has its automobiles driving on the left side of the street, as in their new home of Grand Cayman, they felt much more at home with the increased traffic than if they had attempted this driving endeavor without that experience. They had left Miami at about 10:00 a.m. and it was just now 5:00 p.m., since the flight had picked up three hours.

They scheduled their appointment at Fairline for the next afternoon. Alex was sure that by the time they'd arrived and had driven to their bed and breakfast near Chichester, it would be about 7:00 p.m., and they would be too hungry and tired to have any fun looking at boats. He was right. As they pulled into the gravel drive of the thatched-roof stone cottage, they were ready for a little food and a lot of sleep.

The bed and breakfast was located in a little village only two miles to the west of Chichester, known as Old Bosom. This little village rested on an inlet of the ocean and was a highly visited location for natives as well as tourists. Alex parked the car, checked with the proprietor, and placed their bags in their rooms.

The next morning, feeling well rested, they left their rooms and went to the quaintly decorated dining room. The proprietor had laid out a sideboard with three types of juices, four different cold cereals with a large pitcher of milk, and fresh bananas, apples, and oranges in matching Royal Dalton fruit bowls. In the center of the room was a large, round dining table with an intricately patterned lace tablecloth spread over it. The plates, bread plates, coffee cups, and saucers were all the same Country Rose pattern of Royal Dalton bone china.

As the three of them sat at the table, the proprietor, a very nice lady who appeared to be about forty years of age, with short, light-brown hair, entered the room from the adjacent kitchen and welcomed them. "Good morning. Did you have a pleasant rest?"

"Yes, we did. Thank you. Your rooms are so nicely appointed." Angela always knew how to get the attention of bed and breakfast proprietors. They spent a great deal of time, effort, and money on their accommodations, and it pleased them when their efforts were appreciated. Smiling, their hostess replied, "Thank you very much."

The proprietor of this lovely establishment went about serving them a traditional English breakfast, which consisted of eggs medium served on round-cut toast, English bacon, which was much more like thinly sliced ham, and the ever-present gratuitous slice of tomato. Besides this plateful, there were toast and preserves. Take into account the sideboard filled with cereals and fruits, and you will see it was impossible for anyone to walk away from this breakfast hungry.

After breakfast, the three of them took a walk into Old Bosom. The streets were narrow and lined with houses that looked to be from the mid-1500s. At the end of this small village was a port for small- to medium-sized sailboats and plenty of smaller craft. The waterline was nearly two hundred yards from the edge of the last building on the lane when they first walked through the village. By the time they left, about two hours later, the waterline was two feet high on the far side of that same building. When the water was high, even though there was a chill in the air, the small boats and wind sailors were very active.

After their walk, they returned to the B & B, got into their rented automobile, and headed for the appointment with the Fairline dealer. It only took fifteen minutes to reach the address of the dealership in Chichester. Several boats lined the dock, all looking shiny and new. In the offices of the dealership, the McPhersons met the gentleman with whom they had their appointment. Angela described their needs, while Tony and Alex went into great detail to describe their pleasure-equipment desires. The salesman listened with both ears, feverishly taking notes, and then he put down his pen and began to speak.

"It appears you've done a lot of thinking about the kind of boat you're looking for. But I must say, it sounds like you're speaking of more than one boat. Is this the situation?"

Angela spoke first. "We are looking for more than one boat. Three, to be exact. We would like two larger boats, about the same size, but of somewhat different designs for variety, and the third to be more of a personal pleasure boat rather than something for larger groups. We wish all three to be similarly appointed and of distinctive styling. This is why we have chosen Fairline."

The fire in the eyes of the salesman was blazing like lava. "We certainly have what you're looking for. Let's walk out to our docks and look at the boats up close."

The three of them examined boats for more than an hour and had apparently convinced the salesman they had now decided not to buy. They had questioned and searched and prodded through all of the boats in the docks—it had been fun. Alex looked at Angela at the same time that she and Tony looked at him.

"We've decided," Alex said abruptly. "We want the Squadron 59, the Squadron 56, and the Targa 42."

"You're quite serious, aren't you?" questioned the salesman in amazement. "Those are the three best boats we have in the docks."

"We know; that's why we want them," replied Tony in a calm, businesslike tone. Angela and Alex looked at Tony at the same time, with pride and astonishment.

"When can we take delivery?"

"Well, Mrs. McPherson, we can have your boats ready in one week. Where shall they be delivered?"

Alex chimed in, "Rum Bay, Grand Cayman."

"Grand Cayman—we have a delivery scheduled for there at the end of this next week, and these three—I should say *your* three boats— would fit on that delivery nicely. Let us go to the office and sign the papers."

Following some haggling over price, a deal was struck with the Fairline dealership, and after a couple of extra days in England, the McPhersons returned to their home in Grand Cayman.

The first two boats, the Squadron 59 and Squadron 56, would become the *Blackthorn* and the *Strongbow*. These two boats would be used primarily for their dive charters. Each of the two had two 680 hp diesels, accommodations for six to eight people in separate cabins, enough rear-deck space to provide for ten divers making ready for dives, and all of the possible accessories that made these two boats the top of the line that they looked to be.

The Targa 42, a forty-two-foot power boat with twin 500 hp diesels, was the sleek sport boat that Angela and Alex would use for their personal boating. It had a seaworthy displacement and the accommodation accessories that would allow for nearly any use they might have for it, either around the island, or when they would go from island to island or even to the States.

Following their return from England, Alex and Angela continued experimenting with some measurable testing of Alex and his new mental and physical strengths. Thus far Alex had not found a limitation on his physical strength. They had gone to the local Nautilus club on the island, and Alex had bench-pressed 750 pounds and had maxed out all of the Nautilus machines for lifting, stretching, bending, tugging, or pulling.

Lifting the front of the Camaro had been a fluke, a bit of a joke. "Hey, Angela, watch this." Grasping the front of Angela's Camaro, Alex had placed his left hand beneath the bumper and lifted the front end of this heavy American car a full two feet off the ground. The look of surprise on Angela's face was only surpassed by the look of surprise on Alex's. But even at that point, they had only felt this was a miracle, something that had saved his life. They hadn't really looked into the future to see what other benefits might come from it.

Also, over the past couple of months, Angela had felt that Alex might need to get his hearing checked. On several occasions when the room had been quite quiet, Alex had turned to Angela and asked, "What was that you said?" or had answered a question that she had not asked. It was after he had lifted the car that Angela began to concentrate on these seemingly untimely comments of Alex's. Angela decided to test this peculiar occurrence. She sat quietly, with Alex on the other side of the room. He was reading through one of the books from their collection, a book he hadn't read in years but somehow was finding great interest in today.

Angela sat quietly saying to herself, *I'm thirsty. I'm thirsty.*

Alex spoke up from across the room. "Can I get you something to drink?"

"What did you say?" Angela replied.

Alex repeated, "Can I get you something to drink? I thought you might be thirsty."

"Why would you think I was thirsty?" Angela asked.

"I'm not sure; I just thought for a moment there you might be thirsty."

Angela decided to try this a second time. Not more than five minutes later, she thought to herself, *I wish I had a five-dollar bill. I wish I had a five-dollar bill.*

After she had repeated this thought to herself for only a couple of minutes, Alex said, "How are you on pocket cash? Do you need some money? Five dollars, or something?"

Angela now knew her tests were a success/ But this was something new they hadn't counted on. The changes in Alex's body had also changed functional processes of his mind. He now had a telepathic ability. She couldn't be sure how far reaching this would be, but there should be other ways they could test, exercise, or possibly even train some of the these abilities.

Angela described the two different tests that she had just performed. Alex was amazed. They tried four other situations, each of them coming up just as clearly as the first two had. On the last two, in fact, Alex was concentrating so well that he was able to speak to her immediately after she had the first thought, as if he were answering her question in normal conversation. This was truly an ability that he could train and exercise with.

Alex had not utilized the e-reg. He had not even given it a test during any of the dives of the last several months since his return home from the encounter with the hammerheads. It had stayed in a lockbox in Alex and Angela's bedroom. What Alex did notice was that his consumption of air during dives had decreased compared to prior dives. Alex had attributed this in his conversations with Angela to the efficiency of the organic oxygen concentrator. The two of them decided to take a private dive. There they would experiment with the e-reg.

With the e-reg hung securely around his neck, Alex suited up with all of his normal equipment, as did Angela. They had determined to go to a depth of forty feet and stop there. Trying to be as cautious as possible, they had decided to experiment with the e-reg at that depth first, with Angela present in case an additional air supply were necessary. Alex placed the e-reg in his mouth. It worked just as efficiently as it had the first time he'd used it, when he'd come back from the twelve-hundred-foot dive. They had also decided to experiment briefly at the shallow depths with Angela utilizing the e-reg. Having full supplemental air supply, they felt there was no danger in trying this. Angela placed the e-reg in her mouth and began breathing quite regularly. She was able to breathe just as effortlessly as Alex had moments before. The e-reg could be used by anyone, it seemed. Their next step was to experiment with the e-reg at a depth of one hundred feet. Slowly making their way to that depth, Alex and Angela each again tried the e-reg, and it worked flawlessly.

Alex and Angela returned to the boat, and they began discussing what their next step should be. They had already discussed the ease with which Alex had been able to breathe and move around at the depth of twelve hundred feet when he'd first left the cave, now three months ago. Alex felt he should return to that depth and even attempt to go deeper to fully test himself and to test the e-reg.

Angela's first response was "Absolutely not! We have no idea if you could be killed or injured at that depth. We don't even know if you were truly at that depth. Again, you could have hallucinated some of this. It is so bizarre to think this could be true."

Alex replied, "I agree, but there is no better way to find out than to test it. We will look around and obtain a depth gauge that can measure the great depths we are talking about. We will find a way to connect, so I can communicate directly with you when I am on the test dive."

All at once, Alex thought of something—a possibility he hadn't considered. He thought to himself, *Angela.*

Angela turned and replied, "What?"

Alex said, "It works! I was able to telepathically call for you. So it is not just me being able to hear your thoughts, but I can actually communicate to you with mine! I am going to dive right now and test this."

Angela replied "My tanks are too low; I can't dive."

"No, Angela, I want you to stay on board. I'm going to solo dive; first at a shallow depth to see if we can communicate through the water, and then I will go a little deeper and see how it works. I will go just below the surface and try it there, and then we will try it at ten-foot intervals. My tanks are full of air, and I have the e-reg with me, so I will be fine."

Alex rolled backward off the side of the boat into the water. He gave Angela the okay sign that he was fine. Then, as he had outlined, he went just below the surface and called out in his mind *Angela, can you hear me?"*

It had been their plan for him to call out in his mind telepathically first, expecting to perceive Angela's reply telepathically. Then he would call out a second time in his mind, and she would then reply verbally.

They would do this on each of their attempts so that they could test whether he could hear Angela when she was speaking or whether he could hear Angela when she was thinking. They would test both methods.

Again, just below the surface, he said, "Angela, can you hear me?'

Yes, Alex, I can hear you. Then Angela spoke out loud: "Yes, Alex, I can hear you."

Alex was amazed—he could hear in both situations. "I heard you both times. I am going now to a depth of twenty feet." At twenty feet they repeated the test. Alex then communicated to Angela, "This is great, Angela! I heard you both times. Both times! I'm going to skip thirty feet and I'm going to go to a depth of forty."

It worked successfully at forty, and it worked successfully at fifty, sixty, seventy, eighty, ninety, and one hundred feet. At each ten-foot increment Alex and Angela could hear one another just as clearly as they could at ten feet.

"Angela?" Alex began.

"Yes, Alex?"

"I'm placing the e-reg in my mouth now, and I'm going to go to two hundred feet."

"Alex, we're not ready for that!" Angela exclaimed.

"You know and I know that we are as ready now as we will ever be."

"I know you're right Alex," she whispered apprehensively.

"Angela, we are having a conversation, and I am a hundred feet below the surface, and we are merely thinking one another's thoughts. We have to test this at a greater depth."

Alex slowly descended, and when he reached two hundred feet he began speaking to Angela. "Angela, can you hear me?"

"You are at two hundred feet?"

"Yes, two hundred feet precisely."

Angela replied, "I can hear you as clearly as when we were just under the surface. This is the way that we can stay in contact."

"Angela, I am going to go to three hundred feet, and we are going to try this until we can't hear one another."

"Alex!" Angela said with a sigh.

"I know your concerns, but you mustn't worry. I don't want my two-tank assembly destroyed like the last one was, so I am going to take it off, pump some air into my BCD, and let it float to the surface. If you can't reach it with the hook, I'll retrieve it when I come back up."

"Aren't you scared?" Angela queried.

"I'm anxious, but I am so curious I can't resist."

They tested three hundred, four, five, six, seven, and eight hundred feet. Nine, ten; they tested to twelve hundred feet; this was how deep Alex had been three months ago. At each level, they spoke very clearly. In fact, they were now speaking back and forth in between the levels as if they were standing next to one another holding an open conversation.

Since the unknowns had informed Alex that the e-reg would work at extreme depths, Alex pressed it to two thousand feet. Ever since the twelve-hundred-foot mark, Alex and Angela had stayed in constant communication. Not a moment went by in silence. Alex was describing the wondrous sites he was seeing. Alex looked around in awe at the colorful sea life that surrounded him at this depth. They could hear one another as clearly as if they been standing topside on the boat deck with each other.

Alex exclaimed, "Do you realize, Angela, the possibilities this opens up? I am at a depth of some two thousand feet. I don't feel any pressure on my body at all. You and I are communicating as if we were standing next to one another. It is hard for me to imagine all we can do with these new powers, these new abilities."

Angela replied, "I know. My mind is running wild. But right now, Alex, my mind is mostly concerned for you. You are doing something no one ever imagined a man could do. Let's call it a day."

"That's wise. Hey, Angela?" Alex questioned.

"Yes, Alex."

"I suppose I should have taken my dive watch off?"

She laughed. He laughed. At two thousand feet, his dive watch had long since cracked and flooded, but Alex had been so amazed with all that he was seeing and discovering that he hadn't noticed until this moment when he thought to check the time. Unsure whether this depth would affect the way he would surface, Alex came up very slowly.

Upon reaching the surface, Alex gathered up his floating dive gear and climbed onto the boat.

"How do you feel?" Angela asked.

"I feel great! This is so exciting I don't know where to begin."

"Well, we will begin by me taking your pulse." Angela proceeded to do so, and it was just as steady as it had been days before when she'd checked it while they were sitting and relaxing in their home. Steady and strong.

CHAPTER 6

Alex was rinsing off the breakfast dishes in the kitchen, and Angela was lounging on the wicker chaise lounge on the back deck. He smiled as he replayed the events of the morning in his mind.

Alex had awakened early this morning, earlier than Angela, which was not usually the case. This particular morning, Alex had a plan. While Angela was still sleeping, Alex had quietly strewn rose petals of red, pink, and white all around the bed and around where she was lying. Quietly opening the venetian blinds and allowing ever so little of the morning sunlight into the bedroom, Alex walked quietly across the room and turned on the CD player with Bette Midler's *Bed of Roses* CD already loaded. The new morning light blended with the shadows of the venetian blinds. Bette Midler softly crooned love songs of caring and heartfelt emotion.

"Good morning," Alex said.

"Good morning," she replied.

Those were the last words other than "I love you" said over the next hour and a half. The shadows changing on their bodies as the sun slowly rose further into the sky seemed to ride on the same wild roller coaster of emotion both Alex and Angela were feeling during their time that morning. Alex had taken some floral-scented baby oil and had given Angela a complete back rub. He'd caressed her arms and legs with the baby oil. As Angela moved across all four corners of the bed, the oil on her body picked up the rose petals, decorating her with different-colored petals from head to toe. This encounter, of course, caused the need for

41

a complete shower to get the baby oil and the rose petals off. Alex and Angela spent the next hour in the shower together.

The dishes now complete, Alex joined Angela on the patio deck.

"Good morning again, my love," she said.

"I thought you and I might do some pleasure diving today, if you'd like to," Alex said. "Go do some shallows, and just see what the fishies are doing today."

"Sounds great."

For the next hour, Angela and Alex moved through the house slowly and peacefully. Any time they came within ten feet of one another, they would change directions and give each other a little brush of the hand across a shoulder, a little kiss on the cheek, a touch of the hand.

They had decided to take a drive to the dive shop today to pick up a boat rather than to cut across to Governor's Bay. Most often they would boat across Governor's Bay and not see what was going on in the neighborhoods between Rum Bay and the town of Georgetown. A second set of their gear was down at the dive shop, so they didn't need to load up any gear, but they took a couple of cold soft drinks to enjoy along the drive. During the drive they listened to the radio, music being played by some of the local bands.

The news broadcast came on at its regular noon-hour time, with the day's news of a terrible disaster in which an airliner had crashed into the Caribbean. The report told of the 140 individuals that had been on the plane and that there had been no survivors. As the reporter continued the broadcast, he pointed out that at that moment there was no known reason for the crash. The plane had been flying without incident, on its proper flight plan, visible on radar, and all of a sudden, as far as they could tell, the right wing had dipped and it had gone into a steep dive, crashing headlong into an awaiting ocean grave.

The impact of the plane left scattered debris along the surface, which assisted the Air National Guard in their search. The news reporter closed with a statement describing the difficulty the navy and all other assisting sources were having in trying to discover what had caused the disaster. The difficulty was that in this portion of the Caribbean, the waters went as deep as six to seven thousand feet. As usual with a crash of a commercial airliner, the infamous black box needed to be found to help determine the cause of this particular disaster.

A dilemma now existed—locating the black box at such extreme depths. The elements of probable depth and the initial impact of the crash made up an additional problem. The box might be damaged even if found.

"What an atrocious disaster," Angela said. "I can understand how the families feel. I thought I had lost you, and I can understand the weight of their loss. But at least I had some resolution, because I knew what had happened. I knew what had caused what I thought was your death."

Alex joined in, "The not knowing is an ugly emotional problem. Without finding the black box, the airlines are going to have an information deficit, allowing for the same problem to potentially happen again. If they had the black box, they could determine what caused the incident, make adjustments, make changes to prevent it from occurring again, and decrease the possibility of this event repeating itself."

The two of them drove silently then for the next twenty minutes, until they pulled into the parking lot near the dive shop.

"Alex?"

"Babe?"

"Do you think it wise to have you and I go and try to find that black box?"

"That was precisely what I was thinking, Angela."

"What if it actually went to six thousand?"

"Well, Angela, the information I was given about the e-reg was that it had no depth limitations, and I'm sure I could feel the pressure of depth limitation or depth difference on my body just as I did when I was diving before. If the pressure became too much, I would know that was a depth I needed to rise from."

"But it scares me. You're diving these depths alone—all alone! No partner to help in case there is an emergency!"

"There had to be a reason of fate, though, Angela—a reason for me to have my life saved in the manner it was. I can't imagine it was just for my life to have been saved and that's all. I'm not saying I think the unknowns did this to enable me to go after this black box in particular. They did this to save my life, plain and simple. But I'm looking at a much higher thought now. Be it fate, be it God, be it providence, there is some higher reason and higher purpose for this to have happened. Angela, I think we should go after the black box. We should go after it and bring it to a level where it will be found by the navy investigators. If we do it right, we can be over there, pretending to be regular divers, and then once we're done, we can be out of there and no one will know we ever assisted."

They sat in the car for the next thirty minutes and discussed how they could go about this. They had a basic idea of the location of the crash from the news reports. During the afternoon, the beginning of their plan was for Angela to research the exact location while Alex put together the equipment he would need for this particular dive. At that depth, daylight didn't matter, so they planned to do a night dive to try to draw as little attention to themselves as possible.

After Angela identified the location, they determined it was going to take two hours for them to travel from Grand Cayman to the crash location. They were taking the larger of their boats, the fifty-nine-foot Fairline Squadron, which would be much more stable in the open sea. So the *Blackthorn* was loaded with Angela's dive gear as well as Alex's, which included several special items they had put together during recent weeks with the intent of making deep dives.

During the two-hour trek to the crash location, Alex and Angela discussed in more detail their plans for the dive. They would take the *Blackthorn* to a point marked on their sea map that should put them about one mile from the actual crash location. There they would lower the sea anchor, and Alex would utilize the aqua sled to take him from the *Blackthorn*'s location to the crash location. This would keep them, they estimated, at least a mile from the crash location and should make their alibi of just being pleasure divers a lot more believable.

The next part of the plan, again to make the alibi more believable, was that Alex would begin his dive in full gear. Two tank systems, the works. They would lower a long sea rope over the side of the *Blackthorn*, which would reach down to a depth of a hundred feet. Alex would go to that depth, remove his gear, maintain the e-reg and the equipment he needed, and tie off his tanks and BC to the end of the sea rope. Upon completion of the dive, Alex could then return to the rope, get into his gear, and surface looking like a normal scuba diver. They had determined they would attempt to communicate through Alex's telepathic ability for as long as they could. Their plan included contact on every quarter hour. Alex would check in, identify his location to Angela, and thus they would measure at what point the telepathic contact was broken.

Alex and Angela lowered to the aqua sled off the rear of the *Blackthorn.* The craft looked like a small bobsled. On the front of the transport rested a motor housing where an electric motor was encased in a waterproof container. A joystick was wired to control the positioning of the propeller located on the bottom side of the transport. This gave Alex the ability to change directions and steer his way along the trek. Coming back from the motor housing in a flat platform, nearly the length of Alex's body, was an area designed for the diver to lie upon. Small spring clips were located on either side of the flat platform. These spring clips would attach to the diver's BCD. This would give the diver stability as he turned and changed directions with the aqua sled. The transport was rated at a depth of two hundred feet. Alex decided he would push the aqua sled beyond the one-fifty mark, since he would really like to have the transport for his trek back. Beneath the motor housing was a small cargo area. It was here that Alex placed the fishnet cargo bag containing the underwater diving torches. Each torch had a burning duration of ten minutes, and Alex had brought two dozen. The torches were advertised to burn at any depth.

Just before Alex lowered himself into the water, he took off his mask, looked at Angela, moved in very close, and gave her a gentle kiss.

Angela said, "Now, you'll check in every fifteen minutes, and I'll monitor the time and distance of your location as you report it, so we can measure just how long we communicate. With the speed of the transport and your making a cautious descent once you have reached the crash site, I roughly calculate it will take you between sixty and seventy minutes to make it to a depth where you will start noticing some of the wreckage."

"You've made a calculation of what depth you believe that will be?"

"Yes, I have, if the navy is correct on their debris field and the longitude and latitude points they have given. I have studied the oceanography map for the undersea formations, and right at that point, the deepest area I see is forty-two hundred feet. I pray it is not that deep. This is an untested depth, but at least it shouldn't be the six thousand some of that area could actually have provided. So, if you find the wreckage in seventy minutes, and it takes you much too long to find the black box, that would add another hour and then seventy minutes back. I expect you back, then, in three hours and twenty minutes."

"It took us a little more than the two hours to get here with the current. It's now 8:00 p.m., so my calculated return would be about 1:00 a.m."

"Precisely. Good luck, my love, and be safe."

With the compass on the aqua sled, a compass wristband, and the compass tethered to the BC and tank assembly, Alex set his course for the airliner wreckage.

The aqua sled had the computerized ability to slowly take on ballast and thus control the depth it would then maintain. Additionally, there was an air nozzle hookup whereby, if necessary, a diver could connect one of his pressure hoses and pump some of the compressed air from his tanks into the tanks of the aqua sled. This would enable to aqua sled to stay at the surface no matter what its cargo. Alex placed himself onto the aqua sled and connected the two spring clips, one on either side of his waist. He then started the electric motor of the transport sled and began to submerge, taking ballast into the tanks located all along the right and left sides of the aqua sled. Upon reaching the depth of one hundred feet, still directly beneath the boat, Alex released the spring clips from his outer BC. He tied off the sled with the other front loading spring clip to the sea rope now suspended one hundred feet below the *Blackthorn*. Next, he placed the e-reg securely in his mouth and began breathing just as effortlessly as he always had with the wonderful breathing device. Alex released the front clips on his BC, slipped out of his tank and BC assembly, and connected the BC firmly onto the sea ropes. With no air trapped in the bladder pockets of the BC, his equipment would hang steady on the sea rope. Additionally, since it was a night dive, Alex had taken two of the chemical light plastic tubes and connected them to his BC unit so that it could be seen even if he came back to them without any light.

After his equipment was secured to the sea rope, Alex placed himself back on the aqua sled and released it from the sea rope. Alex wore a vest that had rings on either side, so the clips of the aqua sled could connect to those rings on the scuba vest. This vest was made out of the same two-mil dive suit material Alex would normally wear, which caused no undue buoyancy.

Now traveling away from the anchored point of the *Blackthorn*, Alex steered the aqua sled toward the coordinates of the airline wreckage. The sled was equipped with two small halogen headlights on the front of the motor housing. They lit up his trek with great beauty. The sea life was brightly colored. With the clarity of the water, the lights would shine some sixty to eighty feet in front of him. Alex had brought two of his flashlights, but he knew those would only be good to a depth of around 160 to 170 feet. His intent was to use them if necessary on his trek to the coordinates but to leave them with the transport sled and take only the underwater torches for his lighting as he began looking for the black box.

The transport sled had a convenient device that would help determine the distance it had traveled. It did this by measuring the water flow through a pinwheel that measured the feet traveled with the speed of the transport traveling at one hundred feet with very little water disturbance. Alex had traveled eight-tenths of a mile when the first fifteen minute check-in time arrived.

He concentrated his thoughts and spoke in his mind: *Angela?*

Right on the button. You know, he heard in his mind, "*sometimes you seem to be just wonderfully conscientious. That amazes me from time to time, my love.*

Do I detect a note of sarcasm?

None intended—just trying to stay lighthearted. I am a bit worried here. How are you doing?

Everything has gone as planned. My gear is tied off; the lighting on the sled is working well. I know this is only the second time I have tried the sled, but it's maintaining its depth just perfectly, very easy to handle. I think the speed at this depth is a little faster than what we thought it would be. I am at eight-tenths of a mile and currently moving in on nine-tenths just during our conversation. I believe I will be there before long.

Okay, I hear you clearly. Boy, what a way to put that. I think you … I … I … I feel you … I … I … well, I communicate with you clearly.

Don't be too nervous, Angela; everything will be okay. I'll check in with you in another fifteen minutes.

The measurement devices on the transport sled now showed he had traveled one mile. Alex shut down the power on the sled. He disconnected himself while maintaining a good grip on it. He then grabbed the torches from the sled. With one flashlight in his hand, he backed away from the sled about three to four feet to watch the sled and see if it maintained its level and position. To assist it in maintaining the position, Alex had devised a small sea anchor, much like the one used for the *Blackthorn*, utilizing three ropes and sea anchors which would hang some fifty feet beneath the transport sled. It would not maintain its position precisely because of the currents and eddies in the water; but in the short time Alex expected to be gone it would hopefully maintain its position within a close radius.

As with his gear, the chemical lighting tubes were used for the sea sled. Alex had placed the tubes on the underside of the sled. This would provide no light to be seen from above. The underside of the sled had a huge X made by several of the lighting tubes, so when Alex began to surface later in the dive he would see the lighted X and would be able to find the sled more easily.

With the sled properly stabilized, Alex took the dive torches and began his journey downward. As he held the bag and one of the ignited torches in his left hand, Alex's right hand remained free. He was going to depths that no single individual had been before, at least to his knowledge.

Alex had three dive knives in three different sizes, going from a small three-inch blade to a large nine-inch blade, fastened along his right leg in elastic holding clips. Also attached to one of the clips on his vest, hanging just below his chest, was an experimental device that Alex and Angela had devised some six weeks prior. It was a modified depth gauge with a self-contained pressure adjustment unit. It worked on the principle that the dial would continue to progress as the depth increased, much as hour hands would progress around a clock. The circular dial started with a depth of zero and, whether it worked at that depth or not, actually progressed to a depth of ten thousand feet.

The pressure gauge wasn't the problem in devising something that would be able to measure that depth; the difficulty was devising the encasement that would stand up to the pressure and allow the instrument to be taken to that depth. Alex had spent much time in the library prior to them devising this instrument and had read about some research that had been done in the fifties with deep-sea diving bells. They decided to try the method on this small device.

The basic plan consisted of placing the pressure gauge in an inner casing and then tooling a one-quarter inch space between the inner casing and the outer casing. This space was filled with very thick, barely processed petroleum. The casing with that combination should stand depths of two thousand to twenty-five hundred feet. They added an additional modification of a small CO_2 container attached to the backside of the depth gauge; as the pressure on the outside of the unit increased, the CO_2 container would correspondingly disperse CO_2 into the petroleum lining. In theory, this would allow the casing to stand depths up to ten thousand feet before it was crushed by the pressure. Alex was now at fifteen hundred feet, and it was time for his second check-in.

Angela?

Yes, Alex?

I'm at a depth of fifteen hundred feet. I am a mile away from your location, and your thoughts are very clear to me.

Yours are very clear as well, my love, but I can't help but think it has a lot to do with the way we started today off. I think we are very spiritually connected right now, and our thoughts are all the more connected.

You know, I have always heard friends talking about that morning glow and how it seemed to carry throughout the day. It's improved our communication here, hasn't it? Alex continued more matter-of-factly now. *All is well. I'm now at sixteen hundred feet. The pressure gauge seems to be functioning to plan. The torch has worked well also, and I'm ready to start burning the second one. So far I've seen nothing but open water. I haven't seen the bottom yet. All is well. My dear, I love you. I'll check back in another fifteen minutes.*

You be safe, my love.

I intend to.

Alex continued to descend, constantly monitoring the depth gauge. Now at a depth of two thousand feet, Alex was feeling no pressure resistance on his body. He felt as good at this depth as he had at one hundred feet. This was good, because he still had quite a ways to go, and he was going to be quite concerned if the effects of the depth of two thousand feet were going to be a problem. The sea life became sparse and more unusual at two thousand feet.

The movement of the light coming off the torch created shadows where light had been just seconds before. This also had an effect of staying off any of the sea life approaching Alex to investigate. Checking the depth gauge again, Alex found he was now at a depth of thirty-one hundred feet. Now on his third torch, Alex began to see signs of the airline wreckage. The e-reg was working fine, and the pressure of the depth was not bothering Alex at all. Physically he was feeling quite good, but emotionally and spiritually his heart was ripping in half as he looked at the devastation that lay before him.

Alex hovered for a moment, forgetting the depth he was at, forgetting this miraculous experience of being at that depth. All he could do was concentrate on the wreckage he saw on the ocean floor. What was there didn't look much like an airplane at all. The impact had shredded most of the plane away. What lay before him looked like a patchwork quilt with many of the patches missing. The debris stretched for what appeared to be twice the length of an intact plane. With the torches in hand, Alex saw the shadowy outline of the debris in the darkness.

Alex entered the area from the nose of the plane. He descended to that point and began to slowly go along the line of the debris as he viewed the sharp-cut pieces of aluminum barely connected to the pieces next to them. There was no sign humans had ever had any part of what lay before him. The exception to that picture came about every three to four feet, where Alex would see a small piece of material. Each piece was different; probably they were pieces of clothing worn by the doomed riders of this flight.

As Alex continued down the line of the wreckage toward the rear of the plane, he remembered the feelings he had every time he did any form of wreck dive. Usually those had consisted of ships that had sailed the seas years before and had sunk as the result of a storm, war, or some other long-ago catastrophe. But the feeling Alex now had was different. This was a feeling of memorial, a feeling of honor to those who had once sat in this airship, the precious cargo it had carried on each of its flights, and most especially, the precious cargo it had carried on its final flight.

After going the full length of the debris to the rear of the plane, Alex made a turnaround and went back toward the cockpit area. On this particular design of plane, the black box was maintained in a special compartment below the copilot's seat. When he returned to the front of the plane, he saw, as he had noticed before, that there were no seats in what once had once been the cockpit area. The copilot's seat was missing, but what appeared to be a locked compartment did rest beneath the spot where the seat should have been.

This compartment had been designed to be airtight, thus protecting the contents of the black box. Additionally, the black box was designed to be airtight, watertight, and to contain the computer recording device. All recordings, all conversations, all computer-registered indicator lights and so on would be stored in the program memory of the black box. The compartment was not locked. It was tightly secured with three closed hasps, one on each of three sides of the compartment, with hinges along the fourth.

Alex had decided to bring along a sealable plastic bag. It was his hope that some of the trapped air inside the compartment, if the compartment were still sealed, would go into the bag as he released the compartment's locks. He could then store the black box inside a partially dry package until he reached a more shallow depth.

The compartment looked badly battered. Before he reached for any of the three hasps, he took a good close look all around the compartment. It did appear that the left side of one of the hasps had been sheared off. There was probably already leakage into the black-box holding area. Reaching into the utility pocket on his suit, Alex pulled out the thick clear plastic bag and positioned it over the holding compartment so if any air were there it would be caught. He released the other two remaining hasps, and a small bubble of air did come up into the bag as the compartment opened. It was not enough to fill the entire bag, so he knew the black box had been resting in seawater for some time now.

Pulling loose the connecting wires from the outer portion of the black box, Alex placed the black box into the plastic bag. This would be good enough for the short time it would take him to take it to the more shallow depth. He decided to do a full circle around the wreckage just before his ascent, so he checked his compass at zero from the nose of the plane and decided to go out and do a full 360 degrees and return to the nose of the plane. This way he could keep his bearings and be able to ascend to the location that he had left the aqua sled.

Just before closing off the circle and returning to the nose of the plane, Alex noticed some glitter shining in his peripheral vision off to the right. He stopped, checked his bearings back to where the plane was, and then went the next ten yards to where the glint was coming from. He found another piece of wreckage.

From the small piece of wing still attached to this housing, it was obvious to Alex that this was the jet engine housing from the right-side engine assembly of the plane. He looked at it in awe, surprised by what his eyes were trying to tell him. On the anterior portion of the jet engine housing was a large, jagged hole. The hole penetrated the housing and bent the metal inward toward the engine. It was four to six inches in diameter and was circular in shape. On the interior portion of the jet engine housing was exactly the opposite kind of configuration to the metal. The metal on this side was all bent away and pushed open as if a large explosive shell had entered the anterior portion of the housing and on the impact had caused an explosion. It had then exploded the interior housing as it separated from the plane.

Alex thought to himself, *This plane was shot down! But who—and why?* These were scary questions, but he had no answers. Alex stayed as knowledgeable as he could about the politics of the world, but he could not imagine why a plane carrying vacationing passengers and flying in what was considered peaceful airspace would be shot down. These were things the navy was going to have to investigate. Hopefully, with the contents of the black box, if it weren't too damaged, they would discover the reasons behind this disaster. Surely the contents would reveal the reports from the captain, the copilot, and the computer as they began to feel the pitch of the plane and felt the explosion.

Alex contained his thoughts and returned to the front of the airplane, completing the 360-degree observation dive he had made to circle the airplane's debris field. At this point he decided it was time to check in with Angela prior to going up to where he had left the aqua sled.

Angela, he thought. *Angela.*

Yes, Alex. Are you okay?

I'm fine. I'm just beginning to ascend to the aqua sled. I've found the box, and I'm finished here.

Was it awful? Angela asked.

The view itself, Angela, wasn't awful. Knowing what must have taken place was awful. I'll be ascending now to the aqua sled. From this depth, taking it easy, I should be there in twenty-five minutes. I'll check in with you as soon as I reach the aqua sled.

That's fine, Alex. I'll look forward to your message at that point.

As Alex was ascending he was realizing how tiring it was to communicate with Angela from this distance. This wasn't something he had contemplated, but it took an extreme amount of concentration on his part to generate the conditions that would allow them to communicate through their thoughts. He knew he needed to make mental notes of this and report this back to Angela when they reviewed all of this later today. This would be something that they would need to consider for any such future dives. In fact, Alex noticed as he began to ascend, the conversation with Angela from this distance was more exhausting than any of the physical efforts he was making on the dive. As he continued to slowly ascend, he seemed to recover from that fatigue very quickly. He continued to feel his full strength, both mentally and physically, returning.

The torches Alex had taken with him had burned a little more quickly at the depths than he'd expected. He was now using his last one. Surfacing slowly using a method of inhaling with extremely deep breaths to create buoyancy inside his lungs, Alex was peering around at the different sea life as he rose from the thirty-five hundred-foot depth. The water was so clear and pristine that Alex could now see the lights he'd left lit from the liquid luminescence tubes at the aqua sled still some eighty feet away.

As Alex noticed the small lights on the aqua sled, the hand-held torch burned out. Almost instantly, Alex could see his way as if it were daylight. Surprised, he suddenly remembered his eyes had the ability to adjust to this lack-of-light situation. He had experienced this on the day of his return home, but had not been in a situation where it was tested again until now.

He couldn't tell for sure; he thought the sled had drifted just a little, even with the three sea anchors hanging from it, but it had maintained its position well enough that he found it with no problem. Alex placed the black box firmly on the sled. He then placed himself on the sled, pulled up the sea anchors, and placed them in their holding containers. Alex then attached both sides of the sled's clasps, right side and left side, to the rings on his suit. Alex turned on the sled and began progressing to where he remembered a 150-foot sea formation; this would be a good spot to place the black box. It had occurred to him that they might not look for it at that shallow a depth, and even though he was trying to keep a pure anonymity, he wanted them to find the box.

For that reason, Alex had also taken from the cockpit area the homing beacon from under the equipment area of the pilot's seat. This homing beacon was used as an airplane signature beacon, so whoever was monitoring the different airplanes in the air could distinguish one from another and its general location by the radio signal being emitted from the beacon. Placing the two items together would assure the black box being found. It only took Alex five minutes to find the right formation.

He laid the black box and the homing beacon on the formation. They were firmly in place and would not be washed off by the movement of the water. Checking his compass, he turned the aqua sled in the correct direction so that he had bearing on the location of Angela and the *Blackthorn*. Alex began the slow trip back to the dive boat.

Angela? Alex contemplated.

Yes, Alex?

The reply back from Angela seemed less clear than before, which made no sense to Alex at first, since he was now at a depth of 150 feet rather than at the 3,500 feet when they'd last communicated. He told her, *I just placed the black box and the beacon on the formation, and I'm heading back to the boat.*

That would be good. Please hurry.

What's going on, Angela? You don't sound right.

It is hard for me to … She stopped.

Angela, are you okay?

It is hard for me to talk right now … it is hard for me to concentrate and think right now, Alex. I'm in a conversation with a navy patrolman.

A navy patrolman?

Yes, Alex, a navy patrolman. A boat pulled up just a moment ago, and her captain is speaking to me ship to ship. He is questioning why we are here. Questioning what we are doing because we are so close to the search area for the airline crash. You hurry back, and I'll deal with this. Check in with me as you get closer.

Alex set the electric motor on the aqua sled for full output. He had not used full output before because of the enormous strain it put on the motor. He knew if he had engaged full output on the way out, he would have only made it halfway back on the original journey. But, judging from the amount still registered on the meter, he should have plenty of power to get him all the way back to his gear tied beneath the *Blackthorn*.

Full output still didn't send him at a terrific speed. In fact, the best estimate that he could get was it would cut the time by maybe ten minutes on his return. That was still ten minutes quicker so that he could return and help Angela with her explanation of why they were there.

Now only ten minutes from where the *Blackthorn* was and where his gear was tied, Alex started his contemplation to contact Angela.

Angela? They are still there I suppose?

Yes, they are. Things are fine. I have explained to them who we are, I've shown them our passports, and explained to them that we run a dive shop and you and I on occasion will go out and inspect particular locations for recreational divers. Since we credit ourselves for being a dive shop for the more experienced diver, we occasionally look for those very unusual locations other divers don't usually go to. That's what brought us here, and you are now down below the boat at some 120 feet checking around. They questioned me about your air supply and why you had been down there, so far as they know, some forty-five minutes.

What was your reply to that one?

My reply was that you have a two-tank system and that you are an experienced diver. Since you were doing just the one dive, you had intended to stay down until your air was nearly exhausted. From time to time, that would take you an hour and a half, sometimes an hour and forty-five minutes per dive. I tried to buy you as much time as I could, Alex.

Well, I should be climbing up to the back of the boat in about ten minutes now. I just now reached the gear. I am going to tie the sea sled off to the sea rope and then put my equipment on. You say they think I've been down about forty-five, fifty minutes?

Yes, Alex, that's about the calculation ... that's how long they have been here, and I said you had just gone down.

Well, I'm going to release enough air from my tanks to make it look like I have been down even longer. I'll be right up. You can look for me on the ladder platform any moment now.

As good as his word, no sooner had Alex and Angela disconnected their thoughts from their telepathic communication than Alex's bubbles were visible at the rear of the boat. Alex had taken the e-reg off and placed it in one of the larger pouches attached to his BC.

As he grew closer to the surface he could see the large hull of the navy patrol boat alongside the *Blackthorn*. The sea was quick and was moving the boat around at a greater speed than when Alex had first began the dive, so the ladder was moving in a five-foot distance from point A to point B. Alex had to time this just right to grab the ladder as it went onto the downstroke and then get up onto the ladder before it went to the upstroke. Otherwise, he would suffer a severe beating from the ladder as it began to rise and fall with the water. Doing this rhythmically, Alex got onto the ladder after pulling off his fins and handing the fins up to Angela, who was at the rear of the boat waiting for his equipment. Alex climbed up onto the ladder platform and sat down on the rear of the boat.

"Well, it looks like we have guests!" Alex said.

"Yes, this is Captain Smith. Captain Smith is in charge of the navy patrol boat alongside. They are part of the team out looking for the wreckage of that airplane that crashed a week or so ago."

"Oh, yeah—I guess that was pretty close to here."

"Yeah, from what they've told me, it is not a great distance from here, only a few miles."

"Wow, if I'd have known that ... well, this isn't going to be a good dive site for us anyway, Angela."

"Oh, why is that?"

"Well, I could tell there are some really interesting wall dives, and there are going to be some really interesting formations, but from what I could see from a distance, they weren't going to begin until about 180 to 200 feet; just too deep for the recreation divers we are going to be bringing out."

"Mr. McPherson?"

"Yes."

"I'm Captain Smith. Let me help you with those tanks."

Alex released his BCD hasp from his vest area as Captain Smith's left hand grasped the connecting valve between the two tanks, pulling them up onto the deck of the boat while slipping the tanks off Alex's back. As Captain Smith did so, his right hand reached to give Alex a hand onto the boat deck. His left hand was pulling the BC around to give him a full clear view of the air gauge. He checked the remaining air pressure in the two-tank system that he had just taken from Alex.

"Your wife here tells me," Captain Smith began, "that this two-tank system holds about 5,000 psi. Is that true?"

"Yes, sir, it is."

"Boy, I see you cut it pretty close. You are at about 750 psi."

"Yeah, it is a rule of mine, Captain Smith: I never stay in the water past 500 psi. You never know what is going to happen, especially in sea conditions like this. You don't know how long you might have to wait until you can catch that ladder just right."

"Well, sir," Captain Smith said, "I don't really want to tell you what you can or can't do; after all, this is open water and you are not breaking any boating rules. But you might be looked at a little harshly if anyone found out you were this close to the site until we're through. There are a lot of scavengers that think they can find something even though the depths have been reported quite honestly to everyone. There is no one around going to go that deep. We are going to have to send our remotes down to find anything ourselves. Well, if you two are fine, I'm going to wish you a good night," the captain began as he starting walking toward the connecting ramp connecting the two boats, "and we'll be shoving off."

"Thank you for keeping me company this past hour," Angela said to the captain.

"It was my pleasure, ma'am, and thank you for the coffee. Sir, ma'am," the captain called as he waved and left.

The patrol boat slowly went back toward the area just above where Alex had left the wreckage not more than twenty-five minutes before.

On the boat trip back, Alex shared with Angela the different things he'd seen, specifically the observations he'd made of the right jet engine housing. The two of them quietly sat sipping coffee as the auto pilot steered the *Blackthorn* toward home.

The next day the news was full of an Associated Press story carried on CNN. CNN was reporting the black box from the missing airliner had now been discovered by a Navy SEAL team. It would still be some time before they could report on the contents of the box; the FAA were controlling the next stages of their investigation. Alex and Angela were pleased with what they had done. Since the navy had recovered the box, the FAA would have enough information to look into the matter. They could now discover the information concerning the plane having been shot down. Maybe they could find out who had caused this and bring the proper people to justice.

CHAPTER 7

Alex had been planning a little event for Angela for a few weeks now. He had spoken with his friends at their favorite pub, the Hog Sty, and they were going to throw an island party to celebrate Alex and Angela's wedding anniversary.

Trying to keep his plans a surprise from Angela, Alex had said on the day of the party, "Why don't we go to town, get a sandwich, and just relax for the evening with the gang over at the Hog Sty?"

They took their Targa cabin cruiser from their personal dock on Rum Bay, cut across the inlet, and went into Governor's Bay, docking in one of the private slips. A car had been parked there for times like these. When they arrived at the Hog Sty, it looked like the typical crowd there, but it was quite obvious to Angela now that the place was decorated a little bit differently. It's more than likely the giveaway was the streamers and big sign across the back that said "Happy Anniversary Angela." Their friend behind the bar brought out two drinks as soon as they walked in: Alex's favorite pint of hard English cider and a special mudslide the proprietor always made for Angela, including the little signature touch of a few drops of Kahlua poured in the top end of the straw just before serving. After giving them their drinks, their friend starting tapping a stainless-steel mixing container to get everyone's attention.

"I need your attention!" he said in his thick Liverpool accent. "Everyone! Alex McPherson has something he'd like to say to his Angela."

As they looked around the room, which had surprisingly quieted down, they saw beaming smiles everywhere, from their boat crews, their friends, and a lot of people they had never seen before who just happened to be there for their own evening out. All eyes were intent on Alex. Alex turned to Angela and, in one fluid motion, lifted her and seated her on the bar.

"I wrote a little song for you. This isn't the most appropriate place to have romantic music. I'm sorry," he said, turning to his friend behind the bar, "but it's not a performing arts kind of joint. However, the proprietor of this fine establishment has kindly allowed me to set the stage to sing to you in my best vibrato. Angela, however it sounds, this is from my heart."

Alex began his song with these words:

> "I see you, all the time,
> Not with my eyes but with my mind.
> I touch you from far behind,
> Not on your skin, but that inside.
>
> Lady you're the one,
> The girl I've waited for.
> With you by my side,
> What man could ask for more?
> I wonder what you think of me
> As I go down life's way.
> I want your heart to sing of me
> In a very special way.
>
> I hear you as you sigh,
> Not with my ears, but with my eyes.
> As you walk toward me
> With your head held so high,
> I see your face, I feel your smile.

> Lady you're the one,
> The girl I've waited for.
> With you by my side,
> How could I ask for more?
> I wonder what you think of me
> As I go down life's way.
> I want your heart to sing of me
> In a very special way.

When Alex had completed his song, all Angela could do was cry tears of joy as she leaped off the bar into his arms.

"Hear, hear!" said the proprietor from behind the bar. "Hear, hear! That was excellent! I'd say drinks are on the house, but I'm no fool, so everyone drink up at your own cost, and let's have a party here!" He turned around and cranked up the CD player, which started playing some ZZ Top from the 1970s.

The evening turned into a swinging party, with everyone laughing, playing darts, and singing to the music for the next several hours.

When Alex had planned this evening, he'd arranged for one of the island cabs to come by and pick them up at about eleven o'clock to take them home. He would come and get the car the next day; it would be safe enough at the Hog Sty. As the cab drove them to their home in Rum Point, Angela was leaning her head over on Alex's shoulder.

"You know I love you very much, mister," Angela said.

"I had an inkling that was on your mind. I am looking forward to a lot of years together."

"Me too."

The tenderness of the moment and the celebration they'd had that evening carried Angela and Alex on wings of joy. Arriving home, their shared exhilaration propelled them into waves of passion that were barely subsiding as the morning sun peered onto Rum Bay.

Angela, who had pushed herself to exhaustion, stared down into Alex's eyes. She then collapsed beside him, whispering, "Happy anniversary, my love. I hope you enjoyed how I unwrapped your gift. I know I enjoyed how you unwrapped mine."

CHAPTER 8

I t was one of those island evenings that mainlanders in the States could only dream about. The sun was setting across the horizon as a large colorful balloon of molten metal blending with the ocean and disappearing into the night. Alex and Angela were sitting quietly in the gazebo on their private dock. The dock provided a serene location to sit and listen to the water lapping against the aged wooden piles it securely rested on while taking in the view of this lovely sunset.

"Angela, I've been giving something quite a bit of thought. Since we found the black box and I made the dive and saw the wreckage of the airliner, I've had thoughts of how to possibly use these abilities I now have. I've given thoughts to diver rescue and the salvage of shipwrecks to try to help explain why they sank. Maybe even search for the final resting place of the crew, if the crew was never found. There are a lot of possibilities where we could provide service."

Angela replied soberly and spoke very slowly, "I think you're right, Alex. This would be a great opportunity, but we would have to be very careful. We would want to make sure we still had control over our lives and not allow someone to discover your skills and abilities for what they are. They might want to steal you away to some lab and try to dissect you. Just the thought of that …"

"Yeah, with the changes in my molecular structure, they're going to have to find an awfully sharp knife to be able to even give that one a try," he said with a smirk. "But I do see what you mean, in all seriousness. I think I've got an idea of how we can keep some anonymity, as well as provide some service and have some fun and adventure along the way."

Angela and Alex continued to talk through the evening, sipping wine, looking at the sunset as it finally crested into the ocean, and then gazing at the stars. Only in the highest points of the Rocky Mountains could you match the stars and the magnificent view from Rum Bay. When there were no city lights and no light pollution blocking your view, the sky looked alive and vibrant, as if it had been waiting patiently to come out and play.

When the evening was over, they had formed a plan. They would begin preparation the next morning toward the creation of a new corporation. This corporation would be named TESS, for Terran Exploration & Salvage Society. They intentionally picked a bland name, a name that wouldn't draw much attention if people happened to be searching for something and trying to dig up information about it. With the magic of computers and corporate ownership, they would be able to bury the information about who the members of TESS were, as well as the contact information.

Over the next several months following the formation of TESS, they acquired a very large, French-built salvage vessel and began doing some private salvage. Alex and Angela christened the salvage vessel the *Tessa*. They found their experiences quite interesting in locating, identifying, and even bringing up some of the small airplanes and vessels that over the last 100 to 150 years had been lost because of the depths they had fallen to. By utilizing the *Tessa*, they were able to find and transport the discoveries. They had established a small waterfront warehouse on the backside of the island of Cayman Brac, the smallest of the three islands in the Caymans. In that warehouse they placed their discoveries in dry dock with an elaborately built structure that Angela had designed.

TESS would be an entity of the United States Corporate Law Division and would be an invited guest in this particular location by the Cayman government. This was a common corporate structure.

The next step would be a little bit trickier. They had also discussed this second step on that balmy evening, but nothing had been put into place until some thirty days after that pleasant twilight of wine and sunset with the stellar light show going on. Now Alex and Angela boarded the *Blackthorn* and headed out for the Gulf of Mexico. Before leaving, they had made arrangements for Tony to stay with some friends, since they knew this trip was probably going to last a couple of weeks. Their destination was the island of Galveston, in the northwest part of the Gulf of Mexico. On Galveston there was a US naval base, one of the largest in the area.

After a pleasant but uneventful cruise, the two sailors, Angela and Alex, docked and tied off at one of the piers in the southern part of Galveston. They made some inquiries and found out that the senior officer at the naval base was an admiral. They knew nothing of the admiral, only that his name was Admiral Sterling. They also discovered that the naval base, since it had several ships docked along its pier, gave daily tours of these ships. This was something Alex and Angela were going to use to their advantage.

They made their way to the main gate of the base, found that the next tour would begin in about thirty minutes, and obtained a small tour map of the base. Locating on the map the administrative building, where Admiral Sterling's offices would surely be located, they found it was on the direct path of the tour. Trying to maintain the anonymity they were seeking, for Alex especially, they determined they would try to contact Admiral Sterling while walking around with the other tourists in the group. Alex would attempt to utilize his telepathic communication abilities.

With this in mind over the last thirty days, Alex had been experimenting with contacting other people, placing thoughts in their minds and trying to read their thoughts. He hadn't considered this prior to this particular plan. Alex and Angela had utilized this particular ability on several occasions throughout many of their dives, but it had only been Alex contacting Angela and Angela communicating in return. Alex found if he could concentrate in the specific geographic area where the individual was at that moment, concentrating on sending out a message of "hello," then once he heard a response from that individual he would be able to zero in on the mind pattern of that particular individual. It seemed the mind pattern was as distinctive as a person's voice. Once he heard a particular voice or heard a particular sound, he could block out a lot of the other sounds around and concentrate on that singular sound.

The tour began. From their study of the map, they found that they would never be more than one hundred yards away from the administrative building. The tour would last about thirty minutes. Alex determined he needed to try to make contact with Admiral Sterling right from the start. Angela held Alex's hand and guided him while they walked with the tour group.

Alex began to look directly at the administrative building, merely calling out in his mind, *Admiral Sterling, can you hear me? Admiral Sterling, can you hear me?* Alex repeated this silent questioning, *Admiral Sterling, can you hear me?* three times.

Then he heard a reply in his own thoughts, *Is there someone speaking to me?*

Alex had made contact! From the beginning he'd known this was going to be a very peculiar way of communicating with someone, especially when they didn't expect it. So the first thing Alex needed to do was explain as quickly as possible how this contact was occurring.

Admiral Sterling? Yes, I am speaking to you, but I am communicating with you in an unusual manner. Please don't be frightened. I have an ability, a talent, to communicate telepathically with others. Do you understand me?

Yes I do, but I've got to tell you, this has caught me totally off guard. I don't know I can believe what's happening, and I'm not sure I like it, but go ahead.

Are you alone, Admiral Sterling?

Yes, I am.

Good, I need a few moments of your time. There are a few things I'd like to discuss with you.

Well, where can we meet?

No sir, I'm afraid this must be the way we discuss. It will be safest for the both of us, and apparently we are able to communicate quite well in this manner.

I still don't believe it, but go ahead.

I'm a member of a society that has dedicated much effort toward undersea exploration and salvage. Along with that, we have made efforts toward rescue of several different varieties. This group is called TESS, the Terran Exploration and Salvage Society. There's nothing secretive about this group. The information we're trying to keep secret applies to a few of its members and a few of the ways we are able to help. The reason I'm making this contact is that we at TESS have decided to offer our services to the United States, especially to the United States military, but not for military purposes. We want to offer our services to help protect some of our country's military personnel who may find themselves in dangerous situations while at sea. That is what we do; this is what we wish to offer. It doesn't necessarily have to be a United States situation, but since we are US citizens, we felt our best and safest contacts would be through the US government. If our government were to be called upon to help in another country's sea-based incident, then we hope you would contact TESS and discover whether there is any way we can intervene and help with the rescue.

Wait just a minute here, interrupted Admiral Sterling. *Let me get this straight. I'm sitting here in my office, alone, and I'm having a conversation with someone who tells me he's the member of some kind of salvage and rescue group who wants to offer his services to do something in a sea-rescue arena that the entire United States military and naval forces can't do? Do I have what you've told me fairly correct?*

I know it sounds quite hard to believe; that's why I wanted to offer some information to you. We have already helped you once. We didn't make our presence known to anyone. We assisted with the airline tragedy in the Caribbean, where days of searching had taken place in attempts to locate the black box, with no success. Divers found the black box in only 150 feet of water with a homing beacon, apart from any other wreckage, resting on an underwater rock ledge. Do you recall this information?

Yes, and that's classified. How did you—

Just a second, please, Admiral Sterling. I know about the box and its whereabouts because I was the one who placed the box there.

You what? *How could you have—*

Admiral Sterling, please let me continue. I went to the site of the wreckage. The wreckage was far deeper than any of your people were able to go. I pored over the wreckage of that airplane, and when I located the black box, I brought it up to where it could be found. I wanted the answers to be known to try to prevent another tragedy. I didn't need the box, though, and judging by the information your people let out into the newspapers, you didn't need the box either, because you didn't use the correct information.

What do you mean by that? To my knowledge the correct information was presented. This was a terrible tragedy, but it involved no outside force.

Sir, in all due respect, I saw the damage, I saw the wreckage, I saw the engine panels. This plane was hit with a ground-to-air missile. I saw the burn marks. I saw the evidence, and I'm sure the black box was able to report enough information that the conclusion could have been drawn from its contents.

Okay, my friend, you've made your point. I'm a little more convinced that you can do at least some of what you say you can, but I've got to tell you, I'm still in great disbelief about our method of communication. Why won't you speak to me personally, and what are your ulterior motives are in all of this?

Admiral, you've been in the military too long. Not everyone has an ulterior motive. My motives are plain and simple. I have explained them in brief here today. My motives are that TESS and the members of TESS wish to help. Help rescue, help salvage, help explore situations that might educate or protect people. The only services we can offer are services that have to do with the world's oceans. This is our specialty. My time is almost up, Admiral, so let me please make one final statement. I've made the offer. I've made it for TESS. It is now up to you. If you and the people you confide in choose to call on us when the need presents itself, I'd like to provide you with a way. Do you have a pen and paper nearby?

Yes, I do.

Please write this down. It is an e-mail address. The address is manta@ mixi.net. *Do you have that, Admiral? That's* manta@mixi.net.

Excuse me, son, but if you want to be so secretive, why are you giving me an e-mail address you know I can trace?

Good question, but it is a question we answered long before. That is an e-mail address, and yes, you can trace it, but you'll trace it to a town in northeastern Indiana. You'll trace it to a land-based server where there will be no idea, no whereabouts, and no ability to trace beyond that point. Contact through that particular e-mail address is made through an anonymous remailer unit that no one can trace. So you can place information on that e-mail address and only TESS will be able to pull the information. If you choose to use us, that is to say, to call on us to see if we might be able to help, contact that e-mail address and place the coordinates of latitude and longitude for the ocean-related location. We will then move our ship to that location, contact your people at the site, and find out what circumstances exist. We will then share with you our opinion of the potential success or failure of that particular mission. Admiral, by placing the coordinates on the e-mail address, you will not be breaching any security issues concerning any specifics about the situation. The particular server we have will notify us almost immediately that there is an e-mail message sitting in the box. We will then move our equipment to the location and, as I said, make our determination of the potential success of the mission at that point. My time is done now, Admiral. I must break this communication.

Now, wait a minute son, there are a lot of questions I still have. I need to meet you. I've gotten this e-mail address written down, but that's not a ... how am I ...

Admiral, sir, you and I cannot meet at this point. You will in the future, if you choose to use our help, meet some of the members of TESS, but I am an individual who must stay hidden and behind the scenes for the time being. This is something important to us. In a lighthearted sense, the members of TESS have given me a little nickname. This will be the name that you can use to contact me through the e-mail address if you need to get a message directly to me. Since I like the water so much, the members of TESS have chosen the code name of Manta. Admiral, please accept our offer. This is something we've discussed at great length. This is something we want to do. We have no idea specifically what kind of mission you may call on us to assist with, but we do want to help. Thank you very much, Admiral, for your time, and I hope this particular method of communication and the information I have shared has not caught you too off guard. Again, do consider our offer.

Right at the moment Alex had broken off his telepathic communication with the admiral, he and Angela had approached the gate where the tour ended. They had engineered a nice thirty-minute tour and a nice thirty-minute conversation with the Admiral without ever meeting him. As the tour group was passing through the exit gate, Alex and Angela noticed an increased amount of activity around the administration building. People were pouring out of all the doors and looking all around. The security guards at the gate were picking up their phones and listening to messages of some sort. The activity was high; apparently the admiral was trying to search out who it was that he had been talking to, but Alex and Angela were already well beyond the gate's walkway, headed out to make their way back toward the pier.

They would dine that evening on Galveston's special recipe of Texas hot chili. One of the restaurants along the pier boasted it was their claim to fame. While dining and still somewhat worn from spending the last week on the boat, they decided they would stay in the Radisson, on the beach, and relax for a couple of days before making their journey back to Rum Bay.

CHAPTER 9

One evening, while Tony was chatting with a few of his international friends through a teen-related Internet chat room, the e-mail indicator on the screen illuminated. We had instructed Tony to inform us as soon as possible if he noticed any e-mail on the system.

"Dad—hey, Dad. There's a new piece of mail coming in. You want to look at it now or later?"

"If you're at a stopping place, I'll look at it now."

Tony vacated the chair and Alex moved in front of the screen. Alex and Angela had several friends in the states who primarily contacted them with e-mail since the cost was so much less and it was always a lot more fun than just snail-mailing a letter. Alex opened the mailbox in the Internet software and entered the required password to receive the message. This was not from one of their friends. On the screen, starkly shown with no explanation, was a set of map coordinates.

"Angela, you'd better come in here. I think you're gonna want to see this."

"What's up? Oh my God! It's happening. It's been three months since we offered, and now they're calling for us. I'll get the map."

While Angela went for the map to plot the two sets of numbers, Alex printed out the e-mail and cleared the screen.

Angela had spread the map over the kitchen table, and the two of them correlated the numbers and found the crossing point of the coordinates.

"Right in the middle of the Atlantic. What do you think the problem is?"

"Impossible to guess at this point, Angela. We did offer, and Admiral Sterling is calling for help."

"I can have the *Tessa* ready to head out in two hours, by 9:00 p.m. at the latest. But in looking at these coordinates, it's gonna take us eighteen hours, at full speed, to get there. That would put the *Tessa* at those coordinates at about 3:00 p.m. tomorrow." Angela said this as she began pulling out the needed charts for the journey.

"I'll need to fly out ahead of you, Angela." Alex continued, "If I get there early, I can assess the situation and began to formulate a plan."

"You could take the seaplane, but that part of the ocean may be too rough for the plane to land, and even if you land it safely, it may be swept away after you set it down."

"What if I have Rene fly me out there, and I can parachute to the surface with minimal gear?" Before Angela could swing completely around to argue this part of the plan, Alex continued, "If I leave within the hour, Rene can have me over the coordinates in less than three hours. I can take a full utility belt, a set of submersible lights, my scuba gear, and tanks to make it look good. With my equipment and my e-reg, I'll be able to begin to recon the area. The situation may require greater speed than an eighteen-hour response time."

Angela looked at Alex with a serious and thoughtful expression. "You're right. I hate it when you're right. You pull your gear together, and I'll drop you at the airport on my way to the dock."

Alex went to the phone and called Rene. Rene had piloted jets in Vietnam in the latter part of the war. Right after the war, he had gone to work for a small commercial airline in the southwestern part of the states. Rene had flown for them for ten years, long enough for him to buy a *Bonanza* twin engine and set up a charter service based out of the Caymans. Rene now had four planes, with three additional pilots, for the active trade of his charter service, but he still kept the *Bonanza* for his own use. Alex had befriended Rene shortly after coming to the islands through the diving the two of them enjoyed. When Alex had apparently been lost to the sharks, Rene had been one of the divers who'd searched for days after the attack. Rene had found pieces of Alex's bloodied wetsuit—which was the closest anyone had come to finding Alex. Following Alex's return, he and Rene had grown even closer. When Alex and Angela had decided to try to use Alex's aquatic abilities in the rescue arena, they had approached Rene about assisting them. Rene, now in his early fifties, had offered to help in any way he could.

Rene had told Alex, "I don't understand how you survived the shark attack and came back to your family and dry land. I do know one thing, though—there was a reason for all of this. If you're going to help separate others from the ocean's deep grip, then I want to be there and be a part of it in any way I can."

Alex now called him up. "Rene, I've got an emergency. I need you to fly me about seven hundred miles north-northeast and parachute drop me into the ocean. No, I've not been hitting the cider all night. There's a ship in trouble, and we've been asked to help. It will take Angela and the boys much longer to get there, and I need to assess the situation ASAP. I'll be at the airport in thirty minutes." With that, Alex hung up, went to the storeroom, and began gathering his gear. He also thought to bring a large inflatable raft and a full length of nylon cord to attach to a sea anchor to help keep the inflatable in position until Angela could arrive.

Angela had taken the opportunity to call Mark and Dan to have them go to the *Tessa* and begin preparing her for sea. The *Tessa* was always in readiness, fully stocked and equipped for nearly any salvage expedition, but all of the computer and mechanical systems would need to be initiated and checked out before setting out. With Mark and Dan on their way to the ship, Angela gathered the rest of her gear into their launch and set out to deliver Alex to the airport. By cutting across the bay, they would save a half an hour over driving. They spent this time discussing Alex's plans for discovery prior to Angela bringing the *Tessa* into position.

Angela sat quietly for a moment as she watched the twin-engine *Bonanza* leave the tarmac and take a north-northeastern heading. She whispered, "Be careful, my love."

Alex had heard her thoughts, and he replied, "I will—I'll see you tomorrow afternoon."

As the *Bonanza* flew close to the targeted drop point, Alex was awakening from a brief nap. Sleep wasn't easy with an unknown mission awaiting him, but he knew at least a little sleep would be necessary.

"We're here, my friend," reported Rene. "I feel a bit awful just dropping you out here, but I trust you know what you're doing."

"I have the same trust, Rene. Is that a ship up ahead?"

"Looks to be," replied Rene. "Navy—US—but I can't make out the name yet."

"Better let me out just before we get to her. I'll prepare the raft for the jump."

"Alex, if we get much closer to that ship she'll start hailing us, and I have no idea why we're here. I don't think they're going to buy pleasure flying in this area. Better let you out here."

"You're right. I'm opening the side door."

With that, Alex opened the side door of the plane, positioned the raft package, and pushed it through the opening. As it fell, the long pull cord still trailing from the side of the plane opened the attached parachute. The chute opened, and the package began slowly targeting the ocean for a wet, yet fairly soft, landing.

"I'm next. Thank you, my friend. I'll buy you a pint of cider when we get back."

"You'll buy me more than one pint, and then I'll buy you a few. Geronimo and good luck!" were the last words Alex heard as he jumped through the opening of the Bonanza.

Alex sailed through the air. He began to free-fall until he had successfully targeted the raft package's chute, now floating on the ocean's surface. Pulling his main cord, Alex felt the strain of the main chute opening. The enveloping air slowed Alex's decent so quickly that the straps of the chute made a cracking sound, like that of a whip against rough leather. About twenty feet above the water, not wanting to become tangled in the chute, Alex released himself from the shoulder connections. Alex fell quickly into the sea, watching as the wind pulled the chute up quickly at first and then wrestled the yards of blanketing material onto the surface about ten yards from Alex's entry point.

Alex made his way to the floating raft package and released it from its own parachute. The chute material billowed across the water as if someone had pulled it neatly out of the way. First checking that all of the outer seals were in place, Alex pulled the inflation cord, and the raft quickly took form before him. Alex rolled into the nearly inflated raft, and then the side became firm and fully inflated. The packing had succeeded. All of Alex's gear was securely displayed before him. Having anticipated the cold temperatures of this area of the sea, Alex had packed a warm jacket and had parachuted in a full-body drysuit with a Thinsulate lining. With Alex's enhanced stamina and molecular structure, he had no need for this warming equipment, but he thought it would still be more comfortable to stay as warm and dry as possible.

Alex first set out to secure his position. Loosening the clamps from around the sea-anchor pack, he pulled the three sea anchors and the nylon cords from their pouches. Using his best sailor's knots, he fastened the ends of the cords through the rings of the anchors and secured the other ends to the three points of the raft. With the anchor cords secure, Alex lowered the three anchors over the side. These anchors would not hold the raft in a single position, but they would prevent the raft from drifting more than a few yards in a day's passing.

With the anchors in place and the raft's position secured, Alex went about his next task. He needed to establish radio contact with either Admiral Sterling or whoever was in charge of this particular naval operation. Since he and Rene had spotted the ships from the air before Alex's plunge to the sea, he was sure he could raise them on his radio. He had considered trying to contact them telepathically. In fact, he and Angela had discussed this contingency in great detail. Their conclusion was that Alex would use all normal means of contact with those they might work with, unless he was assured to be out of view. When he was in contact with anyone, in a normal manner, he would use his own name. When he contacted anyone telepathically, he would use his TESS moniker, Manta. By communicating in this manner, Manta, the one who would perform the seemingly impossible feats, would be able to stay anonymous. Likewise, Alex, who could be traced and spotted easily by any form of investigation, would be a more upfront, obvious player in the rescue scheme.

Removing the straps from the radio pack and pulling the marine radio from the pouch, Alex was able to power the radio up in only a few moments. He checked his dive watch to confirm the current time. It was 11:45 p.m. He began. "TESS calling naval rescue vessel, TESS calling naval rescue vessel."

"This is the USSN *Discovery*. Go ahead TESS."

"*Discovery*, I'm a member of the requested supplemental rescue team, TESS. The balance of my team is on its way. I need to speak with someone who can bring me up to speed on this situation."

"TESS, this is Admiral Sterling. Is Manta with you yet?"

"Admiral Sterling, good to hear you're involved. Manta is on site, but he is unavailable to speak at this time. My name is Alex McPherson, and I'm in charge right now. What are the current circumstances, and how can we be of assistance?"

"Alex," replied Admiral Sterling, "we have a very serious situation here, and I'm not sure anyone can help us. Three days ago, one of our Los Angeles-class subs scraped the side of a deep canyon wall. This caused falling rock to quickly encase the sub, which caused the sub to become trapped. That was three days ago. We sent for and subsequently deployed the *NR-1, that's Nuclear Research 1*, and its support ship the, USS *Sunbird*. We've successfully used the *NR-1* in situations like this in the past. While the *NR-1* was approaching the LA-class sub to assess the situation, the same wall collapsed further and succeeded in trapping the *NR-1* as well. We don't know if there has been any structural damage to either vessel. What we do know is both boats are trapped, and we have no plan of how to save either boat."

"Admiral," Alex began," I need the location of the two boats, depth included, and we'll begin a recognizance dive to determine what options exist for the two boats."

"Forgive me, Mr. McPherson, but how the hell do you intend to dive on two subs that currently sit below their respective crush depths?"

"As I'm sure Manta relayed to you in his last communication, we have unique methods of rescue to offer as help. If you are interested in our help, I would ask you please refrain from questioning us about our methods."

"Understood—I think. I'm going to put our operations officer on with you. He'll share with you the information we have to help you locate the subs. Mr. McPherson, I appreciate your coming to the site and will appreciate whatever help you can offer. Those are my men down there. Do what you can."

During the next few minutes, Alex jotted notes from the information the operations officer shared with him. The subs were trapped beneath in excess of three thousand feet of ocean. The *NR-1* was rated safe up to twenty-six hundred feet, with the Los Angeles-class boat having a maximum depth of fifteen hundred feet. The LA-class boat had a predicted collapse depth that exceeded their operating depth by a factor of 1.7 to 2.0, which made its maximum capability three thousand feet. The *NR-1* had a less forgiving collapse rating, since it traveled so slowly and was rated as highly as possible to make it more acceptable as a rescue vessel. It, too, was at its limit at three thousand feet. The location was not clear, but it now rested somewhere beneath the *Discovery*.

"*Discovery*, I now have enough information to proceed. Our surface ship and the balance of our crew will arrive in the morning. They will contact you upon their arrival. If we discover anything new prior to their arrival, we'll contact you at that time."

CHAPTER 10

Alex retrieved the homing beacon from its pouch and initiated its signal. This would allow Angela to find the raft tomorrow afternoon. It was now 12:45 a.m. and time for Manta to go for a little swim. With a weighted utility belt, fins, and his e-reg, Alex rolled over the side of the raft. He calculated that he was still three miles from the navy surface ship, and based on that information, he triangulated the course he should take to place him at the site of the two trapped subs. His strength and stamina would prove invaluable over the next several hours.

Angela and Alex had been experimenting with liquid-filled encasements for certain pieces of diving equipment, including his depth gauge, a hand-held high power flashlight, and a compass. They believed these new encasements would allow the devices to perform accurately as deep as five thousand feet. These had only been tested in their lab to that depth. This would be the true proving ground. Alex was now passing a depth of two thousand feet and estimated he would reach the location of the subs within the next ten minutes.

Alex was familiar with the two submarines, their structures, capabilities, and crew complements. The LA-class sub would afford no access panels for the crew to see him as he investigated their predicament. The *NR-1* had no viewing panels either, but it was a deepwater research sub that had, on occasion, been used to assist in deepwater retrieval of items such as wreckage for study. It had, most notably, been used to retrieve wreckage from the Challenger Space Shuttle. Since this vessel was a research and retrieval vehicle, it was equipped with external cameras and a mechanical arm. These items were the reason it had been sent to assist the LA-class, and it was the external cameras that concerned Alex. They would easily identify him and capture his image on videotape. Alex had determined to approach the *NR-1* and cover the lenses of each of the cameras with a few of the dark plastic bags he had brought along for just that purpose.

Now approaching three thousand feet, Alex could just make out the outline of the *NR-1*. His triangular course had been on target. "I only hope a few other parts of this venture work out as well." Since his eyes had adjusted to the dim light given off by the micro-biotic sea life, he had not yet tried his flashlight. This was intentional, since he wanted to sneak up on the *NR-1* and disable its cameras before making himself too visible. Alex presumed that as soon as he made contact with the crew of the *NR-1*, they would try to look for him with their cameras. Additionally, they would begin to look for causes with the other two cameras when they recognized a problem with the first. With these two thoughts in mind, Alex had planned to go to the front of the *NR-1*, approaching from the underside and covering the two front-mounted units first. Then he would return to the rear of the *NR-1* by the same path and place the dark bag over its lens. After he had blinded the research sub, he would then make his first contact with its crew.

It was a good plan except for one discovery made from his initial examination of the *NR-1*'s status. The rear of the sub was buried under several extremely large boulders, which completely covered the rear camera and completely locked it in place. Alex approached the *NR-1* along the sea wall it had unintendedly become a firm part of. Staying close to the wall would allow him to reach the underside of the sub and approach the front-mounted cameras unnoticed. As he made his way to the front of the *NR-1*, it appeared to him that the structure of the sub was intact. It was firmly held from the rear and well out of reach of the front-mounted mechanical arm, but it did appear undamaged otherwise. Stopping just short of the front, Alex noticed the cameras were swirling in a slow circular motion. He waited for them to both point in the opposite direction and then made a quick move for the first camera. He slipped the little bag over the lens and tightened the attached fastener. As he had predicted, the second camera began to quickly turn in the direction of the now-disabled unit. With one swift motion, Alex forced the bag over the second of the front cameras. With the two units now blind, he felt it was time to open communication with the *NR-1*'s crew.

Commander, NR-1. Do you hear me? Alex questioned the commander telepathically.

"This is Commander Rogers of the *NR-1*," responded the commander verbally. "I do hear you, but you'll need to explain your method of communication."

I've been sent by Admiral Sterling to assess your situation and make recommendation of what alternatives exist to free your boat.

"I hear you and understand your orders, but you did not answer my question," retorted the commander. "Also, did you have anything to do with the malfunction of our video equipment?"

Your video has been temporarily disabled, answered Alex. *As to answering your question, let me pose this question: which is more important to you at this juncture, how I am communicating or that I am communicating?*

"I see your point," the commander replied with a more accepting tone. "What information or effort do you need from us?"

I'm not sure yet. I've just begun the examination of your situation. My first question is to the status of you and your crew. How are you holding up?

"My crew and I are fine at present," replied the commander. "We have assessed our damage and found it to be minimal. If we were free from the rocks, we could surface under our own power."

I'm going to ask you to be patient for a little while longer. I need you to establish contact with the LA-class sub and inform her captain a rescue team has been sent to assess the situation and I will be in contact with him in a few moments. Commander Rogers, I think it best if you describe to the captain of the LA-class that he should expect an unusual method of communication. I would appreciate your assistance in that matter.

"I understand and will follow your request. I would like to be able to give him a name of who would be contacting him, as well as my own desire for a name."

Alex replied to the commander's request, *Understood. My service name is Manta.*

"Understood," replied the commander of the *NR-1*. "We appreciate all the help you can offer, Manta. I'll contact the commander of the LA-class, Captain Dart, and inform him of your presence in the area."

With the *NR-1* now making contact with the LA-class captain, Alex began his search for the second sub. He had seen the *NR-1* immediately upon arrival to the area; its vivid green body and burnt-orange tower made it stand out against its darkly lit background. The LA-class, on the other hand was not a vivid-looking boat. It was designed sleek and gray and would tend to blend in with these rocky surroundings. Alex knew he would need to test the new flashlight to expedite this search. Reaching into one of the compartments of the utility belt fastened around his waist, he pulled the light from its pouch. After he fastened the clip to one of the holding rings on his buoyancy control vest, Alex was pleased when the light shot strongly from the hand-held unit.

Staying along the same wall and at the same depth, Alex slowly kicked his fins and moved gracefully through the water, moving the light slowly from left to right and back again. There were signs of recently fallen rock all around this wall—it was no surprise that the rock had captured its prizes. As he was almost ready to turn around and retrace his path toward the *NR-1*, Alex noticed a slight glimmer below his position and around a turn in the sea wall. This sheer rock face, dropping at least another ten thousand feet into the darkness, nearly hid the dull color of the boat. Alex changed his angle and began to descend to the area of the glimmer. As he came closer to the boat, it slowly became obvious to him that this was not the LA-class sub he was looking for.

Sitting squarely on an edge of the wall was a smaller sub, smaller than the LA-class would be. He moved in to see the ghostly appearance of an intact submarine. It was sitting as if it were waiting for the captain to give the order to power up the screws and move on. Here, resting at 3300 feet, was a submarine about 250 to 260 feet in length. It would be exciting to study this apparent relic, intact, from times gone past, but Alex needed to resume his search for the LA-class. Before leaving the site, he pulled his dive slate and grease pencil from his utility belt and jotted down the compass coordinates of this sub. It would be an adventure to come back to this spot later and research this find.

Alex reversed his direction and took a direct bearing on the *NR-1*. When he had made it back to the green-and-orange research sub, he again contacted Commander Rogers.

Commander Rogers, this is Manta. Can you hear me?

"Yes, Manta, I can hear you."

Were you able to contact Captain Dart of the LA-class?

"Yes, Manta, I informed him of your arrival and purpose. Did you find her yet?"

Alex spoke to the commander in a perplexed fashion. *No, Commander, I have not. Had you sighted her before you ran into trouble?*

No, we had not," answered the commander. "We ran into trouble almost immediately with our running so close to this wall."

Commander, why were you running so close? Didn't you believe that to be a risky course? questioned Alex.

"Yes, it was quite risky, obviously," replied the commander. "But the information we received from the LA-class was that she was trapped by fallen rock at these coordinates, and we came directly to this point with the hope of spotting her quickly."

Understood, replied Alex to the commander. *I will continue my search and update you when I have found her.*

Alex contemplated his moves. He had come to the *NR-1* from her rear and from the near underside. He had then gone from her position further down the wall at the same depth as the *NR-1*, since the report he had been given was that the two subs were thought to be at the same depth. He reasoned he should go back to the underside of the *NR-1* and increase the depth of his search directly beneath the *NR-1*'s location. Taking his bearing, Alex descended another three hundred feet and found nothing. This left only one direction, above the *NR-1*'s location. As he began to ascend again toward the *NR-1*, Alex was feeling confused, since the report from the admiral had been that the two boats were at the same depth and the *NR-1*'s commander thought the LA-class was near or at those coordinates.

Alex went around the outer surface of the *NR-1* as he began to inspect the area above the burnt-orange tower of the *NR-1*, when he stopped abruptly. He was not prepared for this discovery—he had found the LA-class submarine. It was barely ten meters above the *NR-1*, in a perpendicular position to the small research sub and separated only by the rock that rested on the tail of the *NR-1*. Its dark-gray color was hardly visible through the irregular edges of the fallen rock that had all but buried the LA-class submarine, leaving only about 20 percent of its surface exposed.

Alex's initial assessment was that neither sub could move without placing the other in jeopardy.

Now that he had found the LA-class sub, it was time to contact her captain. With the proximity of the two captured boats, Alex floated gently between them, being careful not to touch either boat, since the strength of their rocky grasps had not yet been determined.

Captain Dart, this is Manta. Are you reading me?

"Yes, Manta," the captain of the LA-class sub replied. "I had been briefed you would contact me somewhat unusually. But like Rogers in the *NR-1*, I don't care how you choose to communicate with me."

I hear you sir. What is the current status of your boat?

The captain of the LA-class replied, "It's not very promising. We've had a leak in the reactor cooling system, which forced us to shut the reactor down. We're on battery power, and that will last us another twenty hours with minimal systems operating. Structurally, we seem solid. We've maintained all watertight doors in their locked position since the first collision with the falling rock."

The first collision, sir?

"We were held by the rock at two thousand feet when we first called for help. About ten minutes after that point, we discovered the coolant leak and shut down the reactor. As Murphy's luck would have it, not more than an hour beyond that action, we felt the boat shift. When she shifted, I ordered the tanks to be pumped—I thought we might surface if we were free. I'm guessing there was too much rock on top of us to compensate with batteries only. We continued to fall to our current location. We haven't budged since that shift, and I've ordered minimal movement from my crew."

It appears your assessment of the rock is accurate, Captain Dart. Alex continued his telepathic communication. *Were you able to blow the tanks clean?*

"About 50 percent," replied the captain. "I saw we were burning energy, and the ballast tanks were unchanged, so I ceased the attempt. I needed to save some power for eventualities."

Understood. You know your boat, sir. If you were freed from the rock, would you float with 50 percent ballast?

"I'm afraid not. The best we could hope for at that level would be neutral buoyancy."

Frankly, sir, continued Alex, *I believe it was your attempt to blow the tanks and the fact that you did as well as you did that saved both boats. Are you aware of the position of the NR-1, sir?*

"Not precisely," replied the captain, "but we knew she was near."

Captain Dart, you are no more than thirty feet above her, both held by the same wall. If you had not blown you ballast, you would have sheared her tail off and caused severe structural damage to your own boat, which at this depth would have finished you both.

"I see your point. Well, if we get out of this one, I'll need to write an article on the proper timing of blowing your ballast and why," the captain said with an ironic snicker. "Manta, what do we do now?"

I'm still assessing the entire situation at this point. Sir, I would ask you and your officers meet and discuss alternatives. When I contact you, I'd like to discuss any options you have come up with.

"From my vantage, Manta, we have very few. What is our coverage status?"

Sir, your boat is covered fore and aft; about 20 percent of the boat's surface is visible.

"Understood. When should I expect to hear from you again?"

I'll check back with you in an hour, Alex replied. *Captain, will you contact the* Discovery *and let them know we are in contact and are currently assessing the situation?*

"It's good to know the timing, Manta," retorted the captain, "since my crew would lock me in my quarters if they saw me talking to myself. I look forward to hearing from you at 03:45—and yes, I'll update the *Discovery*."

Alex began to assess the rock face in close detail. The goal was obvious—to free both subs with no loss of life and to have both of them surface and end this calamity. The goal may have been obvious, but as Alex slowly kicked his fins to move around the two subs and began to examine the newly formed rock formations, he could see the level of difficulty shoot off the chart. Starting from his current position near the rear of the LA-class, Alex slowly propelled and ascended about one hundred feet. As he ascended, he made mental notes of the angles of the rocks and paid attention to the apparent stability of those rocks. At one hundred feet above the LA-class sub, the wall looked solid and free of loose boulders. Alex pulled his dive slate and grease pencil from his utility belt and began a rudimentary sketch of the loose-rock formation as he descended again toward the LA-class. He was second-guessing the mental notes and observations he made during his assent as he sketched the labyrinth of stone that held the LA-class sub like the hand of Poseidon himself.

Upon close examination, he saw that each stone had points where it relied on the stone beneath it for its stability. If a certain point of stone *A*, for example, which rested beneath stone *B*, were to be moved, then stone *A* would fall further toward the LA-class's hold point. Alex's drawing was basic, but he had given it detail where these stability points were concerned. After he had detailed his sketch of the rock above the LA-class and the rock that surrounded it, he directed his attention to the rock between the LA-class and the *NR-1*, especially the formation around the tail section of the *NR-1*. If a plan were to be devised successfully, it would have to include freeing both boats.

There were fewer pieces of rock between, even given the distance between the two boats, than there were surrounding the LA-class. To some that might seem a good thing, but to Alex this was not good at all. It appeared to him during his examination of the few large stones separating the two boats that if any movement of the LA-class were caused, the two large stones would shift just enough to fall. Their falling would allow all of the stone that held the LA-class in place, including the LA-class herself, to fall cleanly through the *NR-1*. Alex was sure they would fall with such force and such tremendous weight that the *NR-1* would be sheared from its hold and cut into two pieces, virtually like a warm knife cutting through cold butter.

His sketch of the two areas was complete. Alex was ready to establish contact with the two subs again. He was ahead of his expected schedule, still a full thirty minutes before the captain of the LA-class was expecting him. Alex's curiosity had been so completely squelched by the seriousness of the rescue attempt that he had placed the discovery of the older submarine nearby out of his mind. With this additional half-hour before he was expected to make contact, he decided to go the short distance down the sea wall and examine the outer framing of the relic.

Kicking his fins in a smooth, rhythmic motion, Alex reached the location of the seemingly forgotten submarine in only a brief moment. He started at her rear section, studying her structure. It seemed as though she had been parked here—quite gracefully, in fact. The edge of the sea wall she rested on was no larger than her roughly thirty-foot beam. She had a single screw, with the shaft disappearing into her rear section like a piece of nouveau metal sculpture. Slowly kicking down along her side, Alex saw the signs of wear from what was surely ten to fifteen years in this seabed of hers. The cold of this deep location had slowed the process to a crawl, but surface deterioration was evident. As Alex came around to her bow, he saw the doors to her six torpedo tubes. He reasoned she had been designed with close-quarters battle in mind. Still amazed with her hull integrity, Alex came over the top of her bow and slowly moved to her tower. As he approached the tower, he was happily surprised to see that he could still make out most of the name painted on the side of tower. He saw, HMS *readno ght*. He took out his second dive slate and wrote down the letters as he saw them.

He checked his dive watch and saw it was time to contact Captain Dart. *Captain Dart, this is Manta.*

"Yes, Manta. Dart here. My staff and I have discussed the situation as we see it from our vantage, and the choices are limited, as we thought they would be."

I understand, sir. What did you come up with? questioned Alex as he moved away from the location of the older sub's resting place and back toward the LA-class and the *NR-1*.

"I need to mention, we did a conference call with the *NR-1* crew during this process. If we are guessing correctly about the circumstances outside our respective boats, we are locked in a great-wall situation that brings to mind a Humpty Dumpty story."

Your positive attitude is great, Captain, commented Alex. *And your assessment is correct.*

"That would mean that if either boat moves, it will cause problems for the second boat. With that in mind, we have determined that both boats must move simultaneously—"

Alex interrupted. *That appears to be much easier said than done.*

"Agreed. That's as far as we could take it, with any type of reality attached," commented the captain.

What if you thought outside of reality for a moment? What would that allow you to conceive? questioned Alex as he rested in a neutrally buoyant posture facing the two boats from about thirty feet away.

The captain of the LA-class replied almost playfully. "Thought outside of reality? Well then, we'd have two other subs chance coming to this depth, attach one to each boat, and power-tow us both out of here before the rocks slide again."

That's not bad, Captain. I see your point about how unlikely that might be as a possibility, but it is quite interesting.

"Before you get a plan formulated to follow my seemingly ingenious suggestion, let me inform you that we were on open-sea surveillance before being trapped here." The captain continued, "Since that was our mission, I can effectively tell you that there are no subs that can descend below eighteen hundred feet within two days' journey of our position. My unrealistic plan included two subs, one for each of us, to pull us free. That would prevent being pulled together during the towing. And frankly, Manta, my men and I would rather stay here for the rest of lives than to have a 'needs of the many' plan that included saving my boat at the cost of the lives on Captain Roger's boat."

I would not contrive a plan that intentionally allowed the NR-1 to be sacrificed, replied Alex.

"Well, sir, Captain Rogers offered the lives of himself and his crew if that's what it would take to save my boat. The way they see it, it was their mission to come down here and rescue us, and it would just be an extension of those orders. Rogers and his crew are good men."

Alex spoke firmly. *And that's a good reason to make sure that our plan is good of the all and not just the many. Captain Dart, I am going to take my assessments and meet with the rest of my people. They are going to arrive onsite in a few hours. We'll do the best we can to help. I'll be out of contact until about around noon tomorrow. If you need to contact me, the* Discovery *can raise me on my surface radio. Is the status of your batteries stable?*

"Yes, sir. The power consumption from them is steady," replied the captain. "I calculate we have power to utilize at this current level until 22:50 tomorrow."

We plan to have you free from these rocks before then.

"And I plan to attend the Colts' next Super Bowl appearance," laughingly replied the captain. "You and I both have dreams, now, don't we?"

Yes, sir, we do. I'll do my best to achieve my dream. That Colts thing, well that's in God's hands.

"So are we, my friend; so are we." The captain continued, "12:00 tomorrow; Godspeed."

Alex pulled his compass from his utility belt and attached it to the clamping ring on the front of his BCD vest. Holding the compass directly in front of him and placing the nose of the *NR-1* directly at his rear, Alex was able to adjust slightly to determine his return course. During the time it took him to return to his sea-anchored raft, he reviewed each detail of the situation. He studied the rock sketches on his dive slate and noted how the rocks rested on and surrounded the two boats. He contemplated the remaining battery power of the LA-class boat and the report of no power fall-off with the *NR-1*. Each of the details and dozens more would affect any decision made toward a rescue attempt.

When Alex surfaced, he was pleased to see that his sea anchors had worked and the raft had barely drifted. He was also pleased his training in underwater navigation had taken and he'd been able to find the raft without trouble. He rolled himself into the raft and began to take off his gear. With Alex's newfound stamina, he was only slightly tapped after his dive. He had started this dive at 11:00 p.m. and it was now 5:30 a.m. With his gear off and the warm, waterproof parka wrapped around him, he contacted the *Discovery* to update them. He informed them that he and his staff would evaluate the options and that the captain of his surface ship would recontact the *Discovery* upon their arrival and the formulation of a plan. Much to Alex's dismay, he confirmed with the *Discovery* the lack of any appropriate submarines anywhere in the area.

Alex finished his communication with the *Discovery* and searched through his provisions for something to eat. Along with his new stamina—maybe his new strength and ability actually inflated it—his appetite was ferocious. He found a few cans of kipper snacks and peeled them open. Finding a package of saltines, he used the crackers as spoons and scooped out the herring from the cans and ate the morsels "spoon" and all. Following the kippers, Alex pulled the tabs off three cans of orange juice, gulped down the first two, and slowly savored the third. When he had finished the feast that any good sailor would have enjoyed, he pulled himself to the other side of the raft and opened the watertight pouch that held the radio. He adjusted the dial and began to hail Angela.

"Alex! It's good to hear from you. I've calculated we should be at your position very near 3:00 p.m. What have you discovered?" questioned Angela.

"Well, I've missed you too, my dear," Alex quipped back. "I've completed a cursory examination of the area the boats are in, and I have some information to share from that exam. First off, have one of the boys do a search on a missing submarine of about twenty years ago. It would be from Great Britain, and the lettering on her tower—what was left of the lettering—read 'HMS readno ght.' See what you can find on her and let me know. As to what I've found …"

Alex and Angela discussed the situation for the next forty-five minutes with Alex sharing all he had seen and Angela posing questions that Alex had not considered. But from the research he had done, they were able to obtain the answers.

"Wait a minute, Alex. Dan just brought the information in about the sub you found. It's the HMS *Dreadnought*, out of Brighton. She was reported laid down at Vickers in 1989."

"Well, she's laid down all right, pretty as you please, but not at Vickers."

"It gets better. Dan found that out after about a ten-minute search. He didn't buy it, since you were questioning it, so he broke into the Royal Navy's computer bank. That's what took so long. They have a pretty good system—IBM, I think. Anyway, Dan discovered that the *Dreadnought* was originally commissioned in 1963, the only one like her built, and received a refit in 1974. In 1982, she was reported taken out of service, and here's where the good part begins. She received a new Westinghouse S5W reactor and a new computer package that was designed to be the prototype of the unit they were testing to replace manned submarines."

Alex interrupted, "They were designing a robotically operated submarine?"

"Seems like it," continued Angela. "They, of course, were doing all of this in secrecy, and set out for their maiden voyage in the spring of 1989."

"Let me guess," said Alex. "Not to Vickers?"

"You got it! Right to this area."

Alex asked, "Okay, why is she here—parked?"

"Apparently, and it's a bit sketchy at this point, they had placed a small crew of four—a submarine captain, a pilot, and the two computer engineers who gave birth to this idea. They had reported back to Brighton that all was going as planned and they would instruct the computer to complete a deep dive. The report goes on to say that when the captain reported they had just reached fifteen hundred feet, he began to shout that the computer was now indicating it had armed the four UUM-44A missiles it carried."

"Angela, are you familiar with those missiles?"

"You bet. I read about those when I was in school. They're more commonly called 'subroc' since they are designed as rockets to be launched from the sending submarine. They leave the water and travel about thirty miles maximum, reenter the water, and target another submarine. You get it? Subroc—submarine rocket."

"So these things armed themselves?"

"No, the new computer armed them. The report then says the computer engineers could not reverse the order to arm; further, they discovered they had new direction coordinates to return to Brighton, at flank speed, with target coordinates to launch the four subrocs on downtown Brighton. They tried to override the orders held by the computer, but to no avail. They determined they had been sabotaged."

"So they scuttled her?"

"Not entirely correct," continued Angela. "They were cruising at a depth of fifteen hundred feet, and they had decided to set a charge to blow the *Dreadnought* to pieces. They had added an escape pod that resembled a small diving bell to the forward escape trunk of the *Dreadnought*. They planned to set the charge with a timer, enter the escape pod, and separate themselves from Brighton's apparent doomsday machine."

"What happen to the crew, and why is that part of the report so sketchy?"

"The crew was never heard from again. Many of the details beyond this point are assumptions." Angela continued, "The report has a closing assumption the *Dreadnought* took her crew with her when she was blown to the bottom of the sea."

"Well, well, now. Angela, are you thinking what I'm thinking?"

"I hope not! You would be foolish to try that!"

"Let's do the research. We only have two hours before I need to head back down there. There's so much to do before the LA-class runs out of battery power or that wall decides to shift again. Plus, I need to get a few minutes sleep before I go down again."

"Then what's this 'let's do the research' stuff?"

"Angela, my dear, this is your specialty. I'll sleep for the next two hours while you work your magic."

"You're real funny, Alex. I'll call you in two hours, 9:30 a.m. Stay warm, my love."

"Of course; I brought along your new parka. Thanks for the loan."

"So that's where it went off to! Thief! You just go to sleep, and I'll stay on this cold, damp—"

Alex interrupted, "Signing off for now."

CHAPTER 11

A lex was again approaching the area of the three submarines—the LA-class, the *NR-1* and the H.M.S. *Dreadnought*. After Alex had half-slept for a little over an hour, he and Angela had discussed the research Angela had completed in the meantime. Alex had no equipment with him to record the information; none would be able to withstand the depths to which he would soon return. He had to commit to memory the specifics, with the exception of a few key bits he recorded on his dive slate. Angela had confirmed that she expected to arrive at the surface location where Alex's inflated life raft was resting at or just before 3:00 p.m. The two of them had reasoned that Alex would complete as much of the plan as he could prior to her arrival. She would be bringing materials necessary to the balance of the rescue attempt, and they both knew they would have precious little time to complete the preparation before 3:00 p.m., and thus Angela, arrived. He was now at the location of the LA-class and *NR-1*. Slowly Alex reviewed the rock formations that held tight the two boats, comparing them to the drawing he had made earlier. It appeared that the rocks had not shifted.

In order for their plan to work and allow the two subs to be freed before the batteries went dead on the LA-class, Alex was going to have to enlist the assistance of the H.M.S. *Dreadnought*. His first task was to enter her. As he approached the *Dreadnought*, he went immediately to her forward topside. Angela had informed him that the escape pod had been attached to the forward escape trunk. The escape hatch was clear. There had been some concern from Angela that maybe the pod had never separated from the boat, and the pod itself would cover the hatch. She hadn't been too far off. What was left of the escape pod was sitting ominously twenty feet in front of the *Dreadnought*. A large deepwater Jew fish, a common type of sea bass, was leaving through the escape pod portal. It appeared that when the pod had separated, its hatch had been blown to the inside. Its design was to have the hatch open to the inside. That design relied on the strength of the hinges and not the hatch itself. The water pressure at this depth had been too much for the hinges. Alex chose not to inspect the inside of the pod. It had been years since the latch had given way to the sea, and its guests, the four-man crew of that last test voyage, would have died instantly.

Alex went ahead with the mission at hand. He began to inspect the outer hatch of the *Dreadnought*. It had been closed and sealed appropriately. How odd that the crew would have sealed the escape hatch tightly when they had intended it to be destroyed by the explosives they had set before leaving.

Angela had educated Alex on the design of the escape system. The outer hatch of the *Dreadnought* opened to the outside, into the escape pod, since the escape pod hatchway was a larger diameter than that of her escape hatch. Beyond the sub's escape hatch, there was a small compartment, designed much like a tunnel, which connected the outer hatch to the inner hatch, which opened into the sub to an area known as the forward escape platform. Angela said the specs on the sub listed a manual/power-assisted pump in the tunnel, so that when the two hatches were closed, the water could be pumped from the connecting tube, allowing the inner hatch to be opened without flooding the boat.

Alex moved his hands around the outside edges of the outer escape hatch of the *Dreadnought*, trying to detect whether the seal was infiltrated. It appeared to be intact. With the power-assisted pump controls on the inside of the tube, he was sure the tube was still filled with water. That would assist in his opening the hatch. Even with Alex's enhanced strength from his tightly packed molecular structure, he did not want to test its maximum ability and then fall short of the strength needed to save the lives on board the two trapped subs. Alex firmly grasped the outer turn handle and began to put pressure against it. As he did, the handle slowly turned, giving off a metal-to-metal scraping sound as it did. Alex had heard another sound as well, like something rubbing against the inner portion of the turning handle and being moved as the wheel turned.

Alex stopped for a moment, knowing he was near to opening the hatch. If something was on the other side of this hatch, was he sure he was prepared to see it? Had one of the crew stayed behind to secure the hatch? Had this crewmember then been trapped in the tunnel, unable to escape back into the *Dreadnought*? In the end, none of this mattered anymore. There were more than a hundred sailors, between the *NR-1* and the LA-class, whose lives might depend on the opening of this hatch. Alex positioned his hands again on the turning wheel of the hatch and gave the wheel its final half turn.

The hatch slowly swung upward on its hinges and opened. As it did, Alex moved quickly away from the opening. He was pleasantly surprised, at first, to see that there was no former member of the crew to be seen. What appeared was a box with dimensions of about two feet per side. It floated from the hatchway and first bumped against what was left of the Acoustic Intercept Receiver just aft of the forward escape trunk. When it impacted the AIR, a flush of air was released from the cubical container, and then it came to rest on the foredeck of the *Dreadnought*. Alex moved toward the box, and as he did, he could see that where it had been dull in color, it was now lighted and pulsating. He moved to it more quickly now and saw that it was not a box at all but rather a bundle of what appeared to be high-power explosives wrapped together with an illuminated timer attached.

Alex could now clearly see the timer. It read 19:14 … 19:13 … 19:12. It was counting down to initiate the trigger of the explosive with its original intent of destroying the *Dreadnought* herself.

Alex thought to himself, *Oh, now this is special! I've got to get this out of here.* Alex thought about his surroundings. He could go either direction, but which would be the best direction for the subs? He was sure of one thing. If he took it deeper, chances were high the timer would implode and cause the explosive to release its wrath on Alex and whatever he was near at the time. He decided to take the explosive above and away from the two subs at a forty-five degree angle toward the surface. By doing this, he could lessen the compression effect the explosion would have on the subs as well as the wall of rock surrounding the boats. As Alex began his speed run, he telepathically sent a message to the *Discovery*.

Discovery *Captain, this is Manta. I have no time to explain. I need for you to attach a deflated buoyancy vest to about thirty feet of cord and suspend them from a floating buoy marker. The marker needs to be placed half a mile from your location, due east. Place a strobe on the vest to better indicate its location. Do you have all of this?*

"Manta, this is *Discovery*. I have no idea how you are communicating with me, but I have orders to follow any instruction that comes from you. I have your message. When do you need this in place?"

Discovery, Alex replied as he glanced down at the counter that now read 18:53, *I need it in place in five minutes—no later. And then you need to inform your crew that there is likely to be a large explosion at that spot. So you'll need to take whatever measures you see fit.*

"Five minutes? You said five minutes?"

Less than that now—I suggest you hurry! warned Alex.

All the while, Alex had been kicking with large, full strokes of his fins. He knew his power had been greatly increased by the molecular changes he had gone through, but until this time he had not tested his swimming speed or the speed with which he could surface from three thousand feet. He knew by the rapidity with which he was passing the sea life and the reef formations that his speed was extraordinary. Thus far, he felt no repercussions from the rapid surfacing.

Alex reasoned that when the explosive timer had been set by one of the now-dead crew of four, it had been set for twenty minutes. The package had been placed with the timer activated and the large hatch closed. He figured it was possible the initial jarring of placing the makeshift timer in the holding tunnel could have caused the timer to electronically freeze in its starting position. Since it had experienced no movement until Alex had opened the door, it had patiently waited until now. Now it was quite active.

His depth gauge indicated that he was now at one thousand feet. The counter on the explosive read 12:32. It was Alex's plan, made during a few frantic moments, that he would reach the BCD placed below the marker by the *Discovery* and wrap it around the device. Having the BCD suspended below the surface would allow Alex to approach it without being seen by the crew of the *Discovery*. If he could reach the BCD, wrap it around the device, and manually inflate the BCD to raise the device to the surface with 9:00 minutes remaining, then he might have enough time to go deep enough and far enough away from the explosion to save himself from the effects of the demolition device.

Alex was now at five hundred feet, and the counter was showing 11:30. He should be able to see the strobe from this point. He saw nothing. Alex continued to kick toward the expected location of the marker. He was now at three hundred feet and the counter read 10:58.

Where is that marker? Discovery, *can you hear me?*

"Manta, the marker should be dropped within two minutes. The sea is choppy, and the skiff is traveling as quickly as it can to your location."

You'd better get that skiff out here faster than it's getting here or you won't have a skiff.

"Understood, Manta."

Alex was now floating helplessly at fifty feet, holding on to the device, with the counter showing 9:53. If he just let the explosive go from there, it would only get to about one thousand feet deep before it exploded. But an explosion at a depth anywhere near there would put the subs and their crews in danger.

The counter now read 9:10. It had taken Alex a little over nine minutes to get the device to this point, and he was now on hold, waiting for the BCD. He was not sure he could make it back to the sub's location before the explosion.

The counter now read 8:45. Alex looked up to see the small splash in the water and the sharp turn of the skiff making a break to return to the safety of the *Discovery*. Alex rushed to the now-submerged BCD. As he reached the deflated BCD, Alex wrapped the vest around the device and connected the Velcro clasps. Next he grabbed the manual inflator, and with one large exhale, he firmly inflated it, causing it to quickly dart for the surface. It only took the inflated BCD about three seconds to reach the surface, but to Alex it seemed much longer. He wanted to wait and see it at the surface to make sure the BCD contained it appropriately. The counter had read 8:15 just before he released it. Knowing it had taken him nine minutes to get to the surface, Alex had to kick with all of his strength if he expected to get back to the subs before the explosion.

His urgency to get back to the subs was not just to put as much distance between himself and the exploding device as possible; it was also to be there when the explosion occurred, to see if the compression caused by the explosion would change the position of any of the three boats. He kicked with all of his new strength. He kicked so hard that he could hear the water being displaced by his fins as he quickly motored forward. According to his dive watch, the device had less than thirty seconds before it would explode. He had returned to twenty-six hundred feet, but the subs were not in view yet.

As he reached twenty-eight hundred feet, the faint outline of the *Dreadnought* came into view. His dive watch indicated that the device should explode now. He heard nothing. Alex was still traveling at his full strength when he felt a sudden powerful push downward. The push caused such a sensation that, even with his dense molecular structure, it almost registered as pain on the back of his head. As he felt the push, he was just reaching three thousand feet, and the *NR-1* and LA-class were in clear view.

As if pushed by the some large, slow-moving hand, an enormous boulder from above the LA-class began to fall. Alex judged it would cleanly miss the LA-class and would hit the *NR-1* squarely on her tower with such a force that it would rip the small research submarine in half. Alex pushed himself beyond what he felt was his limit. He kicked as if some evil monster possessed him. If he could just … could just …

When Alex impacted the side of the falling rock, he felt the direction of the rock suddenly change. He had crashed into the near side of the tumbling boulder with the intent of pushing it clear of the *NR-1*. It was working. The rock, now clear of the *NR-1*'s position, would fall harmlessly into the depths of the sea.

Captain Dart, this is Manta. Are you and your crew all right?

"Yes, Manta," replied the captain of the LA-class. "We were warned by the *Discovery* to be alert. We rode through it just fine. What was the cause?"

Captain Dart, I'll need to go into that with you later. I still plan to contact you around noon today with a further update.

Captain Rogers, are you and your crew all right?

"Yes, Manta. We're fine," replied the captain of the *NR-1*. "Manta," beckoned the captain.

Yes, Captain Rogers, replied Alex.

"Manta, we just wanted to say thank you. We owe you our lives."

You are quite welcome. I'll recontact you around noon with an update.

Alex started to slowly head back toward the *Dreadnought*. He considered the tone and content of the message from Captain Rogers. It was as if he knew. Alex didn't give it another thought.

He went to the rear of the *Dreadnought* first. He had not yet inspected the screw or the external portion of the shaft. If these have been badly damaged during *Dreadnought*'s last mission, she would be of no help to the current one. Approaching the rear, he began to smile. The screw was clear of any obstruction, and the shaft appeared straight and operable. But merely because they appeared fine to his untrained eyes did not mean they were in fact going to work. Alex would need a bit more good luck than that—they all would need a great deal more luck.

As Alex moved topside and began to slowly kick his way along the top deck of *Dreadnought*, he studied the periscope tower. He arrived at the tower and wiped the seaweed from the optics. He could see light and hoped it was the refraction of the light from the control room. Turning around from the scope to the opposite side of the tower, he looked at the various masts standing straight up in the darkness of the deep. Each appeared to be intact and undamaged. Again, this discovery meant nothing in itself. But it was a good start. Alex left the tower of the bridge and swam a few feet further to the foredeck.

When he returned to the foredeck of the *Dreadnought*, he found the forward escape trunk hatch still open, as he had left it. He first peered inside the short tunnel and then moved to dive the tube. Alex entered the tube feet first and sealed the hatch firmly behind him. Not sure what he might find in the interior of the British sub, Alex kept his e-reg active in his mouth as he turned the manual crank that began to replace the water in the tube with air from attached storage tanks—just as the designer, decades earlier, had hoped it would. Alex rechecked the outer hatch. It still appeared to be watertight.

Now was the moment of truth. Alex placed his hand on the inner hatch wheel and turned it until the hatch was free to pull up and open. No surprises. That was a relief. Alex stepped cautiously down the ladder from the escape trunk into the forward escape platform—a room used for the preparation for those intending to escape by diving the tube.

Now standing inside the sub, Alex looked around to see a brightly-lighted area. Along a near wall to the left were shelves with four neatly stacked deepwater escape suits. Angela had informed Alex that the refit of *Dreadnought* had updated her with many of the experimental items the Royal Navy has since made standard equipment on her newer boats. These were probably prototypes. Along the near wall to the right were shelves of dry provisions—cans and cardboard boxes of food intended to be eaten long ago.

After this quick immediate survey, Alex decided to test the air. He pulled the e-reg from his mouth and took a small breath. Seemed all right—he took a larger breath and felt just as comfortable. This area was dry and well lighted, and the air was breathable. Things were looking good.

Angela had surmised that if the *Dreadnought* had been sealed properly when left and the reactor core had stayed sealed and dry, then the power would remain up. The air—since the boat had sat undisturbed for these past years, with no one expelling new CO_2—would at worst have a faint, stale odor to it but would be quite breathable. Alex was appreciative to Angela for her correct summation. He was also appreciative to the *Dreadnought* herself and thanked her in a quiet whisper.

Leaving the small area toward the aft, Alex walked carefully along the passageway out of the forward platform and past the officers' upper bunk area. He looked in as he walked by to see the bunks unmade with the mattresses rolled up at the foot of each bunk. Still further down the passageway, Alex found the first room of importance for his mission.

The control room looked as if the crew had just stepped out to allow a photographer to take a few equipment shots. Alex walked to the center of the control room, and with his back to the main periscope, he turned slowly to survey the area. His eyes traveled from the driving station in the front of the room, around the panels of gauges of steady needles, to the back of the room, where he first saw his newest enemy, the *Dreadnought's* computer.

Alex walked over to the station and leaned over the seat where the crewman responsible for computer operations would have normally sat. From this point Alex could see the computer was on and active. It was no doubt one function of the computer to maintain the cabin conditions of breathable air and a comfortable temperature. On the screen were the words that had sent the four silently honored crewman on their ill-fated mission: "Missiles Locked—Brighton. Temporary Interrupt—Simulated System Crash."

Alex would return to this station after he had inspected the rest of the vital areas and assessed their functionality. Walking still aft, Alex left the control room and entered the passageway. The next area Alex encountered was the CO's cabin. Alex looked inside the CO's cabin but did not enter. It was neat and tidy except for the area around the CO's private desk. That area was covered with scattered papers, and the desk had sketches of the escape pod lying on top of several other pages.

Just past the entrance to the CO's cabin was a stairway that went to the mid-ship power-plant control area on the mid deck. This area was where the nuclear engineers would have monitored the various gauges that helped them maintain a safely running boat even though it was being powered by one of the most powerful energy sources known to mankind. This area was now of major importance to Alex's mission. Alex entered the area and went first to the wall behind which he knew the reactor was contained—at least he hoped it was still contained.

The gauges all along the wall had their needles resting steadily and fully in the green areas of the dials. This green area indicated that power was nominal, the energy readings were nominal, and the seals of the confined areas were holding well. No radiation leaks were noted, and the sub still had power. Alex was thrilled. If he and Angela were successful in retaking control of the computer, then they would have the use of the *Dreadnought* to assist in the rescue of the two trapped boats.

Alex checked his dive watch. It was now noon and time to contact the captains of the *NR-1* and the LA-class. Alex made his way from the power-plant control area back to the main deck and in short time was back in the main control room. Alex went over to the radio station, quickly surveyed the current settings, and made the needed adjustments by dialing the frequency up to the highest point of the settings.

Alex then concentrated and contacted the captains of the two subs using his telepathic link. *Captain Dart, Captain Rogers, this is Manta. I would like for each of you to have your radios settings changed to 103.7 megahertz and await further communication.*

Without hesitation the two captains ordered the settings changed, and as this was being done, they began hearing a transmission. "LA-class, *NR-1*, please respond. LA-class, *NR-1*, please respond."

The *NR-1* was the first to respond, and since the three were on the same frequency, all three could monitor each of the transmissions. "This is *NR-1*. We copy. Come back."

"LA-class responding also. Over."

"Excellent. Captains, this is Manta. I have made it possible for us to now speak via our radios. I have some very interesting news for each of you. I have borrowed the property of the Royal Navy to assist us in our upcoming efforts to free your boats from their current dilemmas. Over."

"Manta, this is Captain Dart. Somehow I expected your voice to be a little more like my own. It no doubt was due to hearing my own voice as I translated your incoming thoughts into language. Wow—what an experience! Over."

"Same here, Manta," responded Captain Rogers. "I imagined your voice to be more like Dart's too."

"Don't let go of that sense of humor. I'm sure when I describe the next part of this plan of ours, you'll believe I'm telling you both a big one. As I said, I have borrowed property of the Royal Navy that they misplaced a few years ago. Are either of you familiar with the HMS *Dreadnought?*"

"Yeah, I remember the name," replied Captain Rogers. "Wasn't she the series of wooden fighting ships the Brits used to achieve dominance of the seas about two hundred years ago?"

"Captain Rogers," interrupted captain Dart, "If you want to share an ancient-history lesson with us later, I'll buy the beer—but for now, we could only be considering the Brit's first nuclear sub that was retired in '89. That the boat you're talking about, Manta?"

"Correct, Captain Dart. The *Dreadnought* is resting a short distance from your current position. She was left here in '89 and not truly retired. We really don't have time to discuss the whole issue at the moment, but it's her radio I'm using now. What I intend is to further prepare *Dreadnought* for the mission over the next few hours as we approach our targeted time of 5:30. Here's what I have in mind."

For the next twenty minutes, Alex went on to describe the plan to the two boat captains. They only interrupted a couple of times for clarification. When he had completed his explanation, Alex finished his radio communication with, "Well, Captains, there's the plan. I know it sounds too simple at some points, but as you can well see, a lot depends on a very thin margin of error and a continued generous portion of good luck. Any questions for now?"

"Manta, this is Captain Rogers. We'll be ready and, well, I … uh …"

"Manta, this is Captain Dart. As for me and my crew, we agree with Captain Rogers and his sentiment."

"Let's get to work. I'll contact you again between 4:00 and 4:30, when I have most everything in place. We'll still plan for 5:30 for the plan's final sequence activation point. Over and out."

Angela's arrival time was still three hours away, and Alex knew he would need all of that time for the next stage of the plan. He decided to leave the radio on in case the LA-class or the *NR-1* tried to contact him. But the radio would not reach Angela—it was too outdated for that distance from these depths. Alex knew from the start that he would need to rely on his telepathic abilities and the closeness in thought he and Angela shared.

Alex went to the computer station and sat in the operator's chair. From that point, he began to concentrate his thoughts on Angela. *Angela, can you hear me?*

Alex? Are you all right?

Fine, just fine. In fact, things on the Dreadnought *are better than we could have hoped, so far. There were a couple of difficulties in trying to get in, but those are behind us now.*

Difficulties? We heard a report of a large explosion in your area, and we thought the worst. Was that part of your 'difficulties'?

Angela, my dear, we have a few other fish to fry right now. When this is over, and we have a chance to sit on the beach and share a few pints of cider, I'll tell you every fascinating detail.

Deal. What is your current status?

Alex shared the findings from his initial walk-through of the *Dreadnought*, including the conversation he had just finished with the two boat captains. He concluded with, *I think it's time for us to tackle this on-board computer, don't you?*

Alex, we've done some research on the operating software in that system. It was written in the standardized programming language called ADA. This was the Accepted Defense Application programming language; it's used in all American and English military computers, at least it was until the Dreadnought incident. It was determined the standardization of the applicable operating language was an open door for a saboteur. Shortly after the Dreadnought incident, which no one outside of a very small circle knew about, the military went to PASCAL as their main language.

So we can use PASCAL to rewrite the operating program? Alex questioned.

No, we can't. The engineers on the sub during her trial run knew PASCAL, and they tried it. The saboteur also knew PASCAL and had written protection language into the software to prevent tampering with PASCAL. Since PASCAL was the newest language available, the doomed crew was without options.

Angela, I know I'm not well versed in programming or its history, but wasn't there a new language called C *written to replace PASCAL and do it* in a way that would override PASCAL in an existing system without total replacement of the system itself?

You're right, Alex, but we've already thought that one through. The problem we have is we believe the saboteur didn't merely introduce new language that would redirect the orders of the Dreadnought. That would leave windows of opportunity for the on-board computer engineers to rectify the problem. We've discussed this thoroughly, and we believe the saboteur more than likely changed the programming messages with new orders and then introduced a bug into the system to confuse any attempt to rewrite the programming.

So, what do we do? You've told me a lot of what we can't do—where's the magic?

Well, I'm not sure it's magic, and I'm not sure it will work. The problem is we don't know the extent of the saboteur's efforts. But, we have reasoned if the saboteur were of genius level in 1989, he still could not conceive what we've found as a workable solution. Alex, do you remember me telling you about the work I've done with the Internet and drafting websites for GE and McDonnell-Douglas?

Yeah, well, a little.

I've been working with a new language called BERL. Its qualities have made it a favorite with programmers because it's easy and it overwrites existing programming with a more speedy transformation than anything before. Even BERL has a weakness for what we need, but I have been working on an experimental application that I've called BERL Derivative. It has all of the qualities of BERL, but it also possesses a defragmenter function that works to de-bug as it replaces. It's only experimental, Alex, and I hate to base the success of this endeavor on its feasibility, but we've talked and hammered the thing out up here and we believe we have no better alternative.

What about just pulling the plug on the system and operating it manually?

You can thank the Royal Navy for this one. They have wired the sub to explode if an attempt to disconnect the computer is made. It was one of their safeguards against theft of the boat. Besides, you're going to need the computer to help you operate that boat. Manually, it would be impossible *for one man to do it—even you, my love. Our only hope is to reprogram the computer and enlist its assistance in operating the* Dreadnought.

Okay, I'll meet you at 3:00 on the surface, and you can give me the disks to load the new programming.

Afraid not, love. We've done some depth testing on the disks with information on them, and they are destroyed before they make it to your depth.

Destroyed? questioned Alex. *How are they destroyed?*

The force of the water pressure wipes the data clean. It's a phenomenon no one has written about. Who could have thought someone would want to carry a three-and-a-half-inch disk three thousand feet down and still want it to work. It just wasn't designed to handle that pressure.

Well then, continued Alex, *we'll have to do it manually.*

That was my thinking too, replied Angela. *I can lead you through it from here with you at the operator's station. But it will take us about six hours to go from start to finish.*

You know we don't have that kind of time.

We've tested the reapplication of the BERL Derivative over ADA programming for the amount of material the Dreadnought *computer was originally programmed with. It will take me six hours to read you the language and for you to then input it with the* Dreadnought's *computer keyboard.*

Angela, you've done tests with the actual rewrite for the Dreadnought?

You know me, Alex. I would not just assume something would work without giving it a true test. The only way to truly test it was to rewrite on the Dreadnought's *original programming; so, with a lot of arm twisting from Admiral Sterling, he was able to have the Royal Navy transmit the program package they had used for the trial run, of course, before any tampering had taken place.*

I've got an idea Angela. You've seen how fast I can read and type since I became, well, thick-headed.

Oh, you think you're so funny, don't you?

In fact, I do—but we won't go there for now. I believe I can read the program and then type into the Dreadnought's *system at least twice as fast as you have predicted it would take you and I to do it. Maybe even faster.*

What are you planning to read it from? It's all up here on my system.

Precisely. You can have the programming visible on the screen with you in front of the screen, and I will read the information through your eyes.

You'll what!

I have been practicing something for a while that I haven't shared with you because I felt it might be considered an invasion of your privacy. You and I are so close in our thoughts, and we have communicated so often telepathically, that it has evolved a step further. I can see through your eyes when I concentrate and place my thoughts in line with your thoughts. When I've tested this, I've even had a sensation of feeling when you've touched something. I can't seem to make it work with anyone else. I've surmised it's because we are so close that our thoughts can merge effectively enough that it then becomes possible.

We'll continue this discussion in more depth when we get back to the island. You truly believe you can do this?

I know I can. Right now, I can see the mean little doodle you've just scribbled on the notepad about my not telling you about this until now.

You are in trouble, mister; but for now, I'm extremely pleased with this information. It might be another key to this puzzle we've needed.

Let's get started. I'm in front of the Dreadnought's *computer, and I have the keyboard in place. The screen currently reads "Temporary Interrupt—Simulated Systems Crash."*

That's how they caused Dreadnought *to rest on that ledge. They initiated a routine computer drill that temporarily ceased its original mission against Brighton by taking the boat operationally off-line. It's like asking it to calculate PI to keep it busy, but it caused total propulsion shutdown instead. Okay, Alex, the first thing you need to do is to get into the computer's programming windows. Depress Alt and F4 at the same time. What do you see?*

The screen says, "Good morning Dave."

Very funny. What does it say?

It says, "Programming access—password required." Then it has the cursor blinking below that phrase.

Alex, the password I obtained from Admiral Sterling was "tea party," all in small case.

You're not kidding, are you?

No, that's the password. The English don't forget; they remember and move on.

All right, Angela, I've typed in tea party, and it's all in small case—now what?

This part is unique, Alex. You need to press Enter and Control at the same time.

Done—whoa! The screen has just filled with thousands of characters, and they're all scrolling by at great speed.

That's the way this system loads this function from its memory. It should stop shortly and leave the cursor blinking at the top left.

We're there, Angela. The cursor is at the top left. What's next?

Next, you'll need to type in REPROGRAM OPERATING FORMAT, and all three words must be capitals. When you've typed them in, press Enter, Control, and Alt, all three at the same time.

Done. The screen now reads "enter desired changes." If it was this easy, why did the trial run crew have a problem?

The problem would result from the next function. When they tried to enter new data, the system rejected the data and returned to the start page. When they repeated the process, they experienced the same results again and again. What we are going to do is actually "overtype" the current data in lieu of the new data. This creates an eraser function rather than a rewrite function and, theoretically, should not be rejected by the existing program.

Angela, if you're ready, I need for you to sit squarely in front of the screen and begin to scroll the information you want me to type very slowly. As I become accustomed to this setup, I'll ask for you to scroll faster. Are we ready?

Let's get busy. The information I have on the screen now, Alex, is the beginning of the information you need to type. There will be no need to hit Enter at any time. The mode you have the Dreadnought's computer in will automatically feed the new data to the proper file. There is a timing problem that may exist I should have mentioned earlier.

What timing problem, Angela?

When you start overtyping and replacing data, and the new information enters into the proper file, it will temporarily shut down that system until the new data has been full entered.

This is important. You're right; we should have discussed this earlier. Which systems will this affect?

All that are not vital to the computer's operation. The power plant will stay on line, because the computer needs the electricity it generates.

And?

That's the only system that is vital to the computer's existence. All other systems should be affected.

Alex was silent as he pondered the news. *You're telling me that at several points during the reprogramming of this system, I will experience systems going down and hopefully coming back on line when I've finished with that particular file?*

That's it in a thumbnail speech.

Which system takes the longest to enter?

That would be lighting and environmental, but the computer screen is equipped with its own power feed as well and will not go out with the other lighting.

You owe me an extra pint of cider for that one, Angela. Let's get to it.

I'm good to go, Alex.

Alex began to concentrate on Angela and very quickly was seeing the screen in front of her as if he were there himself. Having been away from her for some time now, he felt himself drawn by her long, slender fingers holding the mouse, with her index finger poised over the left-click button of the mouse. He caught himself drifting and again concentrated on the screen.

Since this was a programming language, it did not have the appearance of any spoken language. Letters and symbols, dots and dashes, back slashes and @ signs were laced throughout. Alex concentrated on the lines, symbol by symbol, at first. As he began to type these symbols, the *Dreadnought's* screen was accepting the input without argument. He heard a noise like a loud click from the other part of the boat. He hoped it had not thrown a circuit breaker. Nonetheless, he continued to enter the data.

As Alex continued, he started seeing the logic in some of the symbol's patterns. And with this revelation, he also noticed that his typing and recognition speeds were both improving. He and Angela had been at it for about thirty minutes by this point, and he had asked Angela to increase the scrolling speed five times. The lines of entry were now scrolling by at a full line per second. This was an incredible speed. Angela had that thought several times but had not interrupted Alex to voice her amazement. Alex knew though—he could hear her thoughts even though he was concentrating on the scrolling information.

Sixty minutes had gone by now. It was approaching 1:30 p.m. Alex continued to hear occasional clicking noises from elsewhere in the boat, but he had not noticed any change in any of the systems around him. He was certain the noise was coming from the switching room, which was located just the other side of the reactor compartment. He was confident that when he had completed this portion of the takeover of the *Dreadnought*, he would need to venture to the main switching room and reset the circuit breakers for the affected systems. He also tried to picture the size of the breakers if he was hearing them kick out from this distance.

Alex was approaching the ninety-minute mark of the reprogramming effort when the lights in the control room went out, and he heard again from a distance the familiar loud click. It startled him, since he was concentrating so intently on the data on the screen in front of Angela. He was so disconcerted that Angela asked, *Are you all right?*

Alex slowed down the keystrokes to reply, *Yeah, the lights around me just went out, and I didn't expect it. It took me so by surprise I must have registered a quick burst of anxiety you picked up on.*

I'll say—I nearly fell from my seat up here.

They were one hundred and twenty minutes into the process, and Alex was feeling the temperature in the *Dreadnought* becoming much cooler, even cold. He now came to the realization that he needed to speed up, if at all possible, since the systems that were shut off by the overtyping function were not coming back on by themselves. The *Dreadnought* was going into hypothermia.

Alex now increased the scrolling speed to two lines of entry per second. The net result was the *Dreadnought*'s computer screen was beginning to have leftover information from the previous line when Alex began the new line of data. He was now up against the archaic speed of the older processor. Even though it was the most advanced military system of its day, its processing speed would have been beaten by many home computers of today.

They were two hours and fifteen minutes into the process. It was now 2:45 p.m. The screen on the *Dreadnought*'s computer was nearly full from the backlog of data. Alex stopped abruptly when he saw the screen in front of Angela go blank. *What's happening Angela? Your screen has gone blank?*

You're done. You've entered all the data I had prepared. You should have control of the Dreadnought *now.*

Not quite yet, my dear; my screen is still inputting the data I typed on it.

The last line of entered data scrolled off the *Dreadnought*'s screen. Alex sat for a moment staring at the screen. He heard the hard drive creaking and shifting as the information was being correlated on it. When he was about to ask Angela what they should attempt next to get a response from the blank screen, he saw "Awaiting New Orders" rhythmically appear across the screen.

The system is ready to respond, Angela.

Great! What's the status of the boat?

I'll need to go to the switching room and close the breakers that were opened when the system shut down. I'll know more in about ten minutes. I'll recontact you in ten.

Alex stood from the computer operator's chair, stretched, and again realized how cold it had become. The temperature from the boat's extreme depth was transferring through the hull. It did not bother Alex, but he was concerned about the effect it might have on the boat's systems. Making his way out of the control room, past the CO's cabin and to a crawl-through tunnel that rested above the reactor compartment, Alex found himself in the large main switching room. His eyes had adjusted to the lack of light, and he could see the majority of the circuits were open. He quickly looked at each of them and found a connected pair of switches, with a label above them that read, "Environmental and Lighting." He took a slow and measured breath and pushed the two breakers upward to their closed position. The click he had heard while sitting in the control room was no longer muffled by the distance between the switching room, aft, and the control room, forward. He was right there, and so was the powerful slamming noise made as the switch connected and reengaged the appropriate systems.

Alex counted thirty opened switches in all. There were another ten that had not been affected. Of the thirty that had opened, he had now closed twenty-two. Alex was in the process of closing the twenty-third circuit breaker when he was showered with an explosion of sparks from the connectors at the top of the switch. The switch then reopened. Alex read "Aft Pumps" above the switch. This switch, or part of the circuitry, had not survived the abrupt disconnect and the freezing temperatures the *Dreadnought* had experienced during the computer's reprogramming. The rest of the circuits closed without incident.

Angela, I have closed all but one of the circuits, the aft pump circuit. All other switches closed, and the temperature in the boat is starting to rise quite nicely. I'll need to begin my trek to the surface to meet you and retrieve the supplies you have brought.

We're just arriving at the rendezvous point. In fact, we have your raft alongside. It's 3:10 p.m. You will no doubt be hurrying to the surface. Be careful, my love.

I'll be on board with you in fifteen minutes.

CHAPTER 12

O n board the *Tessa*, Alex was enjoying his second cup of fresh hazelnut coffee and his fourth Walker English cookie. He and Angela had been discussing nonstop the next several parts to their plan. Angela stopped in midsentence; walked from her mapping table over to the cushioned lounge chair Alex was resting in, and placed her bottom squarely in Alex's lap.

"Are you going to be all right through all of this, my love?"

"I'll be fine. It's the crew of those two boats I'm concerned about. It won't take much to go wrong with either the placement of the explosives or the attempt at pulling the big boat from the wall for one or both of those crews to be lost."

"You are doing your best, Alex. What one man do you know that could do what you're doing?"

"Rest assured, Angela, I have thanked the Almighty more than once for my being able to help here. I just don't want to miss any of the details."

"That's why you have me, my dear. I'm the detail person on this team. You and I have thought through every scenario we could imagine. A lot could go wrong, but so far, more has gone in our favor than we could have imagined. I believe this good luck will continue."

It was now 4:00 p.m., and Alex and Angela were topside, standing next to a ten-by-ten-foot cubed package wrapped in cargo netting. Inside the netting were the two lengths of titanium cable, each measuring one hundred yards in length. Along with the cables were the tools needed to attach them and a container of C-4 explosive, wiring, and radio-controlled detonators. Around the circumference of the package were four buoyancy-control devices. The sheer weight of the package would cause it to sink faster than Alex could control, so they had attached the buoyancy devices and connected a single control valve to allow Alex to control his descent and that of the netted package.

"I should return to the *Dreadnought*'s position with this package at 4:30. It's going to take me the better part of an hour to attach the cables and place the explosive. I should be able to confirm the start of the operation between 5:30 and 5:45."

Angela spoke calmly while slowly brushing her hand across Alex's forehead, "I know that cuts it close for the crew of the LA-class boat. Her battery power is quickly being used up just supporting their environmental systems. I've calculated that if we free her at or near 6:00, she'll have about five hours of battery left, and that's just for her environmental functions. She'll have no power to assist with her ascent. The *NR-1*, on the other hand, will need to get out of the way once she is freed, but she'll have plenty of power to surface."

"Time to go then, Angela. Have them lower the package over the side."

With a long, fiercely strong hug, Angela whispered into Alex's ear, "You bring those hazel eyes back to me safe and sound. Do you hear me, mister?"

"Yes, ma'am. I'm looking forward to a long, restful nap when this is all over. I'll see you later this evening, my love."

With that parting promise, Alex grabbed hold of the swaying package as the winch was swung to the side of the ship and lowered with the package over the side. As he and the package entered the water, Alex made his way to the buoyancy-control valve. He waved to Angela and released the winch hook from the cargo netting. He and the package quickly slipped beneath the surface.

The buoyancy-control device he was using was much like a diver's BCD vest. It was made up of four nylon cloth membranes positioned on the four sides of the netting. The nylon cloth membranes would allow them to withstand the extreme depth. The pressure of the deep water that Alex and the package were now traveling quite quickly toward would continue to compress the membranes with each additional thirty feet that Alex took the package. He had planned to release all of the compressed air into the membranes prior to reaching the maximum depth for the air tank attached to the near side of the cargo-netted package.

Dropping a little faster than a hundred feet per minute, Alex was nearing the resting point close to the rear of the *Dreadnought* at about 4:30. He began to kick his fins firmly through the water against the descent of the package; he found his efforts to be quite adequate to gently bring the package to rest just behind the screw of the *Dreadnought.*

He first released the air from the buoyancy membranes to make sure there would be no undesired movement of the materials and tools. Next Alex pulled the knot loose from the tie at the top of the netting and allowed the netting to fall to the side of the contents. He and Angela had determined it would be safer to place the explosive first, before attaching the boats together. Alex pulled open the box containing the C-4 and the frequency-controlled detonators. He took the needed explosive, wiring, and detonators and made his way to the spot on the rock-wall face he had identified as best for the charge to be placed.

With the *NR-1* resting so close to the bottom of the LA-class, the placement of the explosive was critical, as was the amount of explosive to place. Angela had completed those calculations, and Alex was following that guideline. The rock face was sheer and jagged at the same time, and the closer Alex came to it the more treacherous it appeared. Alex selected a small indention in the wall just below the *NR-1* and placed the C-4 there. A blast at this spot should loosen the rock enough for the *NR-1* to pull away under her own power. With the C-4 placed, Alex then pressed the four detonators in the plastic mass. He was careful to trail the antennas individually from the detonators to allow them free reception when he sent the radio impulse to ignite the detonators and thus explode the C-4.

Alex slowly kicked his way away from the wall face and back to the *Dreadnought.* He went to the first spool of titanium cable, firmly grasped one end of it, and picked up the large toolbox with the other hand. He then went to the front of the British boat and pulled one end of the cable to the front mooring hold of the *Dreadnought*. Slowly running the four-inch cable through the opening, Alex was then able to reposition to pull the end through the top and back to the main line of the cable. At this point, he attached a large holding clamp that attached the end back to the cable itself, creating a clamped loop and thus attaching it firmly to the front mooring hold of the boat.

Having completed the attaching of one end of the cable to the front of the *Dreadnought*, Alex now needed to pull the large strand of cable to the front end of the LA-class boat. The weight of this cable would have prevented any other single individual from even lifting one of the ends. It was Alex's heightened molecular structure and thus his increased strength that made this possible. As Alex pulled the second end of the cable from the spool and toward the front of the LA-class, the coiled stack of cable began to unwind. Slowly, the cable twirled and unraveled until it was a straightened line between the two boats. It was still loosely lying between the two boats and would until Alex had completed the task of attaching the two boats and begun the process of pulling the LA-class free.

Arriving at the front the LA-class, Alex went about repeating the operation he'd used at the other end. Looping through the LA-class's front mooring hold and clamping the end back to the line of cable made the first of the two connections complete.

Alex smoothly kicked his fins, making his way back to where he had left the second strand of cable. Going first to the rear of the *Dreadnought* and attaching to her rear mooring hold, and then pulling the long strand to the rear of the LA-class and attaching the second end of the second cable to her rear mooring hold, Alex felt he had connected the two boats in the best manner possible.

Alex still had one part of the plan to complete before he returned to the dry recesses of the *Dreadnought*. He went back to the remaining box sitting alone on the now-empty cargo netting. From the box Alex pulled two small amounts of the explosive C-4 and proceeded to place one portion on each of the two *Dreadnought* mooring holds. He and Angela had reasoned that if Murphy's Law came into play, it would be prudent to be able to detach the two boats in a great hurry. The C-4 would do just that. After placing a frequency-controlled detonator in each plastic placement of explosive, Alex headed for the forward escape hatch of the *Dreadnought* to return to her control room.

Having entered the *Dreadnought* through the escape trunk tunnel, Alex made his way from the forward escape platform, past the officers' bunk area, and into the control room. He went to the computer operator's station and sat in front of the screen and keyboard. Alex brought up the main menu and highlighted the Systems Check line. Pressing Enter, Alex saw the screen go blank for a second and then brighten with a list of the various systems in the boat, with a status comment to the right of the category.

With the new programming installed, the *Dreadnought*'s system would process with a more modern approach than had been originally designed; nonetheless, the hardware did not have the capability to adapt a mouse to the system. When Alex operated the movement of the sub, he would use the joystick that had been intended for that purpose by the computer's designers. All other functions would be keyboard related.

From the readout on the system's check, he saw that all systems checked as operative except the aft pump system. As he not been able to reset the breaker for that system, this was not a surprise. All other systems had the word *nominal* next to them. Alex now decided he would begin moving the *Dreadnought* into position to begin the freeing of the two boats. He would first need to contact Captain Dart and Captain Rogers.

Adjusting the radio dial to a higher volume, since he had left the channel set to the appropriate frequency, Alex began his update to the two boat commanders at the same time. "Gentlemen, it's time to give it our all. I will be moving the *Dreadnought* into position above the LA-class and then will prepare to ignite the explosive. Are the two of you clear on our next few steps?"

"Manta, this is Captain Dart. Rogers and I have discussed the plan, and it appears to be our best shot. I believe we both have the details understood. I do have some advice from my pilot for you, Manta. He said that the *Dreadnought* would more than likely react to the stick very sluggishly. He said to be patient with her. You will move the stick, and a few heartbeats later you'll feel the reaction to your command of her. Don't expect her to react immediately. She was not designed to be operated by computer."

"Thanks for the guidance. I'll need all the additional advice you can offer as this project continues."

"Manta," queried Captain Dart, "have you ever piloted a sub before?"

"You know, Captain Dart, now is not the best time for me to answer that question. What I will say is that I have been prepared as much as possible in the time allowed."

"We'll keep this line open, Manta, in case you have any questions."

"I'll let the two of you know when it's time to blow the wall loose. Captain Rogers, are you fully powered up?"

"Yes, sir. We're ready when you give the word."

Alex went back to the operator's station. To allow him to stay in contact with the two other boats from the computer piloting station, he plugged in the headphones and attached them to the longest cord available. The screen had returned to the main menu. Alex found the line item labeled Piloting System. He highlighted that item and hit Enter. For the next few seconds, Alex looked at the small panel in front of him that held several command switches. With the joystick to his right, Alex monitored the computer screen straight ahead and manipulated the switches as needed with his left hand. A small slide bar to the left labeled RPM was positioned just next to a short series of buttons labeled Ballast. One row of these buttons was below the word Increase and the second row below the word Decrease.

As with the more modern submarine designs—but very different from the original intent of the *Dreadnought*'s computer engineers—Alex would need to operate the *Dreadnought* with the assistance of the computer rather than to have the computer totally operate the boat. Without the computer's assistance Alex could not perform this mission—with the system in place and with its new programming, Alex had a chance.

Alex pressed the lowest button, 25 percent, on the Decrease Ballast grouping. As he did, he felt the boat move beneath him. He pulled back on the stick and slid the rpm bar slightly forward. Nothing at first, and then as if the messenger had just delivered the message personally, the *Dreadnought* made its first movement in several years. Alex had a sonar screen just above the computer screen, and the sonar was active. In its current position, the *Dreadnought* sonar could not detect the LA-class or the *NR-1*, since the wall stood firmly between them. Alex raised the boat fifty feet from its previous resting place and then began to see the blurry formations on the screen that were the detected forms of the LA-class and the *NR-1*. As he raised the *Dreadnought*, Alex was careful to not pull away from the LA-class's position. He did not want to take the slack out of the cables until he was directly above her.

"Captain Dart," questioned Alex.

"Yes Manta."

"I would like the assistance of your sonar man. I can identify each of the boats and discern them from the formations around, but I would like some assistance in the specific distance between my boat and yours. I'm looking for a measurement as close to inches as possible."

"Understood, Manta. Our man can come close to telling you the color of an object merely from the sonar readings, or so he claims. He's on the line with us now. When you have a question on position or distance, just ask."

Alex moved the *Dreadnought* gently above the location of the LA-class and its trapped neighbor, the *NR-1*. With the assistance of the LA-class's sonar chief, Alex pulled to a distance above the two boats that had now taken all of the slack out of the cables that connected the *Dreadnought* and the larger boat below.

"Gentlemen, it's time. Are you ready, Captain Rogers?"

"Yes, Manta. When you give the signal, I'll throw this little beast into high gear, and we'll pull straight away from the wall, as you have instructed."

"Very good. My friends, the time has come. I'll blow the charge on the wall between your two boats on the count of three: three—two—one—now!"

With that, Alex pressed the frequency detonation transmitter with his left hand and pulled back on the stick of the *Dreadnought*'s controls with his right. He was hoping to maintain the LA-class's position just long enough to allow the *NR-1* to escape; then he would concentrate on the LA-class. Alex felt a rumble from below his boat's position.

"Manta, the charge has blown. I'm giving my boat full thrust forward," stated Captain Rogers. "She's moving! I haven't detected any damage at this point. We're free and fully mobile! Good work, Manta!"

"I'll let you affirm that later. Right now, you have your orders. Get your boat to the surface."

"Yes, sir. We're on our way. God be with you all." With that, the *NR-1* became a moving blip on the sonar screen—slowly, but clearly, ascending.

"Hang on Captain Dart—alert your crew. I'm starting the pull to separate you from the wall." Alex now moved the rpm slide bar to half speed and pushed the stick to the left to cause a power move horizontally to that side. He hoped to pull the LA-class with him and away from the wall. Nothing happened at first, and then again, with a delayed reaction, the *Dreadnought* began accepting power from its forty-year-old shaft and turned the screw at the ordered half speed. It was not enough to pull the LA-class free. Alex pushed the rpm bar to three-quarters. The *Dreadnought* began to groan under the stress. Then, as if a rubber band had released and sprung across the room, the *Dreadnought* was beginning to pull the LA-class free.

"We're free, Manta! Can you hear the cheers from the crew?"

"I certainly can, Captain. I'll start the ascent now. Captain Rogers, what is your current status?"

"We have the *NR-1* nearing fifteen hundred feet, and all is well Manta. You can worry about your task at hand. We're doing fine."

"Great news. Captain Dart, what is your boat's status?'

"We've just checked for leaks or possible areas where the hull may have been compromised and found no damage. Our battery power is now at five hours at its current output, which is providing for the electrical and environmental systems."

"It's 6:00, and we are currently at a depth of three thousand feet. I've prepared to blow my boat's ballast to 75 percent. Stand by." Alex placed his hand cautiously over the ballast controls as if the graceful pressure used on the button would gently coerce the CO_2 release tanks to more carefully release their contents into the ballast tanks while forcing the water from the tanks. The readings on the computer screen showed the ballast had now emptied to 75 percent, evenly dispersed between the forward and aft ballast tanks.

From the depth of three thousand feet, the *Dreadnought* began to move slowly upward with the LA-class beneath her in tow. Alex had slowed the screw's rpm back down to half speed and was pulling the joystick slightly back, trying to guide the two boats to the surface while holding them as level as possible.

"Manta," spoke the voice over the *Dreadnought's* radio.

"Yes, this is Manta."

"This is Specialist Foyt. I pilot the LA-class. If you set your boat for an ascent at fifteen degree up-bubble, you'll put a minimum amount of stress on the connections while still making an aggressive ascent."

"Understood," replied Alex. "Adjusting the stick to a fifteen degree up-bubble. It will take a moment for the old girl to react to the—there she goes. She's at a fifteen-degree ascent angle."

Alex sat in the *Dreadnought's* computer operator's seat, watching the ascent meter to his right stay at a steady fifteen degrees. This boat had a listed top speed of 25 knots submerged, but with the load she was pulling during her fifteen-degree ascent, with the screw's rpm set at half speed, she was barely making ten knots. Alex was quite pleased with that speed—all things considered. He then realized just how anxious he had become during the past few minutes. He quickly calmed himself with the reminder that whatever he was feeling, the crew of the LA-class was experiencing that to the power of ten—and then some, he was sure.

Creaking noises continued coming from all around him—not very loud but very regular. The *Dreadnought's* depth was approaching twenty-five hundred feet; it seemed to have taken an eternity to climb the past five hundred feet. Alex was watching his instrument panel closely. As he kept the ascent at fifteen degrees up-bubble, his speed was slowing to seven knots.

"Manta, we've detected a decrease in speed. Are you reading the same?"

"Foyt, you're right, and I'm having trouble keeping the ascent angle steady."

"Can you see a gauge that shows your trim?" requested the pilot of the LA-class.

"Trim, trim—yes, I see it. It reads eight degrees to aft. That means we are lower in the aft section by eight degrees without any ascent adjustment from the stick, doesn't it?"

"Yes, sir," replied the pilot, "that's exactly what it means. Here's Captain Dart."

"Manta, Dart here. If you're having difficulty keeping a fifteen-degree up-bubble, your speed is decreasing, and your aft trim is at a negative eight degrees, you're taking on water in your aft section. Do you understand?"

"Yes, Captain Dart, loud and clear. When I restarted the electrical system of this boat, one breaker would not reset."

"The aft pump breaker?" questioned Captain Dart.

"Precisely."

"Manta, if I may, I would like to suggest you have two possible courses of action," offered Captain Dart.

"Go ahead."

"Your first choice, as I see it, would be to release the lines and get yourself to safety before that poor old boat takes you down with her."

"Captain Dart, you said you saw two possible courses of action?"

"I think, Manta, you're a true risk taker, and the second course of action is surely a risk. If you blow the remainder of your rear ballast, that should compensate for the additional water you've taken on thus far. You're at 75 percent ballast now; if you blow the rear ballast completely, that will put you at 40 percent ballast retained, and it'll all be in the front. The downside is the age of the superstructure. With the water as ballast in those tanks, they have withstood a great deal of pressure for a very long time. By putting CO_2 in those tanks and shoving the water out—well, you get my meaning."

"Yes, sir, I do. But we've now returned to twenty-six hundred feet during this discussion. I'm going to blow all of the remaining ballast—front and back. If we had other circumstances, I could play it more conservatively. But with our current circumstances, I feel we have precious little time left."

"Manta, I agree. I knew you were a risk taker. A man after my own heart. Blow all of your boat's ballast."

Alex pulled up the area from the computer's main menu and selected the Dump All Ballast action line in the menu. As he did, he felt the boat quiver beneath him. The creaking was interrupted by a scream from the bowels of the *Dreadnought* as she replied to the difficult task of pumping the CO_2 into her fore and aft ballast tanks and displacing the water held for decades in those aging tanks. The readings on the gauges all began to change. The depth quickly went to twenty-four hundred feet, while the trim adjusted to a negative two degrees and the speed increased to eleven knots.

"It's working, Captain Dart. We're now at twenty-one hundred feet and rising."

"Good work, Manta. The cheers on boat were so loud I thought you would have heard them from there. You still have a breach in your aft, and it's gonna continue to take on water. You'll need to watch your aft trim closely. I see we're at twenty-four hundred feet now. We're making it happen."

Alex maintained his fifteen-degree climb toward the surface. The *Dreadnought's* depth was now eighteen hundred feet, with the LA-class hanging below her at the end of the set of one hundred-yard cables that attached the two boats. This difference would put the current depth of the LA-class at twenty-one hundred feet. The stick was becoming difficult to keep steady again. Alex checked the aft trim gauge, which now read six degrees down without the stick. The speed was now down to eight knots, and the climb was again slowing. Alex believed it was time to increase the rpm and put more pressure on the *Dreadnought*.

As he was reaching for the rpm slide bar control, Captain Dart began speaking. "Manta, we're reading a return to the sluggish conditions of earlier. I would suggest that the next logical move would be to increase the rpm on your drive shaft."

"Captain Dart, my hand was on the bar when you called. I'm increasing the rpm to three-quarters capacity." With that, Alex pushed the bar forward. He could feel the slow reaction to the increase in rpm, but more than anything he heard the troubled whining from aft as the main turbine pushed hard against the clutch.

"Manta," called Captain Dart, "have you closed all of your watertight doors?"

Alex had not thought of this, since he did not personally fear the coming of the water. But if he were to keep this boat operational for as long as he could, he would have to keep the water out for as long as possible. "No, sir. I'm on that right now. Thank you."

Alex left the control room, going past the CO's cabin and down the ladder to the reactor control room. He sealed the lower doors and then went further aft beyond the main switching room. He had already secured the aft hatch to that room, but he was curious. Alex walked to the aft hatch and placed his hand against it. It was ice cold. Water had already come in to that point and that door was the only guard against it entering further.

Retracing his path back to the control room, he made sure he'd secured all of the doors along his way. He raced through the control room to the forward area of the boat, past the officers' bunks and into the escape-platform area, Alex went down the ladder to the crew's sleeping area and took the ladder down from there to the weapons storage compartment. He saw no hint of water, but he heard painfully louder creaking noises than he had heard from the control room. After sealing each watertight door along the way, Alex returned to the control room and went immediately to his station.

When he checked the gauges, it was apparent that the increase of rpm was helping. The *Dreadnought*'s depth was now at 1650 feet, with an aft trim of negative three degrees and a speed of ten knots. The best news of all was that she and the LA-class were still climbing toward the surface. Now at 1575 and climbing, the boats were halfway there.

At the same moment that Alex was thrown from his chair onto the floor he heard another scream from the *Dreadnought*. Like a body builder pressing that last repetition and screaming when the muscle tissue ripped in his chest from the energy of the effort, the *Dreadnought* was screaming as the effort she was giving caused the forward ballast tanks, emptied by the replacement of pressurized CO_2, to give way to the pressures of the years and the sea. The quake of the boat and the rippling effect of the forward implosion were felt by the LA-class and her crew.

"Manta, are you still with us?"

"This is Manta. Yes, I am still with you. But my boat, according to the readouts, has experienced a hull breach in both of the forward ballast tanks. Not only are they full again, but about now I would guess they are pushing against the remaining superstructure with amazing aggression."

"Manta, this is Dart. My officers and I have been discussing a gamble we might take. We had tried to consider all of the possibilities and what to do at each of the possible junctures. We have determined that if we could make it this close to the surface and if enough stress was evident in the *Dreadnought*—and it is—we could use our remaining battery reserves to blow the remainder of our own ballast."

"What is your remaining battery reserve, Captain?"

"Providing for electrical and environmental systems only, we have four and a half hours remaining on our reserve. We project it will take 80 percent of the reserve to blow our ballast dry."

"Captain Dart, that will only leave you with about twenty-five minutes of battery reserve for your environmental. It's taken us thirty minutes to bring you halfway, and now we've encountered a possible show stopper."

"Manta ... we believe it's our best chance."

"You want to know something, Dart? You're the real risk taker."

"How do you think I pegged you so quickly?" quipped Captain Dart.

"Captain Dart, let's get with it. If I'm correct in my calculations, you have about 50 percent, one thousand tons of ballast, remaining in your tanks. If you expel all of that at once, becoming more buoyant, I had better adjust my bow planes to a steeper ascent to compensate. What does your pilot suggest?"

"Manta, this is Specialist Foyt. To properly compensate for all of the new variables, I would suggest you set your ascent with the bow planes at a forty degree up-bubble."

"That's a drastic change, Foyt."

"Yes, sir, but without it, our bridge tower will make contact with your lower midsection."

"And that would not be good, Foyt. I'm adjusting the bow plane to forty degrees up-bubble. It takes a moment for her to react. Thirty-five, thirty-eight, forty—she's at forty degrees up-bubble, and she's shaking and quaking violently. You'd better hurry; this additional stress is not good."

"Understood, Manta. Chief," commanded Captain Dart, "make her float. Blow all remaining ballast."

The LA-class, even in her low-powered state, reacted quickly to the command. The ballast tanks were all emptied, and the crew felt a sudden surge upward as the compressed CO_2 replaced the water in the fore and aft ballast tanks.

Alex also felt the surge. As the feeling registered with him physically, the gauges in front of him also registered electronically. They had crawled to a depth of fifteen hundred feet and had slowed to a speed of six knots. Now, following the blowing dry of the LA-class ballast tanks, the *Dreadnought* had swiftly increased her speed to twelve knots and had ascended to thirteen hundred feet in a matter of seconds. "It's working, Dart. What's your status?"

"Just as we had calculated, Manta. All ballast has been emptied, and we have about twenty to twenty-five minutes of battery left."

"Understood. I show we have decreased our depth by five hundred feet since blowing your tanks. We're moving fast enough now. Barring any further problems, we'll have the two boats on the surface in fifteen minutes." Alex finished his comment to Captain Dart and then thought to himself, *This is cutting it awfully close.*

With the *Dreadnought* now at a depth of eight hundred feet, the goal was in sight. Alex had radioed ahead to Angela and the admiral to make ready for the surfacing of the two boats. He advised that the LA-class would need immediate attention to tie her off to the side of the admiral's ship and to provide for her crew. Angela had assured Alex that all preparations were ready and standing by. With the *Dreadnought* improving its climb to only three hundred feet, Alex was sure they were done for the day. But the *Dreadnought* still had other plans.

As the depth gauge in front of Alex reached 150 feet, Alex felt the concussion of another implosion. He instinctively looked at the watertight doors at either end of the control room. They were undisturbed. He then looked at the main menu on the computer screen. While he was staring at the damage report on the screen, he was shaken by the concussion of another implosion.

The damage was extensive. The readout on the screen showed the damage from the forward ballast tanks had spread and had now breached the forward escape platform and the officers' bunk area. The forward control-room door was the only thing holding the water back—from that end.

The second concussion came from aft. The computer was showing systems all over the boat were arcing and shutting down. This could only mean that the aft door of the main switching room had been breached.

Alex checked the other gauges. Speed was down to two knots, and the trim, fore and aft, was even—this was not good. That meant that the *Dreadnought* had taken on just as much seawater in both areas.

The most disturbing reading was the depth gauge. It now read 180 feet and was slowly going deeper. Alex felt he had only one chance to save the crew of the LA-class.

He tried the *Dreadnought*'s radio. It was out. He knew he had to contact Captain Dart in his own way now. *Captain Dart, I've had some additional trouble up here. I only have a few seconds to speak with you.*

When we felt the concussions and could not reach you on the radio, we expected the worst.

I'm going to blow the connections between our boats and free your boat to surface under its own buoyancy. Your boat is at a depth of 480 feet right now. If I can get the Dreadnought *out of the way, your boat will surface within ten minutes by virtue of its own current buoyancy. I know you'll run out of battery power in about eight minutes, but if I stay connected, I'll either pull you down or we'll collide.*

Understood Manta. What are you going to do to save yourself?

I'm covered, Captain. I'm blowing the connection on the count of three. Captain Dart?

Yes, Manta?

When you get up there, find the captain of the Tessa *and assure her that I will see her soon.*

I certainly will, my friend. Manta … Manta … I hope you're still there. God be with you. Alex did not answer. He understood Captain Dart and appreciated the wishes, but now he had to move quickly.

With the *Dreadnought*'s depth now at two hundred feet, Alex counted down from three and triggered the hand-held detonators. The explosions were small but more than adequate.

The aft and forward mooring holds snapped like willing twigs and the cables fell freely from their clutches. At that very moment, Alex set the bow planes for ten degrees down-bubble, pressed the rpm slide bar to full speed, and turned her rudder hard left. This was all in an attempt to get the *Dreadnought* out of the way of the LA-class as quickly as possible. With the sonar now down, Alex could only guess at her location.

The *Dreadnought*, first put into service in 1960, was now quaking hard. The depth gauge showed an additional decline to three hundred feet. At that depth and position, Alex knew he was clear of the path of the LA-class.

He pulled back on the joystick in an attempt to slow the descent. There was no slow reaction this time—there was no reaction at all. The computer was dead. As he realized this, the lights went out in the control room. It took a moment for Alex's eyes to adjust to the lack of light. Just as his eyes had adapted, he beheld an unwelcome sight.

Simultaneously, the fore and aft watertight doors of the *Dreadnought*'s control room burst open. The seawater filled the control room so quickly that Alex barely had the chance to place the e-reg from around his neck into his mouth. Looking around the control room with a blend of appreciation and remorse, Alex began to make his way through the water-filled room to the blown open forward doorway.

At the doorway, he turned, paused, and gazed into the control room of the fine British lady. "Thank you for your help," he said. "Without you, those men would have died."

With all of the doors now blown open, Alex easily made his way past the flooded officers' bunks, through the water-filled hall, and into the awaiting escape hatch. It, too, hung open from the inevitable assault of the sea around it. As Alex passed through the tunnel, he heard Angela's message.

My love, the LA-class has just surfaced. Her captain has passed a message and a warm hug that was to assure me that you were going to see me soon. The captain and his crew are all fine, and the crew of the NR-1 has been up here for some time. They are all fine as well. Captain Rogers, of the NR-1, handed me a videotape and said it was the only copy. His only message as he handed it to me was to tell Manta thank you for saving their lives, and that they saw absolutely nothing of your efforts to help. Captain Rogers then said, "That's our story and we're sticking to it."

Yes, my love, I'm fine. I'm just pausing to watch the Dreadnought *limp back into the depths that have been her home for many years. Have you watched the tape?*

I have. It shows a man with no apparent diving gear pressing against a huge falling rock and shoving it out of a path that would have taken off the entire forward portion of the NR-1. Then the tape goes blank. I guess they turned off their camera at that point.

I thought I had gotten to all of the cameras on that boat. Oh well. Will you put on some hot, sweet, Earl Grey tea and fold down the blankets on the warmest bed on the ship? I'm looking forward to a warm shower, a nice cup of tea, and a good long sleep.

Is that all you're looking forward to, my love?

Angela, is that all you ever think about? Well, I suppose ...

Mister, are you in big trouble!

Alex replied as he made his way gently back to the surface and to Angela, *Baby, I love your kind of trouble.*

BOOK TWO

RELATIVITY

CHAPTER 1

L eaping thirty feet from the side of the large, French-built salvage ship was always a thrill. This particular thrill belonged solely to Alex. The *Tessa*, formally commissioned by the French merchant marine and converted just two years ago by Alex and Angela McPherson for their salvage ventures, was well equipped, with a slight walk-off at her stern rising a mere three feet above the surface. Alex rarely chose the stern.

The three-story drop from the side of the *Tessa* to the surface of the Caribbean waters so exhilarated Alex that he would let out what sounded like a scream of fear that was muffled only when he plunged beneath the surface. But Alex was not afraid. It had been said that there was no fear in this McPherson.

After looking up to his crew, who were still gathered along the ship's railing laughing about his gangly giant leap, Alex gave them the *okay* sign and began to descend. He followed the anchor chain of the *Tessa*, which jetted out from her bow at a gradual ten-degree angle. The current trip had them located in Caribbean waters twenty miles south-southeast of Grand Cayman, with a depth that reached well beyond the length of the *Tessa*'s normal anchor chain. Consequently, they had employed the sea anchor, which swayed gently below the large ship to a depth of one hundred feet.

Written reports existed of a shipwreck suspected to have gone down in this area in the early 1940s. A medium-sized pleasure yacht with all her passengers had been lost. Angela, Alex's wife and the captain of the *Tessa*, had spent a day last week reading about the yacht in a reference publication she'd found in the Grand Cayman library, only a few miles from their Cayman Island home in Rum Bay.

For the past two years, since Alex's encounter with a ravenous group of hammerheads near Trinity Caves, the two of them had been researching several possible finds. They would then set out to locate and hopefully bring their discovery to the surface. Alex and Angela McPherson had an edge over anyone else who might have tried the same method of discovery. They had Alex.

Now reaching the end of the sea-anchor cable, Alex slowed his descent and began to take off his BCD and his scuba tanks. Having first placed the e-reg firmly into his mouth, Alex used the attached D-hooks of his BC to fasten the equipment securely to the end of the cable. After checking the connections a second time before he continued his descent, Alex was confident his two-tank, single-valve scuba system was secure.

It never ceased to amaze Alex how easily he was able to move around in the water with only his shorty wetsuit, fins, and the e-reg in his mouth. Since the encounter with the hammerheads and the series of events that had followed, Alex McPherson had been unrestricted in his diving adventures. He could dive as deeply and as long as he chose without suffering from personal damage or fatigue.

He remembered his feelings of dying that day, and how his feelings had somehow been eased by the knowledge that he had fought off the ten hungry sharks just long enough for his wife, Angela, and their son, Tony, to guide the rest of the divers to safety. His memory was also keenly aware of the binding feeling around his right ankle just as he thought his air supply would run out and the sharks would have their feast.

But the part of the memory still the hardest for Alex to believe was when he'd awakened in the undersea cave still alive. He had known he was alive because physically he felt so awful. He'd rejoiced in this awful feeling, though, for he knew it meant he was alive. Not only was he alive, he'd learned, but he had been saved by an unknown race of beings that lived deep beneath the sea.

This race of unknowns had left Alex a device that looked much like a laptop computer. The device had answered his questions about his ordeal with the hammerheads. He discovered that he had been pulled into the depths of the ocean by a giant squid, sent by the unknowns to save him from the hungry sharks. They had sent the squid to save him because they had observed the sacrifice he had made to save the others. They'd told Alex they could not merely stand by and allow the sharks to have their way with such a courageous man.

The problem the unknowns encountered when saving Alex by the method they had chosen was that his body was badly damaged from the pressure of the ocean depth to which they had brought him. Following a series of procedures, they were able to genetically reengineer him, causing his molecular structure to become a thousand times denser than it had been. This, they thought, would allow Alex to return from the ocean depths unharmed.

Their solution for one problem created a new one, though. With Alex's body structure being denser, thus made up of a concentration of productive cells a thousand times greater than before, his need for oxygen had also dramatically increased. As they'd told him while he was still in the undersea cave, he'd nearly died a second time—but this time from the very efforts they were making to save him.

To solve this problem, they had surgically installed an organic concentrator in Alex's bronchial passages, just above his lungs, so any air he breathed in would be effortlessly concentrated to the level of oxygen he needed for his new molecular structure. Still, he could not return to the surface, even with his increased strength and genetic reengineering. Alex could not extract air from the seawater, and he could not survive on a single breath to make it to the surface.

The unknowns provided Alex with a mechanical device they called an e-reg. This enhanced regulator would extract air from the seawater as if it were attached to air tanks and could be used at any depth, thus surpassing the limited depth ratings of any man-made tank system. The e-reg had what looked to be a bungee cord attached to it, which allowed the device to be worn around the neck. The e-reg resembled many of the standard two-stage diaphragm regulators used with normal scuba equipment.

With his rebirth that day from the process of genetic reengineering, with the surgical implantation of the organic oxygen concentrator, and with the gift of the e-reg, Alex McPherson had been able to return home to his family. But he'd returned home with new strength, new mental capabilities, and telepathic abilities that were a direct result of the increased cellular development and how it affected his brain tissue. As far as they could tell, Alex had been left with the ability to dive in any body of water, to any depth, for as long as he chose.

Only Alex and Angela knew of these abilities and the full events of that day. The fear of an outside force trying to exploit Alex was too great. Nonetheless, they had devised a plan that allowed contact to be made by a highly placed individual in the United States Navy if the services of their salvage company, TESS—the Terran Exploration and Salvage Society—were needed for emergency rescue. There had been one such contact from Admiral Sterling, through the e-mail address of Manta@mixi.net, which was rerouted by an anonymous remailer, for security and secrecy. *Manta* was the code name Alex used when in contact with anyone while he performed his deepwater services.

It had been well over a year since Alex and Angela had performed any salvage work for anyone but themselves. Today was no exception. Alex had now descended to a depth of 350 feet, where the pleasure yacht, the *Belgium*, was thought to be resting. With any luck, they would find her and be able to retrieve her from her watery grave to be restored and sold to a museum as a part of seafaring history.

Angela, I'm approaching three hundred seventy-five feet. Alex was able to communicate quite effectively with Angela, or anyone he chose, by means of his telepathic process. They had tested this ability up to five miles between the two of them, with complete clarity.

Have you come upon her yet? Angela queried mentally from her captain's chair onboard the *Tessa.*

Not yet, but the sea floor is level, and I should be able to find her. I think—yes—I have her! replied Alex. *She's resting on her starboard side.*

It appears the boat and her crew were rammed. There is a hole about three feet across near her bow. Beyond that damage, she is intact. We should make plans for me to temporarily repair the damage on my next dive, and then we'll attach to her and pull her up.

Sounds like a plan, quipped Angela. *Can you make out her name plate?*

Just a minute. Yes, she's the Belgium. I'll be up in about fifteen minutes. I want to have a look around before I start up.

All right mister, responded Angela with her mothering tone played to its maximum effect. *But you had better be careful. There's no one, including me, who can come down there to help if you get yourself into trouble.*

Yes ma'am; I understand.

Alex took his time examining the surrounding area and found nothing remarkable to note. He took his dive slate from his utility belt and, checking his wrist compass, wrote down the coordinates of the *Belgium* to make it easier to find her again.

Returning to the sea anchor of the *Tessa*, Alex put on his BCD and two-tank scuba system. He then followed the anchor chain back to the surface, though there was no need to do so with the clarity of the water and the brightness of the sun. When Alex reached the end of the chain, still one hundred feet below the *Tessa*, he could easily make out the detailed lines and the contours of her hull. He went to the back of her hull and climbed out using the ladder that hung, four rungs below the surface, from her stern platform.

Alex pulled off his gear and went to the bridge cabin, where he found Angela scribbling a few notes on a yellow notepad on her desk. "Did you get lost again, sailor?" Angela teased.

"Not at all," replied Alex. "I went, I found, I noted."

Alex pulled the dive slate from his belt and handed it to Angela, who took the slate and looked at the writings with puzzlement. "I thought I misunderstood you when you communicated you had found the *Belgium*. That's what you have written here. I suppose there could be a second boat with the same registry."

"What do you mean? I went down there specifically looking for the *Belgium*." Alex was the one sounding confused now. "Why would you think there was a second boat with the same name? The *Belgium* was the one you and I were looking for in the first place."

"In the first place?" Angela reacted with amazement. "I had no idea what boat you were looking for on this dive."

"Angela, dear, have you hit your head on something?" questioned Alex as he looked around her cabin. "You researched this pleasure yacht and determined its location before we set out today. These coordinates match your earlier calculations. We're in this location because of your research."

"We can discuss that later, Alex. For now, look at the screen. My research on the pleasure yacht *Belgium* shows she is still owned by descendants of the original owners and is sitting in her slip in Newport in mint condition. See for yourself."

Alex moved around to the other side of the desk and stared with doubt at the well-kept boat that looked too identical to the wreck he had just left nearly four hundred feet below to be a second *Belgium* registry.

"I don't understand," he queried. "That boat looks just like the one I found on the dive. I need to return to her before we plan to make repairs."

"Alex, my love. Are you all right?"

"I don't know. I could have been mistaken about a lot of things. But I can't believe I was mistaken about your research on the *Belgium* and it being your research that brought us out here to these coordinates. And on top of that, I can't have looked at her nameplate wrong; it was too clear. I'll dive on the site again to make confirmation."

Alex went directly to the rear of the *Tessa* and giant-stepped in, with the e-reg firmly placed in his mouth. The crew had gone below for lunch, and he didn't want to take the time to put on his full scuba gear. Alex followed the anchor cable down, to create a direct match to the approach he had taken before. He followed the coordinates he had written on his dive slate to the spot where he had first found the *Belgium*.

She was not there. The *Belgium* was nowhere to be found. Alex floated in a neutrally buoyant position for a moment, asking himself how this was possible. How could he have seen it so clearly only forty-five minutes earlier and now it had vanished?

Angela. Alex contemplated his thoughts to telepathically communicate with his wife. *The* Belgium *is gone.*

Alex, according to the records, she was never there. It must have been a different boat.

But that's another mystery, Angela. There's no wreck here at all. I'm floating over the very same coordinates I have written down for the Belgium—*and neither the* Belgium *nor any other boat is here!*

Alex was getting more confused by the moment, and Angela could sense his frustration by the way his thoughts were being relayed. *My love,* she gently whispered, *why don't you come back to the Tessa, and I'll fix you a cup of Earl Grey and we can think this through after you rest.*

You're right, Angela. There's nothing logical about what I'm telling you. I'll be right up.

I'll be waiting. Don't take too long, or you'll worry me.

No messing around. I'll be there straight away.

CHAPTER 2

The afternoon was chilly, even for early March. The wind had picked up, whipping against the 1962 Impala and gently pushing it around on the winding country road. Young Gayle Beaufort was riding in the backseat, as she and her parents ventured to their relatives' house in upstate New York. Gayle's father was proud of their new car. This model had only been on the market for a few weeks before he'd secured the loan with the bank and made the purchase.

Gayle had just celebrated her fifth birthday two weeks ago; she was playing with her new Barbie doll in the cushioned backseat of their car. She was changing her doll's outfit from the swimsuit it was wearing to something more suited to the cold, blustering wind: a full dress with a matching coat and hat. Of course, the handbag coordinated nicely with the new shoes her doll now modeled.

Gayle's parents were very much in love. They sat next to one another in the front bench seat like teenagers on a Saturday-night date. The young child could feel the love between her parents. They shared that love with her, and the three of them were seemingly inseparable. But all too often, fate has a way of ignoring such things.

Gayle's father guided the robin's egg blue Impala down the winding two-lane highway as he talked to her mother about the events of this past week. He had started a new job with a large construction company, as an entry-level skilled worker. The pay would not be much at first, but he hoped that if he worked very hard for the next couple of years his position in the company would grow, and so would his earnings.

They were people of modest means who had decided it was more important to them that Gayle's mother not take a job outside the home but rather spend time with their daughter and forgo the benefits of a second income. It was a choice they were both very happy with, and Gayle had benefited by having her mother's daily attention, since her father had to work six or seven days a week trying to learn the construction business as thoroughly as he could.

They were all smiles as they enjoyed this rare Saturday drive to the country. They could not have imagined the horror that awaited them just two miles ahead.

Billy Edwards had been out since six the evening before. He and some friends had decided they had worked hard all week and wanted to paint the town. They'd cashed their paychecks and started drinking before seven Friday evening. It was now nearly two on Saturday afternoon. Only ten minutes earlier, Billy had decided to leave his friends' house where they had drunk and played poker until they'd passed out early Saturday morning.

His battered red Ford pickup was swerving violently against the wind, as he tried to maneuver each of the winding curves along the two-lane highway. Matters were worsened by the fact that young Billy Edwards was still quite drunk.

Gayle was quite pleased with Barbie's new dress, hat, and coat. "Mommy, look at Barbie. Isn't she darling? She looks just like you, Mommy, on Sunday mornings at church."

"Gayle, darling," her mother replied as she turned around in her seat and rested her arms and head on the seat back, "you are the one who is so darling. And yes, your doll is beautiful. I don't know that my waist will ever be like hers, but thank you for the compliment, my sweet."

"Oh my God!" were the only words Gayle's father had time to get out of his mouth when the aging red pickup seemed to come from nowhere. It was barreling down on the Impala, head-on, in the Impala's lane on one of the sharp curves of this mountainous stretch of road.

"Oh my God!" were the only words Gayle's father had time to get out of his mouth before Gayle was thrown from her seat, hard, against the padded rear of the front bench seat. Gayle saw her mother's face at that spilt-second moment in time. Her mother had a look of confusion, which moved quickly to fear and then to extreme sadness.

"Oh my God!" were the last words Gayle's mother heard before she was thrown away from her daughter, away from her loving husband, and through the windshield of the Impala onto the unforgiving pavement.

These were the last words Gayle's mother heard before she died and left her husband and five-year-old Gayle behind.

1962 had been key in the life of Gayle Beaufort. It was the year she lost her mother. It was also the year she began to fantasize about having her mother by her side once again.

Gayle Beaufort never stopped fantasizing; she continued to strengthen her fantasy with her intense pain and extreme feelings of loss.

CHAPTER 3

Alex had completed a very busy week in the Miami area. He visited several diving-supply houses to investigate a few items of the newest diving technology that might be incorporated into their business, the Ore Verde Dive Shop. These items would allow Alex and Angela to provide nitrox diving to their patrons.

Since most of their divers were experienced divers with fifty or more dives logged, it was important, or so Angela thought, to have the compressing technology to be able to blend gases for a nitrox diver. These supply houses were exhibiting the best in the field. Alex was confident the mixing compressor he had ordered would surpass any need they would face in the area of gas mixtures for nitrox.

As he still had three hours before his flight back to Grand Cayman, Alex had decided to get his hair trimmed, and he was now relaxing in the barber's chair. He was particular about who cut his hair. Alex was not vain about his hair—or about any other element of his rough-hewed, athletic appearance, for that matter. He had had one bad experience with a barber who Alex swore was blind. Five years ago, Alex had visited the barber his father had gone to for over twenty years. Before Alex knew what was happening, the septuagenarian barber had taken an electric shaver to the left side of Alex's head. When the second barber had finished trying to even out the damage, Alex looked as if he were in boot camp. Since then, Alex had paid quite a bit more attention during his haircuts.

This barber was a short man of slight build. His own hair was cut very short, and he had the look of a two-day-old beard trying its best to finish him with a rough look, which his voice and mannerisms clearly prevented. Nonetheless, Alex had visited this shop on three or four previous occasions and had been quite pleased with the finished product.

The barber, Chris, had finished cutting Alex's hair and had turned around to pick up the dryer from the top of the styling counter. When Chris turned his back, Alex noticed the vibrant green and red of Chris's tropical shirt nearly jumping off the threads. Alex closed his eyes for a moment and promised himself never again to wear his own shirt of nearly the same design, which hung in his closet at home. When Alex opened his eyes, a young, attractive lady had the dryer in her hand and was beginning to dry his hair.

"That was quick. Where did Chris take off to?"

The young lady turned off the dryer and spoke to Alex with a question in her voice. "I'm sorry Mr. McPherson—what did you say?"

"I asked where Chris had taken off to so quickly."

"I don't know a Chris," replied the young blonde, whose deep-blue eyes now looked more confused than before. Shaking her head slowly, she was about to turn the dryer on again to continue the drying process.

Alex stood up and took the protective smock from around his neck. He moved quickly and without hesitation in his movement, which startled the young stylist. Alex's voice had moved from its friendly, noncommittal tone to one of serious indignation. "Hey, I don't want to be a pain, but I've had a long week, and I know I could have easily fallen asleep in this chair. But I didn't! Where did Chris go, and who are you?"

"Mr. McPherson," hesitantly replied the young, five-foot-nothing lady, who was faced with a tall, muscularly built, agitated man staring down at her and demanding answers. "I don't know a Chris and certainly not one that works here. I've cut your hair before, and you didn't have any concerns with any previous visit. Maybe you fell asleep and had a bad dream—I don't know. But I do know I've done nothing to deserve you getting upset with me."

Alex heard what she said, and for a brief moment he felt apologetic for his behavior. More quickly than it takes to blink an eye, Alex let that thought pass and replaced it with another thought—the *Belgium*.

"I think I'd better leave." Alex began a brisk walk toward the front door of the shop.

"If you don't want me to dry your hair, that's fine; but you still owe me for the haircut."

"Why?" replied Alex, "you weren't the one who cut it."

With that, Alex was gone. He had a growing feeling that this issue was somehow related to the experience with the *Belgium* wreck dive a couple of months back. He had found a wreck that had never been wrecked and had his hair cut by someone who might not have been there. Alex was concerned he was suffering from some ill effect related to his genetic remapping. He decided to take an earlier fight back to the islands and get home as soon as he could.

Not hungry at all for dinner, Alex sat at the table with Angela and his son, Tony, and just silently picked at his food. He'd shared his experience at the barbershop with Angela when he'd arrived home. She had not been concerned at all, at first. It had sounded like some kind of mix-up or joke, until she had listened closely to the somber tones in Alex's voice. She knew then that, real or not, it was serious.

After dinner, Tony went to a friend's house to play his friend's newest video game. They had an ongoing competition on a new hockey game, which seesawed back and forth between victory and defeat. Tony had been beaten rather badly just last evening and was anxious to get to his friend's house for the rematch.

Angela brewed fresh sun tea that day and brought the tea service out to the gazebo. Their gazebo was located on a walkway that jetted out about a hundred yards from the rear of their house into the bay. It was right in the center of the walkway and was positioned to see the maximum amount of sky—a great place for relaxing, reading and, on occasion, making love under the stars. Tonight, though, it was a great place to sip tea and talk.

"Angela, what's going on?"

"I'm not sure. You've always had a very vivid—often too creative—imagination, but this is certainly more than just your imagination."

"I have no proof, but Angela, the *Belgium* was there two months ago. And I am just as sure it was Chris who was cutting my hair today. Could it be my genetic rebirth has finally taken its toll on my mind?"

"I'm confident you believe you saw the *Belgium*, and I'm confident you believe Chris cut your hair today." Angela spoke these words with the same meticulous, matter-of-fact tone in her voice Alex was very familiar with when Angela was contemplating pieces to a puzzle. "I'm not confident these events truly happened, though."

"You believe me but you don't believe me?"

"Not at all. I completely believe you. I believe your sincerity and I believe you believe. What I'm saying is if something has happened to your thoughts to make you believe these things, they don't necessarily have to be facts to be real to you."

"I understand." Alex calmed himself and sipped on his iced tea for nearly twenty minutes before speaking again. Then he said, "What do I do about my thoughts apparently not agreeing with reality?"

"Nothing tonight, my love." Angela sat next to Alex, took his hand, and spoke in a near whisper. "Tomorrow is Saturday, and you're going to sleep in. I'm going to go to the library to start researching the symptoms you're displaying. It would be prudent to pull up information on similar occurrences and read what's been done in those cases. It may take me most of the day. I want you to rest around the house for the day. I'll call the guys at the shop and tell them they're on their own. Tony is sleeping over at Jimmy's tonight, and they were going boating with a group from school tomorrow, so he won't be around until the evening. You'll have the place to yourself all day, so take advantage of it and rest."

"It's a deal." Alex and Angela finished their tea and slowly walked back to the house at about eleven in the evening. Alex was in bed and asleep before midnight.

The next morning, Alex awoke feeling rested but still troubled. He looked over to Angela's side of the king-size four-poster bed and saw that she was not there. He then recalled that she had planned to head into town early and go to the library. He also remembered that Tony was at a friend's house.

Alex left the bedroom to have his shower before dressing and getting some toast and coffee for breakfast. Being nearly comatose in the morning was normal for Alex. Angela had often questioned how he made it to the shower without bumping into something along the way, since his eyes didn't even appear to be open. This morning Alex did just that.

As he turned the corner from the master bedroom to enter the connecting bathroom, Alex came face to face with a wicker étagère with bath linens stacked neatly on its shelves. Alex grabbed a clean washcloth from one of the shelves, as well as a clean bath towel. Hanging the towel on the towel rod near the shower door and taking the washcloth with him into the shower, Alex showered slowly, waking up as the hot water beat him to consciousness.

Alex slid the shower door open and took the towel from the rod to dry his face and then began to dry the rest of his body. As he moved the towel from his face, he looked across the bathroom to the étagère. "Where did that come from?" Alex said this aloud, knowing he was alone. "Angela put that in a garage sale ten years ago. I remember buying that when I was in college. She hated it. How could it? It must be a different one—but why?"

He finished grooming and went downstairs to put on the coffee. Alex stopped in his tracks at the foot of the stairs, and his jaw nearly dropped from its socket. Everything was different! All of the wall coverings were different; most of the furniture was different; in fact, all of the walls were different. Each of the walls had a different color treatment on than it had the evening before.

"What is going on? I'm flipping out!" Alex was in shock. "I pray to God this is a dream." Alex stumbled throughout the house, amazed at what he was seeing. There were things there he had had while in college but he and Angela had replaced years before with something newer and more to their joint tastes. There were items he had never seen before. They were very masculine in their design and immediately to his liking, but whose were they?

Alex remembered the étagère and ran upstairs to the bathroom. He roughly pulled the étagère away from the wall, tossing the linens from the shelves, and looked blankly at the back of the aging piece of wicker furniture. There it was: the identifying mark Alex had remembered when he was downstairs. When Alex was in college, he had found the étagère at a discount furniture store where college students were more than likely to find affordable furniture. He had seen the piece during a visit between classes, paid for it, and agreed to return to the store after the day's classes to pick it up. The store manager had marked the item sold for Alex. When Alex got it home to his small, off-campus apartment, he'd discovered the store worker had used a permanent marker on the back of the wicker piece, so the word *Sold* was indelibly visible for years to come.

And there it was. The word *Sold* was still faintly visible, just where it had been for nearly twenty years. Alex's eyes widened, and he ran for Angela's closet. It was empty. He pulled open the closet's side drawers where Angela kept her sweaters. The drawers were empty.

Alex moved over to his closet and opened the expanding doors. His clothes were there. But there was a difference. Alex immediately noticed that things were missing. The Old Navy sweater Angela had bought Alex for his most recent birthday was not there. Other things were different, but Alex plunged into the clothes to pull out a pair of blue jeans, an IU sweater, his shoes, and a pair of athletic socks from his sock drawer. At least he thought it was his sock drawer. The five-drawer chest was also unfamiliar to Alex.

Grabbing his keys, Alex went out to the garage and found that the tropical green Geo Tracker convertible he had bought just after coming to the islands was there, just as he remembered leaving it the afternoon before. He decided to drive to town and find Angela. She had said she was going to the town library, so the library was Alex's target location.

The drive was extremely painful for Alex. Questions were going through his head, but there were no answers for these weird questions. The thirty-minute drive from Rum Bay to Georgetown seemed to take forever.

Upon arriving in Georgetown, Alex went directly to the library. Rushing inside, he took a frantic look throughout the small building. There were very few people in the library, and none of them had seen Angela nor could they remember every seeing her. Alex spoke with the librarian, which also resulted in frustration. Angela had not been to the library.

Alex left the library for the short drive down the seven-mile beach road to the location of the Georgetown Hotel. Alex and Angela's dive shop, the Ore Verde Dive Shop, was located on the beach behind the Georgetown Hotel. Alex briskly ran through the hotel lobby, past the indoor pool and recreation area, and out the back door of the hotel. The dive shop was there, but even it looked different somehow.

Alex cautiously entered the shop to find his two boat captains preparing for the day's trips to take divers out. "Hey, Alex! Qué pasa? We didn't expect you this early."

"Mark, Dan—have either of you seen Angela this morning?"

"Who's Angela? Is this another girl you've picked up and promised a day at sea with God's gift to the ocean-loving blondes of the world?" Both Mark and Dan snickered as if this had happened more than once in the past.

"No, she's not some girl I've picked up," responded Alex, using his talents of self-control to maintain his composure in spite of the mocking laughter from his two friends. "You guys don't know Angela, do you?"

"Sorry, boss. I've never heard of her," answered Mark, with Dan adding, "Me neither. Should we know her?"

"You should, but I can't explain why right now." Alex looked around the shop at the various pictures of the different dive groups that had traveled to the dive sites with him and the boat crews in the past two years. He was searching for a picture of Angela in any of them. He found nothing.

Hesitantly, Alex asked the next question. "I think I'll take the boat back home instead of driving. Mark, can you give me the extra set of keys?"

"Sure, boss," replied Mark as he reached behind him and took a set of keys from the partially opened safe. He then tossed the keys to Alex.

The keys didn't look familiar to Alex. "Which boat do these go to?"

Mark and Dan looked at each other with puzzled looks on their faces, and it was Dan who spoke up first. "Are you okay, Alex?"

"I'm fine enough for now; I just don't remember seeing this set of keys in a while."

"Sure. Okay. That set is to your boat, the *McPherson*." Dan stood and looked out the back window of the shop toward the ocean. "The *McPherson* is the forty-two-foot Fairline Targa on the right side of the dock. Now, the dock is that wooden thing that—"

"Cut it out, Dan," chimed in Mark. "Can't you see Alex is hungover? Are you sure you should take the boat out in your condition, Alex?"

Alex had to work hard at staying calm. "I appreciate your concern, Mark, and your attempt at humor, Dan. I'll be fine. Is she gassed up and ready to go?"

"Aye, Captain," responded Mark in his favorite pirate's brogue.

Alex thought to himself, *Well, some things haven't changed. Mark is still a pirate, and Dan is still unable to take anything seriously.* As he headed out toward the boat, Alex considered the Fairline Targa. This was the boat he and Angela had bought for their personal use, but it had been Alex who had actually signed the check. And the boat had not been named the *McPherson*; it had been the *Angelina*.

Trying to think clearly was impossible for Alex during the boat ride home. The sky was clear, the wind was warm, and the temperature was a pleasant eighty-two degrees. The weather aside, Alex continued feeling psychological chills. He would go home and search the house for anything to do with Angela. He would call to the friend's house where Tony had stayed the evening before—but Alex knew that if no one knew of Angela, then no one would know of Tony.

Alex had been home from the trip to Georgetown for three hours now. He had called Tony's friend's house; they had had no idea who Tony was, and Alex had not pressed the point. Alex pulled all of the photo albums from the cabinets and went quickly through each of them, to no avail. Angela and Tony did not exist. They had somehow been erased from Alex's life.

Alex was feeling extremely low. He decided to call his parents, if for no other reason than to hear their loving voices. Alex wasn't sure what to do next. He felt it best not to share his sudden loss of Angela and Tony with his parents unless they brought up the names of Alex's missing wife and child first. Alex just wanted to talk with his family.

As he dialed the telephone and listened to the ringing tones, Alex started to feel good, since in a moment he would be speaking with his parents. Alex's parents still lived in Indiana. That was where Alex had grown up, and he had attended Indiana University on a football scholarship as well as the Bellamy Scholarship for Educational Achievers.

The line was answered an unfamiliar woman's voice. "Hello."

Alex was caught off guard. "Uh, hello. May I speak with Mr. or Mrs. McPherson?"

"I'm sorry, but you have the wrong number," responded the woman on the other end of the line. "What number are you trying to call?" questioned the woman in an attempt to be helpful.

Alex slowly spoke the number he'd had memorized since he was thirteen years old, when he, his sister, and his parents had moved to their current home.

"Well, that is this number, but we have had this number for the past ten years, and there are no McPhersons at this residence." The lady then promptly said goodbye and hung up the phone.

Had Alex not personally experienced the day he was having, he would not have believed it, even if a trusted friend had described it. He called for directory assistance for Indiana. Alex asked for the number for Russell McPherson, his father. The operator told Alex there wasn't a listing for a Russell McPherson in Indiana.

An hour after his attempt to contact his parents, Alex decided to make one further attempt to contact family. He called directory assistance for Florida and asked for the listing for Mr. Gavin Kind, Angela's father.

"I have that number for you; please wait," responded the operator.

Alex's heart jumped into his throat. He wrote down the number and immediately dialed it. "Hello." The voice on the other end of the call was Angela's father.

He had first met Angela's father while he and Angela were dating in college and had spent a great deal of time around him for nearly twenty years.

"Mr. Kind?" Alex spoke with great hesitation.

"Yes. This is Gavin Kind."

"Mr. Kind." Alex wasn't sure how to approach this telephone call. He couldn't start out with 'Have you seen your daughter? I can't seem to find her.' But Alex had known this man for a long time. Gavin Kind was a logical, straightforward man who had served in the navy as a pilot during WWII and worked as a mechanical engineer and building contractor before retiring. Alex was sure Gavin would answer a few questions even from a stranger, and that is exactly what Alex was sure he would be to Gavin Kind. "My name is Alex McPherson." No response. "I'm calling to ask a few questions that would assist me with some personal research I'm working on. Do you mind giving me a moment? I'd greatly appreciate it."

"Go ahead, young man. Ask your questions."

Alex thought for a moment, and then asked his first question. "I was wondering, Mr. Kind, are you working or retired?"

"I'm retired and have been for the past twenty years."

"Is your wife retired also?"

"I never married," responded Mr. Kind quickly. "I was engaged once, many years ago, but we never married."

"Then I suppose my next question about your children would not be applicable."

"No, young man, I do not have any children."

"I apologize for being so personal, but did you say you *never* married, or that you were currently not married?"

"Young man, you seem a bit shaky about asking questions. Am I the first you've called?"

"Well, sir," replied Alex with an ironic smile on his face, "You're the first person I've been able to get hold of."

"Well, son, I'll answer your question, so there is no doubt about my marital status. I was engaged to a lovely young girl before I entered the navy. She decided to visit her relatives in Switzerland while I was in boot camp. She booked passage on a passenger ship coming out of Brighton, England, in 1943, which the Germans believed was also carrying munitions back and forth from the United States to England.

"A U-boat captain gave the order, and the passenger ship was sunk. It happened so quickly, and the ship was so small, that it sank before half of the passengers could be brought up from the lower decks. My fiancé was lost that evening at sea.

"Funny thing about the whole deal—the passenger ship wasn't carrying munitions at all. It was carrying passengers, as it should, but it was also secretly carrying three of the first German scientists who were defecting to the States to work on the atomic bomb project. They survived, but my fiancé did not.

"So, young man, there it is. I was never married."

Alex was beginning to feel he had overstepped his permission to ask Mr. Kind a few questions. "Mr. Kind, I want to thank you for your time. You've been very helpful."

"I don't see how I could have been. You didn't ask very many questions."

"I realize that, sir. But your answers have been food for thought. I hope to speak with you in the future. Maybe then I can tell you about my research."

Alex hung up the phone, sat back in his chair—at least it was his chair now, even though he had not seen it before this morning—and tried to begin to put all of the information together that he had encountered today, especially the most recent piece of the puzzle.

Alex recalled hearing Angela's parents recount the tale of Anna Kind's trip to Switzerland while Gavin was in flight school. The ship had carried some of the first scientists to work on the Oakridge A-bomb project in Tennessee. But the story had been quite different from this version. In the original one, the passenger ship had completed its journey to the states after sighting a U-boat that was heading away from the passenger ship's bow into the moonlight.

Anna Kind had completed her voyage back to the states. She and Gavin had had two daughters; one of those daughters was Angela. And now Anna had died, Gavin had never married, and Angela did not exist.

What evil from hell was behind all of this?

CHAPTER 4

T he activity in the science building seemed to step up several notches when the news spread through the complex that the dean of the School of Astrophysics had just resigned. Professor Gayle Beaufort had served in the MIT Department of Science since being awarded her first PhD from MIT in astrophysics. Following Dr. Beaufort's completion of her second PhD, this one in electronic engineering, and her third PhD, awarded in computer engineering, the good doctor had served as MIT's Dean of Astrophysics. She held this post for the past ten years. Now, two weeks after her fortieth birthday, she was leaving the school and tendering no notice.

Dr. Beaufort had wrestled with her decision over the previous weekend. Watching her father slowly die from a rare, inoperable brain tumor, which had disabled him for the past six months, had not been easy.

She and her father had lost Gayle's mother when Gayle had just turned five. Her father had remarried when Gayle was ten, to a strong, goal-oriented woman whose father owned the construction company Gayle's father had worked for since Gayle was five. Gayle's new stepmother cared for Gayle with great love, but it was the support and direction she gave Gayle about her future that was her greatest gift.

Gayle's new family structure had a few other advantages that assisted with Gayle's future. The construction business was booming, and

Gayle's father had shown himself to be more than a skilled carpenter or contractor. He had shown himself to be a talented money manager and leader. When he married the boss's daughter, he came clearly into the view of his father-in-law, the owner of the Nor'easter Construction Company. The increased income from the rapid promotions that followed allowed Gayle to attend the best private schools. It was her stepmother's opinion that Gayle showed signs of brilliance and her abilities could best be nurtured if her college preparatory path began early. Gayle attended a preparatory high school located in the Catskills. Gayle learned quickly and sought knowledge with a fervent hunger.

Gayle was eighteen when her father took over the company following the retirement of his father-in-law. Gayle had graduated from high school at the top of her class and had been accepted early to start her undergraduate studies at MIT. She visited her father and stepmother on holidays and during the summer, as she had during her high-school years. This had been her habit from the age of fifteen, until ten years ago, when she'd earned her third doctorate.

For the past ten years, Gayle had kept herself very busy with her study of astrophysics. She'd concentrated her studies on radio telescopes and on the various effects of the ellusive black holes. During the majority of the past ten years, Gayle had seen her parents only on major holidays. When her stepmother had passed away a year ago, her father had seemed to lose interest in life. Gayle had thought it was depression until the diagnosis six months ago.

During the past six months, Gayle had spent every weekend with her father at his home, with the last four weeks' visits being at the hospital instead. With the passing of her father, Gayle became the sole heir to his estate. Gayle had been astounded to discover, just three days ago, that her father had left her with millions.

Dr. Gayle Beaufort, PhD, determined during the last two days of the weekend that it was time to put her years of grueling research into motion. She now had the financial resources to fund the project and had only recently discovered several break-through enlightenments that would give her dream the wings for flight.

CHAPTER 5

T ime seemed to be against Alex. He stayed in or near his home for nearly two months. His state of mind was disastrous for the first few days after he'd spoken with Angela's father. He wasn't angry—who was there to be angry with? Alex felt his entire existence turning numb. His failure to understand what was happening ate at him for weeks.

A call every other day from the guys at the dive shop was the only communication he had with the outside world. The only entertainment he allowed himself was to play thirty-year-old rock and roll loudly from his antique record albums. Yet, it couldn't honestly be called entertainment the way Alex played this music. He would look through the albums and any album newer than 1977 would be quickly ripped open and Frisbeed out the back door.

It was in 1977 that Alex had met Angela. They'd met when Alex had first arrived at the Indiana University campus. He had been scouted to start his freshman year on the school's football team and was there on a full scholarship. Angela was working in the administration office as part of her work/study program to help pay for her education. Having just completed her undergraduate program, with a double major in electrical and mechanical engineering, she was poised to enter the doctoral program in engineering.

She'd sat at the registration desk with a helpful, but somewhat distracted, look on her face. It was not one of her wildest dreams to play counselor to a rowdy group of jocks, for which this special registration area had been designed. General studies and easy courses were the primary choice of the guys in the room. The jocks were here for one purpose—play the sport that brought them here and waste as little time as possible on classes they felt would be of no consequence to their future. Alex was more than a surprise to her—Alex became a puzzle, and puzzles, he found out later, were the most exciting things Angela could ever consider spending her time contemplating.

Alex had stood tall directly in front of Angela's table. Until that moment, he had not paid any attention to who was at the table. Alex was not excited to be there himself; he was more interested in arranging for the most effective schedule he could acquire and spending the least amount of time possible on that endeavor. It wasn't that Alex was or is impatient, but he didn't like spending too much time on one project— some think that to be synonymous—oh well.

But Alex had become speechless. He'd looked into the face of this person patiently waiting for him to tell her his name so she could process the "basket-weaving schedule," as some had called it. At that moment, Alex would have sworn he could the moon in her deep blue eyes. He felt the words of an old song come to his lips: "raven hair and ruby lips."

"Excuse me?" Angela had replied.

"Ah, I was just, ah …" Alex had stammered.

"Let me have your name. I believe I have the perfect schedule already planned for you," she'd stated in a matter-of-fact, assuming tone.

"My name?" he'd stammered on. "Name … my name is Alexander McPherson, Alex."

"Well, Alexander McPherson, Alex, if you will just sign here, you may call it a day." Angela had said this as she'd placed the paper in front of him and held out a pen.

Trying to accommodate any request this beautiful woman would make of him, Alex had taken the pen and aimed it for the dotted line she so delicately indicated with her long, slender finger. Then he'd noticed something other than the contour of her neck.

"There must be some mistake," he'd said, sounding quite confused.

"After meeting you and sharing this enriching moment of conversation, I doubt there is any mistake. This schedule will allow you to play whatever sport you are here for and not spend any unwanted time reading or writing."

That statement had shaken Alex back to reality. "Reading or writing?"

And Angela had apologized. "I'm sorry. I did not mean to sound demeaning. It's been a long day."

"There's no need for you to apologize to me, but if I intend to graduate with a degree in Marine Biology," he'd said as he looked at the page she was offering him, "I might need more than Intro to Preliminary Business Math, don't you think?"

"Excuse me—Marine Biology? What did you say your name was?"

Alex had repeated his name and Angela had quickly gone through the card file in front of her, searching through several 4 x 6 information cards.

Angela began to speak now with a more enlightened tone, "Alexander McPherson. You are here for a Marine Bio degree."

Alex was glad she confirmed this for him. He was beginning to think his instant failure in all brain activity when he first saw this lovely lady was to be a permanent dilemma.

"You're here not only on a football scholarship but a partial assistance grant from the Bellamy Foundation of Educational Achievers."

"You know, you seem to have a lot of information about me on that card; don't you think it only fair you tell me your name. At least then I'd have some information about you."

From the moment Angela had told him her name, Alex had been determined to convince her that a life with him would be a good gamble. They'd dated through the next four years, and following graduation, they'd married. Their son, Anthony, had arrived a year later.

*****

So Alex was not enjoying the music. It was merely a desperate attempt to cling to a time when Alex had had his family, a time when he'd understood his own life and the goings-on around him. It was a time when he'd had a sounding board in Angela: he would describe a situation to her, she would pose her logical questions, as she always seemed to do, and he would have the wherewithal to sort out the solution.

"That's it!" Alex yelled as he was walking through the empty house, which resounded with the heavy bass line of Creedence Clearwater Revival's rendition of "I Heard It Through the Grapevine." "I need a sounding board!"

He walked over to the stereo and turned the volume down to a reasonable roar. *How could I possibly begin to assemble the pieces of this puzzle while locked away in this cave? I need to think of who I can contact to sit with and help me think this thing through. But who? It's got to be somebody I trust and*—laughing to himself, he continued the thought—*I suppose it's important they still exist.*

Alex's attempt at humor brought a small smile to his face. It was the first smile his face had felt in nearly two months.

Alex remembered a professor he'd had at Indiana University. This prof had taught a class he'd used toward his science requirements, even though it had been outside of his major. Dr. Marc Lee had been an associate professor of astrophysics at IU, but that had been twenty years ago.

"It could be he's still there," Alex spoke out loud to himself. "He was a first-year associate during my senior year. That would make him about fifty. He's got to be there!"

With those words, Alex jumped up and nearly ran to the telephone. He called through the international operator to connect with directory assistance for Indiana. After finding the number, dialing it, and hearing someone on the other end answer the phone, "Indiana University, Administration Offices," Alex felt a thrill that the school was still there.

"Yes. Hello. I need to speak with Professor Marc Lee."

"I'm sorry," replied the receptionist, "but we do not have a Professor Marc Lee at this university."

Alex's heart fell through the seat of his pants, while a rumbling scream began to build up from deep inside his gut.

The receptionist continued, "But I do have a forwarding address and telephone number for him. Would that be of any help?"

"You bet it would!" Alex felt the pain that had been rising begin to subside. He took down the number and the other information and quickly ended the call.

The Professor was now at MIT, according to the information the UI receptionist had given him. Alex dialed the number.

"MIT, Astrophysics Department," answered the male voice on the other end of the line.

"I'm trying to get in touch with Professor Marc Lee."

"Just a moment," replied the voice as the on-hold music began to play. The golden oldies station was in the middle of a tribute to CCR. "I Heard It Through the Grapevine" was nearly completed.

"This is Dr. Lee. How can I help you?"

"Dr. Lee. My name is Alex McPherson. I'm curious, Dr. Lee—do you remember that name from about sixteen years ago at IU?"

"No, I'm afraid I don't remember the name. But I'm sure you understand I've had so many students through the years that the names sometimes slip away."

"That's fine, Dr. Lee," responded Alex. "I can understand how names can be easily forgotten. The reason I was calling was to ask a favor of you. I was hoping your could give me a little of your time next week for me to come to your offices and discuss a few theories."

"Are you teaching at a university?" questioned Dr. Lee.

"No, I'm not. I'm involved in a private research project, and I need someone of your reasoning experience and level-headed nature to run a few ideas by, if you can spare the time."

"Next week? Can you make it here on Monday? I'm leaving for the Christmas break on Tuesday."

"Monday is fine," replied Alex.

"How about just after lunch then, say one o'clock?"

"One would be fine. I'll see you then."

With the conclusion of the call, Alex began to feel a new energy. He turned the music's volume down still more but not off. He began to make plans for the trip. Today was Thursday. He would need to get a lot done in the next few hours to arrange his travel from Grand Cayman to the MIT campus. But most of all, he needed a shave and a haircut. It had been a while since he'd had either.

CHAPTER 6

"Susan, have they all assembled in the dining room?" the attractive Gayle Beaufort inquired.

"Finally," replied her administrative assistant, Susan Sanchez. "It's a bit of an ordeal trying to pull sixty-five people together from all areas of this facility without the aid of any form of paging system."

"All in good time, Susan. This is why many of these people are here." Dr. Beaufort continued, "I've been spearheading this project for the past year to get the facility built. It was a nightmare in itself, coordinating the installation of the twenty miles of wiring. I still pray I've done my part to have all of the connectors in each of the departments wired to the correct panels. You think pulling sixty-five people together is an ordeal? Consider trying to trace a half a dozen dead connections through one hundred and twelve panels, each panel potentially wired to another one hundred connectors."

"I get your point, Gayle. I'll try to be happier with our progress and be more patient with our current shortcomings." The smartly dressed Susan Sanchez, who had left her hectic but well organized civilian position with the navy twelve months earlier, continued with, "Well, it's time to address the troops."

The two of them left Dr. Beaufort's office and walked down the short hall that led from the administrative area to the common area with the dining room located in its center. The room was filled beyond its capacity for dining. It was not too crowded for this meeting, though a few people were standing along the back walls.

The members of the group were dressed in similar uniforms. The skirts and pants worn were different, but the smocks, shirts, and blouses were all of the same robin's-egg blue. The ages of the members of the group varied across the board. There were a high number of men in this group, but most of them were part of what Dr. Beaufort called her "temporary" specialists.

As Dr. Beaufort addressed the group, she presented a confident air of command. Her comfort in standing at the front of this makeshift conference room was obvious to all. Still, Gayle was nervous. She had always felt better with small groups or even one-to-one communications. The good doctor had learned many years before that she would often be expected to speak to large groups on numerous topics and she needed to learn to present a positive comfort level no matter what she felt like on the inside. Gayle Beaufort excelled at hiding her true feelings.

"For those who have just joined us this morning, welcome; to those of you who have been on the project since the beginning, good morning." Dr. Beaufort slowly paced back and forth across the front of the room as she talked. "I would like to describe what each of you has to look forward to over the next several months. This building we're standing in encompasses just under eighty thousand square feet, with less than half of that usable space for the staff. The greater portion of the structure contains equipment for future projects. The responsibility of those of you who are part of the temporary specialists' group is to assist the balance of the group with the installation of the equipment.

"For more years than I care to admit to, the culmination of this project has been my dream. When we've completed the equipment installation, that dream will be in reach." Gayle slowed her pacing to a standstill as she looked into the eyes of several of the members of the group. "Each of you has been chosen based on very specific criteria. The first of these is that each of you is the very best at what you do. Your skills may be matched by many of your colleagues, but to my knowledge, none of you are surpassed.

"Another area that caught my attention," she continued, "is the passion each of you has for your work. You see each project as a mission, and you make the necessary efforts to make the project happen. The third criterion used for your selection, which was a must, was your ability move here to this complex for an extended period of time. Many of you are alone in the world, as I am, except for the friends we may make along the way. Since our agenda calls for the complete up-and-running operation of this facility slated for December of this year, coupled with the location of this facility in remote Nevada, we're too far from any town for a brief pleasure visit, and a long visit is out of the question.

"This third criterion affects those of you who are part of the temporary staff specifically for the next year. The rest of you are potentially affected for much longer. Because of this specific criterion, each of you has been put through extensive psychological testing. This was done to determine you are capable of withstanding the rigors of intense project stress while working in an enclosed environment—not to forget the psychological pressure some may feel working in a facility located completely underground."

Dr. Beaufort began her pacing again and made no eye contact, as she continued. "We have the opportunity here to construct a facility filled with specific expertise and the technology that will compassionately benefit mankind in ways that are beyond comprehension. I need for you, the staff of this project, to complete the installation of the remaining elements so the rest of us will be able continue with the project and place the power of this facility into action."

CHAPTER 7

T he trip to MIT took much longer than Alex would have liked. Air travel on short notice often creates flight plans that resemble base lines on a softball field. Leaving Grand Cayman, Alex met his first connecting flight in Miami. No problem. From Miami, Alex rode a jet to Dallas. No problem. Leaving Dallas before noon on Saturday, he headed on the leg of the flight to Chicago. No problem. December in Chicago was a problem. O'Hare was snowed in, and the flight was redirected to St. Louis.

At midnight Saturday, Alex was pacing aimlessly in the St. Louis airport, still waiting for the flight to Chicago to be cleared to land in O'Hare. The announcement was made that the flight, rather than remaining delayed any longer, had been cancelled. The next flight to Chicago was scheduled to leave St. Louis the following morning at 11:00.

It was now 10:00 Monday morning. Alex had rented a car after arriving in Boston, after a layover in Detroit until the red-eye flight at 6:00 a.m. The Chicago flight from St. Louis had been diverted due to hard-to-manage stacking at O'Hare as a result of the previous day's snowstorm. Alex figured to arrive at the off-campus hotel by noon, which would give him time to quickly shower before the 1:00 p.m. appointment with Dr. Lee. Sleep could come later.

"Dr. Lee. I'm Alex McPherson. We spoke last week." Alex walked into the office extending his hand to the nearly bald professor.

"Of course," replied the professor, accepting the hand and responding with a firm, unswerving handclasp. "You're right on time. How was the trip?"

"Have you ever played pinball?"

"Enough said. Please sit and share your reason for seeking me out."

This will be good, Alex thought. *He likes to get right to the point.*

"How is it, Dr. Lee, you wound up at MIT from IU?"

"I find it interesting you know of me well enough to track me down from the Midwest to the East Coast and I still can't place your name or face. No matter. I was contacted in December of 2000. It seems that the school's shining star, a multi-PhD whiz who headed up the School of Astrophysics, left abruptly, leaving the school unprepared. They asked if I would accept the position as an interim, and after the first semester I suppose I was able to show the powers that be that I was right for the position for the long term. I've been here since and hope to retire from here."

"Out of curiosity, what was your predecessor working on when she left?"

"She was working on accelerated radio waves for enhanced communications for NASA. She owned most of her research, or so it seems. She took it with her, and no one is quite sure where she went or what she is doing."

"I've run into more of that than you might believe."

The professor looked truly curious, "What was that?"

"Dr. Lee, let me describe a hypothetical set of circumstances. After I've painted a little of the landscape I'm currently exploring, I would be most interested in your interpretation. I would ask you not to call me crazy until I've finished."

"It's my belief, son, that you have sought me out because you know I will dispel theories only if I feel they are flawed, not because they sound crazy."

Alex began his recounting of the events of the last several months, starting with the dive on the *Belgium*. As he did, Alex watched Dr. Lee's eyes and expression for any signs of disbelief. A few doodles made; three deep, cleansing breaths; and one long, calculating stare at the office ceiling were the only reactions.

As Alex finished the description of the phone call to Angela's father, he sat quietly waiting for Dr. Lee's response. It came—following a full twenty minutes of silence.

"I see three possible explanations to the set of circumstances you have shared. The first, and of course most believable, is that you are mentally ill. You may be suffering from a loss or a rearranging of your memories or maybe even a combination of the two. I doubt this explanation is valid.

"The second possible explanation is that you are a wonderful liar and seek to gain some notoriety from this package of imagination." The look on Dr. Lee's face was deadly serious, and his eyes pierced as they connected directly with Alex's. "But that's not the case either. You are in too much pain for you not to believe what you are telling me is true.

"That, in my opinion, leaves only one explanation. What you are describing is precisely true just as you have spoken it. Now, if what you are telling me is true, then we need to take a scientific leap of faith at this point."

"A scientific leap of faith? I don't follow you, Dr. Lee."

"What I mean is just this. In order to explain the circumstances as you have described them, there must have been a distortion in the fabric of time. A change in one of the threads that leads to each of the situations you have shared has substantially changed that element to alter, or erase, the existence of people you have known.

"But there is a flaw is this theory," continued Dr. Lee.

"What flaw?"

"If threads in time have been altered, we would have no awareness of the changes because we would be involved in the change. Today's awareness would be based on the threads that have led up to the moment. If a thread had been altered, we would have been likewise altered.

"I see your point. I've been meaning to ask you Dr. Lee—have you ever married?"

"No, I haven't." Dr. Lee saw a look in Alex's eyes. "Tell me something, Alex. Have I ever married?"

"Yes. You had. You had twin sons with pictures all over your IU office."

"So," calmly stated Dr. Lee, "my life has been altered also. There's no telling how far this has reached."

The two of them sat silently for nearly thirty minutes. Each stood and began pacing around slowly within the rather tight confines of Dr. Lee's office. Alex thought of some additional information he could spill into the mix. But what would Dr. Lee make of it? At this point, all information was fair game.

"Dr. Lee. Let me add a few ingredients to the soup. What if all I have said is true? Then my existence must in some way be disconnected from the formal threads of time. I don't pretend to understand what I just said, but it sounded good."

"Go on. Is there something about you that is different?"

"Yes, there is." A brief pause later, Alex continued. "If the science existed to genetically reengineer a human, could that set that human apart from the changes in a timeline?"

"Okay, let's look at this for a moment. If a change in one of the threads of time occurred, then all things along that thread or the threads that were intertwined would be affected. But, if someone were born outside of that thread's pathway, then those changes would not directly affect that individual.

"Thus, if an individual were reengineered, then they, theoretically, would be separated from the threads to which they had originally been attached. They would then see the changes around them and recognize them as changes from what was.

"Dr. Lee, let me share with you another set of circumstances." They sat, and Alex began to describe the events that had turned his life inside out a little more than two years earlier—the events that caused the genetic rebirth of Alex McPherson.

Dr. Lee stood again and began to pace in quick, short lines, turning just before he ran out of room or slammed into walls, furniture, or the like. "Whoa, whoa, whoa. Tell me something first, before we go any further. How do you know me?"

"I had you as an instructor for an elective class of astrophysics when you were an associate professor at Indiana University."

"I don't remember you at all, and I believe I should have remembered you. My classes in astrophysics in those days were limited in size to twenty per class."

"I was number fifteen in my class registration. Because of my football practices and the lack of interest I had at the time for astrophysics, I barely passed your course."

"I'm sorry I couldn't keep your attention any better than that, but I still do not remember you. You say you played football for the school? What year?"

"I played four seasons, '90 through '94."

Dr. Lee went to his bookshelves and pulled a school yearbook from the stacks. Turning the pages, Dr. Lee stopped on the varsity football team picture. He searched the caption for Alex's name. It was not there. "You say you called for your parents and they weren't there?"

"That's what happened."

"You must feel awfully alone." Dr. Lee sat leaning forward in his seat with his head down, looking deeply into the carpeted floor. He sat like that for several moments, and then he spoke as if he had just realized something. "These changes in the threads of time did not happen accidentally. Accidents like this have no basis for theory or fact. So, if they were not accidents, they were man-made."

"You mean someone has intentionally made changes?"

"It may be the case. The primary difficulty would be for the person, or persons, that would initiate such changes to be careful not to erase themselves. Now that I think about it, there would be a host of difficulties."

Another long pause created itself in Dr. Lee's office. The two of them looked at one another and both shrugged their shoulders.

"What do we do about this?" asked Alex of Dr. Lee.

"We? We can't do a thing. If I change anything, I won't know I've changed it. If I return anything back to the way it was, I wouldn't realize it. It's up to you, my boy. You're the only one who theoretically is in any position to tackle this problem. I don't know how, but you're the only one."

They sat silently for a few moments longer. Then they stood and wished each other well. Alex left Dr. Lee's office for his hotel room off campus. Alex slept from five that afternoon until nearly five on the afternoon the following day. The next day he would head home. He hoped home was still there.

CHAPTER 8

"Those of you who have worked on this team these last several months have been a godsend." Dr. Beaufort continued as she addressed the group of temporary specialists, "We have worked as a team in all areas of this installation. This would not have been the case had each one of you not given your all to that end. It is with a great deal of sadness I must bid you farewell. You each have completed the goals and projects that were laid before you. I commend you for those efforts."

Gayle Beaufort walked to the large table that rested behind her in the same dining room where she had welcomed this group eight months prior. She took a shoebox-like container from the table and then turned back to the group.

"As each of you leaves today, I would ask that you allow me to present you with this small gift for the outstanding successes accomplished during your tenure here."

The room began to move, as the group of temporary specialists stood and slowly, one by one, walked to the front of the room to receive an envelope from Dr. Beaufort. A check for five thousand dollars from her personal account was neatly tucked into each envelope. She had wished it could be more. But with forty temporaries leaving the complex for their last time, the two hundred thousand dollars parting bonus was what she had limited herself to giving.

The group members reacted in various ways to leaving. When they received their envelopes, and none knew of its contents until later, more than half of the group shared a heartfelt hug with their "Dr. Boss." Of those who did not share a hug, there was still a great deal of emotion in their glances, their brief words of farewell, and the tears that were welling up as they parted.

Their work had felt from day one as if it had a special mission attached to it. Gayle Beaufort had instilled that feeling and done everything to nurture it. She had spared no expense to provide the best materials to work with. She had showered the staff with treats and little extras for their enjoyment during their personal time, which there was plenty of. Gayle believed all should work hard during their watch but they should be allowed to relax fully when their watch was over. It was Dr. Beaufort's opinion that when they fully relaxed during the off hours, the staff would then push much harder during their work shifts.

It worked beautifully. The staff, temporary and permanent members, worked round-the-clock shifts in never-changing teams that picked up the project where their counterparts had left off and carried it as far as they humanly could before it was time to turn the project over to the next shift. With this level of continuity in action, three years of work had been completed in only eight months.

Tomorrow she would address her permanent staff and describe to them some details of the true purpose behind this high-tech installation. But tonight, Dr. Gayle Beaufort would spend a quiet evening alone in her private quarters. She would soak in a warm bubble bath and fall asleep thinking of sunny days, country roads, and her darling mother.

*****

It had been three weeks since Dr. Beaufort had bid farewell to the temporary staff and began a series of meetings and planning sessions with the permanent staff. The level of anticipation was running quite high throughout the facility.

"All right everyone, let's get this meeting of the Historical Research Team underway." Dr. Gayle, as she asked the remaining permanent staff to address her, opened the discussion. "From our daily stand-up meetings, I gather you have reached a final resolve on this, your first project."

"That's correct." Angela Hicks, the Historical Research Team leader, replied confidently. "My team and I have cross-studied all recallable data, and each limb of the family tree has been examined thoroughly."

Dr. Gayle, intently listening to Angela's report, remembered their first meeting, when they had been interviewing for Angela's current post. Angela had looked just as she did today. Nearing sixty, with piercing blue eyes, Angela had gray hair that was loosely gathered with a soft-white hair comb, allowing her ponytail to hang to just above her shoulders. Though she was modestly dressed in the standard project uniform, it was still obvious that Angela was an attractively built woman.

What had caught Dr. Gayle's ear during that first meeting when Angela was being initially considered by the good doctor, was the discovery that Angela was an only child, her parents had long since passed, and she had never married. When questioned about why she'd never married, Angela's response had struck Dr. Gayle as a well-thought out and often-considered reason.

"Why I never married? Very simple, really. When I was in third grade, I had a boyfriend. We were, of course, much too young to know what all was entailed in that label. But we did know consideration for one another. The young boy would walk several blocks out of his way to my house in the morning and then walk with me to school. We held hands, if you can imagine third graders doing that sort of thing, and we were the talk of the school. I felt quite special when I was with him. He would even walk to my parents' house on Saturdays and he and I would go to the drug store across from our grade school. We'd sit at the drug store's lunch counter, share a sandwich, since his allowance was limited, and talk the better part of the day away about being married to each other. Even to the point of what type of refrigerator we would purchase.

"My parents gave me the news of our moving on a Monday. We were to move across the country at the end of that week. I was sitting on my porch step in tears the next morning when my young man arrived to walk me to school. I cried all week. So did he. I didn't know enough at the time to ask my parents for our new address so we could keep in touch; neither did he. That week was painful. We had never kissed. We sat close and held hands. He held my heart as well.

"I did not realize until I was about thirty-five that I was still carrying a torch for that young boy—for that relationship. I dated for years. I socialized often and even came close to accepting the second of the five proposals I have received in my life. I just couldn't, and I didn't know why. Well, a year of counseling and several paychecks later, it became clear that no matter how peculiar it might sound, the first of those five proposals, the one I had warmly accepted while sitting on that drugstore lunch counter stool, was still too important to me to let go. After that realization, I still dated but would never allow myself to get too close. I lost that love, but somehow it was still too real to me to replace."

Dr. Gayle now sat listening to the bright, energetic Angela Hicks discussing the flawless methodology behind the research she and her team had concluded. She thought to herself, *She's perfect for this project: skilled, intelligent, and no connections to the outside world—perfect, just perfect.*

"Very good, Dr. Hicks. Now, tell me the results of your exhaustive research."

"You requested we research Barry and Susan Rutherford and highlight certain aspects of their lives. What we discovered was that these two were in their sixties when they died at sea. They had no children. Barry Rutherford had only one brother, whom he hadn't seen for the ten years prior to Barry and Susan's deaths. Their passing left no inheritance, since there were no survivors. Their will had their assets liquidated and the monies given to a few charities."

"About their deaths," queried Dr. Gayle, "what are the known elements surrounding their demise?"

"They had been sailing around the Cayman Islands for several weeks when they were last heard from." Angela continued, "They traveled on their own pleasure yacht, a motor-powered launch built in 1937. Their last known heading was south-southeast of Grand Cayman, on April

7, 1962. With no radio contact following that date, they were reported lost at sea by the Coast Guard."

"Additionally," continued Angela, "we have completed an exhaustive search on any possible connection between the Rutherfords and any member of our project's staff. Our conclusion is that no connections exist."

"You and you team have done good work here, Angela. Very thorough and concise. It's time for a very well deserved break for a couple of days before you start your next assignment."

"Dr. Gayle," interrupted Angela, "I am aware of your project guideline having each division work independently of one another. Your hope that this will allow for concentration of study and decrease the potential of crossover and duplication of efforts is well founded. I do ask, though, that you update us on how our research benefited the project as a whole. It would mean a lot to me and my team to know the measure of success of the overall effort."

"I fully understand. It's still too early to know, but I can tell you this. If this specific effort does not succeed, it will not be the fault of your research. Much is still to be done and many bridges to cross."

"Thanks, Dr. Gayle. What is the next assignment?"

"Oh no—I know you too well. If I give that to you now, you'll concentrate on it immediately. I'll introduce you and your team to the next assignment during our meeting next week. Until then, take advantage of the relaxation areas of the complex."

This was proving to be a very busy day for Gayle. With the research she had from the Historical Team, she now needed to meet with the Revisionist Team. Their team leader, Celia Roberts, would be eager to begin working with the conclusions of the Historical Team.

Celia was the first person Dr. Gayle had approached about the project. Not only was Celia the head of the Revisionist Theories section, she was also one of a three-member project oversight committee that included Dr. Gayle and her administrative assistant, Susan Sanchez. Gayle and Celia had met while both were studying at MIT. Celia was one of the most studious colleagues Gayle had ever known.

There was one night Gayle recalled when she and Celia had worked late on a joint research paper. They'd decided to go out for some dinner and maybe a drink or two to celebrate the completion of their research. Celia had sat there, very few of her forty plus years showing in her face, and allowed her dark brown eyes to stare off into nowhere.

"What's on your mind, Celia?"

"What? Oh—you caught me staring off. I was just thinking about that couple over there."

"The ones who look connected at the hip?"

Celia smiled softly when she said, "Yes, those two."

"What about them, Celia? They've been in here when we've been here before."

"I know. That's part of my mingled thoughts. They're in here a lot, and they always look just like that—deeply in love with each other. They're so attentive."

"I'm too tired to talk of romance tonight, Celia."

"I've always been too busy for it. Did I ever tell you how I got here, to MIT, I mean?" Most of the time, Celia's face seemed to have no expression on it. No smile, no frown, just the frank look of a constant thinker. But as she took her lightweight wire-framed glasses from her face, in that single moment her entire countenance took on such a childlike persona that the slight gray in her dark-brown hair seemed to disappear.

"No, you haven't."

"I had a twin sister. Well, they told me I did for about five minutes. She and my mother died during the delivery. My mother was extremely malnourished, and my sister and I weighed a total of only five pounds. Can you imagine the size?

"After they died, and since my mother had never told anyone who the biological father was, I was sent to a state-operated orphanage when they felt I was healthy enough to leave the neonatal intensive care unit of the hospital some eight months later. I lived there until I was eighteen.

"Since I was not adopted, I grew very close to the nuns at the orphanage. They were much older than I and into the things of their age group. I adopted those likes as well. I read and I read and they read and they read, and then we would schedule arguments about what we had read. As a result, needless to say, I became very analytical and well read. I received my first scholarship after applying for it only once. It carried me through my undergraduate studies, and then I applied for several other scholarships along the way, received them all, and they carried me to MIT. Did you know I was the first to graduate from MIT with a PhD in theoretical analysis? They created the distinction after I argued with them for an hour on its merit.

"So you see, Gayle, I have studied and put myself entirely through school on one scholarship or another, and I've spent no time cultivating a relationship that even remotely resembles the one those two have." Celia then paused and returned her glasses to their usual position. "What are you ordering for dinner? I'm so hungry. I'm not sure what to have."

*****

"Dr. Roberts," began Gayle, "I have the factual information from which you can now build you scenarios."

"Excellent. I was getting anxious to get started. What's our deadline on this?"

"I want to initiate the first action in five days. I can have the other systems ready by then. Can you be ready?"

"Five days? I'll have it to you in three."

"Celia, you are truly a jewel."

"I know. Now though, I have a myriad of revisionist theories to explore. I'll see you in three days—let's say 9:00 a.m.?"

Gayle knew Celia would assign some initial research to her team and then retire to privacy to look at the results and ponder the theories. She did her best work alone.

Gayle now needed to concentrate her time on the two areas where she was the section team leader. She felt she was best qualified for these posts, and she knew she would literally pound to death anyone else who might head up these sections with hundreds of questions about their progress. Additionally, these were the two areas in which Gayle held her PhDs, and she was confident no one understood these areas better than she.

The first of these two areas was the astrophysics section. Dr. Gayle had two divisions in this area. Each division had a minimum of ten staff members working at any given time, who were constantly monitoring the newly designed devices for any apparent abnormality that should be reported to Dr. Gayle. This section was in a small room adjacent to the computer banks in the main control room.

As Gayle walked through the entryway, she noted the stark whiteness of the walls and floors in both the anteroom she was in and the primary function room it was connected to immediately in front of her. The glass wall that separated the two rooms had just been installed the week before. The room was now sealed and airtight. Access to the contents of the room was no longer necessary. In fact, the only way to access the primary function room at this point was to remove the newly installed glass wall.

"Dr. Gayle. Good to see you in here." The technician nervously stood. He had been taking readings from the wall-mounted gauges. "All systems are nominal. The Argon is pressurized to four atmospheres and has held that level without fluctuation. As you can see, the photon directional tester shows the VLA is precisely set for optimal reflection."

"Good report, Steve." Gayle spoke with such a calming tone in her voice that the technician seemed immediately placed at ease. Gayle stared into the pressurized room, which measured ten feet across by ten feet deep and only four feet from floor to ceiling. The floor was raised to a height of four feet to give a plain view to the staff of the Very Large Array; a misnomer of sorts, since this VLA was located within the confines of a one hundred-square-foot space. The VLA in New Mexico, which worked to detect astrological movement while working as a very large telescope, was positioned on train cars for movement and could be moved over miles of ground in a single setup.

The VLA Dr. Beaufort had designed consisted of 28 six-inch reflective dishes set in two rows of fourteen. The two rows were opposed to each other, with a distance of precisely five feet between them. Each dish had just over two and a half inches between it and the next dish and there were two and a half inches between the outermost four dishes and the perimeter walls. The photon direction tester was used to correctly align the array to provide for a microscopic setting of each dish so it would successfully reflect to the next dish in the sequence.

"Steve, do report even the most minor fluctuation in the Argon pressure. The signal will not reflect appropriately if the pressure is off by even a micro-fraction of psi."

"Understood, Doctor," Steve was nervous again. "I will be sure to report any variance."

Gayle left the anteroom and headed for the doorway on the opposite side of the main control room. This door was standing open, and there were the sounds of hammering and drilling coming from within.

As she entered the room, she was met by a thundering growl from the man just inside the doorway. "How many times do I have to say for you all to stay out of here? Oh, Gayle; I didn't see it was you."

"Well, Karl, are you having another bad day?"

"As a matter of fact, I am."

"What's happened this time?"

"I've found another imperfection in the sphere. It's much smaller than the last one, but it seems every time I am ready to make the final adjustment, some yahoo comes through the door and jars the equipment."

"Was I the yahoo this time, Karl?"

"You almost were." He paused for a brief moment. "You and I both know that even the minutest imperfection and the process will fail. More than that, it might even be a major disaster. I just don't know."

Dr. Gayle had known Karl for only a few years. He had been a team-leading mechanical engineer for NASA for twenty years until he lost most of his left foot in an accident. Some "yahoo," as Karl put it, did not triple-check the locks on the pressurization tubing before opening the release valve that sent thirty thousand psi of liquid oxygen through the titanium alloy pathway. The piping was at the floor level, and when it split, it sent shards of titanium at and through Karl's left foot. Karl said they found the rest of his foot nailed to the wall on the other side of the hanger.

Since then, Karl had absolutely no patience for imperfection when safety was the issue.

Karl was the last member of the temporary staff. He had signed on to see the project through its first test run and then planned to leave the installation with a nice retirement bonus Dr. Gayle had promised him. She had done so because she knew, as did Karl, that no one on this earth but him could construct the spherical room she had designed.

"What can I do for you at this moment, Karl?" Here sincerity was quite clear.

Karl thought hard for a brief moment and then said with confidence, "I need a strong cup of coffee and one of those donuts I saw you scarfing down this morning."

"You got it, soldier; coming right up." Gayle moved toward the kitchen a five-minute walk from the control room at a quick pace. She retrieved the pastry and coffee as requested and returned to Karl with his peace offering.

"By your command."

"Thank you, darlin'," he said with a fake southern drawl. "You're gonna make some man a wonderful wife one of these days."

"Don't hold your breath." Gayle exalted. "No man would ever put up with the hours I keep and with the preoccupation I have with my work."

"Ain't it the truth," Karl replied, slowly shaking his head and taking a full bite of the cream-cheese Danish. "All this beauty and all those brains—what a conflict."

They looked at each other and started to laugh. Karl was blunt. With Gayle, he needed to be. She was warm with the men on her staff, but she made it clear in her tone and demeanor that they worked for her. With Karl, it was never clear who worked for whom.

"When's it going to be finished, Karl?"

"It's finished now, Doc. All you need to do is shut the door, initiate the tidal gravity generators, and in seven hours—*poof*—you have singularity."

"I thought you said you had found another imperfection."

"I just needed the coffee. I knew I could get you to get it for me if I pushed the right buttons."

"You old—"

"Ah, ah! Don't get carried away with insults. You still need me to monitor this monster you've devised, to make sure all we think is well is, in fact, well."

"Right you are, Karl. I've loaded the computers with all of the same history files we have in the main computer here in the control room. If you and I have succeeded with the singularity design, it should allow us to compare the two computers and be able to measure the differences."

They sat quietly for a few moments, just staring at the perfectly spherical metal room beyond the door that separated it from the control room. Inside the sphere, there was a suspended metal floor, on which rested a very short metal table. A massive computer sat on the table, with only a single disk drive. There was no monitor or keyboard in the room. They could not be designed to handle the oscillation of the tidal gravity, so it was determined when Dr. Gayle would go into the room to retrieve data, she would need to take a keyboard in with her.

By next week, Gayle thought, *we will know if this whole project works. All of the pieces hinge so on all of the other pieces.* But without the singularity, she would never know if she had succeeded. No one could know—at least, no one in the earth's present timeline.

CHAPTER 9

T he flight to Grand Cayman was underway. It had left on time, and the flight attendants had just finished serving the midmorning coffee. Although he usually looked out the window with a book opened on his lap, things were different for Alex this trip. Coffee in his right hand and his left index finger slowly rubbing his left temple, he was a million miles away from the airliner.

Dr. Lee had not only made a few critical points but had also helped to stimulate Alex's reasoning. With the absence of Angela, Alex had found his sounding board in Dr. Lee.

The present is certainly being altered. The most likely conclusion is that somehow this is being done by an element of the past being altered, causing subsequent changes related to the first change—but why?

The steady vibration of the 737 and the smooth taste of the sweet coffee gave way to daydreams. Alex thought back to a trip he had taken his family on only a few years ago. They had still been living in northeast Indiana, and the winter had been especially cold. Alex and Angela had planned a week's vacation in mid-December, and after waiting in the grade-school pickup line for Tony, they did a twenty-hour drive to Orlando, Florida. A week at Disney World and the surrounding attractions was on the menu for the McPhersons.

It was the first day at the amusement park that stuck out in Alex's mind. They had stayed only a mile from the park entrance and planned

182

to be up early and open the park first thing Monday morning. Alex and Angela had been just as excited as Tony. It had been years since they had been at the park, and this was Tony's first visit. These two adults loved to play.

As usual, Angela woke first and began her morning grooming in the dressing area of the hotel bathroom. Alex was awake, but lay still in the bed closest to Angela, with his eyes only half open but still trained on his wife. She had brushed her teeth, washed her face, and begun brushing her hair before she noticed Alex's gaze.

"Hey, what's the deal? You should be getting up instead of lying there pretending to be asleep."

"I just love to watch you."

"I'm brushing my teeth, for heaven's sake. How exciting can that be?" Angela slowly moved to Alex and sat on the edge of the bed. "Do you have some kind of tooth fetish I need to know about?"

"I'm not that bad—I don't think. It just brings a smile to my face to watch you do normal things. Especially in that nightshirt, I might add."

"Watch it, mister. Your young son is asleep in the next bed. You'll need to behave yourself this week."

"I can still look, can't I?"

"Not when you look at me like that. You know what that look does to me."

"What does it do to you, Mom?" The voice of the waking young Tony came weakly from under his covers.

"You see what you've done now?" Angela pointed a playful finger at Alex. "You're in trouble now, mister."

"Are you in trouble again, Dad?"

"Looks like I am, son. But I've always loved the kind of trouble I get into with your mother."

They left the hotel and drove the short distance to the park. It was a drizzly day, but it was fairly warm considering the cool rain.

"First order of business," began Angela. "We need to find some ponchos to help keep our clothes dry. That shop there should have them."

So the day started out with the three McPhersons donning yellow Disney ponchos with pictures of Mickey on the back. The day stayed drizzly, and the park was nearly empty. The three of them took full advantage of this situation, and with the ponchos and hot chocolate every other hour, they enjoyed ride after ride and watched show after show with no waiting and no rushing.

Tony was the perfect age for this first trip to the Orlando theme parks. His imagination was wide awake and his energy level was unbridled. Each attraction that held a level of theatrical exhilaration was designed for kids Tony's age. He saw the shark as real, King Kong as a threat, and his father as possessing the ability to ward off all danger just by being near.

They finished up the day with setting a new park record by riding Space Mountain twenty-five times in a row, being stopped only by the park's closing. After an Italian dinner in Epcot, they returned to their hotel, looking forward to the rest of their vacation with excitement.

*****

Alex smiled as he remembered that day most of all from their vacation; in some ways it seemed like only yesterday. Tony was much older now, and they no longer lived in Indiana. He took a sip of his coffee and noticed that it was a strong Colombian blend. "Pardon me, I think I would rather have the hazelnut blend. I believe that's what I ordered."

Smiling, the flight attendant shook her head. "You couldn't have ordered hazelnut. We only have Colombian. Would you like a fresh cup?"

"No, I would like for you to have told me you had made a mistake and given me the wrong coffee. That would have made me happy. I'll keep the Colombian. That's my wife's favorite."

Alex thought to himself, *This is not make-believe. This is really happening.* He paused, took a deep breath, and thought, *I'll find you, Angela and Tony. I'll bring you back somehow.*

CHAPTER 10

The time had arrived. Dr. Beaufort assembled her operations staff in the main control room early in the morning. They had each been busy with their individual preparations for today's big event. For the previous seven hours, the singularity had been building up. There were minimal gauges, so most of the boundaries of operation were based on calculations and mathematics.

"Where are we on time, Karl?"

"We're two minutes away from our first window, Dr. Gayle."

"You heard the man: two minutes and counting. Remember, we will have 180 seconds to complete the process before we will be forced to disengage the singularity."

"We either disengage the singularity, or it rips a hole right through our reality and we are no more." Karl was always to the point.

"Right you are, Karl," remarked Dr. Beaufort. "Let's begin the countdown and the preprocess procedures. Disk message loaded?"

"Disk loaded and message uploaded."

"Good. Carrier frequency up and running?"

"We have Closed Time-like Curves registered through the VLA. Argon levels are stable, and we have perfect alignment."

"CTC is confirmed." Dr. Beaufort continued her checklist. "Transmitter generator to full power?"

"Trans-Gen is operating at 100 percent."

"We have one minute before singularity is achieved."

"Thank you, Karl; one minute and counting, confirmed. Reception target acquired and anomalies accounted for?"

"Structural reflection calculations bearing true; target is acquired."

"Confirmed target acquisition." She takes a long breath. "Karl? Time?"

"Ten seconds before singularity. Eight—six—four—two—now, Doctor."

"You heard the man. Initiate Trans-Gen."

"Trans-Gen initiated; fully operational."

"Confirmed; initiate Communiqué program. Let's upload that message, people."

"Program initiated; message attached to carrier frequency and processing by Rapid Reflection through the VLA."

"Confirmed. Karl, time?"

"1-3-0 seconds remaining."

"Confirmed. Release message from VLA to Trans-Gen."

"VLA releasing to Trans-Gen, Doctor. Message is flying."

"1-1-0 seconds remaining, Doctor."

"Understood, Karl. Each station, check all gauges and monitors. Report."

"Message upload still on line."

"CTC is still active."

"VLA alignment confirmed. Carrier frequency at four times Einstein."

"Transmission readings?"

"Trans-Gen still operating at 100 percent. We are broadcasting."

"We're down to seventy-five seconds, Doc." Karl's tone was becoming greatly concerned. "We have no way to be sure that we even have 180 seconds to work with."

"Understood. Keep the process alive, people. On my mark, disengage Trans-Gen and begin to power down systems. Stay ready, people."

"Sixty seconds, Doc." Karl was beginning to overheat. "Fifty-five seconds."

"Ready, people, ready."

"Gayle, fifty seconds before singularity breach."

"Cease transmission. Shut down the Trans-Gen, now, people."

"Forty seconds before breach."

"Trans-Gen disengaged. Other systems powering down."

"Now, Karl. Disengage the singularity."

Without hesitation, Karl slowly dialed back the primary control for the tidal gravity oscillation within the singularity chamber. "Thirty seconds before breach," Karl stated and then paused while closely studying the singularity chamber's gauges. "Singularity has ceased at twenty-five seconds before breach."

"When can we go in, Karl?"

"By the reaction of the gauges, it should be safe in two hours. Simpson, watch these gauges. If they do anything other than decrease, call me immediately. I need a tall drink."

"I'll join you, Karl."

It was a very quiet two hours. The two of them had gone to the installation's small pub located next to the dining room. The pub was always open, but alcohol was only available on special occasions and other limited times during the week. Dr. Gayle went directly to the locking scanner on the liquor cabinet and ran her ID card through it. The red light on the scanner went cold and the green light illuminated.

"What's you desire, Karl?"

"Scotch, two fingers."

"I thought you wanted a tall drink." Gayle poured two glasses of scotch, both only two fingers, and sat at the table with Karl.

"This isn't over yet. I need to keep a clear head. There are so many laws of physics being bent nearly beyond recognition by that system in there—well, it scares me, Gayle."

Silently, they both slowly sipped their scotch as if each drop was being deeply revered. Looking nowhere, but frozen in studious concentration, neither of them said another word for an hour.

"Of course you must understand the possible ramification if anything goes wrong."

"Karl, we have safeguarded the singularity in every way we could imagine."

"I don't mean the singularity, Gayle. Theoretically, I knew it was possible. In reality, I never thought it could generate enough of a field. Being there and seeing it work as planned, down to the numbers, I'm confident the results will also be as planned. That is what scares me."

"How could the success of the project scare you, Karl? Our whole purpose in being here is to succeed."

"We're wielding an awesome power. The power to control destiny. To erase the broad stroke of fate and replace it with a predetermined outcome tuned by our very own multi-system jeweler's tool. One flawed or rushed effort on the part of your research teams and we could erase neighborhoods."

"Karl, I'm impressed. I didn't realize you had put the whole puzzle together. I had worked to keep the divisions separated, with the intent of preventing any one person from putting it all together. I wasn't sure how they would respond, and I did not want that variable to disrupt progress. I suppose I knew from the first day we discussed creating the singularity; the look in your eyes should have told me you had reasoned the ultimate conclusion."

"Gayle, I joined you for the science involved in this project. I held no moral discussions with myself. I knew that this project would allow me to work in areas of science no other project had—or, for that matter, ever would—without comparison. Our work here has developed into just that."

"Then what's the concern, Karl?"

"It's like the splitting of the atom. There were many possible applications, many of which have proven to be beneficial. Still, other applications immediately went into play and killed millions. If this process stays focused, controlled—and above all, a secret from the outside world—then, mathematically speaking, the good it can produce will greatly outweigh the negative. If not, well …"

"Karl, I have taken mountains of precautions to prevent the loss of control and to maintain the secretive nature of this entire project. As to the focus, that's where I come in. I've been focused on these goals since I was five years old. Nothing will be allowed to divert me from my goal."

"Hey, you're the doc. It's been an hour and fifty-five. Let's go see what our witch's brew has cooked up."

Simpson was still sitting in front of his control panels when Karl and Dr. Gayle returned. "Give us a report, Simpson."

"Yes, sir. All measurables returned to nominal at one hour and thirty minutes following the power being disengaged. There has been no movement in the gauges since that point."

"Good work today, Simpson. It's time for you to call it a day. Time for some R & R."

"Thank you, Dr. Gayle. I do have some plans with a few of the others. Are you sure you don't need me any more today?"

"Quite sure, Simpson. Go have some fun."

After the young technician had left the control room, Gayle and Karl began to work. This was the easy part, at least the part that required the least amount of effort. It was the hardest part as well, since it was time to test all of their efforts with the only trial that truly mattered.

"Releasing the locks of the singularity room entrance."

"Right, Karl," Gayle replied while retrieving a small metal pushcart from the storage on the opposite side of the control room. "I have the keyboard and the monitor ready."

The door opened with a slow, steady movement as it rode its hinges and swung to the inside of the chamber. The two of them walked into the chamber with Karl leading the way. Karl first lifted his head and surveyed the top of the spherical chamber, and then his eyes moved steadily to the center and then to the lower area of the room. It only took fifteen seconds for this cursory visual review, but to Gayle it seemed an eternity.

They went further into the room, walking carefully on the metal walkway that led to the computer bank in the center of the room. Without speaking, Karl connected the monitor and Gayle connected the keyboard. The computer had not been on during the process; it booted up within seconds.

"I need to first go to yesterday's entry relating to today's procedure." Gayle pulled up the word-processing software and opened the file with the previous day's date as its title. "It says here that in 1940 a small pleasure yacht, the *Belgium*, was lost at sea near the Cayman Islands with its owners, a husband and wife. The yacht has never been found, and the cause of the disappearance was never known."

Gayle sat silently looking at the screen.

"Gayle, what's wrong?"

"It's one of my responsibilities in the process to load this information into this file."

"Well, it's here, isn't it?"

"It is at that, Karl. But I have no recollection of doing it, and I am not at all familiar with its content."

Gayle sat quietly for a moment and then said, "Let's pull up the data on a pleasure yacht registered as the *Belgium*."

They walked back into the main control room and sat at the PC, which sat separately from the main bank of computers.

"There she is, Gayle." The Internet search had not taken much effort at all. "She's a beauty."

"It says that she is pictured sitting in her slip in Newport. She is listed to be in mint condition and is the property of the descendants of her original owners. Her construction date was 1937, and she has held the same registration since her purchase early in 1940."

"Did we prevent her from being lost?"

"I believe we did, Karl."

They returned to the computer resting in the spherical chamber. "Let's go back to the file saved yesterday. It was my plan to save the data related to the entire plan in that file. I don't remember doing any of it, but it was part of the plan. Here it is, Karl. A message was sent through the system, back in time, to the owners of the *Belgium* at their Havana hotel. The notes read that the intent of the message was to prevent the owners from departing from Havana as scheduled. By delaying the beginning of their planned sea voyage, it was hoped whatever the *Belgium* encountered that caused her destruction and the loss of life of her owners could be avoided by the two elements not being in the same place at the same time as it was before our intervention. Apparently we succeeded."

"What message was sent, Gayle?"

"The owner was an architect. The file says we sent a message pretending to be from the State Government of Cuba. The message read, 'We have become aware of your visit to Havana. We have also become aware of your expertise as an architect. It is our desire to meet with you and discuss the possibility of your working with our government to design several new buildings for the good of our people. We will contact you during the next few days to examine your interest in such a project.' He took the bait! We delayed the *Belgium*'s departure with this message, and their lives were saved as a result!"

"The singularity worked! We put the files containing the original history in this computer and then surrounded it with the singularity. When you sent the message and, in effect, changed the past, the singularity held this computer separate from the timeline change you generated. This computer and its contents were not affected by the change in history."

"Precisely! This is why I knew we needed the singularity as part of this project. You and I were affected by the change in the timeline. We noticed no difference from one moment to the next because we were attached to the changes as they occurred. We could not have known if we were successful in averting the disaster had the original files not been separated from the timeline by the singularity. Only something or someone who is separated from the timeline would notice the differences. It would seem normal to anyone else. There would be no disruption in their orientation or recollection at all."

"Wow—Gayle this is big! I knew this was where you were headed; I just didn't think it was possible."

"It's not only possible, Karl, it's now a part of history itself."

In awe for the next hour, they calmly walked from the spherical chamber, hugged each other, and then went their own ways for the evening. At the end of the hour following the triumphant success, Dr. Gayle Beaufort sat on the sofa in her own suite and whispered, "It works. Now, Mom, it's your turn."

CHAPTER 11

The jeep was waiting for Alex at the Grand Cayman airport. After clearing customs, he grabbed his bags and headed for the parking lot, looking like a man on a mission.

He was just that, but his mission was still unclear. He knew there was a problem; he didn't understand its scope. He had to intervene, but he had no idea how. "When all else fails, read directions. It's time for me to go to the library. That was always Angela's plan. It's as good a place as any to start."

A short drive from the airport and Alex found himself walking from his jeep toward the front door of the Georgetown library. It was a small building compared to any of the libraries Alex had used while at school in the States. It reminded him most of the small satellite building of the Indianapolis library located in the Broad Ripple area of town. That is, before the expansion.

There were four six-foot study tables with chairs located in the center of the single-room building. Two of them were occupied, with various books scattered across their surfaces. Two rows of books started from one end of the building and went the length of the room to flank the study tables. There was a small cubbyhole of an office at one end of the building, between the rows of books, where the reference librarian's desk rested. The gray-haired lady Alex had seen every time he noticed that desk in the past sat there as always. She was always reading something. One could only hope it was something different each time.

He also noticed the usual low-level hum of the ceiling fans scattered across the library and moving the eighty-degree Cayman air around. None of the public buildings were air-conditioned. The designers felt it detracted from the natural ambiance of island life.

"Angela's mom disappeared because a passenger ship that originally missed being attacked and sunk *was* sunk in this altered reality. I'll start there. Famous shipwrecks. I should be able to discern if that part of history has been altered any more than just my mother-in-law's ship."

Alex went to the history section and pulled a couple of books from the shelves. He returned to one of the open study tables and spread the books, trying to take up space in the hope that he would not be joined by some other library visitor.

"*Titanic*. This is the only time I have ever been happy to see that big boy went down." There was an entire book dedicated to *Titanic*. Alex pushed that off to his right and opened a thick collection of seafaring disasters.

"The *Lusitania* is still gone." Alex continued to read and turn the pages, not seeing any changes in the history of sea disasters that were readily noticeable.

When he raised his head from the book, he saw that there were now six study tables. "Where did those two tables come from? I wasn't reading that intensely. Hey, wait a minute. Who took my book?"

Just then a library staff person walked nearby. "Excuse me, someone has cleared a book from my table. I was still using that book."

"Sorry, sir," she replied with her polite Texas accent that argued gently with her Caribbean features. "We do that a lot. When we clear them, we take them to their correct place on the shelves. Would you like me to retrieve it for you?"

"No, not a problem. I'll go for it in a minute."

"Let me know if you change your mind."

Alex returned to his reading. As he was reading the caption beneath the USS *Arizona*, photographed entering port at Pearl Harbor two weeks before she was sunk, he stopped for a moment and noticed he was feeling a chill. He whispered, "When was the last time I felt a chill on Cayman? Never, that's when!"

He lifted his head from the book and looked around the room. Except for the extra two study tables, it seemed the same. And then he turned his head to the other end of the room, between the two rows of books, to the reference librarian's office. Where was she, and who was the man sitting there instead?

"Excuse me," he said to the same staff member he had asked about the missing book. "It's no big deal, but where did the reference librarian go to? I mean, she was just in her office a minute ago."

The voice that came from the young lady's throat sent a shudder through Alex. It was no longer the sweet Texas drawl that immediately labeled her as from the States. Now she spoke just as pleasantly but with the broken Caribbean accent that purely matched her features. "I'm sorry, sir. She left for lunch earlier. Can I help you?"

"She's out to lunch. That's a relief."

"Sorry, sir?"

"Oh, nothing." Alex paused for a moment to recollect his thoughts while the staffer waited patiently. "This may sound weird, but did you feel the chill that went through here a few moments ago?"

"Chill? I'll have the manager turn the air-conditioning down, if you like."

"Air-conditioning?" Alex looked around and then listened. The fans were gone, sound and all. The chill was the A/C. "No, no—let it go. I'll bear with it."

"As you say, sir."

Alex looked around the room. The walls seemed different, but he couldn't quite figure out how. While he was looking at the far wall and all of the maps covering it, the maps disappeared. Right in front of him, they disappeared.

"What—how?"

He was now looking at a blank wall covered with cotton candy-pink wallpaper. He shook his head and looked back to the reference librarian's office. It was gone—the whole office. It just wasn't there.

Alex pulled the picture of the *Arizona* back into his sight. The caption caught his eye, because it was much longer than before.

It read, "The USS *Arizona* as she began to take port just two weeks before the Japanese attack on Pearl Harbor. Receiving new orders upon her arrival, she left port only three hours later. The *Arizona* has been credited with single-handedly saving untold lives as she returned to sea and ran straight into the flight path of the Japanese fighter squads. The *Arizona* reportedly took out a full third of the attacking planes and sent a warning back to Pearl, allowing them to prepare for the balance of the attacking fighters. Although the *Arizona* was lost during that conflict, she and her crew are credited with staving off the surprise enemy attack long enough to allow the US Navy to set most of its ships from Pearl to sea. They chased down the attacking Japanese warships and fought a decisively victorious sea battle, which caused the Japanese government to surrender no more than seventy-two hours after their attack of Pearl Harbor."

Alex lifted his head slowly from the book. He noticed the map wall again—the map wall with no maps that had changed to cotton candy-pink wallpaper. Now it was dark blue.

"Blue?" Just as Alex whispered the color, it changed. While he was staring at the blue wall, it turned green.

"The book!" Alex ran to the history section to retrieve the book that had been replaced by the staffer. It wasn't there. Alex now knew better than to ask about the book. In this reality, it had never existed. In this reality, Pearl Harbor was an American victory and the *Titanic* never sank or maybe never even existed.

"I've got to get out of here before this whole building disappears." Alex ran to the parking, got into his jeep, and began the drive to Rum Point and his home—he hoped.

CHAPTER 12

T he bronze paperweight flew through the air of the office and obliterated what had been Dr. Beaufort's framed PhD in astrophysics.

"You're wrong, Celia. You are all wrong."

"No, Gayle, the revisionist team's conclusions are flawless in this matter."

"Then rework the conclusions until they are right. I will not have this high level of incompetence involved with my project."

Celia Roberts turned to the two members of her team who had been a part of the presentation to this point. "You two can return to your quarters and call it a day. Dr. Beaufort and I need a few moments to work through these results. I'll get with you tomorrow morning and let you know what our next research assignment will be."

Now the two were alone: Dr. Gayle and the dark messenger she was finding it difficult to look at.

"Gayle, we go back a lot of years. What is going on?"

"Celia, your research and the outcome of your revisionist theory, it has to be wrong. This was my reason for all of this. This one project was what fueled me."

"Gayle, listen to me. You were five years old, and you watched your mother thrown from your reach through the front windshield of a car and onto a highway. How in God's name could you feel good about any of that? But that was forty years ago! You are older and extremely well educated."

"But—"

"Wait, Gayle; let me continue."

Gayle twisted her high-backed leather chair to where her eyes were out of reach of Celia's piercing intrusion.

"Your father remarried, Gayle. Married into money. Your new mother."

"Stepmother."

"Fine. Stepmother. The new female in your father's life brought more than money to the relationship. She brought drive, determination, and connections. The kind of connections that opened doors for you. The kind of doors that allowed you to enter the most prestigious schools from prep school through grad school. Your father's new wife pushed you to learn and excel in all of your endeavors, and especially in school. Did you ever finish a school below the top five? You don't need to answer that. I already know you were the top of the top at every level you attempted."

"So, I earned good grades; big deal. That has nothing to do with this."

"It has everything to do with this. You earned the education that gave you the know-how to create the various sciences contained in this installation. Without that education, only your dreams could house these ideas; and that's all they would be too—ideas and dreams."

"What's your point, Celia?"

"You know my point, and your blindness to my point worries me to no end. You can in no way use this process to prevent the death of your mother. If you do, then it will be as our theories have tested out. This installation and all that is in it would not exist. All that you said you wanted this project to be built for would be out of reach. You would instead grow up with your mother and not have the resources and urging of your stepmother to allow you to create these tools and systems you endlessly preached to me would save countless lives with minimal disturbance in the original timelines."

"But my mother—"

"Gayle, I'm sorry. This research project was painful for me, as well. I knew from the start where it was going, but I followed the protocol to prove out the theories. You and I sit on the Oversight Committee. Aside from Susan, and it appears Karl should be added to our short list, you and I are the only ones who know what this entire installation was built for. Don't tell me it was only to bring back your dead mother."

"Watch it, Dr. Roberts."

"Dr. Roberts? Why do you suddenly feel the need to be formal? It's true, then. You built all of this to avert only one disaster. The death of your mother. Wow! I'm not sure where this leaves us, then."

The silence of these brief moments felt much longer to Celia. When Gayle broke the silence, Celia wasn't sure she felt much better.

"Celia, I lost control for a moment. You can rest assured it won't happen again."

"Why do I feel I'm hearing the offer of Confederate money, Gayle?"

"I'm tired, Celia; that's why. I think we should all back away for a few weeks and relax before we enter into our next research projects. Your news hit me hard, but I'll recover. After all, we still have a lot of work to do."

"Maybe, Gayle—maybe."

"Sure. We'll catch up on our sleep and on our reading, and in a couple of weeks we'll be ready to push on with the next project. You'll see, Celia. After a couple weeks, I'll be a different woman. You may not even recognize me I'll be so relaxed."

"Maybe so …"

"Celia," Gayle said as she moved her gaze to the center of her desk and her day planner, "Mark your calendar for, let's say, the day after New Year's to begin our next project. That gives the whole place a chance to kick back for a little over three weeks through the holidays and enjoy some much-deserved R & R."

"That does sound good, Gayle. We've all been pushing hard around here for a long time. R & R may be the medicine we need to refocus our efforts."

"I know it is. That settles it. I'll see you, for work that is, on the morning of January second of the new year. Until then, I'll see you around the lounges and studies with novels and not research texts in your hands, and that's an order."

Celia left the office, and Gayle moved to the broken glass from the fallen degree and began picking up the pieces. "I'll sleep and I'll rest as well," Gayle said quietly to herself. "As someone once said in the past, tomorrow is another day. How right they were. In fact, when I'm through, no one will recognize tomorrow."

CHAPTER 13

Returning to his home usually felt reassuring to Alex. Not today, though. He knew he would not find Angela or Tony anywhere near home. As he pulled into his drive, he saw the large open lot three hundred yards from his home. "That's where the Richardson's house was. Doesn't even look like a house has ever been on that property."

As he walked through the house, things seemed to be as Alex had left them. It was still overwhelming not to have the obvious touches of style and preference that had prevailed through the house before Angela's disappearance.

"What's my next move?" Alex found that, being alone so often, he was now talking to himself much more than ever before. "Things were changed over the past couple of months, but at a different rate. What seemed to start slowly, with alterations being few and far between, has now begun to change so quickly it's making me dizzy. The same questions remain: who and why? But now a new question's gotta be added to the list. Why has the rate of the changes increased just now?"

With music playing softly from the family-room sound system, Alex browsed around the kitchen for a while, going through the dry goods of his pantry, looking for something for dinner. He had not been to the grocery store since Angela had disappeared, and he had gone through all of the frozen meats and vegetables.

"Looks like a pasta night." Boiling spaghetti on the back burner and simmering a homemade concoction for a sauce on the front looked to be his task for this evening. The sauce was well seasoned, but it lacked a few of Alex's regular components. Alex was known for an abundance of diced onion and extra ground beef in his pasta sauces. Neither item was to be had, but he did give dried, minced onion a chance to fill in part of that gap.

The meal was over, dishes were washed, and the two hundred-CD changer was working through a hodgepodge of music in its random selection mode. Alex decided to walk to the remote box and check the mail. Nothing in the mail was addressed to Alex, with the exception of a utility bill. The rest he trashed as he reentered his house. The bills were normally placed in a holding slot in his office on the second story of the house, so he robotically climbed the stairs to place the electricity bill in its proper place.

As he walked into the office, his computer was quietly signaling there was unread e-mail. Alex hadn't thought to look lately. There was one message with the sending address of "unknown." The note was dated the evening of Alex's departure to meet with Dr. Lee at MIT. This meant the message was now five days old. It had two parts; the opening note and an attached file.

The opening looked very familiar. It was the same as other messages he and Angela had received from Admiral Sterling over the past couple of years. Due to the special talents Alex possessed from his biological changes and the salvaging resources he and Angela had amassed, the MacPhersons had been called upon by the admiral to assist with various rescue missions. The greatest of these had been the first, when Alex, working under his code name of Manta, had worked to rescue two navy submarines trapped well below their respective crush depths.

The success of that mission had set the stage for Admiral Sterling to contact Alex and Angela by e-mail through an anonymous remailer addressed to Manta. The protocol was simple. The admiral would contact Alex and Angela with a set of oceanic coordinates where a problem existed. Alex and Angela would then trek to those coordinates, assess the circumstances, and report to the admiral's representative on the site what potential for success Manta's intervention would offer.

There they were; a new set of coordinates. "I don't feel much like reaching out a helping hand with all that's been going on." He turned and started to walk out of the room, but something nagged at him and he stopped. "What were those numbers?" With the scribbled latitude and longitude on a notepad, he went to the reference map hung on the far-left wall of the office. "This must be a mistake," he muttered to himself. Checking the numbers displayed on the monitor again against the numbers on the note and then returning to the reference map, he said to himself, "This position is in Nevada! Twenty miles south-southeast of Emigrant Pass in north-central Nevada. Why would the admiral be involved in a land-based project?"

He returned to the computer. "Let's see if the attachment sheds any light on this." The note was not from the admiral but rather from his assistant, Susan Sanchez.

It was brief and painfully fractured. It read, "Please come. Need your help. She's crazy. I know what happened to your wife."

CHAPTER 14

Susan thought her computer was the only one in the installation that had Internet access. She was wrong. She thought her e-mail could not be detected. She was wrong on that point, as well. Dr. Gayle had networked the two computers, hers and Susan's, to improve communications between the installation's chief administrator and her assistant. A piece to that network was the pop-up notice on Dr. Gayle's screen notifying her of unauthorized contact with the outside world. Within two hours of Susan's e-mail, Dr. Beaufort had confined Susan to her quarters.

Confinement took on the full meaning where Dr. Beaufort was concerned. No contact was allowed with anyone, not even with the kitchen staff who delivered Susan's meals to her quarters. They were ordered to maintain complete silence or suffer the same punishment. Not just ostracized, Susan had been sealed off from the rest of the installation, just as Karl had been the day before.

Susan had broken the ordered silence with Karl by bribing the kitchen orderly into allowing her to deliver Karl's noon meal. The guard unlocked the door to Karl's quarters, and Susan walked in carrying the food tray.

Karl looked like he was about to speak, and Susan frowned at him, hoping he would remain silent. He did, at least until the guard left the doorway and went back to the hall.

"What are you doing? She'll lock you up for this."

"Why? What is going on? Why are you confined, and who are these security guards?"

"I'm sure we only have a minute, Susan, so listen. Gayle has lost it. She has bypassed all of the safeguarding perimeters established to prevent dramatic alterations to the primary timelines."

"*What?* How?"

"You knew she had an argument with Celia. Celia was so troubled by the ramifications of Gayle's mood that she came to me and we talked it over for hours. Celia was deathly concerned about how Gayle had taken the results of the last research Celia and her team worked on."

"What research? And it couldn't have been her last, because Gayle has initiated the Trans-Gen process twice a day for the past few days."

"Which is precisely the problem," Karl continued. "It was the last research Celia did. It determined that Gayle could not prevent the death of her own mother when Gayle was five. Gayle told Celia to take a few weeks off and Gayle said she would tell the other departments to do the same."

Susan's eyes opened wide. "But she didn't. She had the Trans-Gen team working double shifts."

Karl shook his head slowly. "I went to her when I saw that was the case. I asked her why we weren't using the singularity. She told me she had put together a few dry runs for the Trans-Gen team; we weren't actually sending communiqué to the past. I left the control room and went directly to her office. I found some notes in her trashcan about alterations to Pearl Harbor. She had scribbled next to it, 'This could save millions.'"

"Millions?" questioned Susan. "It said *millions*? That would change history in a cataclysmic way."

"I think she already did. She has been nearly giddy at moments and then downright vicious at other times. There's no way we would know if she did, but if she's doing that, she's got to be stopped."

Susan whispered, "Did you talk this over with Celia?"

Karl paused and lowered his head. "I couldn't find her. I looked for her and asked for her. No one has seen her since the morning after she talked with Gayle and then with me. I went to Gayle about Celia."

"And?"

"And, I'm in here. She had her private guards, wherever they came from, escort me to this jail she called my quarters. As I was walking from the control room, I turned and asked her point-blank if she had done something to shut Celia up. I'll never forget the look on Gayle's face. She was torn between explosive anger and a burst of tears."

"What did she say?"

"She said, 'Be content to know I've chosen to deal with you differently.' I took that in the worst way possible, Susan."

Susan shook her head in disbelief. "Oh no—not Celia! Gayle wouldn't—?"

"I never would have thought so, but this is not the Gayle we signed on with."

"I'm sure I only have another minute. What can I do Karl?"

"You need to send for help."

"Send for help? From who?"

"I have no idea. She has covered this installation so well that if anyone came out to these empty acres they would never find the entrance and wouldn't believe the installation was buried beneath their feet."

Susan quickly pondered, and then she said, "I know of someone who may be able to help. I'm not sure why I think they could, but when I was with the navy, Admiral Sterling described this group that worked miracles in oceanic rescues."

"What?"

"That's not it, though. The admiral was sure they had a member of their team with some kind of superpowers or something. It's all I can think of."

"Do you know how to get in touch with them?"

"I still have my address book and the method of contact was through the e-mail. I'll send a message in the morning. But—"

"What?"

"What if Gayle's reckless actions have already erased them?"

"Then we're cooked."

Susan hesitated and then said, "What should I say?"

"Tell the truth at first to let them know what they're in for. Tell 'em she's crazy, and we need help, and then—" Karl stared straight into Susan's eyes, "Then, God forgive us, lie."

"Lie? About what?"

"Was it a man or woman who the admiral thought had some kind of powers?"

"A man. He had a code name of Manta."

"Tell this Manta you know what happened to his wife."

Susan seemed puzzled. "His wife? Why his wife?"

"It's a calculated guess, Susan. With all of the alterations Gayle must have generated with her rampant Trans-Gen messages, maybe she has affected this Manta's group as well. It's a gamble, but we need a hook to draw help—and quickly."

"Do you think she'll make us disappear with a message to the past?"

"No," Karl was firm about this. "That would disrupt the installation itself. We helped to build the place. Take us out in the past, and we were never here. Then the place would not be here either. But she could take us out now, and it would only affect her and us. We'd be dead, and she'd be our executioner."

"You believe she killed Celia?" Susan spoke sadly.

"Yes, I do. Since we remember Celia, she did exist and was not erased by a past intervention from Gayle. She can't keep me locked up forever. She'll have to kill me, too."

"But Gayle is not a killer."

"Susan, this is not Gayle. Gayle snapped when Celia proved her mother had to stay dead for the installation and the plans to continue. This is a quite changed Dr. Beaufort, and oh dear God, how the winds have changed."

"You done in there?" bellowed the guard, now sticking his head through the doorway.

Karl whispered in Susan's ear. "You'd better go. Good luck. I hope to see you again."

Susan now found herself sitting idly in her quarters, reviewing her conversation with Karl time and again. She fell into a shallow sleep several times, only to be awakened by a recurring nightmare of being in a large room with thousands of people, strangers, whose faces were different each time Susan looked at them.

"I hope Manta will respond to my message. I hope he still exists."

CHAPTER 15

Alex didn't want to travel by plane, just in case the pilot disappeared. But from Cayman to north-central Nevada would take nearly three days nonstop by boat and car. He had to chance flying. The next connecting flight to Reno left the Georgetown airport in two hours. Alex showered and grabbed an overnight bag. Reno would place him less than three hours from Emigrant Pass by car.

Sleep was impossible during the flight, yet Alex kept his eyes closed for most of the trip. It seemed something or someone changed every couple of minutes.

Alex thought, *This is maddening. Stay focused, Alex; stay focused.*

The flight captain came on the overhead to announce the landing. "Good afternoon, ladies and gentlemen. I hope your flight was a comfortable one. Our flight took a little less time in the air than we had planned, so we will be landing in Salt Lake City in about five minutes."

Alex still had his eyes closed, and he thought to himself, *It could have been worse. That's still only a four-hour drive. I just pray it doesn't change again before we land.*

The plane taxied to the terminal. Alex disembarked and headed straight for the rental-car desk. "I need to rent a car."

"Yes, sir. We have several available. I will need to see your driver's license and a major credit card."

Silently, Alex handed the two items over to the rental clerk.

After a moment with the credit card scanner, the clerk returned. "I'm sorry, sir, but your credit card is reading invalid."

"Excuse me?" While the clerk was repeating the same words, Alex remembered it had been Angela who had completed the application for the card. The clerk was more right than he could possibly know. "How about cash?"

"I'm sorry, sir, but we must have a major credit card to rent any of our vehicles."

Alex whispered, "Some things still haven't changed."

"Excuse me, sir?"

Alex had not spoken with anyone telepathically since Angela had disappeared. Now might be the time to put that tool to use. With a gentle intensity to his thoughts, Alex began talking to the second young man behind the counter. He had been standing with his back to Alex while the front clerk was explaining again how a major credit card was required.

"You see the man in the denim shirt in front of the counter? He just rented," Alex looked at the board for a remaining set of keys, "car 2487. Could you get him the keys for me? I need to run to the back for a minute."

Alex then looked at the young man he had been trying to rent from and aimed a very different message in his direction. "Your need to get to the bathroom now, before you wet yourself in front of all of these people."

Alex watched as the front clerk stopped in midsentence, his eyes opening wide. "Please excuse me for a minute." He left the area as though on a mission.

Alex watched the second clerk look up at the key storage board just as the front clerk was leaving the area. Alex thought again, "Yes, 2487. He's all done and just needs the keys. I'll be right back." The second clerk took the 2487 keys from the board, turned, handed them to Alex, and said, "When you gotta go, I guess you gotta go."

"So it seems. Thank you. Which way to the car?"

Alex drove the rented Lincoln Town Car west on Interstate 80 from Salt Lake City. After about two hours of constantly changing billboards, he left Utah and entered northeastern Nevada, where the scenery was full of unchanging landscapes not yet developed by man. This left them unaffected by the changing winds of time.

Before leaving the Salt Lake City airport terminal, Alex had purchased a Nevada state map. Just past Wells, Nevada, he was glad he had the map.

Alex pulled over at a small diner at the junction of two two-lane, blacktop roads; he had to gather his wits. He had been speeding along at eighty miles an hour on a four-lane highway when all of a sudden the highway had disappeared and he'd found himself speeding in the wrong lane of this altered reality's version of the road to Emigrant Pass. The narrow miss with the oncoming semi had sent the Town Car into a spin, and it came to a jolting halt along the roadside.

Much to Alex's delight, Emigrant Pass was still clearly marked on the map. But the road to Emigrant Pass from his current position was quite different than the map had shown earlier. His hope in buying the map was that if any changes took place along his trek, the map would change as well. It would change to the altered reality's layout of the roads to Emigrant Pass. And so it did.

Alex now had a series of secondary roads to traverse. It even appeared a county dirt road made up a small part of the total trip. The final part, in fact.

The diner was well placed. It stood at the end of the primary road, at the crossing of two secondary roads. Food—food was the order of business. And a bathroom; this needed to be first, and then food.

With the diner still in the rearview mirror as he headed east on State Road 213, he had already eaten both sandwiches and the onion rings, and the large diet Coke was nearly gone as well. *I don't want to take any chances,* he thought. *I ordered cheeseburgers, and I want to eat cheeseburgers. I don't want to wait too long and have these sandwiches change into some kind of local delicacy. I don't even want to think about what the onion rings might have changed into.* He was laughing to himself, when he noticed the label on the diner's to-go bag had changed color and design. It still read Buck's Diner, but the dull red had been replaced with a pea green, and the letters were italic script instead of small-case block.

After a total driving time of five and a half hours, Alex passed the sign announcing Now Entering Emigrant Pass. A small hotel was just ahead on the right. "Time for a shower and a change of clothes," he told himself.

The room was neatly appointed with no remarkable characteristics. It had a clean shower, with plenty of hot water and soft, large towels. That was all that mattered for the moment.

I think I need to be prepared for running into strangers at the coordinates. I won't know what to say until I get there. Any eventuality is possible. It's late. I'll start out first thing in the morning. I need to sleep for now. Gotta be sharp. Seconds later, Alex was asleep.

Dressed in blue jeans and a forest-green polo shirt, overnight bag over his shoulder, he started out the day with a tall cup of coffee from the cafe as he walked to the hotel parking lot. The Town Car was not in the parking spot where Alex had left it the night before. There was an arctic-blue VW Beetle in that spot. Not the new version Alex was familiar with; it was what he thought was the old body style. It looked brand new. He reached into his pocket for the key and found he had a VW key on the ring. The key fit the door and the ignition, so Alex took the Bug. It *was* brand new. The odometer read three hundred and forty-two miles, and the interior was filled with gauges and amenities that hadn't even been thought of when this body style of Bug was sold. It also handled like new. The steering and handling were nothing like the 1971 Beetle he'd once owned. Apparently, in this altered reality the new body style never came to market because the old style never left.

Before dressing, Alex had studied the map for the final path to take to the coordinates received from the e-mail message. It looked to be about an hour from the hotel. The drive was pleasant in the early morning light. The road was a straight dirt one that was barely a dotted line on the map. But it was there and appeared to go directly to the map coordinates. That was good enough this morning.

An hour from the hotel, Alex found himself looking at a small, white, twenty-by-twenty building with a very tall transmitting tower positioned next to it. The outbuilding behind it was four times larger than the front structure. The outbuilding had four garage doors along one side, which were all closed. A ten-foot metal fence, with jagged barbed wire on the top-most portion, encircled both buildings, and what appeared to be a radio or cell tower was located within the fencing. The fenced area was as large as a baseball field, and the buildings and the tower were right in the middle.

Alex wasn't sure whether he was in the right place or not. From the coordinates on the map, he should be. He missed Angela's unswerving sense of direction. He carefully looked over the little complex. On the primary building, just to the right of the left edge of the roof, nestled a small surveillance camera. It was just high enough that it could slowly rotate a full 360 degrees and take in the view of the small compound. "This must be the place. I need to find whoever sent me that message."

Alex opened the door of the little blue Beetle and got out to stand near the front of the car. With his eyes closed, he thought to himself, as if he were shouting, *Manta is here!* The overwhelming, if garbled, response to his telepathic message shook him. His knees became shaky and he needed to lean back against the car.

As if from behind a curtain, there was one nearly hidden cry of "Thank God, Manta! Are you really here?"

Alex concentrated intensely on the lonely cry. He sent another message, but this time he targeted the single thought pattern that had called out for him. *Yes, I'm here; but I'm not sure where here is and, for that matter, where you are, either.*

"Manta, Admiral Sterling said you could communicate telepathically. Should I speak out loud or can I just think what I wish to say?"

Just think your sentences. How do you know Sterling?

I was his administrative secretary. My name is Susan Sanchez. I sent you the e-mail message. Did you bring your team with you?

No. I'm alone. My team, well...

They're gone, aren't they?

Who's doing this? Yeah, they're gone. Well, the key members anyway. But how?

And you know they're gone? How can you know that? The admiral was right; there's something very special about you, Manta.

Stop. Where are you?

I'm sorry. I'm in a science complex below ground. If you are at the coordinates I sent you, then you are standing just above the complex. There's a couple of buildings and a two-hundred foot high-gain antenna above the complex.

How do I get to you?

If you are to be of any help, you'll want to stay away from me. I've been locked away in a security holding area for asking too many questions.

Questions about what?

Let me try to update you from the beginning. This will take a while. You'd better sit down. Susan began with the phone call that Gayle had first placed to invite Susan to join the project.

It had been an hour since Susan began her description of the workings and purpose of the complex. With each new element, Alex was able to fill in the holes in what he had experienced since August. Alex spent the next forty-five minutes asking Susan questions about the key staff and other specifics that came to mind as she was painting the picture of the past months.

Wait a minute, Manta. Someone's at the door. It's the guard with a meal tray. I haven't eaten for days. I've been afraid to. I mean, what's to keep Gayle from poisoning me?

You said she was a caring and compassionate person. Why would she want to hurt you?

Wait a minute.

Alex was out of the Bug at this point and pacing in front of it for a few yards before turning and going the other way.

Manta. It was the food tray. I'm too hungry. I'm going to go ahead and eat while we're talking. Gayle is a compassionate person, but something happened to her. She went mad. She began to treat us all with anger and paranoia. I think she is capable of almost anything at this point.

I need to get into the complex, Susan. Where's the entrance?

There are two entrances. One by way of a passenger elevator in the small white building, and the second is in the outbuilding. That entrance was built for equipment. There is a long concrete ramp from one of the garage doors that goes down to the complex. The ramp is big enough for

213

medium-sized trucks to negotiate. But Manta, she will have you arrested the moment you try to use either of the entrances.

Arrested by who?

She has a security staff that she brought in just after she started acting differently. It was not part of the original plan to have a security staff. This was an unexpected and unwanted wrinkle.

Has she mentioned the source she used to hire the security?

No, but they do have an emblem on their shoulders. A patch of some kind. It reads Carson City Security.

Does there appear to be a supervisor in the security ranks?

I haven't seen any. They all refer to Gayle as their boss.

Maybe I can gain access as a visiting supervisor from Carson City. I need access to be able to take any action. What do you think, Susan?

What? I can't make out your words, Manta.

I said, do you think I could gain access as a visiting supervisor from the security company?

Manta. Susan spoke weakly. *Oh my God, she did it! There was something in the food. My legs are numb, and I can't … I can't. My head feels so heavy.*

Susan!

I can't breathe. Oh my God! She's killed me. Help … I … I …

Susan!

Susan.

CHAPTER 16

A lex leaned back against the Beetle and stared off into the Nevada sky. It seemed forever before the two security guards appeared from the front door of the primary building.

"It's about time. Did someone turn the surveillance monitors off, or were you guys just too busy to pay any attention?"

Alex's comments caught the two guards by surprise. "You're trespassing on private property. You'll have to leave—now," one of them ordered.

"Wrong, boys. It's time for you to introduce me to your boss, Dr. Beaufort."

"And why should we do that? She's not expecting any visitors."

"That's why it took you this long to come up here and investigate some stranger wandering around the compound? Now, boys, contact the good doctor. Her new head of security has just arrived and would like to meet with her."

With a hand-held radio, one of the guards called to the complex and asked for Dr. Beaufort. "Dr. Beaufort, there's a man up here who says he's your new head of security."

The puzzled female voice came from the radio. "I've made no arrangements for a head of security. What's his name?"

215

Before the guard could ask, Alex informed him, "My name is Alex. I don't use a last name anymore. I've been in security too long to be too personal with people I work with."

"Get rid of him. I have no need for a head of security."

Before the radio communication was broken, Alex continued, "Your security is a joke. I know about as much about your project as you do."

The detached voiced nearly bellowed from the hand-held. "You what?"

The two guards stood motionless as the conversation continued between Alex and their boss through the radio in the hand of one of the guards.

"How else could I know about the singularity?"

A brief moment of silence passed before the voice from the radio continued, in a much more accepting tone. "Well, Alex, you've become a puzzle. Gentlemen, please escort our visitor to my office."

"I'll take him in. You take his car in and put it in storage." The guards separated, with one leading the way into the main building. "Follow me."

Alex studied the inside of the main building. The walls were painted, but there was no separation of rooms. There was nothing in this building except for an entrance to an elevator. There were no buttons on the wall on either side of the elevator door. The guard pulled a remote switch from his pocket and using the remote to call the elevator.

"So you think you're the new head of security?" The guard spoke smugly. "Wait until you meet with the good doctor. You'll find out real quick she's the boss."

Alex gave the guard a cold stare. "Did I speak to you? The next time you share your opinion when I didn't ask for it will be the beginning of your end. Do I make myself understood?"

The guard dropped his eyes and didn't utter another sound.

The elevator door opened and the two of them entered. There were only two buttons. They were labeled Surface and Complex. The guard pushed the lower of the two, and the doors swooshed shut.

Gayle had her back to the door when Alex entered her office. "Would you like a cup of coffee?" She spoke pleasantly, still with her back to Alex. She was facing the credenza behind her desk, where the coffee maker sat.

Alex studied her. Was she truly the one causing all of the temporal disruptions? From behind, she was quite attractive. Even though she was wearing her three-quarter-length white lab coat, her shape was pleasingly evident. "What blend?"

"French Roast."

"That will be fine. I'll need a little cream with that, though. It cuts the bitter aftertaste of an Americanized French Roast."

"Ah, a man of discerning taste." Gayle added the cream to both cups and turned to look at Alex for the first time. She flinched when his eyes initially struck her. "Ouch."

"Spill the coffee?"

"No. It's your eyes. I feel like they have pierced right through me."

Alex took the cup of coffee and began forcing himself to calm down. So much had happened to lead up to this meeting. But he had to change his tone if he was to succeed in gaining her trust.

"I apologize." He paused. "I didn't expect you to be beautiful."

Gayle replied calmly. "So, my security is a joke and you have confidential information concerning the functions of this complex." She finished her statement with a wry smile. "But there seem to be some things about this installation that aren't public knowledge."

Alex tipped his head as if tipping a hat. "Well put. Right to the point without drawing blood."

"Then tell me, Alex. Why are you here?"

"Fair enough. I'm a mercenary of sorts: talent for hire. Since my military days, I never stay in one place for very long. I keep on the move. So, being a nomad, I'm in and out of all kinds of circles. I was doing a little work for a small group at MIT when I first heard about you. The information didn't mean anything to me at the time, but as usual, I filed it away for possible future use. I found myself without a contract and in Nevada. It was time to look you up."

"And so you did. But to what purpose? Surely you're not serious about heading up my security?"

"I'm quite serious. My plan is to be here for only a short time. But in that brief stay, I'll clean up your security and tune it to continue without me. Then, I'll move on."

"What makes you so sure that I need your services?" She sipped at her coffee.

"Now you're playing games with me, Doc." Alex sat his cup down on the desk and leaned forward in his chair. "You've gone to a lot of trouble to bury this complex. I'm sure you wanted the knowledge of its existence to be buried just as well. I found you. I found you quite easily. And that bothers you. It should bother you. I can fix the situation and protect your secret. When I'm done, no one will be able to find you out again."

"Your point is well taken." Gayle rose from her chair and turned to the coffeepot, with her back again to Alex. As she refilled her cup, she said, "Can you start immediately?" She turned to face Alex with the coffeepot in her hand waiting for his answer.

"I already have."

Gayle stepped to the desk and poured a refill into Alex's cup that was still sitting on her desk. "Yes, I believe you have."

CHAPTER 17

Alex had been assigned his own room in the complex. Nothing fancy, but it would meet all of his needs. After his shower, he dressed and began his first rounding tour of the complex as the new chief of security.

Gayle had offered to give him a grand tour. Alex told her he wanted to make the first rounds on his own to get a fresh feel for what was going on before he heard her describe how it was supposed to be. His ploy worked. She had a badge pass created for him that would give him access to the bulk of the complex, with the obvious exception of the main control room.

He spent the better part of the morning roaming around, asking no questions, and only replying to questions from others with sounds like "Um" or "Oh." After seeing nothing in the balance of the complex, Alex knew he had to have access to the control room.

But how? Gayle would be very protective concerning access to the control room. He reasoned he would need to gain her trust, cause her to drop her guard, and then make his move.

"Alex." Gayle was approaching him from the other end of the corridor. "How has your morning gone? Any blatant security issues discovered?"

"It's too soon to say. I saw a few things I want to observe to see if they present a common pattern. If they do, then there may be a problem. Beyond that, the morning has been uneventful."

"Join me for lunch, and I'll try to answer any questions you may have from today."

"Good idea."

Gayle led the way to her private quarters. Her living quarters were spacious. As she and Alex entered the rooms, two of the kitchen staff were already setting the table for two in the dining room and placing the table service and food out in an array that would compete with that of any four-star restaurant. When they were finished, they rolled their dining cart back into the corridor, closed the door, and left without saying a word.

"Awfully quiet, aren't they?"

"I've asked that they have all of the details planned to set the table and leave without a need for my intervention. There are times when I change my mind about what I want. They're quick to respond. I just don't want them hanging around while I'm trying to enjoy a meal."

"I see your point. Efficient, effective, and out of the way."

Gayle turned her head to Alex; there was an amazed look on her face. "Yes. Precisely! I'm pleased you saw my goal so quickly. Maybe there will be additional benefits to your being here, Alex. I've not had anyone to talk with in a while that didn't act like a subordinate."

"They are subordinate. Why shouldn't they act as such?"

"True. So are you, for that matter. But you don't act like a subordinate. Why's that, Alex?"

"Because I'm not. I work for you, but I am not your subordinate. In fact, you should at times consider yourself *my* subordinate."

Gayle again twisted her head to look right into Alex's eyes. "*Your* subordinate? And how could that be the case?"

Alex pulled out Gayle's chair, allowing her to sit before he responded. He then went to his chair, stood directly behind it, and said, "My spirit is too strong to be subordinate to anyone. Your spirit is exceptionally strong as well, but I think it would relinquish to my spirit to at least consider my point of view. I would bet I'm the only one in this complex who can safely say that."

Alex sat, pulled his napkin from the table, and placed it on his lap. Then he continued, "And I do mean safely."

Gayle took her napkin, placed it on her lap, and began eating her salad.

"'Safely,' you say? What a peculiar choice of words. Would you care to elaborate?"

"Of course," he said with a half laugh in his voice. "I always enjoy elaborating on my own opinions."

They both smiled.

"Your spirit, like mine, can overpower a person with the tone in your voice. The responsibility and control bares itself in the choice of conversational content. Knowing this, the conversational content of others is also controlled by the tone in your voice. They hear your tone and adjust their content to meet those demands."

"Interesting. So it is your opinion that I limit the content of others by my approach?"

"Not just your approach; that's too general. As I've said, the tone of your voice dictates the extent of conversations with those in this complex. So, they are subordinate to you as their boss and subordinate to you as their 'strength-of-character superior.'"

"And you would have me believe you are, as you call it, my strength-of-character superior?"

Alex resisted responding for a long, contemplative moment. "Let's call us equals. And as equals, I suggest we open that bottle of wine and toast our newfound relationship."

"Relationship?"

"Well, let's at least toast to world peace. Surely you have no question about toasting to world peace?"

"You are quite the speaker, Alex. Quite so, indeed. Yes, let's toast to world peace. In fact, let's toast to an accord of peace between you and me. I think I'd like that. I think I'd like that very much."

"Agreed. To our personal accord of peace."

They toasted and continued with their meal. Nothing of substance came up again during their lunch. They discussed the food and wine, and Alex brought up the question of why the salad fork went to the far left and not to the top of the entrée plate where the desert utensil would normally reside.

When Gayle broke into laughter from their exchange over the placement of the salad fork, Alex could tell he was getting through to her. He could also see she was no monster, as he had supposed. She was a tender woman with a need to laugh and a need to be heard. He could use this to achieve his goal.

They had completed their lunch, and Alex was excusing himself to continue his freelance observations when Gayle made her invitation. "Alex, I would be interested in your observations after a full day. Could you be available for dinner, let's say around eight this evening?"

As he turned from the door to answer Gayle's invitation, Alex caught Gayle's eyes nearly reaching out to him. When Gayle realized this as well, she tilted her head away ever so slightly and broke her gaze.

"I'd enjoy that. Eight it is. I'd bring a bottle of wine, but my card limits my access to the common areas only."

"Just a minute." Gayle disappeared into her bedroom and returned quickly with a key card in her hand. "I have an extra you can use."

She handed the card to Alex, and as she did, he noticed the words imprinted on it: Full Access. One step closer.

"White."

"White it is. Until then." Alex put his hand out, palm up, to grasp Gayle's hand in a gentleman's handshake. Gayle responded by placing her hand atop Alex's. Her hand was warm and strong, and it hesitated in letting go of Alex's.

CHAPTER 18

Alex spent the rest of the afternoon searching each room that had been inaccessible when he was using his common area passkey. Now, with Gayle's Full Access card, he could go anywhere.

Because of time, at first, he stayed away from any of the staff's private quarters. He stayed away from the main control room for now, as well. He would need to have Gayle occupied before he could chance entering the control room.

He found nothing. Each room was neatly kept and sparsely appointed. It would be difficult for anyone to hide and a bit more difficult than usual for anyone to hide something. He wasn't sure what it was he was looking for. Just something out of the ordinary.

It was about six in the evening and he was expected for dinner in a couple of hours. Alex had seen the pub in his early tour and headed there for the wine. Finding the pub just next to the dining room, Alex noticed the liquor cabinet behind the small wet bar.

It was locked with a scanner lock. After he passed the Full Access card through the scanner, the red light went cold and the green light illuminated. The door opened with a gentle click.

Alex thought to himself, "White wine was the request for the evening. Pouilly Fuisee will do the trick for dinner. And this," as he reached for the bottle of Beaujolais Village, '84, "will do the trick for after dinner. Bottle of white, bottle of red."

Alex returned to his room for a shower and a change of clothes. He was ready for dinner by seven, when he sat in the chair by his bed, stared at the ceiling, and thought about his plan for the evening.

"Eight o'clock. Right on time. Not fashionably late?"

"I've always had a problem with that term." Alex walked into Gayle's rooms carrying the two bottles of wine. "Late is late, and if I'm so rich and fashionable I'm always late, then maybe I should fire my chauffer."

She smiled at his comment. "Two bottles of wine?"

"You requested white for dinner, and I thought red would do well for talk, after dinner."

"Good choice. I'll set the red aside for now."

Gayle walked into the kitchen and placed the bottle of white wine on the sideboard near the wineglasses. Alex's eyes followed her. He couldn't help himself. She had made a superb effort to dress in a manner that would get Alex's attention. Her blonde hair was pulled up and back from her face, with her shoulders left pleasantly visible by the strapless evening dress. The front of Gayle's dress fit smoothly across her breasts, with the material rising up and around her neck. This neckline left her back beautifully exposed down to her hips. The dress flowed the full length of Gayle's curved body to just above her feet.

In sharp contrast to the dress, Gayle was barefoot. It was after noticing this that Alex realized this alluring dress, which fit with a natural smoothness, was all Gayle was wearing, and her shoes were not the only items of clothing she had chosen to go without for the evening.

"Would you please pour us a glass of the white? It sounds like a refreshing move before dinner."

"Happy to." Alex found the opener on the sideboard. He poured the glasses as Gayle returned to the dining room.

"Thank you." She toasted, "To the evening."

Alex responded, "To the evening and to that dress."

"A bit forward, aren't you?"

"Yes, I am. But I believe that dress gives me license to be forward."

"Touché. Thank you for the compliment. Shall we sit?"

During the early part of the dinner, they discussed the food, the wine, the china, and very little else. During desert, a sweet, cream-filled torte with a powdered-sugar glaze, Gayle ate very slowly and spoke very little. After each bite, she slowly touched the tip of her tongue to each corner of her mouth to remove the excess sweet cream, whether it was there or not.

"Shall we move to the sitting room for our after-dinner red?" Gayle did not wait for a reply. She stood slowly, without removing her gaze from Alex for a moment, until she turned and walked fluidly into the kitchen to retrieve the bottle of red.

Alex went to the sideboard, where he gathered two fresh wineglasses and the corkscrew. He stood quietly awaiting Gayle's arrival.

Gayle smoothly glided across the floor as she entered the living room. Alex took the wine from her, opened it, and poured two glasses. Gayle moved to the cushioned loveseat and sat in the middle, leaving space on either side—Alex's choice—but nowhere else.

Alex sat to Gayle's right and handed her a glass. After filling both of their glasses, he began his plan for the evening.

Gently, Alex began to speak to Gayle telepathically. He spoke gentle words like *This feels very good, very relaxing; I feel like I just want to lie down.* Alex repeated the phrase as he watched Gayle begin to lean back against the loveseat. Her eyes smiled deeply, as did the corners of her mouth. Both smiles were inviting, almost to the point of offering no alternative.

Alex repeated a third time, *This feels very good, very relaxing; I feel like I just want to lie down.* Gayle began to apologize and then gently laid her head onto Alex's chest and was fast asleep.

Alex then spoke a different telepathic message to the now-sleeping Gayle. *You are asleep, and you will dream until I count to three. After I count to three, you will enter a normal sleep pattern and dream anything you choose. When you awake, you will remember you were dreaming of a romantic encounter on a sandy Caribbean beach. You will feel rested, but you will have an uncontrollable urge to return to this dream at your first opportunity. You will be sure you are having this dream because of the romantic encounter you had with Alex before falling to sleep. You will remember your encounter with Alex ended with the two of you taking a shower together and sharing a tender exchange in the shower as well. You will desire to repeat that encounter before falling to sleep to dream again.*

Alex saw the smile grow on Gayle's face with each new thought he shared with her. He lifted her from the loveseat, carried her to the bedroom, and laid her gently on her bed. In order for the hypnotically induced dream to work, she would need to awaken in her bed without clothing. As her took her evening dress off and placed her under the bedcovers, he saw her beauty was not an illusion. She was a beautiful woman. He also saw he was correct about her having more bare than just her feet.

For this first evening, Alex decided he would stay in her room to see how long she stayed asleep from the telepathic hypnosis. He sat in the side chair near her bed and rested his eyes, making sure not to fall asleep himself. As he sat there, he saw Gayle's face maintain a brilliant smile, which changed only when she was making soft sounds of pleasure.

After three hours, Alex was sure the dream trance she was in would be deep enough for him to leave the room and go search the main control room. That was his plan for tomorrow evening. He would woo her to sleep and then continue his investigation.

Leaving a note on her bedside thanking her for a wonderful evening and telling her he thought it best they both be seen leaving from their own rooms the next morning, Alex was prepared to return to his quarters.

Counting out loud to three, Alex noticed Gayle's face. She first lost her full smile. Two heartbeats later, a new smile returned to her sleeping face.

"I wonder what's she's dreaming now. Sleep, Gayle, sleep."

CHAPTER 19

Alex awoke early, showered, and began his tour of the complex with breakfast in the common cafeteria. It was about 6:30, and the room was full. He took his time while listening to the conversations throughout the room. He heard nothing of work. They talked of what they were doing recreationally; they talked of times in their past; no one talked of anything that could possibly be work related.

That's when Alex put it together. The day before, he had walked the entire complex, and with the exception of the custodial and dining service staff, no one had been working. The complex had gone dormant.

"Can I get you more coffee?" The cafeteria hostess was smiling but seemed cautious in her offer.

"Please. I seem to be a bit more sleepy than usual this morning, so the coffee is really hitting the spot."

"If you need anything else, you just let me know." As she walked from Alex's table, a second hostess urged her to the far side of the dining room and began whispering anxiously. The friendly hostess bearing the gift of fresh coffee listened intently to the whispered message. As she did, her face contorted from its wide-open smile to a troubled, frightened look. She gave only a slight glance in Alex's direction before looking straight into the face of her coworker and then nearly running from the dining room, through the double doors, and into the kitchen. She did not return.

"Excuse me," Alex called out to the remaining hostess. "May get some coffee?"

She quickly crossed the room to Alex. "Yes, sir." She topped off the coffee without making another sound.

"What happened to the other hostess? She looked ill when she left the room."

"No, sir. She's fine. She just forgot her place. I hope you will forgive her. She meant nothing by her comments." The hostess lowered her gaze and left the dining room as well.

Alex suspected the dining rules Gayle expected were now being applied to him. The second hostess must have informed the first that Alex had been spending time with Gayle and she should treat him in like manner or suffer the consequences.

As he left the dining room, he knew he wouldn't be able to see anything with all eyes watching. He decided to go to the exercise room and spend as much time there as he could.

Pleasant music was playing in the weight room. Alex immediately noticed the two men who were using the room as he entered quickly put their weights back on the racks and left the room without saying a word to Alex. They wouldn't even make eye contact.

Apparently, Alex thought, it was not only the dining staff that was to keep their distance from Gayle. They were all afraid of her.

It was a small complex. They probably knew a lot more than they would ever say, especially to an outsider that was "making time" with their tyrannical boss. He began his workout and continued to think.

With his enhanced strength, he didn't work up a sweat with the weights available in the room, but it was enjoyable to push the weights around as if they were mere paperweights. He was in the middle of his tenth set of bench-pressing four hundred pounds when Gayle's face appeared above the rising free weights.

"Good morning." She spoke with tender, alluring, and submissive tones. "I think I'll watch for a moment, if you don't mind?"

Alex continued the slow motion of lowering the weight bar to his chest, touching, and then pushing it to the full extension of his arms. "Please do. I always appreciate an interested audience."

She moved around to his side and let her hand drag across his chest, gently touching his stomach and then feather-touching his right thigh before she lifted her hand away and stood at his feet. "Trust me, I'm interested. You may not make it out of this weight room before I show you just how interested I am."

This was going to be difficult. Alex continued his bench-pressing while he thought this situation through. Gayle was obviously feeling her hypnosis-induced dream was a reality, as Alex had intended. He wanted her to yearn to be with him again, and she had obviously responded to that suggestion. But this was not the timing Alex had planned. He had hoped to put her to sleep again for a second evening and spend time in the control room.

As he was thinking, she moved to another part of the room and out of his sight. Alex heard the weight room door click shut. He then saw Gayle reenter his field of vision. This was not good. She had taken her clothes off and was now standing at Alex's feet, wearing nothing but a smile.

"After last night, I didn't think you'd mind if I joined you in working up a little sweat." She moved to the butterfly weight machine. She moved in slow motion, enhancing every gesture of her body for Alex's benefit. She sat leaning against the back support, stretched her arms out to either side to grasp the extended hand grips, and with a tightening motion of her chest and shoulder muscles, she slowly moved her raised arms toward each other until her elbows touched.

"Is this the way I should be doing this?" She asked Alex this question as she allowed her arms to part and then slowly moved the weights to where her arms were now fully extended again, but this time her chest and shoulder muscles were flexed against the pressure of the butterfly extensions.

"I can uncomfortably say I have never seen it done more effectively." Alex closed his eyes, regained his concentration, and before he knew it, he was saying Angela's name gently to himself.

"Did you say something, Alex?"

Gayle's movement was now more than Alex could bear. He had to end this session now. "I did at that. Why don't you and I return to your rooms for a therapeutic shower?"

"'Therapeutic.' Now there's a word I don't believe I've heard used quite in that context before." Gayle's movement with the butterfly extensions continued, and the tones in her voice were as alluring as the vision of her body flexing against the weights. "There are showers here in the weight room. Why not try them out?"

"I can't stand what you're doing to me, Gayle." Alex sat his weights on the crossbar, pivoted to the side of the bench, stood, and walked deliberately toward Gayle. When he was in front of her, she allowed the butterfly extensions to extend fully to the sides, exposing her in the fullest possible view. "Gayle, I can't take this much longer. You're affecting me more than I could ever tell you."

"That's my plan." She released her grip from the butterfly extensions. "Okay, I'll turn off the switch until we get back to my rooms. But when we get there, I'm going to do to you everything I did to you last night—twice."

Standing behind her, Alex commented as he helped her with her lab coat. "Last night times two? Under those terms, I'd be thrilled to accept your offer."

CHAPTER 20

G ayle didn't accept the hypnotic suggestion as easily this time. They returned to her rooms, and she immediately took control. Alex maneuvered to his best ability to keep Gayle at arm's reach until she collapsed in his arms from the sleep-inducing suggestions.

Since she had begun her moves the moment they reached her rooms, unlike the night before, they shared no wine. Nonetheless, her sleep seemed content enough, and with Alex's added suggestions, she was smiling from ear to ear.

He laid her on her bed, covered her, and went about his change of plans. She had been very susceptible to his telepathic suggestions, but he had not counted on her loneliness being so extreme. He was sure her years of perpetual loneliness were feeding her desire for romance. He could not count on being able to put off her advances much longer.

It was now eleven o'clock in the morning, and Alex was headed to the control room.

He passed his key through the security lock of the control room door. The red light went out and the green light began to glow just as the door swooshed open. Alex entered the room and quickly spotted the banks of computers. He walked down the row and saw they were all on but sitting dormant. Just as the staff of the complex had been—there, but not busy.

He stopped in front of the glass wall containing several small reflective dishes facing each other in two precisely measured rows. "Wow." The room was sealed, with no apparent access. The only door in the control room, other than its entry door, was on the opposite side of the room.

It, too, had a security pass lock. Alex passed the key through, and it unlocked. The door did not swoosh open as the entry door had. Instead, it opened to the inside, suspended on hinges. He had never come across a room such as this before. *This must be the singularity,* he told himself.

The room was a perfect sphere, with a walkway going from the entry door to a table with a massive computer. There was only a single disk drive visible, and Alex saw no monitor or keyboard.

The spherical room was stark. The walls were smooth and uninterrupted by seams or joints. With the exception of the walkway and the computer, the room was empty—or so he thought until he turned and was ready to leave the singularity.

Above the door, hardly visible with its color nearly blending with the surrounding surfaces, was a computer disk taped to the wall. "I bet that's not part of the original design," Alex murmured.

He took the disk from the wall and looked at the description written on its memo side. "Three files," he said to himself. "One labeled 'Karl,' one labeled 'Auto Initiation,' and the third labeled 'Gayle's Mom.'"

With no monitor or keyboard in the singularity, Alex had to take the disk out into the control room. Off to the side was a small PC that looked separate from the bank of other computers. He placed the disk in, and it automatically opened the first file. Alex was surprised at first when the images of Karl came onto the computer monitor and begin talking.

"Who I am is not important. What is important is that if this is found by anyone other than Gayle, I must be dead, since we are the only two allowed in the singularity." His face was ashen and filled with concern. Karl continued, "I put the disk in the singularity to protect it from any changes Gayle may make, or have made, to past time-lines. I have suspected for a few days now that Gayle's mental health was on the verge of a collapse. When I spoke with Celia and then the next day couldn't find her anywhere in the complex, I created this disk.

"I will not try to justify this complex nor my involvement. My reasons were my reasons. What I will do is offer the finder of the disk a way to put everything back as it was, or at least as close as I can get it."

"The second file on this disk is a start-up file that will cause the entire system to function as planned, with the exception of the singularity. It's been designed to be operated manually with no exception. But, if the plan contained in the third file works as designed, then the singularity won't be an issue.

"Do this for everyone. Initiate the second file, and have the computer pull and send the contents of the third file. The entire process will take precisely two minutes. I apologize for my part in any harm this complex may have caused you. God be with you."

The monitor went blank. And that was the first moment Alex noticed Gayle standing behind him in the control room.

"Surprised to see me? I'll bet you are." She stood there, cutting at Alex with her stare. She had tears in her eyes and a nine-millimeter Beretta in her hand pointed directly at Alex. "Do you think me such a fool?"

"No, Gayle. I don't. I find you a troubled woman with a heart full of passion and a mind full of pain."

"So now you're a psychologist as well. A security chief, a psychologist, and a Don Juan, all rolled together. I'm sure there is more, but right now, I just don't have the energy to care."

Gayle walked over to the singularity doorway and closed the door. "You've been prowling around haven't you? You're not as good a security guru as you thought, though. I had a special sensor installed on the singularity door to enunciate in two remote rooms in the complex. My room is one of those two rooms. It woke me from what I thought was a moment of passion—passion with someone who I thought was in the room with me—passion with someone when I thought I was awake."

"Gayle."

"Shut up. I'm in control now. You've played me all too well. It's my move, Alex—if that's really your name."

She moved to the bank of computers, the keyboard closest to the singularity doorway. She placed her hand on the keyboard and with a quick flick of her wrist the lights on the computer began to pulsate."

"Now we'll see who plays whom. In about five minutes you and I won't even be dust. We'll be nothing."

"What have you done, Gayle?"

"Oh, mister know-it-all is at a loss. Well then, there's one for the books." Tears were still streaming down her face and the gun still pointed at Alex. "In about five minutes, the singularity will breach and this reality, if you can call it that, will cease to exist. Not even boom— just gone."

"You need to shut it down, Gayle—now."

"Too late," she said as she turned and blasted three shots into the singularity computer. "It's all over now, big boy. Want to be romantic now? Or is it time for me to be put to sleep again?"

Alex turned and took the disk from the PC. "We're going to deal with this once and for all, Gayle." He reached the disk toward the drive on the center computer.

"Stop, Alex, or I'll make your end sooner than mine."

"Then that's what you're gonna need to do. I'm putting this in the computer."

He put it in the slot as Gayle fired the next shot. Alex heard it whiz by his head—a near miss.

Gayle's crying was changing. It was now more frantic. She was losing her control. "Stop, you fool! I'll put the next one through your head."

The singularity computer was now screaming a regular, insistent warning. A mechanical voice came from the speakers in the corners of the control room. "Singularity breach warning. Two minutes from breach—repeat—two minutes from breach."

Alex saw the computer he had placed Karl's disk in come alive. It, too, voiced an update: "Trans-Gen initiation underway. Communiqué program loaded and ready for transmission."

"What are you doing, Alex? How did you—?"

"Give me the gun, Gayle. Let it be over."

"No! It was over years ago. I don't know why I pretended all these years it wasn't.'

"You mean your mom's death, don't you?"

The two computer voices rang out in the background.

"Singularity breach in sixty seconds."

"Trans-Gen progressing on schedule."

"Gayle, you don't want to die. Give me the gun."

"I wanted, I want ... I'm not sure what I want anymore." Gayle's tears continued to fall, and her voice now changed to a whimper. "Hold me, Alex. Just hold me."

She walked over to Alex, handed him the gun, and he took her into his arms, "Gayle, stop the breach."

"I can't. It now has a mind of its own. But, I can do this."

Gayle reached out to the Trans-Gen computer. Alex pulled her hand back from it.

"It's okay, Alex. Let me set things right."

Alex looked into her eyes and released her arm. She reached out, and before depressing the green transmission switch, she said, "Is the communiqué loaded, Alex?"

"I believe it is."

"Let's hope so."

Gayle depressed the green switch as the computer rang out with two messages.

"Singularity breach in ten seconds."

"Communiqué program complete. Message sent as recorded."

"Goodbye, Alex. One way or another, I'm going to see my mom now."

The last sounds Alex heard were from the computer: "Singularity breach in five ... four ... three ... two ..."

Then darkness ...

CHAPTER 21

The effect had been enough to knock Alex unconscious. He awoke slowly and then realized he was alone. Gayle was gone. The complex was gone, and he was lying on the ground in the open country of Nevada.

The VW he had driven to the complex was not in sight. If things had gone as they should have, he had never rented it—that is, if the timeline had now been altered as planned. But since the change he hoped to initiate was long before his biological reengineering, Alex could still detect the changes.

It was going to be a long hike to the nearest town. It was still midday, and the sun was high. Alex would need to make tracks if he hoped to make it to the nearest town by nightfall. So he started out.

The small ten-room hotel was closer than he could have hoped. It was only seven in the evening, and he was already standing in a cool shower. There was a cold bottle of Coke sitting on the small dining table in the room next to an opened bag of chips.

He toweled off and sat on the bed next to the phone. Dialing the number with some trepidation, Alex felt his heart jump when he heard the voice on the other end of the line.

"Hello."

"Angela! Oh how I've missed you! Is Tony okay?"

"Alex! Where are you? Are you all right? Where have you been? You've been gone for weeks!"

"The question would be more correct, Angela dear, if I were to ask, Where were you?"

"What?"

"I'll tell you all about it when I get home. It's so good to hear your voice. I'm in Nevada, and I'll be heading home tomorrow. I should be there before the evening."

"You're in a lot of trouble, mister—you know that, don't you?"

"I know that, and I've always loved the kind of trouble I get into with you. I have a few other things to check out this evening. I love you, Angela."

Alex quickly finished his Coke and chips, grabbed the telephone, and made a few phone calls to numbers he remembered from the notes Karl had left for him with the disk. The third call, the one to Denver, was the charm.

"Hello," answered the familiar female voice.

"Hello. My name is Alex. I was calling for Gayle Beaufort."

"This is Gayle. But it's Gayle Beaufort Francis."

"I am calling for the *Denver Times*, completing a survey. May I ask you a couple of questions?"

"I have a minute. Sure, go ahead."

"Thank you. Are you married?"

"Yes. For the past twenty years."

"Do you have any children?"

"We have two. A son and a daughter."

"Did your parents used to own a robin's-egg blue Chevy?"

"Yes, they did. What a peculiar question."

"I suppose it was. Are your parents still living?"

"Yes, they are. They live in Florida now that they have retired."

"Thank you for your help, Mrs. Francis. I just have one more question. It is a bit personal, but it is critical."

"Go ahead, I suppose."

"Do you have a strawberry-shaped birthmark on your upper right thigh?"

"Yes, in fact, I do. How would you possibly know that?"

"In all honesty, I believe I knew you in another life. But I am so happy you're in this life instead. Again, I thank you for your time."

Alex hung up the phone and spoke out loud in his empty hotel room, "*Your time.* At one point, Gayle Beaufort, everyone's time was yours."

BOOK THREE

ICE

CHAPTER 1

Frigid was not the word for the bone-biting cold clearly evident through the windshield of the new Range Rover. The Thinsulate Alaskan parkas could keep the Rover's passengers warm only with both front and rear heater fans blowing at full power. Normally quiet, the sound of the 6.4 liter V-8 roared as it resounded from the ice highway beneath the Rover's cleated tires. A look out either of the Rover's side windows would find another Rover keeping pace—there were three in all—four-wheel drives activated, plowing across the frozen straits of northern Alaska, strangely vibrating the icy pathway.

Only two months out of the year was such travel possible. At midseason, the narrow straits of the Bering Sea were frozen six feet thick, allowing semi tractors to pull their trailers filled with needed supplies for the villages to the north of the straits.

But these vehicles weren't tractor-trailers carrying supplies to the villagers. The three four-wheelers, ripping through the two inches of new snowfall that lay powder-like on the frozen roadway, carried four passengers each. The passengers held Uzis—loaded and ready to be cocked, as they sped toward the Bering Diamond Mine operation.

It usually took the tractor-trailers about an hour to traverse the ice highway. Today, the wind was calm, and the racing four-wheelers faced no resistance. They would cross the tundra in just under forty-five minutes.

*****

The miners had just settled down for lunch. It had been a tedious morning at Bering. The mining operation had been shut down for the season last Friday afternoon. After relaxing for the weekend, they'd begun work early Monday morning to package the raw diamonds carved from the frigid, subterranean mines.

These charcoal-colored chunks, ranging from golf-ball size to baseball size, were placed in plastic milk crates and sealed with five layers of heat-shrunk Visqueen. Each crate, which normally carried four one-gallon milk jugs and weighed no more than fifteen pounds, was instead filled level with the raw diamonds and now weighed between seventy and eighty-five pounds.

The miners had finished sealing the last of the crates and had stacked them in the locked warehouse, awaiting the Huey cargo chopper scheduled to arrive the next morning. One trip by the Huey would transport all one hundred and twenty crates. The weight and space taken up by the crates would require a second trip to extract the miners since there was no other safe way to get back to the real land of central Alaska now that the thaw had begun.

"I see the camp. Get ready to party." The growl came loudly from the lead Rover's two-way radio to the second and third Rovers. "No witnesses, clear?"

"Oh yeah, we're clear. Blood on the rocks, hey, boss?"

"That's right, mate. No witnesses, no wasted time. Shoot and then shoot some more—that's all."

The two outside Rovers split to the right and the left with the lead four-wheeler going straight in. The camp would be swept from all points.

*****

"I hear motors. Do I hear motors?" The miners looked at each other in amazement. As if on cue, they all moved to the windows and tried to find the source of the throaty engine noises. Too late. The lead Rover had already passed the dining hut and parked near the warehouse.

The miners turned from the windows and moved slowly back to their chairs, reaching for their coats. "I know I heard—" Their comments were cut short. The hut door flew open, funneling six armed men through the opening, one after another, with their fingers pressed firmly on their sensitive triggers. The noise was deafening, but the noise lasted only twenty seconds. The miners, ten in all, were on the floor and dead before they could even look to the open door.

"Oh man!" The gunman at the rear of the line nearly giggled. "Can we do that again?"

"You find any more miners and you can shoot all you want. Until then, let's load the Rovers."

They turned from the raw carnage of the dining hut and headed for the warehouse.

Whistling lighthearted tunes, the band of killers started loading the crates into the cargo areas of the three Range Rovers. It was painfully obvious that the massacre they'd left in the dining building was a normal experience for them. "It was awfully nice of the miners to package our goods. Sure makes it easy to load."

"Hurry it up," barked their first mate. "We need to get out of here and back to the boat by nightfall."

"Don't get keeled over some talk about wiping out these feebs and takin' their loot. I'm still workin', boss."

With a little over three hours of daylight left, they loaded the diamond-filled crates into the Rovers. There were a total of a hundred and twenty crates and they were working to put forty crates in the cargo area of each Rover.

"Ain't gonna fit," barked one of the unshaven robbers. "I got thirty-seven crates in the back here, and it's full."

"Then put the other three up front. Put one on the floorboard of the three riders." The first mate added, "Our orders are to take it all, and I'm not going to be the one to tell the Skipper that we left anything behind. Anyone else want to volunteer?" All heads quickly shook as the last of the heavy crates were loaded onto the Rover's passenger area floorboards.

With the Rovers loaded and a few minutes to spare, the three teams walked back toward the dining building to see if there was anything worth eating in the kitchen.

Evie saw them heading her way. She had been in the walk-in refrigerator, getting more salad dressing, when the killers had arrived. She'd heard the gunfire but been too frightened to leave the cooler until several shivering minutes of silence had passed by.

"Why are they coming back?" she nervously whispered to herself. She was standing in the dining room, surrounded by her dead and mutilated friends, looking out the lower corner of the front window. "Food!" she said. "They want food. They might look in the cooler this time." With no place to hide, Evie looked back at the mangled group of bodies. Then she moved into action.

Evie ran to the edge of the carnage where two of her fellow miners were lying in bloody pieces, having been ripped apart by the automatic weapons. She dipped her hand into the pooled blood between the two bodies and wiped the blood over her face, chest, and arms. She had to use three dips to cover herself fully, and the still-warm blood made her nauseous. Holding back as well as she could, Evie lay on the floor between the two bodies and pulled their lifeless limbs onto hers. With that, her stomach gave way as she lay there between the warm massacre of her friends, and she vomited, the stream of stomach contents escaping her mouth and running down the side of her face to the floor.

"Nobody get up. We'll take care of ourselves." The ghoulish figure laughed to his buddies as he entered the dining room and headed for the kitchen. The members of the troupe were all relaxed, with their weapons slung over their shoulders. They were certain they were the only living things for miles.

"Hey, Bob, look. That one over there threw up. I hope that's not a reflection of the quality of food in this place." The six-foot-three, broad-shouldered man laughed, moving his attention away from Evie's bloodied, seemingly dead, body. "Too bad; that one would have been fun for a few hours, until I broke her in half. What can I say? It happens."

The robbers stayed in the kitchen for what seemed a nightmarish eternity to Evie. They were laughing and throwing things around for about twenty minutes before they walked through the dining room again to leave. Evie waited and waited, until she heard them drive off.

Evie just lay there and sobbed. In shock, feeling more connected to her mining companions now than ever before, she no longer felt revolted by their condition. Soon she would get up, she told herself. She would make her way to the barracks and would scrub off their blood and her vomit. She would then radio a report to the mining office in Nome.

For now, though, she would just lie there and cry. There seemed to be no reason to hurry.

The CD player in the lead Rover was playing loud, with the heavy bass line of "Burnin' Down the House" booming. None of the riders were singing along, but they were all moving to the music in some small way. They had left the campsite of the Bering Mining operation behind some minutes ago and were just starting their return trip across the ice highway.

The wind had picked up, and the Rovers were being blown from the northwest, making handling a little tough. Visibility was limited. As they traveled in a line rather than side by side, the first mate in the lead Rover could just make out the second Rover through the rearview mirror. The load was packed so tightly in the rear of the Rover that even with the strong winds, the load was not moving at all. Still, they should make it to the boat ahead of schedule.

The radio cracked, and then a voice yelled out, "They're gone!"

"This is Rick," answered the first mate from the front passenger seat of the lead Rover. "What do you mean, they're gone?"

"The rear Rover; it's gone—it's disappeared!"

"Belay that, sailor. With this crap blowin' around, they could easily be hidden by the snow cover." With that, the first mate tried to raise the rear Rover on the radio. "Chester? Do you read me? Pick up." He waited. "Chester, turn the radio down and pick up the microphone."

There was no answer. The first mate started to call out to the rear Rover again, but the sight in his rearview mirror stopped him cold.

The middle Rover was gone. He attempted a call, "Jack? Come back." There was no answer.

That's when he saw it. Racing up behind the lead Rover was the hungry monster that had deftly swallowed the other two Rovers. Stretching a hundred feet wide if it was a foot was a ferocious crack in the ice highway—unsatisfied, and grasping for the rear of the only remaining Rover.

"We're too heavy. Floor it man! Put your foot through the floor if you have to, but get us out of here!" The first mate saw the crack begin to disappear under the rear of the Rover. Its speed was far quicker than the loaded-down Rover could move.

It was too late. The rear of the Rover began to sink while the snow cloud created by the racing crack in the ice swept past the vehicle. Being quickly replaced by the icy ocean water, the snow cloud disappeared as did the third and final Rover into the depths beneath the thawing and cracking ice highway.

The last sound coming from the cabin of the lead Rover was from the dying CD player, still playing the tune from the Talking Heads. "Cool Baby," they sang, and then even the pulsing bass line froze silent.

The Rover sank in a rush. On top of its factory weight of five thousand pounds, it also carried four men and over three thousand pounds of raw diamonds. Nearly five tons of once surface-dwelling mass was plummeting to the ocean floor nearly five hundred feet below.

The Rover settled upright, as if it were ready to drive across the ocean floor, just as the other two Rovers before it. The weight distribution of the massive engine in the front and the diamond-filled crates in the rear made them sink level.

The engines drowned out early, but the headlights of the all-weather vehicles still blazed. Fifty yards back, the middle Rover's lights were succumbing to the sea. The dark sight was eerie as the Rover sat upright on the cold ocean floor, headlights reaching forward. Imploding from the pressure, one light burst, shorting the electrical system and quickly plunging the last Rover into total darkness.

The cargo of men was insignificant to the laws of physics, just as the lives of the miners had seemed insignificant to the cold-blooded killers only hours before.

Now, they were cold blooded indeed—cold as ice.

CHAPTER 2

T he morning sun seemed to gently breathe as the ocean water from St. George's Bay danced against the boat dock. Tony was already making the boat ready for the morning dive trip. He had left his mom and dad still relaxing in the open-air restaurant as they enjoyed the light breeze and casually finished their coffee. Tony had begun to come into his own over the past year. He'd been only fifteen when they'd moved to Grand Cayman, but that had been two years ago—two years filled with such unusual experiences for Tony and his family. It was enough to last most teenagers a lifetime.

But this wasn't Grand Cayman, this was Malta—the town of St. Julian's, to be exact. Tony and his family had been on this island for three days now. They were on a mission, a secret mission, as Tony liked to say. In truth, it was just that.

Tony saw his parents approaching. "She's ready to go," he informed them.

"I knew there was a reason to have kids." Alex had half turned to Angela with a wry smile.

"You mean other than to take out the trash?" Angela remarked.

"Ha, ha, guys." Tony had heard these slams before. "Do either of you old folks need help getting into the boat?"

"Watch it, boy," Alex quipped, "your mother's aged like a fine wine." With that, Alex leaped into the boat from the dock, bypassing the walkway and just dodging a shoulder punch from Angela.

They had rented this boat, a sleek forty-foot twin-diesel cabin cruiser, from a local dealer. It was necessary to their plans. The McPhersons had been sent to Malta with a goal. After being contacted by Admiral Sterling, of the US Navy, some ten days ago, they had set out on a journey to Malta to vacation and ask a few questions. The high-priced, highly visible boat was key to their being noticed by the right people.

"Let's shove off, son."

"Right, Dad. I'll get the fore rope."

Alex went to the aft rope, and Angela went to the wheelhouse and started the engines. After hearing the "all free" from both Alex and Tony, Angela began backing the cruiser out of her slip. With a quick look topside, it was immediately clear to Alex that Tony had the gear stowed and the boat was shipshape and ready to travel.

The McPhersons were a normal family in many ways, but there were differences beyond most people's imaginations. Tony and Angela were both bright and very fit, but it was Alex who truly set this family apart—or, more to the point, what Alex had experienced and the changes that resulted that set him apart—apart from the rest of the world.

It never ceased to amaze Alex how easily he was able to move around in the water with only his shorty wetsuit, fins, and the e-reg in his mouth. Since the encounter with the hammerheads and the series of events that had followed, Alex McPherson had been unrestricted in his diving adventures. Since then, he had been able to dive as deeply and as long as he chose without suffering from personal damage or fatigue.

He remembered his feelings of dying and how his feelings had somehow been eased by the knowledge that he had fought off ten hungry sharks just long enough for his wife, Angela, and their son, Tony, to guide the rest of the divers to safety. He was also keenly remembered the binding feeling around his right ankle just as he'd thought his air supply would run out and the sharks would have their feast.

But the part of the memory that was still the hardest for Alex to believe was when he'd awakened in the undersea cave, still alive. He'd known he was alive because physically he'd felt so awful. He'd rejoiced in this awful feeling, though, for it meant he was alive. Not only was he alive, he'd learned, but he had been saved by an unknown race of beings that lived deep beneath the sea.

This race of unknowns had left Alex a device, which looked much like a laptop computer. The device had answered his questions about his ordeal with the hammerheads. He'd discovered that he had been pulled into the depths of the ocean by a giant squid sent by the unknowns to save him from the hungry sharks. They'd sent the squid to save Alex because they had observed the sacrifice he had made to save the others. They told Alex they had not been able to merely stand by and allow the sharks to have their way with such a courageous man.

The problem the unknowns had encountered when saving Alex by the method they had chosen was that they badly damaged his body as a result of the bone-crushing pressure from the ocean depth to which they'd brought him. They had been able, following a series of procedures, to genetically reengineer him, causing his molecular structure to become a thousand times denser than it had been. This, they'd thought, would allow Alex to return from the ocean depths unharmed.

Their solution for the one problem had created a new one, though. With Alex's molecular structure being more dense, thus made up of a concentration of productive cells a thousand times greater than before, his need for oxygen had dramatically increased as well. As they'd told him while he was still in the undersea cave, he'd nearly died a second time, this time from the direct efforts they were using to save him.

To solve this challenge, they'd surgically installed an organic concentrator in Alex's bronchial passages just above his lungs, causing any air he breathed in to be effortlessly concentrated to the amount of oxygen he needed for his new molecular structure. Still, he hadn't been able to return to the surface even with his increased strength and genetic reengineering. Alex could not extract air from the seawater, and he could not survive on a single breath to make it from five miles deep to the surface.

The unknowns had then provided Alex with a mechanical device they called an e-reg. This enhanced regulator extracted air from the seawater as if it were attached to air tanks and could be used at any depth, thus surpassing the limited depth ratings of any man-made tank system. The e-reg had what looked to be a bungee cord attached to it, which allowed the device to be worn around the neck. The e-reg resembled many of the standard two-stage diaphragm regulators used with normal scuba equipment.

With his rebirth that day from the process of genetic reengineering, with the surgical implantation of the organic oxygen concentrator, and with the gift of the e-reg, Alex McPherson had been able to return home to his family. But he had returned home with new strength, new mental capabilities, and telepathic abilities that were a direct result of the increased cellular development and its effects on his brain tissue. As far as Alex could tell, he was left with the ability to dive in any body of water, to any depth, for as long as he chose.

It was because of these special abilities that Admiral Sterling had called upon the McPhersons in the past. They had formed a company called TESS, the Terran Exploration & Salvage Service, to perform as a salvage company but to also act as a front for the talents and skills that only the McPherson team could offer.

*****

The first two days of the trip had been very pleasant. They were staying at the Corinthia Beach Resort in St. Julian's. Alex and Angela shared the Ambassador Suite and Tony was across the walkway in a junior suite. There was an adjoining dining room that was used exclusively by those who stayed in the suites of this five-star, indulgent resort. The dining room and each of the suites had private balconies that looked out to the sea.

Admiral Sterling had asked Alex if he and his family would pretend to be vacationing in the islands of the Maltese archipelago. The McPhersons were to act as a wealthy family who were in the market to buy an exceptional cabin cruiser. Sterling said he would foot the bill for this venture as well as commit to owing the McPhersons some future favors they could discuss at a later time.

The request by Sterling was simple enough. While vacationing and using a top-of-the-line rental cruiser, they were to make it quietly known that Alex was in the market to buy a boat of exceptional quality but was also interested in paying less than fair market price. This was based on information that Sterling had acquired about a group of modern-day pirates who combed the open seas boarding boats of all types, looting them all, and relieving the owners of the best ones. There was also talk that these pirates were involved in smuggling and drug running, often using the stolen boats for their illegal ventures. On two occasions it had cost the boats' owners their lives, but most of the time the thievery was so well planned that the owners were nowhere near their boats at the time the pirates were boarding them.

Sterling had asked Alex to plant a few seeds of interest, listen for any response, and hopefully obtain a name that Sterling could follow up on through a more overt investigation. Alex and his family were not being asked to investigate any further. Once they heard a name, they were to leave and get that information back to Sterling's office.

After three days, there had been no response to the comments and questions Alex had shared around St. Julian's. They had stayed close to the island of Malta for those days, hoping for a contact. When there was none, they planned a day trip to one of the smaller islands in the Maltese group. The island of Comino was only an hour's boat ride from Malta and contained one of the most colorful cavern dives in the world. The caverns and other dive spots were riddled throughout the Cominotto reef.

It was time for a good boat dive. Alex and Angela had spent most of an hour sitting on the front deck chairs, hardly saying a word. Even though they had become island dwellers two years ago, their amazement with the beauty of the sea was still unbridled.

Tony had served as the captain for this trip, much as he had on several trips during recent months. Their son was growing into a man and was showing the early signs of a solid maturity guided by a young but level head.

The little island of Comino began to rise above the horizon about forty-five minutes into the trip. It seemed to maintain its distance for nearly fifteen more minutes before it raced within reach. "Well, let's get our gear in line." Alex led the way as he and Angela went around the wheelhouse along the side deck to the rear of the boat.

Now anchored, the three were in the water with their BCs filled with air. These buoyancy compensator vests allowed them to rest on the surface. Tony and Angela wore their single-tank systems, while Alex was fitted with his twin-tank system. With his e-reg, he did not need to wear the tanks at all. But, with the possibility of meeting up with other divers, Alex always wore his scuba gear in these situations, keeping his e-reg hung around his neck by its long, bungee cord-like necklace.

They submerged and headed for a depth of sixty feet. Directly beneath the boat was the entrance of the Comino caves. Reaching sixty-two feet, Alex led the way to the cave entrance. These caves were unique throughout the world for the sea life that made its home on the walls, floor, and ceiling. Bright-yellow coral layered the cave surfaces with constant movement from the living decoration. And a brilliant contrast to the glistening yellow came from the well-developed red sponges that attached themselves to the coral and lived among the thousands of other life forms in the coral cave.

The cave they entered had been viewed by many a diver in years past. The pathway was well known. Remaining at a depth of about sixty feet, the single tunnel would gently twist and turn for about one hundred feet before opening up to a small lagoon. The lagoon was open to the sea through a deeper, less diver-friendly cave. It was through this less-traveled cave that the amazing collection of sea creatures gained access to the lagoon.

Upon leaving the cave, the McPhersons maintained their buoyancy at sixty feet and hovered there as motionlessly as possible. In this Comino lagoon, a diverse community existed, shared by large, slow-moving grouper, sea tuna, and vibrantly colored amberjack, with a small school of shiny-teethed barracuda slowly circling just overhead. The walls of the lagoon were coral encrusted as well, but these walls were also covered with bright-green tube worms and bristle worms, peppered with gently pulsating starfish.

Alex looked at Angela, and she and Tony looked back to Alex. They took their regulators out and each formed the word *Wow!* into the surrounding water. Replacing and clearing their regulators, they continued to float motionlessly as visitors to this bigger-than-life natural aquarium, until Angela and Tony's air reached 1000 psi. At that point, as they had discussed in their dive plan, they slowly turned and reentered the Comino cave, with Angela leading the way.

As they climbed from the water and began to take off their gear, they couldn't stop talking about the marvelous sights they had seen and the experience they'd shared with the lagoon neighborhood. When all their gear had been cleaned and stowed, they went into the galley and retrieved sandwiches and pop for lunch. The boat gracefully swayed and moved with the water as they casually lunched, feet propped up along sidewalls of the boat, relaxed after their dive.

After lunch, Alex took the wheel while they cruised along the shoreline of little Comino. The beauty was incomparable, and in many places it was so natural and raw that there were no signs of the effect of human intrusion. They cruised all around the backside of this small island, staying away from the main dock. Alex then checked the compass, engaged the GPS, and turned the boat back toward Malta and St. Julian's.

The evening was warm and breezy. The outlook from the balcony of the Ambassador Suite was of the sunset, with an unencumbered view of the sun melting into the sea. Tony had camped out at the pool for the late afternoon with several of the other teens also staying at the hotel. Angela and Alex had lazily drifted back to their suite, immersing themselves in the oversized seawater hot tub. Easily finding their way into each other's arms, they made love with passion and pause, with caressing and adventure, rivaled only by the receding and coming of the ocean waves just beyond the reach of their suite's private balcony.

Two hours later, they felt so connected to each other they could have melted into the sea itself and become one with Mother Earth.

Alex showered first. then, while Angela showered, he walked down to the pool to remind Tony of their dinner plans. As he was still standing poolside, a hotel page approached Alex.

"Mr. McPherson?"

"Yes?"

He handed Alex a portable phone, "There is a call for you, sir."

"Thank you." Alex took the phone and began, "Yes?"

"Mr. McPherson," a sweetly aromatic female voice spoke though the receiver. "My name is Brigitte," she said with a French accent. "I understand you may be in the market for a pleasure cruiser or possibly a personal yacht?"

"I might be."

"Good. May I come and meet with you and your wife tomorrow, just following breakfast? If you are agreeable, I could be at your suite at around ten o'clock in the morning?"

"Tomorrow morning at ten o'clock would be fine."

"Excellent. I will bring complete information on what may be available through our consortium. I look forward to meeting with you."

"Until the morning, then." Folding the phone, Alex whispered to himself, "They've taken the bait. Time to snap the line and bury the hook."

Alex stood in the hotel lobby and looked in amazement. He had known Angela since his freshman year of college. He had seen her adorned in clothing for all occasions, from pearls and plunging necklines to T-shirts and blue jeans. But as Angela seemingly floated through the carpeted hotel foyer, barely touching the floor, Alex was reminded how easily she could surprise him. She wore a two-piece outfit, the skirt glistened with sequins. The contoured blouse hung from her shoulders by dainty spaghetti straps. Her skirt, cut well above her knees, shimmered even when she wasn't moving. This seemingly alive, wonderfully short skirt seemed to caress Angela's upper thighs as she moved purposefully toward Alex.

"Wow! Are you for real?"

Angela offered a small half smile and then purred, "You're the only one who matters, so this outfit is for you."

Dinner was excellent. The Hilton on St. Julian's had an open-air dining courtyard surrounded by and set within baroque palazzos. It was known for its authentic Maltese cuisine, and the menu held recipes offering a blend of Sicilian and Moorish flavors.

"I'll have the sea bass with snow peas and pesto bread. My wife will have the barracuda fillet with snow peas and spinach soufflé. We'd like a chilled bottle of Beaujolais, a vintage earlier than '89, before dinner as well." Alex reveled at the look in Angela's eyes as he ordered for her.

"You haven't ordered for me in a long time. Trying to impress me or the waiter?"

Capped off with slow dance after slow dance until midnight, the evening continued to flow as well as the perfectly chilled wine had on this warm evening.

Tony met them for breakfast just after 8:30 the next morning on the shared dining balcony. There were two other families there as well, but they were just finishing and left the dining balcony before the McPhersons were served.

"Good time last evening?" Tony almost snickered. "You both came in pretty late. Do I need to set a curfew?"

"Listen, mister," jested Angela, "when your father is in the mood to dance, I'm up for it, no matter how late."

"Just checking, Mom; don't get too wild, though. I'm not sure if I can break you two out of jail in this country."

Finished with breakfast, they'd stepped back to their suite just as the gentle knock on the door softly resounded.

"Mr. McPherson? I'm Brigitte. May I come in?"

"Yes, please. We can sit at the balcony table for after-breakfast coffee." Alex directed the young lady over to their table, now cleared by the hotel staff of any sign of their breakfast, and pulled out a chair. Brigitte was an attractive woman, almost a young lady, in her early twenties. Her dark, well-tanned skin went well with her minimal jewelry and her professional attire, which showed no overt intent to flaunt her obviously attractive features.

Tony spoke up, "Mom, Dad, I'm going to my rooms. Let me know when you're ready to dive." Tony turned to the attractive female visitor, "Pleasure to meet you. Please excuse me."

Brigitte smiled warmly at Tony and replied graciously, "Of course."

Alex felt he needed to explain Tony's comment. "We're planning to dive on the *Um El Faroud* early this afternoon. We've been told she is an excellent wreck dive, with great access for the interested diver. "But that's not why you're here," he continued. "So, tell me what you have to offer."

"You Americans do like to get down to business. Let's do. Our consortium has access to five spectacular boats that might be of interest to you. Each has its own selling points. The decision of which, if any, will of course be yours, based on your wishes and desires."

The young visitor began to describe the five boats, starting with the most modest and moving up the scale of both amenities and price. As she finished with the fourth description, her cell phone chirped like a well-trained parakeet. "Please excuse me." Brigitte stood and walked to the far side of the balcony, with her back half turned away from her potential customers.

From the very start of her call, she was subdued. She answered only in yes or no replies, and her tone could not have been more submissive. The call lasted only two to three minutes, but the effect was monumental.

"I must apologize, but I'm being called away. I would have liked to share more with you about our seagoing properties, but this recent intrusion has directed me otherwise."

"When should we plan to hear from you?"

"Let me give you my card. I would like for you to think about what you've heard so far, and if tomorrow morning you are still interested, give me a call, and we'll schedule another meeting."

Alex decided to throw out a piece of bait. "Will we meet with 'the Skipper' before we finalize a deal?"

Brigitte's eyes flinched suddenly at Alex's mention of the Skipper. She had not mentioned that the Skipper was a part of the consortium. She tried to backpedal, "The Skipper? I'm not sure who you mean."

Alex had struck a nerve. That was all he needed to know, all he needed to pass on to Admiral Sterling. With this information, the McPhersons could enjoy the rest of the day and plan to leave the next afternoon. They had achieved their goal.

"I must have been mistaken. Please pardon me."

"Think nothing of it. Good day, then." The previously calm young lady turned and almost ran from their room.

CHAPTER 3

The rented cabin cruiser rode high in the water as Alex guided it toward their planned dive site, the *Um El Faroud*. The *Faroud* sat southwest of the Maltese coastal town of Wied iz-Zurrieq, directly south of Malta, having been strategically sunk as an artificial reef at that location in 1998. She had been docked in Wied for repairs when an explosion had ripped through her engine room. The explosion of the *Um El Faroud* that day had killed nine dockworkers.

Adequate repairs were made to raise her from the shallow dock waters and she was successfully relocated to her current and permanent resting place. With a length of three hundred feet and a weight of ten thousand tons, she went down fast. As she rested upright, the *Faroud*'s bridge was only forty feet deep. The really exciting part of this dive, though, was to enter her from the bridge and journey through her structure. The main areas of the *Faroud* rested between eighty and one hundred feet deep.

It only takes a few years for the sea and its natural inhabitants to move into a new home, especially one as accommodating as the *Faroud*. With her open bridge, large stairways, and all the doors removed from her forty staterooms, the *Faroud* was a ready-made neighborhood for the sea. The *Faroud* was not without problems for divers. Even with her easy access, she was big and could be confusing for the inexperienced wreck diver. But the McPhersons were not at all inexperienced wreck divers. It promised to be an exciting dive.

"We're there," Alex called out to Angela and Tony as he slowed their boat.

Tony came from below. "Do you see the anchor flag yet, Dad?"

"Off to starboard about ten degrees."

Tony turned his head in that direction. "I see it, Dad. When you shut down, I'll go in and tie off."

"Good plan, son."

Tony hit the water with a giant step, with his head hardly going below the surface. Only ten feet from the anchor flag, Tony had their anchor rope connected in moments. He lifted his hand toward Alex in an okay signal and began to swim to the rear of their boat.

The three of them had reviewed the layout of the *Faroud* over lunch before setting out for the site. But a good dive plan is always open for more review.

"I still think it wise to enter from the main bridge here." Alex pointed to the layout stretched on the wheelhouse chart table. "We can then go deep inside her through the main passageway until one of your psi readings hits 60 percent. At that point, we turn and follow the same path out."

"I'll lead going in," Angela continued their review, "and your father will lead coming out. The *Faroud* is supposed to be open enough to have some filtered light, especially with her doors removed. Nonetheless, let's lead with our bright light and the other two moving with our smaller lights in hand."

"Good plan," Tony added. "Let's get wet."

They checked each other's gear, front and back. Alex checked his gear primarily to make sure that nothing was loose that could get snagged by a piece of the *Faroud*. It wouldn't cause him trouble, but it could cause something to tumble down and either hurt Angela or Tony or, at the very least, disturb the site itself.

"Everything checks. I'm in." With that, Tony jumped from the back of the boat into the water.

Alex looked at Angela and said, "Kids," followed by a running leap off the back of the boat accompanied by a loud "Geronimo!" Angela, shaking her head, was not far behind.

Being careful to equalize as they descended, they marveled at the clarity of the water. From the moment they entered the water, they could see the outlined form of the *Faroud*. She was big, all right. She appeared to be about fifty feet wide on her center deck just in front of the bridge.

Angela indicated that she was ready to enter the bridge's main door. She turned on her big light and slowly floated through the passageway. How eerie it looked at first to see the wheel standing alone, surrounded by small fish of three or four different varieties. Tony easily took care of the eerie feeling. Making his way through the bridge compartment, he rested buoyant in front of the wheel, taking hold of it with both hands; he looked back and moved his shoulders in a little dance as if he were singing a sailor's tune while on watch.

Angela pointed at Tony and then put her hand on her stomach as if she were belly laughing. Alex, with his telepathic ability, went a step further. *I think your mother thinks you're funny; should I tell her that you're just plain insane?*

Alex heard Tony's reply. "You're just sore, Dad, because you didn't think of it first."

Alex nodded affirmatively to Tony, followed by Angela waving to them to follow her and continue further into the *Faroud*.

A thin cover of coral was making its home on the surfaces of the *Faroud*. Where gray had been the only color, the *Faroud* now was taking on yellow and red on her floors and walls, with a predominance of orange on her ceilings. Angela had led them to the *Faroud*'s mid decks and they had made their way through about a third of her length when she noticed that her air gauge was just reading 60 percent. She stopped and buoyantly pivoted to face Tony and Alex. She pointed to her air gauge and showed six fingers followed by a zero shaped by her right hand. Tony looked at his gauge and indicated he had 70 percent remaining. Alex had been using his e-reg, so he had not consumed any of the 5000 psi in his twin-tank system.

Alex spoke telepathically to Angela and Tony. *Let's head back. I'll lead the way.*

He turned and then stopped immediately, saying to himself, *Oh my God!* Apparently his thoughts were intense enough that he sent that thought to both Angela and Tony. Looking to his right and left, Alex chose the open stateroom to the right and pushed Tony in. Angela quickly followed Tony without hesitation.

It's a mako. Alex was calm, but it was obvious to Angela and Tony as they received his message that his concern was real. It was not the first encounter Alex had experienced with sharks, but in these confines his alternatives were limited. Alex began to take off his BC. "Angela, take this. Use the air for you and Tony if you need it. I'll try to lead the mako away."

Angela would have been terrified for him if Alex had been anyone but Alex. Still, she did not know what the limits of his bio reengineering were. He could be hurt; they just didn't know what it would take.

Crap! Alex's thoughts were clear. The mako had rushed down the passageway and slammed into Alex full force, sending him against the wall at the rear of the passageway. Pulling his six-inch dive knife from its thigh-mounted holder, Alex pushed his way to the underside of the ten-foot mako. With a quick jerk, the knife penetrated the underbelly of the shark, causing the gyrating mako to collapse. With its belly opened from the four-foot slit, the shark died instantly as its life spilled onto the passageway floor.

Angela started out of the stateroom only to have Tony grab her BC and jerk her back into the room so hard she dropped her dive light. A second mako had nearly closed its mouth onto Angela's head as she'd stuck it through the stateroom doorway. Alex saw the second mako and headed toward it. This one was twice the size of the first and seemed to be angry at the sight of its dead comrade, if such anger were possible for a mako.

Alex was tied in a wrestling match with this one. He could not gain an advantage over this larger, stronger shark while contained in this tight passageway. The two were as one as they rolled and tumbled against the walls and floor. It was as if Alex was gripping the back of a bucking bronco in some bizarre underwater rodeo.

That's when Tony saw an opening. With his own dive knife firmly held in his hand, he stretched through the doorway and slashed at the belly of the mako. Not having Alex's strength, Tony was only able to inflict a small wound. The slashing attempt worked just enough, causing the mako to jerk away. As it did, it exposed more of its head to Alex and less of its opened mouth. Alex took advantage and forced his knife to the top of the shark's head, near the center. Tony made another slashing move, and the shark jerked more violently. But this time its jerking caused it to surge abruptly in the direction of Alex's already plunging knife.

With his six-inch blade buried deep into the skull of the mako, Alex gave it a brutal twist. At the same moment, while its underside was fully exposed, Tony held his knife with both hands and opened up the second mako as his father had the first. The second mako collapsed.

Tony smiled with a triumphant expression, just as he began struggling to breathe. He checked his gauge. It read empty. His assistance in the battle had caused him to rapidly burn his air.

Angela saw him look to his gauge and read his body movement. She yanked his regulator from his mouth and forced his father's regulator into Tony's mouth, while depressing the clearing diaphragm. This movement pushed the water from the regulator and Tony's mouth at the same time. Tony quickly recovered, grabbed the regulator that was attached to his father's two-tank set from his mother's grasp, and began to breathe regularly.

Angela then checked her own air gauge and found it at 10 percent. She called out to Alex, who was still looking down the passageway, not wanting to be surprised again. *Alex, we need to get out of here. Tony's air is gone and I'm down to 10 percent. We're both using your tank through your regulator and its octopus regulator.*

Let me take a look. Stay here until I get back.

Alex began cautiously down the passageway, looking into each of the staterooms as he passed. Kicking gently, he barely disturbed the water. He did not want to draw attention to his presence in case there were other mako in the area. As he came to the low point of the stairwell that led to the bridge, he noticed something small and roughly square was slowly falling down the stairs.

You're kidding me, he thought. He took the ripped piece of flesh in his hand. *Chum.* Nearly crawling up the stairs, Alex saw a shower of chum gently sinking in the entire area surrounding the *Faroud*'s bridge.

He didn't see any other sharks, but he knew they were either there or on the way. Chum was their bait: easy food falling from the surface.

Keeping an eye over his shoulder, Alex returned to Angela and Tony, still waiting in the midlevel stateroom. To make sure they understood what was in front of them, he shared that the area had been pelted with chum. *We'll talk about it later. For now, wait again for me to return.*

Alex, our air is down to 50 percent. Both of us anxious and on the same tank are making it go pretty fast.

Force yourself to stay calm, if you can. I'll just be a moment. With that, Alex took hold of the smaller of the two sharks and began dragging it down the passageway toward the bridge.

He returned in what seemed like seconds to Angela and Tony. *I threw that carcass over the side near the rear of the Faroud. I saw three more head for it in a flash. I'll lead the way.* Alex grabbed the second recently vicious mako. *Stay close. When we are ready to leave the bridge for open water, I want to use this beast to shield us from view for as long as we can.*

Both Angel and Tony nodded. They needed to stay close to each other anyway, since they were sharing the air supply, so they put the BC that held Alex's two-tank system between them, each with their own regulator.

Moving slowly through the passageway behind Alex, who was dragging the twenty-foot mako's lifeless body, Tony and Angela could see nothing else. They stayed in this order until they reached the top of the stairs leading onto the bridge of the *Faroud*.

Alex looked all around. He saw no other sharks from this vantage. *Stay up against this shark; stay close.*

With that, they left the confines of the *Faroud*. They were only forty feet below the surface and their boat, but they were out in the open and easy targets. Alex continued a 360-degree search for more killers. As they left the deck of the *Faroud*, he saw nothing.

At thirty feet, he saw them: three new arrivals coming from their right. Placing Angela and Tony behind him, Alex firmly gripped the dead mako, placing it between the three new killers and the humans trying to surface.

At twenty feet, they hit. If not for the glancing blow they gave each other before making contact with the dead mako, they would have torn the dead mako from Alex's grip. They came about for another quick strike at fifteen feet from the boat ladder. This time, they timed it well. One hit high on the mako carcass, one hit low, and the third made a delayed hit as the first released its grip. This move wrenched the dead mako from Alex's grasp.

"Now—break for the ladder! Go! Go!"

All three went for the ladder. Tony and Angela swam in tandem, still surviving from the same air source, with Alex turning his back to his family and keeping an eye on the savage disposal of the once-fearless mako by his former comrades.

Rolling onto the boat's wet deck, which rested about six inches into the water, Angela and Tony were out of danger. Before Alex turned to make for the wet deck, one of the three attacking makos had his attention caught by Alex's presence. Like lightning, the mako turned and blazed full speed into Alex, forcing him against the bottom of the boat. The mako seemed surprised by the collision with the boat's hull, and for a split second it ceased its attack.

Alex did not hesitate. His knife was already drawn, and pulling with all of his energy, Alex pierced the shark's head just behind the left eye and twisted viciously as the knife flew through the mako flesh, under the neck, past the shark's right eye, and met up with the original stab wound. The mako was stunned and its body fell away, tail still churning in the water as the head slowly followed. The remaining two sharks made chase—one on each piece.

Just before collapsing on their boat's deck, the McPhersons had seen the water surrounding the boat. Remnants of fresh chum were still peppered all around their location, but there was no sign of another boat.

With a tone of pride in his voice, Alex said in a near whisper, "Good work down there; both of you. You held your cool, and you held your own."

"Dad, we'd have been dead if it wasn't for you being, you know, weird."

"Well put, bud. Thanks, I think."

"This was deliberate," Angela concluded. "Let's go home to Cayman. I don't want to be here anymore."

"Not yet," replied Alex. There was a somber, almost murderous, timbre to his voice. "We still have a dinner to attend this evening. I want to see who views us as surprise guests."

CHAPTER 4

The dining room decor at the St. Julian's Hilton was of the same style they had grown accustomed to at their resort at the Corinthia Beach. But the Hilton was more opulent and pretentious. Tonight's dinner-dance was sponsored by the St. Julian's Chamber of Commerce as a kick-off event for Malta's Carnival. After showering and just sitting by the pool for the afternoon, the McPhersons held to their plan to attend this five-star, invitation-only event.

"Not hungry, Tony, or is there something wrong with the sea bass?"

"I tell ya, Mom, when you almost become seafood yourself, it kind of takes away your appetite."

"Well, your father doesn't seem to have lost his desire for fish."

"I worked up an appetite this afternoon. Maybe we should have ordered shark steaks."

"Now, that would have been fair." Tony's comment trailed off, and the three of them went silent again as the dinner music whispered Beethoven's Ninth.

Tony regained his appetite when dessert was served. "Strawberry shortcake has nothing to do with seafood," could barely be understood as he wolfed down the last bite of cake and whipped cream.

"Mom, I see a girl I met the other day. Mind if I go dance?"

"Go ahead, but stay in sight. This has been a precarious day." Angela turned her head slightly sideways toward Alex, "Don't worry, dear, I won't ask you to dance tonight. Fact is I'm too tired to kick up my feet."

Alex seemed to be a mile away as Angela made her comment. His reply proved he was off somewhere else. "Right, perfect. Dear, would you like to dance?"

He stood and offered his hand but was still looking across the dance floor away from Angela altogether.

Quietly surprised and a bit confused, Angela answered Alex's invitation. "I'd love to, I guess."

They danced gracefully, yet they were moving across the floor with more determination than Angela had remembered Alex leading with the night before.

"Are we going someplace, or are we dancing?"

"Hang on, babe. I think there's someone we need to meet."

Angela looked around and saw the young lady, Brigitte, who had begun to discuss the sale of boats with them before she'd been called away. Now she was dancing with an older man, an attractive man in what appeared to be a very expensive silk suit. She found it interesting that the personal space this dancing couple was being given by the others on the dance floor was unusually expansive.

"She's just seen us," Angela whispered to Alex as they had made their way within fifteen feet of the pair. "She looked directly into my eyes and then darted her head away and down as if I had cursed her." Angela thought for a moment and then looked directly at Alex. "Do you think she—?"

"Yes, I do. I think she works for the Skipper, and I think she told him of our dive plans for this afternoon. I think she's now dancing with the lead shark."

Angela now began to lead, and she moved them even closer to Brigitte and the man who might possibly be the infamous Skipper.

"Slow down, Angela. Keep it cool."

"But they're evil!"

"He might be evil. She's just a minion."

Brigitte had whispered something to the man she was dancing with just after the eye contact with Angela. Their dance pace or pattern did not change in the slightest. When Alex and Angela came within five feet of the pair, the song ended. The two couples politely applauded the live band that had replaced the prerecorded classical dinner music.

The man turned to Alex, saying, "Mr. McFearson. What a surprise to see you here. I had heard that you had left our little island."

Alex looked into eyes that were as empty and dead black as the eyes of the killer makos he'd fought with earlier in the afternoon. Maintaining a controlled half smile, Alex replied, "The name is pronounced McPherson. There's no fear in a McPherson."

The man's smile was wide. "I see what you mean. Let me introduce myself. My name is Helio Peregrine. My friends around the world call me 'the Skipper.'"

Angela responded with her best diva voice, "Of which I'm sure you have many."

Peregrine smiled at Angela and began to reply as a new slow-dance number began. He turned to Alex. "Do you mind if I share this dance with your lovely wife?"

Alex did not hesitate. "As a matter of fact, I do mind."

A quiet affront moved across the Skipper's face. "I must take your refusal as an insult." He paused. "But as a visitor to our little island, I will give you the chance to reconsider."

Again, Alex didn't hesitate. "Allowing you to dance with my wife would at the very least make me a fool."

"Maybe sometime in the future, when you better understand who it is you are refusing."

Alex slowly shook his head, moved his face within inches of Peregrine's face, and growled, "What part of *no* are you having trouble understanding? Now, back off, while you still can."

Without a ripple in his demeanor, Peregrine replied, "Until our next meeting, then." The Skipper backed away from Alex, leaving the dance floor and the Hilton.

It wasn't until that moment that Alex noticed that the attention of the room had been centered on the whispered exchange. Tony had noticed the reaction of the locals and had positioned himself behind Peregrine, only a heartbeat from his parents.

A waiter they had spoken with earlier came over to them and whispered, "Don't you know who that is? He's the Skipper. What he asks, people do. What he wants, he gets."

Alex looked kindly into the waiter's eyes and calmly and politely replied, "Not this time, my friend. Not this time."

CHAPTER 5

"**D**ad, there's an e-mail for you from Admiral Sterling." Tony noticed the inbox on the screen was showing the sender's name only.

"Your dad's outside trying to keep tabs on Sophie. She's running the full circle of the cay again." Angela walked into the office with her arms filled with folded linens.

"I wonder what she'll bring back to Dad this time. Last week that golden brought him a piece of driftwood twice her size. She looked pretty dumb hobbling up to Dad with that wood sticking so far out of each side of her mouth."

Setting the linens on the side table, Angela opened the e-mail and found a note with a set of coordinates. Reading the note, she became very solemn. "You'd better get your father. This is serious." Tony quickly left the room, and Angela moved over to the world map they had on the back wall of the office to check to coordinates. "Arctic Sea. Wow."

"What is it?" Alex bolted up the stairs to the second-level office. Tony had apparently delivered his Mom's sense of urgency with the message.

"A message from Sterling; there's a Russian sub in the Arctic Sea that has run into trouble. His note says that it has gone down with all hands with no contact for over twenty hours."

Alex began staring at the wall map as Angela placed the stickpin on the spot of the coordinates. "The Russians asking for help?"

"No. Sterling says he's offered four times, and they keep saying they have it under control, but the satellite photos show no activity at the site—none."

Silent for a brief moment, the two sat in the opposing office side chairs with their eyes locked on one another. "Let me guess. Sterling wants us to go as independents."

"That's right. He knows his hands are tied, but you know Sterling. He can't sit by and let those submariners die over political hogwash."

Alex whispered, "Good man."

The two sat for another moment staring at the map before Alex spoke up. "We'll need a cutter with a decompression chamber and salvage capability. It'd take us weeks to get the *Tessa* up there and through the ice. That sub has hours, maybe days, but not weeks."

Alex continued, "You get Sterling on the phone and make the arrangements for the boat. I'll call Rene and have him gas up his plane. He can get the three of us to Anchorage. Have Sterling plan to pick us up in Anchorage."

"The three of us?" Tony had just made it back in after placing Sophie in the large, fenced-in side yard with Dobie, their older golden retriever. "I can go?"

"You were a lot of help in Malta. I'd say we could use some extra help on this one."

"Cool. What'll I need to pack?"

Two hours later, Alex, Angela, and Tony were in the air. Connections in Anchorage were being arranged by Sterling, and the Coast Guard cutter *Expedition* was moving to the location. It was only five miles away from the site, having been unofficially, yet intentionally, en route since the night before.

"I'll need to dive on the sub and take a look. Did Sterling know anything else?"

"He said reports were sketchy. Someone on a nearby surveillance trawler detected what could have been an explosion around eight last night, but they couldn't be sure."

"Explosion? Any US boats in the area?"

Angela snickered, "You mean other than the CIA-manned trawler? None. There are two surface ships carrying salvage materials and a sub on its way, but they have to keep their distance, since the US has not been asked to help."

Tony spoke up for the first time since their departure from Grand Cayman. "That's bull! The politicians are going to kill that crew."

"We hope you're wrong," replied Angela. "That's why the three of us are heading north to help the crew."

The flight to Anchorage required a fuel stop in Ardmore, Oklahoma.

"Now, tell me again why we're stopping in Ardmore at this little municipal airport rather than Tulsa International?"

"Alex," began Rene, "When you have a chance to have one of the Ardmore Airport cafe's cheeseburgers, you take that opportunity. They're good and they're quick. Pilots fly for hundreds of miles to eat here. It's one of the most famous two hundred-dollar hamburger joints in the Western US. We'll be done eating just as the refueling is finished."

Alex twisted his face. "Two hundred-dollar hamburger joints?"

Rene continued, "Right. Amateur pilots want a reason to go flying, so they tell themselves they're going to Ardmore for the cheeseburgers. It may cost them a couple hundred bucks in fuel for the day's flight. So, it's a two hundred-dollar cheeseburger."

Rene was right. The cheeseburger was simply amazing. It was a single half-pound burger topped with sliced fresh mushrooms and a circle of sliced Vandalia onion, covered with fully melted mozzarella cheese and resting open faced on an oversized bun. The lazy Susan in the middle of the table was filled with all types of toppings, from mustard to real warmed bacon bits. On a separate plate was a generous portion of fries that were waffle-cut thick and cooked in an English chips style.

It was obvious that Rene had been there before. As they finished their meals—as much of their meals as they could finish—the mechanic came in with the news that the twin engine *Bonanza* was refueled and ready to go.

*****

Bundled in their Thinsulate ski jackets, Alex, Angela, and Tony braced against the Alaskan wind as they walked the short distance from Rene's plane to the awaiting Chevy Avalanche.

A sailor, walking up to Alex, Tony and Angela, addresses them, "Admiral Sterling sent me to bring you to his location at Elmendorf Air Force Base in King Salmon. Can I get you anything before we head that way?"

Angela replied, "I'd like to freshen up. How far are we from the base?"

The sailor responded, "Only fifteen minutes, ma'am."

"I can wait." Angela looked to Alex and Tony. They nodded. "Take us to the base, sailor."

"Yes, ma'am." With that, the sailor maneuvered the four-wheel-drive vehicle out of the airport and down the two-lane coastal highway.

A short drive later, they were in King Salmon, Alaska. Elmendorf AFB is the largest airbase in Alaska. The sailor drove the Avalanche to the back of what appeared to be the main administrative building. As the Avalanche came to a stop, two soldiers came from the building and opened the doors for the McPhersons.

"Admiral Sterling is waiting for you inside. We will transfer your bags to the helicopter. Is there anything you require from us at this time?"

Angela spoke up, "I think we'd like to freshen up before meeting with the Admiral. Could you direct us?"

"Of course, ma'am. If you'll follow me."

Ten minutes later, they were in an office with Admiral Sterling, his aide, and two other officers that neither Alex nor Angela had met before.

"It's a rough one. We know that sub's in trouble, and we can't get their government to open the gate and let us help."

Alex spoke up. "Any change in information?"

"Nothing from their side. We have moved our ships into close proximity. A Canadian cutter has already plowed the way for our rescue ship, but we've not moved her into position yet. The cutter is equipped with state-of-the-art sonar and has been monitoring the position of the

Russian sub. She's picked up muffled sounds. Some voices; some minor creaks, and metal-shifting groans, but nothing definitive. That crew's only chance rests with your group."

"Well do what we can." Angela continued, "Tony and I need to get to the rescue ship ASAP. I'll, excuse me, *we'll* need to assess what they have available in case we need to improvise." Then Angela turned her attention to Alex. "And you'll …?"

"I'll need to be dropped off just above the site."

Alex's comments drew strange looks from the two officers. Sterling raised his hand before they could make a comment. "Get Mr. McPherson to the site now—no questions, just get him there."

"Yes, sir. I have two HH-60G Helos fueled and standing by at Eielson."

"Well, that's it. We should get our butts moving." The admiral stood and started walking toward the office door. "We'll all fly to Eielson together. From there, Alex will go to the site and the rest of us will fly on to Shemya and deploy from there."

The big Hueys were loud, but they were quick and dependable in this climate. They had been chosen especially for service in this environment and had been used for years in numerous rescues in the Alaskan interior. To get to Eielson Air Force Base, they needed to cross the interior. The HH-60G was the best at this trip, the very best.

"Admiral?"

"Yes, Alex?"

"I understood that Shemya Air Force Base closed down a number of years ago. It's still active?"

"As with anything we've worked on, all that I share is Top Secret. Shemya was restructured under NORAD. There are no surface operations on that hunk of rock anymore. But we have constructed an Arctic NORAD base underground at that location. It's location on the edge of the Bering Sea has proven critical on more than one occasion— too critical to close down operations and too critical to allow normal surface operations to be visible from orbiting satellites."

"Sir, we'll land at Eielson in ten minutes."

"Thank you, airman." The admiral thought for a moment, "Have the captain set us down next to the two waiting Hueys."

"Yes, sir. I'll inform the captain immediately."

"We'll set down there, Alex. I suspect you'll want to get to it without delay. Do you need anything, or can you just change rides and go?"

"I'm prepared. Is there ice they can set me on? It might make it easier to explain."

"That's the plan. They hover at about five feet and let you deploy. They leave the area for you to—well, for you to do your thing."

"Interesting choice of words, Admiral," quipped Angela. Directing her attention back to Alex, she said, "I want to hear from you when you set down, before you dive, and intermittently during the dive. This water is cold and I—"

"Angela," Alex interrupted her, "I won't—"

Now Angela was interrupting Alex. "I don't care what you think you can do. I need to—"

Tony spoke up and directed his comments to the admiral. "You see what I have to put up with. And these are my role models? I don't have a chance—I'm doomed."

Tony and the admiral smiled widely at each other.

"We're beginning our approach at Eielson, sir."

"Thank you, airman. Well, team, let's do some good today."

CHAPTER 6

The blades on the Huey 60 were whirling at a fast idle, awaiting Alex's boarding. Moments after he was in, the large helo lifted from the tarmac and set off toward the frigid Arctic Sea. Even with the doors closed, the supercharged helicopter was loud. Each of the chopper's human cargo were wearing headphones to muffle out some of the motor noise and enable them to communicate with each other.

"We have an e.t.a. to the coordinates of forty-five minutes. It's a straight flight, sir. We'll make good time."

"Thank you, Lieutenant. You wouldn't happen to have any music we could listen to during the flight, would you?"

The lieutenant turned his head back from his pilot's seat and smiled at Alex. "That's not within regulations, sir." He paused. "But I do have an ancient CD I confiscated from Airman Shepherd there." The Airman to the right of Alex smiled. "I suppose since we have it here, we should review it to assure it doesn't contain anything contrary to the public good."

With that, each passenger's headphones were filled with the opening notes from Led Zeppelin's "Misty Mountain Hop." The next forty-five minutes rocked the Huey as the Zeppelin Greatest Hits CD unfolded its driving beat.

The last song trailed off, and the lieutenant spoke. "Sir, we have reached the coordinates. It appears the ice is in worse shape than we had reported to us in our briefing. We're not going to be able to set down anywhere near the coordinates."

"Just get about five feet from the ice, and I'll deploy from there."

"Sorry, sir, we're not going to be able to do that either. There's a crosswind over the ice that has created an updraft with a floor of thirty feet. We may need to abort your deployment."

"Not possible, Lieutenant." Alex thought for a moment, and then he continued. "Forget reason for a moment Lieutenant. Look to your right, about thirty yards. Do you see that large opening in the ice floe?"

"Yes, sir, I see the opening."

"Lieutenant, I want you to hover above that opening. I'll deploy to that point."

"But, sir, I still can only get to thirty feet."

"I understand that, Lieutenant. That'll do."

Looks were exchanged throughout the Huey, with all eyes resolving on the lieutenant. "Forget reason, you say, sir?"

"Yes, Lieutenant, forget reason. I will offer no explanation, but I can assure you with the utmost confidence that you will be performing your assignment within acceptable parameters and expectations of Admiral Sterling."

The lieutenant hesitated only for a moment. He looked into Alex's eyes and a split second later made the adjustment in the Huey's position, locating it directly above the large opening. "What else do you need from me, sir?"

"Just keep praying for the men on that sub."

"Yes, sir; that I will." The lieutenant stuck out his hand to shake Alex's hand. "You take care, sir. Deploy at will."

"Thank you, Lieutenant. Now is as good as it gets."

The Huey door was opened, and Alex positioned himself in its doorway, with his fins held firmly in his left hand. Thirty feet would not be a problem for Alex, but if he slammed into the ice—well, pain is pain, no matter who you are.

Pushing off while gripping his mask in his right hand and his fins in his left, Alex went through the door like a skydiver. He then immediately adjusted his body position to hit the water feet first, with his legs pulled tightly together. Not using a giant-step form would cause him to go further below the surface, but keeping his legs together would lessen the impact on his stomach and groin areas.

In only a second and a half, Alex had pierced the chilly surface and plummeted twenty feet below the surface. Quickly stroking, he returned to the icy surface. Deployment had gone as planned. No problem.

Lifting his arm toward the Huey that still hovered over the thirty-foot opening in the arctic ice floe, Alex gave a two-handed, double okay sign. The lieutenant dipped the Huey's nose slightly as a return signal and pulled the hovering bird off to the right to return to Eielson.

With the Huey out of sight, Alex donned his mask and unzipped one of the cargo pockets in his Arctic dry suit, just beneath his dive vest, and retrieved his e-reg. Alex had chosen this particular dry suit based on a few factors. First, it was light and flexible and clung close to his body. This provided the freedom of movement Alex would need. Next, there were several D-rings on the chest, arms, and legs of the suit to attach other gear or accessories. The Arctic dry suit also possessed a thin inner layer of finely woven alpaca fur, known for its warming properties. The fur was so tightly woven that it was calculated to lose only 5 percent of the human body's generated heat, making it the warmest dry suit on the market.

It was a custom-made suit that Angela had given him on his last birthday. The fact that it was arctic blue in color was a plus, seeing how deep blue had always been Alex's favorite color. Angela's goal with this gift was a simple one. Neither she nor Alex had any experience with his newly acquired diving abilities and the extreme cold, especially for any extended period of time. The simple truth was that Angela didn't want her husband getting cold.

Placing the e-reg firmly in his mouth and reaching down to put on his US Divers fins, he knew he was ready to dive. It was time to attempt to contact Angela.

Concentrating, Alex placed his thoughts on his wife. *Angela, can you hear me?*

Alex! You're late. What went wrong?

Nothing went wrong. The weather conditions caused a need to alter my entry into the water.

Do I want to know what you mean by that?

Maybe later, but for now it's safe to say that I'm in the water and ready to begin my first dive on the sub. I'll contact you when I find her or in thirty minutes, whichever comes first.

Understood. Be careful, Alex. She paused for a moment. *I just hate it when you're out there alone.*

I'll stay out of trouble, dear.

You'd better, mister, or you'll get yourself into trouble with me.

I just love your kind of trouble. Thirty minutes or less.

Alex checked the time on his dive watch, twisting the bezel to the current position of the minute hand, and then he started headfirst for the last known position of the sub.

The first hundred feet had floating pieces of ice drifting through the water, like solidified clouds through a deep-blue sky. The light was almost gone, but Alex's eyes had adjusted. To him, it still seemed like bright daylight, but he knew at his current depth of two hundred feet, the sea was now black.

The ice was thick in this area of the sea. At three hundred and fifteen feet, the ice became a ceiling to dive under rather than a wall to swim beside. The sub should be very near this depth. The sea could be very deep in this area, but it was thought that the Russian sub was resting in relatively shallow water of about four hundred feet.

Alex checked his compass to make a correction to his course now that he was below the ice floe. Reaching four hundred and twenty-five feet below the Arctic surface, Alex could make out the faint outline of the still-distant nuclear submarine.

Twenty minutes into his dive, he concentrated his thoughts again on Angela. *Angela, am I reaching you?*

You're early. All is well?

Yeah, all is well. I've found the boat. All of a sudden, I feel very somber just looking at her sitting there.

How close are you?

I'm still about fifty yards away. I have her in full view from this point. She's resting on the bottom. I don't see any ice immediately above her. Unsure what the thickness of ice is at the surface here. I guess we'll find that out later.

Alex calmed his thoughts for a moment as he came closer to the N1. He reviewed the briefing about the boat in his mind as he came to a buoyant stop just to the side of her bridge. The N1 was one of the latest series of Russian submarines. It was designed in a post-Cold War climate and thus included fewer weapons and a greater number of surveillance devices.

The N1 was smaller and sleeker than her earlier Russian cousins. Her hull resembled the US LA class in size and shape, except for her bridge. It was almost nonexistent.

The topside of the N1 was smooth fore and aft, with only the slightest bubble one-fourth of the way back from her forward torpedo doors. And a bubble is exactly what it resembled. Raised approximately four feet from her hull, with an elongated shape measuring a width of ten feet and length of twenty, this perfectly smooth, clear-view port would serve her captain well as an observation port either above or below the surface. It also provided less drag, which allowed the N1 to be the quickest fish in the sea.

But not this N1. She was belly-down on the ocean floor.

Alex started at the front and did a slow kick survey of the lower right half of the N1. Seeing no damage to her smooth metal hull along her lower right side, Alex began a slow kick from back to front of her lower left side. He noted no damage during his five-minute examination of her hull.

Now back at the front of the boat, Alex started upward over her nose to assess her top deck. Her rounded nose was smooth and without flaw. Alex kicked his way to the front of her bridge level view port. Cautiously peering into the front edge, not wanting to be seen by the Russian submariners, Alex discovered another detail about the N1 not mentioned in the briefing. Her clear bridge-level view port had a pressure door separating that viewing area from what was certainly the internal bridge area. This door was sealed, and the view port area was not occupied.

Alex examined it thoroughly, expecting to find a flaw in its design as the culprit. The area within appeared to be dry, and the clear port structure was intact.

Gracefully kicking his way further along the topside of the N1, Alex came upon the main hatch positioned in the center of the top deck. At first it appeared intact, but as Alex looked closer, he found something very strange about this main hatch.

It appeared to be welded shut.

Resting buoyantly above the main hatch of the N1, Alex pondered the sight. The weld was clean and effective. There was no way that hatch had been planned for use. Shaking his head slowly back and forth, Alex continued his assessment of the topside of the N1.

As he neared the rear section, just above the power plant but still in front of the rear torpedo section, the rear escape trunk came into view.

Wow! Alex stopped all movement to fully take in the site. *What happened here?*

Angela, can you hear me?

Yes, Alex. Go ahead.

I believe I've found part of the problem. I'm positioned just above the rear escape trunk area of the N1. There appears to have been an internal explosion. The escape trunk hatch is open, hanging by a single hinge, and twisted so badly that it looks nearly folded in half. The top deck plating surrounding the escape trunk is bubbled outward but intact.

It sounds like an explosion in either her torpedo room or in the power plant.

I've got to tell you, Angela, with the condition of that hatch and the surrounding bulkhead, it must have been a whale of an explosion. Hold on for a minute, Angela. I want to take a look down into the escape trunk tunnel.

With that, Alex cautiously moved across the top deck surface, approaching the trunk tunnel. Sticking his head over the edge and into the tunnel, he saw more damage.

Angela, the tunnel is shattered above the lower entry hatch. That hatch seems to be intact; at least it's in place. There's a hole from the rear side of the tunnel piercing the front side of the tunnel.

Do you think a torpedo shot through there? How is that possible? Hold on a minute, Alex.

While Alex hovered over the damaged N1, Angel was having a conversation with Admiral Sterling back at the Shemya NORAD base.

From what Alex has described to you, Angela, it sounds like one of their newest torpedo designs went foul. It's a sea-based torpedo with a new propulsion unit that resembles an ICBM propulsion system. If the thing had a better wing system, it could fly.

That's what happened, Admiral, isn't it? Their new rocket torpedo design got out of control somehow and ripped through sections of that N1.

That's a solid theory. You said that Alex described the surrounding bulkhead as bubbled outward but still intact?

That's what he conveyed.

Then it was not armed. It must have been a drone gone bad. They're supposed to have been working on a new directional deployment system as well. A way to fire above or below the sub's position. It would require a rotating tube system for the torpedo, to provide for either above or below targeting.

Well, Admiral, what should I tell Alex about this?

You, of course, can share all you want later, but for now, to conserve time, just tell him that the damage sounds consistent with new torpedo designs the Russians were thought to be working with.

Angela shared some of the details with Alex and asked that he continue his assessment.

Okay, but ask the admiral if he has any idea why the N1 would have welded her main hatch shut from the outside.

What the———?

Uh, Alex, I think it's safe to say that the admiral has no clue at this time.

CHAPTER 7

ngela and Tony were now aboard the Canadian ice cutter *Blade*. The *Blade* was the newest cutter of the Canadian fleet, and she sparkled as the morning sun turned the surrounding area into a field of floating ice-diamonds. The *Blade* was not only equipped as a cutter, but she had also been put to sea to assist with the Alaskan pipeline. Many a time she would be the first responder to a new leak in the line and successfully make repairs before loss of oil and the disruption of ecological balance became measurable.

The ship's ready room, just off the bridge, was made available to Angela and Tony. They reviewed current charts of ice floe while they awaited Alex's next contact.

"Yes, ma'am. That's correct. There are fifteen small to moderate icebergs in the area at this time."

"But none caught in the currents and heading this way?"

"Correct. They're either somewhat stationary or they're moving away from our position."

"Thank you, Ensign. Could you point me to some more coffee?"

"I'll get that for you, ma'am. No problem."

"Thank you, Ensign."

With that, the ensign walked slowly out of the ready room.

Go ahead, my love. We're alone now.

It's a mess down here Angela. The rear of the sub is porous, and the only other hatch is welded shut.

We'll have to cut the hatch open to get them out of there.

It'll take a while. They put a thick bead on that hatch. I think they did it in a hurry—a last-minute thing or something. Alex paused. *Is there a submersible with the cutter?*

No. She's a good, well-equipped ship, but no deep-sea unit.

I'll need a dry room built around the hatch. When I cut through, if it's still wet, she'll flood in a heartbeat. Alex paused. *Tony, how you holding up?*

No prob, Dad. Just anxious to get at it, but we don't know what it *is yet.*

That's all too true. She's too damaged to raise. Besides, we don't have anything big enough to raise her. Well, first things first. What do they have that we can use to construct a dry room? I need to get at that hatch.

Angela replied, *I believe that we're in luck there. The* Blade *provides emergency service to the oil pipeline, so she has a supply of man-sized tube. The pipeline has a diameter of four feet. It's high-volume pipe. We can drop a section to you that's been sealed shut on one end up here. We'll attach a transfer pump to the section, so you can pump her dry after you weld her to the N1. Voila! You then have a dry welding area.*

Good plan. When can they be ready?

About half an hour from the point we order the job. They truly are well equipped on board.

Dad.

What's up, Tony?

What if we connect the pipeline to the sub and run a tube all the way up to the Blade? *We could bring the crew of the N1 up through the tube.*

Nice idea, Tony, but the pressure the sub is under right now would cause the sub to implode the moment we connect a tube from the surface to the opened hatch.

Angela whispered, "Unless we control the pressure."

What, Angela? I couldn't make out your thoughts. Alex realized he was feeling a bit cold, and he shivered slightly. He hadn't experienced that feeling to this degree since his changes. He had been in the Arctic Sea for about an hour now. He shrugged it off, thinking to himself, *I suppose it's only natural.*

Alex now heard in his thoughts Tony asking Angela, *How, Mom?*

It could work. Angela stood and started pacing methodically around the ready room. *We could attach the topside end of the tube to the ship's decompression chamber, weld the depth-side end of the tube to the N1, and then adjust the pressure in the tube to that of the sub.*

Angela turned to her son and said, "Good work, Tony; good work."

Angela and Tony went to work organizing the needed supplies and assorted materials. Within an hour, the ship's crew had amassed all the supplies topside. With over a mile of replacement pipeline on board, there was no shortage of tube. After just over an hour diving on the sub's site, Alex had returned to the surface, where Angela and he agreed that he would be of greatest service on board the *Blade* as another hand helping with the welding.

Angela had the captain quietly order a cargo net to be thrown over the port side of the *Blade* while at the same time shifting the assignments so the port side was evacuated for a few minutes. This would allow Alex time to surface and climb the net unnoticed.

The next three hours were as hectic as it could get on board ship. Both sides of the *Blade*'s main deck became work areas for tube welding. The sections were in twenty-foot lengths. Each connection was made first in the same manner as it would be for pipeline use. Beyond that, each joint was then large-bead welded around the outer seam of the joint.

Their plan was to construct sections of tube consisting of three sections of pipe—sixty feet in length each. They would need eight of these welded sections to reach the *N1* at her depth of 480 feet below the *Blade*. When finished, they would have four sections along each side of the main deck ready to be lowered into place.

Angela was working with the ship's chief engineer on adapting the decompression chamber. One section of the pipeline was already connected and welded around the main hatch; it went from the chamber and out over the edge of the *Blade*, with a ninety-degree angle elbow aiming downward toward the sea. The hatch had a diameter of three feet and fit well within the circumference of the pipeline. The decom chamber had a second hatch, much like a door, on the backside of the chamber. As the chief engineer and Angela worked on the tube, they discussed other details of the plan as well.

"The chamber is designed to hold twenty at a time. She'll hold a few more for our purposes." The chief went on, "We'll bring 'em up and into the chamber, close the hatch, do a quick decom—as quick as we can, and let that group out the back door of the chamber. When they're out, we'll repressurize the chamber, open the hatch, and start over." The chief paused and then asked Angela, "How many you think are still alive?"

"It's hard to know, Chief. The rear end of that boat is destroyed. Hopefully most of the crew members were mid-boat to forward. I would imagine we're looking at forty to fifty of her crew that could still be alive."

"That'd mean two or three cycles of our plan." The chief looked concerned.

"What's wrong, Chief?"

"We'll need to hurry. These welds are good, but the sea is unforgiving. She'll certainly move on us and break those welds—we just don't know when."

"That raises another problem, Chief. We need to bolt an electric winch inside the chamber to pull the sub's crew topside through the tube. That's forty-eight stories. Ladders won't be fast enough—even if we had that many—and we have no idea of the condition of the *NI*'s crew."

"Sailor!" cried out the chief. "Take four men with you and go to D hold, and bring that Cummins winch to the front door of the chamber—and don't let me see you walking, either!"

They heard, "Yes, Chief!" followed by the sound of a sailor running to the cargo lift to head below decks.

"That winch has an adjustable speed control and a lift capacity of four thousand pounds. Once she's up here, I'll have it installed in under thirty minutes. She'll do the trick, ma'am."

"Good work, Chief."

"Ma'am, I have a question that I have hesitated to ask."

"What's that, Chief?"

"After we have this constructed, how is it going to be aligned with the hatch of the *N1*, and who is going to align it?"

"Chief, I can't answer that. I know the answer, and we do have that part under control; I just can't share those details."

"Ma'am, I'm career military. You say we have it covered; I don't need to know. I just want to make sure it's covered."

"It is, Chief. But thank you for your concern. If we weren't able to connect to the *N1*, all of this effort would be worthless."

"Yes, ma'am."

Angela left the chief and took the long way around, surveying both decks, before finding Alex and Tony. As she approached, she saw Alex on the left side of the pipe and Tony on the right side, both with welding masks down and laying large beads on the outside of what appeared to be the last section. A large smile grew across Angela's face. As both a wife and a mother, she was proud.

With the first three sections completed, Alex placed his e-reg into his mouth and went into the water with a giant step. Wearing his distinctive Arctic Blue drysuit, and with his mask and fins already on, Alex took one end of the guide line and a tool kit, which included a six-inch eye hook and a portable handheld underwater welder. *Angela, I've arrived and am sitting on the* N1. *I will start welding the guiding eye hook to the sub's outer skin just to the right of the welded hatch.*

Alex started the torch and began the weld. Almost immediately, he felt more than heard a hammering from inside the sub. He shut off his torch, and the hammering became very clear. A repeating series of three hits—metal to metal—was clearly coming from within the sub. Alex forged an ear-to-ear grin on his face. He took a hammer from his own tool belt and rapidly hammered about twenty hits against the sub's hull. It was answered by the same rapid series.

Angela, I've made contact. They're alive! Alex heard Angela share with the chief on board the cutter, which was followed by a chorus of yelps and applause from its crew. Sailors are sailors; a man in the water takes precedence over all political points of view. *Good news, my love; good news. Now get back to work and finish that weld.*

Yes'm. Alex relit his torch and continued his task.

Thirty minutes into this dive, Alex let Angela know he'd finished the eye-hook weld. *I'm running the guide line through the eye hook. There. Now to bolt the cable's wraparound clamp and secure the guide cable end back to the cable—there, done. Tell the chief he can start lowering the first section down the guide line. Make sure the winch cable and its redundant are secured firmly to the sections. I don't want a few thousand pounds of tubing arriving too quickly down here. Once I have the first section welded to the hull of the N1, I'll release the lowering cables for the next sections.*

Alex saw the shadows of the six-story piping moving smoothly down the guide cable. When it was about one hundred yards away, it obviously began slowing. *Very good timing. You are about 250 feet from goal. I'll let you know when you get to about one hundred feet, and we can begin slowing down to a crawl.*

Roger that, Angela replied. She was wearing a wireless headset with only a right-side ear speaker, to give the illusion to the crew around her that she was in communication with Alex in some normal, yet secure, manner. "Chief, prepare to slow the descent to two feet per second." Angela held a stopwatch, concentrating on the clicking second hand. "Ready, ready—now, Chief—two feet per second."

"Yes, ma'am. Crewman!"

"Two feet per second, Chief. Roger that."

Looking good from here, Angela. The lower end is about fifty feet away now.

Roger that, Alex. "Chief, prepare to slow to one foot per second on my mark." Still gazing at her stop watch she directed, "Now, Chief."

"Crewman," gently spoke the chief.

"Roger that, Chief; slowed to one foot per second."

"Chief, prepare to stop on my mark. We'll get close, and then we'll nudge it in."

"Yes, ma'am. Crewman."

"Ready, Chief."

Angela, the end is within ten feet of the hull.

Roger that, Alex. "Chief, now."

"Crewman."

"All stop, Chief."

Alex watched as the enormous tube gradually came to a dead stop only two feet from the hull. *Nice driving. Two feet from the hull.*

"Chief."

"Ma'am?"

"Give me precisely two feet of further progression."

"Crewman, you heard the lady."

"Yes, Chief. Two feet of progression it is." And with that, the crewman almost imperceptibly moved his hand on the control joystick. At the moment Angela heard the crewman confirm the two feet progression, she also heard Alex confirm, *We have hard contact. I'll start the weld. Hold on for confirmation of hard connection.*

It was a full thirty minutes later when Alex confirmed, *Hard connection made. Looks like a solid weld, best we can do. Ready to release both winch cables. Done. You can have the chief pull up the winch cables and send me another piece.*

Roger that, Alex.

Alex had been on this dive for nearly five hours. During this time Alex had connected the guiding eye hook to the hull of the *N1* and welded the 480 feet of escape tubing into one continuous piece. During this endeavor, Alex noticed he was visibly shaking from the cold. But he pushed on, never mentioning it to Angela.

"Never in my career have I been a part of this type of construction," exhaled the chief. "I'm making mental notes, ma'am."

"That's good, Chief. I'll need you to explain why this seems to be working when they are all safe topside, just not now."

"Yes, ma'am."

"All right, Chief, you and I need to pump the tube dry while watching the numbers for the decompression chamber attached topside, and keep an eye on the balance between the two. It's make it or break it time, Chief—literally."

"Yes, ma'am. Crewman, I'll take this. Let me relieve you of your chair for a while."

"Yes, Chief."

The chief of the boat sat at the control panel. He began slowly adjusting the pump pressure with his left hand, bumping a small joystick, while holding his right hand on the calibrating dial. He readied himself to adjust the pressure in the decom chamber, to balance the increasing pressure from outside of the newly constructed escape tube to the decreasing pressure created by the escaping water from within.

It was a slow process, but in an hour the five-hundred-foot tube was dry, empty of seawater, and ready for use.

"Not in my entire lifetime ma'am; not in my entire lifetime."

"Roger that, Chief," Angela replied. In her mind she spoke with Alex. *Time to surface. Take a look at the construction on your way up for any obvious flaws.*

On my way. It seemed to Alex that his thoughts were emitting an almost quivering voice.

Alex, are you all right?

I'm fine. Be topside in a few minutes. How about a nice, quick cup of coffee when I get there?

I'll have it ready and waiting, sailor. Chief, can you have someone get a thermos of coffee ready for Alex? He likes it sweet and creamy.

The chief stood to leave the control room. "I'll get it myself, ma'am. Sounds like he likes his coffee the way I do; I wouldn't trust it to anyone else."

Finding no obvious leaks, Alex came topside and was now working with the crew. He had the thermos of coffee in his hand and appeared to be savoring every gulp. The chief of the boat decided to stay at his post at the control panel, monitoring and adjusting the pressure inside the tube. Angela, Tony, and Alex helped ready the winch cable for the work inside the tube.

"It may take me a while to cut through that hatch weld. It looks solid. I'll take the winch cable down with me and let you know when I'm through."

"Looking forward to hearing that, dear. Borrowed time is an understatement we may have to face if we expect this tubular escape path to withstand the sea for very long."

"I get your message. I'll hurry." He handed the empty thermos to Angela and smiled.

Tony gripped the winch cable and began lowering Alex into the dry tube, carrying his torch and large ball pein hammer.

Alex finished the controlled lowering through the 480 feet of dry tubing and arrived to rest his feet on the welded hatch of the *N1*. He took the hammer, knelt on the hatch, rapped the hatch hard three times, and waited. What he heard as an almost immediate response sounded like music to his ears—three hammered sounds in reply. *Angela, I have signaled the sailors and received a return signal. They are at the hatch. I was hoping they would be ready.*

It didn't seem long before Alex announced, *I'm through.* This was followed by, *Hello to you as well, Captain. I am glad you speak English.* Alex explained to the captain that they had no time for discussion but needed to start the evacuation of the crew with haste. The captain agreed as he stared wide-eyed at the towering tube above the escape hatch.

The cable was lowered into the sub, allowing one crewman to take hold at the top and successive crewmen to each take hold just beneath the feet of the crewman above. By doing this, when the end of the winch cable reached topside, twenty crewmen would be brought to the surface.

The ship's doctor had calculated the minimum time each twenty crewmen would need to stay in the decom chamber before being evacuated from the chamber, thus allowing for the second bunch to surface. This was a down-and-dirty thirty minutes. Once the remaining crew of sixty was topside and each had gone through their initial thirty-minute quick decom, each group would successively rotate in thirty-minute intervals until reaching shore, where all sixty could go through a slower, complete decompression. "This should work," claimed the ship's doctor. "I pray it does."

It took an hour for this first group to cycle out and the winch cable to be fully lowered and ready for the second group. Two hours into the escape, and the third group was ready. The captain was the sixty-first person; he would need to wait. Alex waited with him, as he had during the other rounds.

Angela, the last group of crewmen is on the way up. The captain and I are the only ones remaining.

Understood; give us thirty minutes. How's the captain holding up?

He's tougher that I am. He's calm, and I'm getting anxious. I don't like the sounds this tube has been making down here.

Hang in there, dear. Thirty minutes for this group to quick-decom, and we'll start bringing you two up.

I'll follow the captain's example and try to be calmer than I feel.

Won't be much longer, my love.

Thirty minutes had passed when, true to her word, Angela gave the command for the winch cable to be lowered to Alex and the captain. *Here comes the cable, Alex.*

Great. I think it's going to be just in time. We've sprung a leak in one of the welds holding the tube to the hull. It's the tiniest dribble right now, but—

With that, Alex stopped communicating to Angela. He looked into the captain's eyes and for the first time saw fear. Alex grabbed the captain around the waist, pulled him close, and as the words "Hang On!" came screaming out of Alex's mouth, the weld broke, and the tube began to explode with frigid seawater from beneath, pluming like fast-motion photography, rushing over Alex and the captain.

Alex began kicking his feet with all of his might. He could withstand the pressure of the sea, but he knew the captain would surely die. *Angela!* Alex communicated in a mental scream. *Hurry—close the door of the chamber, or we'll destroy it!*

"Tony!" Angela yelled at her son who was inside the chamber, assisting the final crew members to vacate. "Slam the door—now!"

Without hesitation, Tony followed Angela's instruction and slammed the door shut, just as the first of the exploding water reached the surface point, made the turn toward the awaiting chamber, and pelted the outside of the chamber door as if hitting it with a sledgehammer. The door held, and the water subsided back to sea level.

Angela yelled again at Tony, "Tony! Open the door—now!" Again Tony followed the order without question. The door opened just as his father appeared and pulled the sub's captain from the water and into the awaiting chamber. Tony then slammed shut both doors to the chamber, hit the emergency engage button, and sat down next to the other two, very wet, very haggard looking occupants.

"Captain," spoke Alex with strained tones of exhaustion, "let me introduce you to my son, Tony."

The captain barely, but clearly, responded in English with, "Very honored to meet you, Tony." He then collapsed onto the waiting bench and appeared to lose consciousness.

CHAPTER 8

After a good night's sleep, the McPhersons walked from their private quarters to the military hospital, which also served the adjacent community. They wanted to check one last time with the Russian submariners before flying south.

They were standing in an area of the cafeteria where four makeshift rows of hospital beds were aligned, with narrow walking rows between them. The rows of white sheets and white thermal blankets reflecting the overhead fluorescent lighting created a crispness only matched by the snow-covered landscape seen through the many windows in three walls of the improvised recovery unit.

Alex was shaking the hand of the Russian boat's captain when his face visibly winced. "I beg your pardon," commented the Russian captain. "I did not mean to crush your hand so hard. I am just so thankful for your team's assistance in saving the lives of my crew."

"It's not you, Captain," Alex calmly replied. "Please excuse me, sir."

Alex moved quickly over to Angela. "Something's wrong in the hospital. I hear someone struggling for their life."

"I didn't hear—you heard them in your mind?"

"Yeah. I've got to track it down. Cover for me."

Alex moved quickly from the four-rowed area to the hallway to his left. Once in the hallway, he felt the silent scream in his mind once more. It was weaker now, but this time Alex could sense the direction of the cry.

He ran at full speed down the hall, turned right at the small nurse's station and left into the room across from the nurse's station, and bolted through the room door. What he found did not surprise him, given the intensity of the silent scream he'd heard.

One man was pressing a pillow down over the face of someone lying in a hospital bed with the head section of the bed slightly raised. There was a second man standing guard near the room's door.

With one fluid motion, Alex turned to his right and open-handedly swiped the guard across the face, sending him flying into the wall opposite the bed. He followed this with a two-step bolt toward the man still holding the pillow over the patient's face. Alex grabbed the second man by the back of his shoulders. The man growled, "You're makin' a big mistake, mister; you have no idea who you're messin' with. The Skipper will have his revenge."

"Is that right? Well not today." With that, Alex heaved him through the air into the first man, who was just beginning to get to his feet.

A nurse entered the room as the two men collided in a pile against the far wall. She only looked briefly at the fracas, and then turned all of her attention to the young woman in the bed, who was now coughing loudly.

When Angela and Tony arrived to the young woman's room, three armed MPs were escorting the two handcuffed men from the room and into the hallway past Alex.

The young woman yelled from her bed at the two men as they were leaving, "You tell your 'Skipper' those diamonds were never his! No matter how many people he kills, the diamonds are still sitting at the bottom of the Arctic Sea. I know it breaks your skipper's heart, but there they'll stay. They're as cold as all of his henchmen who went down with the diamonds."

"You don't get it, lady," blurted one of the handcuffed henchmen. "The Skipper has no heart; even if he did, it's a lot colder than those diamonds could ever be."

Then the second henchman spouted, "No matter what, lady, you're dead. And anybody else that gets in the Skipper's way is gonna be dead too." He looked at Alex and continued, "And that means you, too, tough guy."

Alex replied to the threat with just enough energy to form words, "This is twice your Skipper has wanted to dance; he's been denied both times. I've got a message for your skipper—bring it on!"

CHAPTER 9

H ome was always good. This return was especially good because they knew the sailors were safe. Relaxation came easily to Alex and Tony. They found themselves back in the water the very morning following their return from Alaska.

Angela, on the other hand, seemed preoccupied almost to the point of distraction. She was cordial but quiet. After two days back home, Alex approached her about it.

"What's on your mind?"

"I've been out of it, haven't I?"

"Well, you've missed the point behind several jokes."

"Maybe my mood has protected me, then."

"Whoa there, girl; don't start making me think you're not hanging onto my every word."

"Honestly though, I know I've been distracted. I just can't get Evie out of my mind and what she said."

"You mean about the diamonds?"

"Indirectly, but more to the point, what she said about the cold and the Skipper's henchmen."

"She's safe, Angela. The navy moved her the next day to an undisclosed hospital. She'll recoup and then get on with her life."

"Will she? With what she went through, how is she going to just move on?"

"I don't know. Some people can't. But I think Evie's a fighter. I can see her moving on without much trouble."

"I suppose you're right."

"I usually am."

"You're hard to believe, you know that?"

"I know. I'd be perfect if I didn't lack humility."

"You're so full of yourself, aren't you?"

"Well, I'm full of something."

"That's for sure."

Later in the day, Angela and Alex went into town, cutting across Governor's Bay. Alex drove the boat at a relaxing pace that had them taking about an hour to get across the bay. Angela took advantage of the smooth, relaxing ride by lounging on the bow in her coral-green, one-piece swimsuit. She rarely sunned herself anymore, but today it was for her psychological health and not to get rid of tan lines.

It worked. Both Alex and Angela were quite relaxed by the time they docked in Georgetown. Angela grabbed Alex's hand, "Let's walk to town."

"You got it."

It was a short walk to the restaurant section of town from the dock. Arriving at the Hog Sty Pub about a half hour after docking, Alex was the first to speak up. "How about a pint of cider?"

"You've missed that, haven't you?" She watched Alex nod quickly. "Well, you go ahead. A cool Mudslide sounds more to my speed this evening."

Alex looked to the proprietor and prepared to request the drinks when he noticed some commotion going on in the middle of the bar. A local had been drinking a bit too much and was having words with one of the visiting divers out with his friends for the evening. Alex delayed his order and began moving from the barstool on Angela's left side toward the stool on her right side.

Angela placed her hand on Alex's forearm, "Oh no, mister. Stay out of this one."

"No need for me to join in. Just getting between you and the action—in case it goes bad."

"What do you mean?"

"Do you see our talented proprietor now talking with the local who's had one too many? He has solid eye contact with the guy—he has him fully engaged. Now you see Steve over by the left wall, and Jack over by the right wall, both moving slowly? They have a plan in play. I just want to be between you and their plan in case it goes awry."

As Alex finished his explanation to Angela, Steve and Jack made their way slowly along the outside walls and were now quietly coming up behind the local. In one fluid movement, Steve and Jack moved in on the local, each scooping him under one arm, and swiftly carried him out through the front door. They carried him about ten feet from the door, released him, and stood there talking with him. After about five minutes, the local shook hands with Steve and Jack and headed away from the bar, watched only for a minute by the two peacemakers, who then returned to the bar and blending in with the crowd as they had before.

"You see, they had a plan, a good one. Ole Bob had too many tonight, so they took him outside, talked him down, and sent him home to his wife. They had it under control; they didn't need me tonight."

"Well then, it seems I have you all to myself for the rest of the night."

"Indeed you do, my lady."

It had been a week since their return, and Angela had settled. In fact, she was beginning to plan the small bird sanctuary she dreamed of attaching to the back of their home. The sanctuary would resemble a moderately sized greenhouse but would teem with perches and troughs. She already had five birds in different cages throughout the house, and she had no intention of buying any new ones. But she had her sights on at least three more from people on the island who had grown tired of caring for them. Angela was known for having a house full of rescues— Alex included.

With plans and drawings spread across the kitchen table, Angela was talking to herself about including areas in the enclosure for the birds to find privacy when they felt the need. Talking to no one in particular, she was carrying on an active conversation nonetheless. Tony walked by her during her talk, slowing down because he wasn't sure whether she was speaking to him or not. When he saw her go on without any reply, he remained silent and moved on. As he did, he caught the eye of his father, who was sitting in the kitchen breakfast area with the morning paper. They exchanged a wry grin, both slowly shaking their heads in silence.

"I saw that," spouted Angela. "Remember, there's out of it and there's *out of it*."

"With you we're never sure, Mom."

"You just remember that, mister. You need to also remember that, sometimes, being too much like your father is not a good thing."

Both Alex and Tony laughed out loud as Tony left the house for the beach and Alex returned to his paper.

It was later that afternoon when the call came through from the States.

"Mr. McPherson, my name is Samuel Alt. I represent the US Diver's research division. Your name was passed on to me as someone who may be able to help us find a few answers about a new regulator line we're working on."

"May I ask who it was that passed on my name?"

"Of course. It was Admiral Sterling out of Norfolk. My boss spoke with him about trying to find a private researcher who might be interested in helping us test a couple of new designs we're very excited about. Your name came up immediately. The admiral speaks very highly of you."

"Well, I'm sure he went too far with his compliments; he usually does."

"Mr. McPherson, before you say no, may I ask that you at least accept our invitation to come to our research center on Galveston and take a look at what we have? We'll have tickets waiting for you at the Grand Cayman airport within five minutes of your acceptance to at least come to our offices and hear what we have to say."

"How long were you wanting me to be there?"

"One day to hear what we have to say. Beyond that, it's up to you. We'll pay top dollar for the day and then be open to negotiation for your fee to participate with the rest of our research process."

"Well ..."

"Please say yes. It would mean so much to our plans to have you in Galveston as soon as tomorrow—if that's not rushing you too much?"

"Tomorrow's fine, but—"

"Excellent! I'll call the airport myself to arrange for your flight directly to Galveston. Thank you so much, Mr. McPherson. I look forward to meeting in the US Diver offices tomorrow. Safe passage then. Goodbye."

Angela came into the room just as Alex was finishing his call. "What's up?"

"It seems the admiral has been dropping my name to the research department at US Diver. One of their people, a Samuel Alt, just talked me into going to their offices in Galveston tomorrow to discuss my being a part of their final testing phase for a new line of regulators."

"Did you mention that you only use somebody else's regulators when it is absolutely necessary?"

"Very funny; but no, I didn't."

"So you said yes?"

"I think I did. You know sales people—they seem to talk you into something before you know it. What could it hurt? I'll fly up there tomorrow, hear what they have to say, and be back late in the evening. Even if their pitch is not something I want to be a part of, it'll only be a day."

Alex called the airport and discovered that Samuel Alt had indeed immediately called and had a ticket waiting for Alex on a flight leaving at 8:00 a.m.

The next day, about an hour after Alex's flight had left the Grand Cayman airport, Angela received a call from the dive shop. "Angela, this is Stacy. I just got a call from Mark. They left the shop early this morning to test the boat and the new depth finders. Well, it seems that the electrical system on the boat has gone out, and the engines won't fire. They're stuck just beyond Stingray City and asked if you could come out and give them a tow back to the island."

"Is Tony with Mark?"

"I believe he is. Yes, I remember Mark saying that Tony had been working on the system for the past hour but couldn't figure out what the problem was without the testing equipment he has here in the shop."

"Okay, Stacy, give them a call and let them know I'll head out from here. I'll be there within the hour."

"Thanks, Angela. I'll give them a call now."

It was a little after nine when Angela released the ropes and started up their boat. She knew there was no rush or emergency, so she didn't push the twin diesels. She cruised at about half speed, which would still put her at Mark and Tony's location in about thirty-five minutes.

Alex's flight was uneventful from Cayman to Galveston. It took the usual hour, with most of the short flight either ascending or descending. Upon his arrival, Alex got a cab and directed the driver to the US Diver's office complex in downtown Galveston. The cab pulled into the half-circle drive at the main entrance of the four-storied offices of one of the diving community's oldest businesses. Alex had thought it might be fun to be a part of this project. He had never done any work with US Diver before. But knowing that its tradition was built on Jacques Cousteau and his research, from the magazine to the line of dive equipment, he thought it might be fun to be a small part of that tradition.

Alex stepped to the front reception counter. "Hello. I'm Alex McPherson. I have an appointment to see Samuel Alt this morning."

"Thank you. Just a moment sir." After looking to her computer screen, the receptionist looked back to Alex. "I'm sorry, sir, you said Samuel Alt?"

"Yes, he and I were to meet today to discuss a project in the research department."

"I'll contact that department sir. Just another moment, please."

A few moments later, a casually dressed man came toward Alex with the relaxed stride of a fit man. "Hello, I'm Sam Alt. Can I help you?"

"Hello. Alex McPherson." Alex watched the puzzled look on the man's face and then continued, "It appears you've not heard my name before."

"I'm sorry, sir, I've not. I understand you believed we were to meet concerning a research project."

"That's what I understood."

"I do head up our research department at this location, but I didn't make a call or authorize any calls to you concerning any project we're working on. I'm sorry for any confusion we may have been a part of."

"No, don't apologize. It appears that someone has been playing a joke on me. May I use a phone?"

"Of course, come on into my office. I can offer you some privacy there."

Mark's body was almost entirely in the boat's engine compartment staring at the carburetor assembly when he started cussing.

"What?" Tony questioned.

"The stupid fuel line's been cut," shouted Mark. "It's only a small cut, cut really low on the line, but it's a cut, all right. We're lucky it leaked directly into the runoff basin and away from the block. That's why we didn't have a fire." Mark paused for a moment, still staring at the engine, and then continued, "But who would cut the line? And why was it cut just at that point?" After another thoughtful pause, Mark started climbing out of the engine compartment proclaiming, "This was not luck; this was timed." He did a slow 360, looking out across the sea. "Probably by *them*. Get your gear on—now!"

Tony looked where Mark had looked and saw the barely visible image of three dots growing larger as they came closer, cutting swiftly across the waves. Without any further hesitation, the two donned their scuba gear.

"Here," Mark told Tony hurriedly, "take two extra tanks each, and wrap these bungee cords around them to hold them together in case we need to stay down for a while. Attach a surfacing bladder to each set. They'll get heavy after a while, and we can keep them buoyant with these."

Just as the two were slipping over the far side of the boat, they heard cracking sounds from the boat's hull. Mark looked and then shoved Tony off the rail and into the water. "They're shooting at us!"

Tony and Mark submerged and went under the boat, resting just beneath their hull. They knew they would be visible otherwise. The water was very clear in this part of the ocean. A diver could be eighty feet down, look up at two boats on the surface and easily distinguish which boat was his.

Each with a dive slate, they could communicate if needed. But for now, a slate wasn't necessary. The look in their eyes said it all: "Wait—stay still—what is going on?—wait."

They saw the three smaller speedboats converge on their boat. They heard more thumping sounds they guessed to be more shots being fired at their boat. Then one of the three speedboats came close enough to touch the hull of their boat. They saw the boats moving in rhythm, swaying as one with the ocean.

Both Mark and Tony had their hands up against the bottom of their boat's hull, trying to get a sense of what was happening topside. When they felt their boat being boarded, Mark and Tony looked at one another and each could feel the rage the other was exuding by their expressions through their masks.

They felt more than one of the pirates moving around, apparently searching the entire boat. They heard what sounded like abrupt metal to metal contact, followed by a *ker-plunk* splash sound at the rear of the boat. Looking intently to see what hit the water and began sinking quickly, Mark and Tony mouthed the same word "carburetor."

Soon after that, two of the boats turned away and headed back in the direction they had come from—not toward the island but further out to sea. There was still movement on their boat as they watched the third speedboat begin to follow the other two. They'd left someone behind, maybe more than one.

Mark and Tony watched each other's faces as they tried to work out this puzzle they were in the middle of, when Tony's eyes went wide. He pulled his slate out and wrote, "They're waiting for Mom!"

Tony started away from their position beneath the hull, but Mark grabbed his arm and gave him a "wait" sign. Mark pulled out his own slate. "You may be right. What do you think you're going to do?"

Tony wrote on his own slate, "Have to get this guy before Mom gets here!"

Mark returned, "No. They're armed. We need to wait."

"For what?" Tony wrote in exasperation.

Before Mark could respond, they heard the sound of twin diesels approaching. They turned toward the direction of the island to see the hull of Angela's boat gently moving closer to their own boat. Mark had to hold Tony back while shaking his head feverishly "No!"

Angela's boat gently bumped their boat's side rail. A moment later they heard and then saw the three speedboats racing back toward them. Through the hull of their boat they felt the quick movement of the pirate who had stayed behind, apparently struggling with Angela.

Tony's face was livid; it showed both fear and rage as he faced Mark. Mark was no coward—anything but. Mark was ex-military, British Navy Seal, and he would often judge how successful a party was by the quality of the fight that broke out. But Mark knew when to fight and when not to fight. Mark's call was that now was not the time.

Mark gave Tony a pleading "wait" sign with his right hand as well as with his eyes. Tony relaxed some. They became more attuned to the activity topside. There was no movement on their boat—none at all. Mark pointed to Angela's boat, and the two of them kicked their way beneath its hull while continuing to use their own hull as cover.

They again sensed movement. At least three, maybe four, people were on Angela's boat.

Mark pulled out his slate and began writing quickly. He handed it to Tony. It read, "They plan on taking her with them on her boat. They think we are diving, and they have thrown away our carburetor to keep us stranded here."

Tony wrote in response, "I think you're right. What do we do?"

Mark wrote, "We stay with them. We have air for hours. We're shallow—no problem."

Tony wrote, "Stay with them?"

Mark wrote, "Until it's our turn to make a move."

Tony wrote, "Make a move?"

Mark wrote, "Of course. We're not waiting out of fear. We're waiting for our best chance to be most effective."

Tony wrote, "Then what?"

Mark wrote, "We move, and we move hard!"

Tony nodded in agreement as they felt the twin diesels of Angela's boat start. Mark shot a look at the two O-ring clamps attached to the hull of Angela's boat, one on either side of the center line. These clamps were normally used for group dives. The team would attach cables to the clamps and dangle a couple of extra tanks of compressed air about twenty feet down for the divers who were nearing the completion of their dives and might be running low on air for their final decompression stop.

Mark reached into one of the pockets of his dive vest and pulled out a strap about three feet long with clips on either end. Tony understood and began doing the same. They each clipped one end of their personal strap to the hull and the other end to an O-ring on their dive vests. Almost immediately the boat began to move. Now attached to Angela's hull, they began to move as well, further out to sea.

CHAPTER 10

Alex had dialed and was waiting when he heard, "Admiral Sterling here." His voice was more gruff than normal for this time of day. It was still midmorning, but the admiral sounded as if he had been sleep-deprived for a day or two.

"Admiral, this is Alex McPherson. Admiral—"

"Alex, give me your number. I'll return your call on a secure line."

Following the end of the first call, Alex asked if he could have privacy from the man whose office he had just commandeered. After a brief moment, Admiral Sterling was back on the line. "We appear to have a situation here," he told Alex. "I've just received a call reporting that the pirates are now active in the waters surrounding the Cayman Islands. The report comes from the Coast Guard, who just found an unmanned dive boat adrift near the Stingray City dive sites. Alex, she's one of yours. Now, before you say anything, I've had my secretary trying to get Angela on the line at your home, with no success. I was just handed the message that we got hold of with the girl in your dive shop, Stacy, who said she called Angela to let her know that Mark and Tony had some mechanical trouble near the Stingray City dive location and that Angela was going out to give them a tow back to the shop. That's the last she heard."

"I'm in Galveston. It'll take me a couple of hours to get back home. I'm headed there as soon as we hang up. If you hear anything—"

"I'll call you that very minute."

Alex went directly to the local airport's private booking hanger and arranged with a pilot for an immediate departure back to Grand

306

Cayman on a small seaplane. That way Alex could land near their home on Rum Bay rather than face the delay of going to the island's airport.

In ninety minutes Alex was walking into his front door. During the flight, Alex had tried to telepathically connect with Angela, hoping she was near enough. He felt nothing, nothing but concern. These circumstances did not sit well. As he thought about the diversion pulling him to Galveston, the mechanical failure on Mark and Tony's boat, and Angela's disappearance, Alex shook violently at his core.

He went to the phone and read the indicator telling him there had been six missed calls. Before he had the chance to think about them, the phone rang. Almost without the hint of any emotion, Alex answered the phone, "Hello."

A voice that spoke like a helpful hotel attendant addressing a valued customer said, "Mister McFearson, good; you are home at last."

Still very cold and in flat tones, Alex answered, "My name is McPherson. Who is this?"

Unfazed by Alex's retort, the caller continued, "We have your wife, whatever you choose to call yourself. You will need to listen closely if you plan on seeing her lovely eyes again."

Alex slowly growled, "I'm waiting."

"Yes, you are. The Skipper needs a favor. From what he tells us, you can perform this favor for him better and faster than anyone else. This is to your advantage. For you see, if you refuse or fail the Skipper," his tone slowing contorted, and he sounded like a lustful voyeur, "you will never see your wife's lovely eyes, legs, hips, and so on—either dead or alive."

Alex was still slowly growling. "What do you want?"

Completely returning to his helpful-hotel-clerk voice, the man replied, "Good; we have your attention. The Skipper, as I said, needs a favor. It seems a team assigned to a project of some importance to the Skipper experienced a disastrous calamity that prevented it from reaching a successful conclusion. As a result of this calamity, the Skipper has lost possession of his property. The Skipper would like for you to do whatever it takes to retrieve his property and return it safely to him. A simple request, to say the least."

The growling tone was still there in Alex's voice. "I want to speak with Angela."

"No. That is simple as well. No games, no negotiations, no playing ball, as you Americans like to say. If this is not acceptable, we will erase your wife and seek other means of retrieving the Skipper's property."

Without the growl, Alex responded painfully with "Wait. Where's the property?"

"The location of the Skipper's property will be discussed with you in a moment. Do we have your commitment in this matter? If not—"

Alex's voice went from the pained tone it had slipped temporarily into back to its slow, low growl. "Yes, you have my undivided attention and my unswerving commitment in this matter."

"Excellent. A deal has been established, then. You retrieve and return to the Skipper his property within seventy-two hours, and we will then rejoin you with your lovely wife."

The man continued, after a brief pause, "You will find placed on your kitchen counter an envelope containing the coordinates of the Skipper's property. It is in Alaska, so delaying the start of your endeavor would not be wise, given the short amount of time available to you. I will give you a moment to find and open the envelope."

Alex went quickly to the kitchen and found a crisp, white letter-size envelope on the counter. He saw nothing else in the kitchen that appeared to be disturbed.

While the man was silent and Alex was starting to open the envelope, Alex sensed Angela. His thoughts began to speak to her, *Angela?*

Alex! It's you. Oh, thank God! I'm all right. Tony and Mark were not in sight when I arrived to their boat. These people drugged me before we left the area. I have no idea where I am, except for the strong smell of the sea, and we're on a dressed-up oil rig. Do what they want and then come get us the hell out of here!

Alex's face contorted a bit as he asked, *Angela, what do you mean by "us"?*

Tony and Mark attached themselves to the underside of my boat and rode here with me. Mark was able to sneak his way to the door of this room, in the middle of the night, and tell me he and Tony were hiding out on my boat. Mark said my boat's tied to the oil rig's undergirding. He said he would keep an eye out for you—he knew you would come. But he says the security is too tight for the two of them to try anything on their own. I'm worried for them, but I feel a bit better knowing they are at least safe for the moment. I wasn't sure when I found their boat.

It was at this moment that Alex first sensed, only briefly, the existence and depth Angela's physical pain. She must have shut those feelings off before to keep them from Alex. *Are you sure you're all right?*

Oh, I hurt a bit. You know how much I like to be forced to do something I don't want to do. I let a few of them have it when I woke from my druggy nap. But there were too many of them, and the Skipper, well, when he heard what I had done, he honored me with a personal visit.

Painfully, Alex asked, *Angela, what did he do?*

I was tied to this chair by then. He hit me a couple of times to show his crew he was still in charge. He hasn't been back since.

Alex's thoughts were interrupted by the Skipper's henchman, "Mister McFearson, have you reviewed the contents of the envelope? Do you understand the location requirements?"

Growling again, but with more energy, Alex replied, "I said, the name is McPherson." With that Alex heard Angela laugh. She obviously was still connected to Alex through the phone. "And yes, I understand where the property is located. Where do I take it once I have it?"

"You will be contacted at your home again in three days. Take the property there, and we will give you further instructions at that time." The man's voice changed again to that of the lustful voyeur. "Make no mistake—if you fail, you will never see your wife again, but the things she will see will frighten and enlighten her to no end."

Alex sent one last thought to Angela: *I love you. I will come and get you all. Stay strong.* Then Alex responded to the man, saying in his now-controlled tiger growl, "Tell Peregrine I'll get his diamonds—I promise. Yes, I know the property we're talking about is diamonds. And tell your Skipper I'm making him a second promise—he's dead."

With that, Alex ended the call.

CHAPTER 11

"**A**dmiral, I need your help."

"Whatever you need is yours."

"I need a flying boat waiting for me in Alaska, at the Juneau air field, fully fueled and ready to go at 6:00 a.m. tomorrow."

"Do you have capacity requirements?"

"It needs to be capable of carrying a ten-thousand pound payload within at least a one hundred-cubic-foot cargo area."

The admiral only paused for a moment. "The Antilles G-21G Super Goose can do that easily, especially if we pull all her passenger seats. How many passengers?"

"Just two of us, Rene and me."

"It's obvious you'll need their cold-weather package if you want her in Alaska. What else do you need?"

"Thank you, Admiral. I don't know at this point."

"First off, you're welcome. I figure if you wanted my help in any other way, you knew all you needed to do was ask. You didn't, so I'm not asking questions. About the plane, you'll be able to easily identify the Antilles. She's a bright blue-and-yellow twin turbo prop, about forty feet long, with about a fifty-foot wingspan. You'll need a flight plan; I'll make one up. You taking the plane somewhere other than back to Juneau?"

"Back to Grand Cayman."

"Okay. I'll have papers waiting to certify your pilot for that plan and that area."

"Thank you again. I'll let you know when I have Angela and Tony back and this is over."

"Alex, if you need anything else—anything else—all you need to do is ask."

Alex had already called Rene, found him at home, and explained the situation. Rene assured Alex he would arrange for a leased personal jet and have it fueled and ready to go by the time Alex made it to the Grand Cayman airport. Grand Cayman was a common location for personal jet travel, and there was lots of availability.

True to his word, Rene had Alex in the air within an hour of Alex's call. Rene's flight plan was direct, and the fuel capacity of this twin jet-powered Elite 275 would take them to just south of the Canadian border for refueling. They might have been able to make it all the way to Juneau without a refuel, but it was better to be safe than sorry, and better in the States than in Canada—there would be fewer questions.

Alex and Rene landed in Juneau at 5:00 a.m. local time. They had traded off flight time and slept in shifts. Going directly to the outgoing terminal, they found the Antilles Super Goose fueled and ready, with two navy guards watching her. "Mister McPherson, the admiral sends his regards. The plane has been readied and checked out. You're good to go, sirs." With that, the two navy guards walked away from the plane, allowing them to board.

Airborne, Rene and Alex remained as silent as they had been for the journey from Cayman to Juneau. Alex had explained to Rene that Angela and Tony were in trouble and that Alex needed to go to Alaska, make a series of dives to bring up cargo, and then make the return flight to Cayman with the cargo. Beyond that, Alex hardly spoke, and Rene didn't ask.

"GPS says we've arrived at the coordinates. We're two hours out from Juneau, about 7:30 a.m." Rene continued, "Now, let's find a place to set this Goose down."

"There're patches of open water, but it's riddled with floating ice. I'm gonna have to bounce her down into a landing. Ready?"

"Let's do it."

Rene turned the plane toward the most-open patches above the coordinates and began taking the Goose to the water. Rene now brought her to about five feet above the surface.

"This is gonna sound painful." The seaplane lowered to the surface and began scraping across floating ice to water and back to floating ice. The sound was like a crying whale being slashed at with a chain saw. The Goose bounced and slowed; cried, bounced, and slowed; and cried some more, until Rene was able to pull her slowly up onto a larger piece of ice about the size of a basketball court and stop her there.

"Best I could do," he said as he turned to Alex.

"You're good, man. Wow!"

"Now what?"

"It's just before 9:00 a.m. our time. We have until noon tomorrow to get this done and get home to Rum Bay. I'll need your help when I bring the packages up and get them into the plane. It may take a while. As I understand, there are 120 milk crates of rocks down there, weighing about eighty pounds each. I'll find them, float them to the top with these buoyancy carriers, and you and I can get them into the plane. First, I've got to go find them. Be back when I've found some."

In his Arctic Blue dry suit, wearing his mask and with his e-reg in his mouth, carrying ten flattened inflatables and a couple of small compressed air canisters connected to D-rings on his suit, Alex went into the water.

Alex went slowly toward the bottom, scanning methodically from left to right and right to left, searching for the vehicles loaded with the cargo he was after. The bottom didn't present itself until Alex was five hundred feet down. He checked his diver's GPS and confirmed that they were at the given coordinates. There was nothing here.

The sea bed was smooth and cluttered with sea creatures looking quite at home in this thirty-eight degree saltwater landscape. But nothing looked out of place. The water temperature was a bit warmer as Alex went deeper, closer to the earth and further from the Arctic air, but the deep-freeze chill was still evident—even to Alex. "Where are they?" he asked himself.

Alex marked the spot directly beneath the flying boat with a brightly colored flag from one of his cargo pockets. He then took a second flag out and placed it directly north of the base flag. He then set off in that direction, searching unsuccessfully for fifteen minutes. He returned to the flag's location and moved the second flag to the south side of the primary flag and set off in that direction.

Using his oversized dive light, Alex fanned it slowly from left to right. Though Alex's vision had adjusted to the darkness and the dive light seemed needless, he chose to use it for ultimate vision opportunity. Alex went south from his base flag, continuously fanning the dive light for fifteen minutes, to no avail.

Returning to the base flag's position, he adjusted the second flag to the east and set out. After fifteen minutes to the east, he had seen nothing. As he began to turn, he saw a slight glitter reflected by his dive light, just a bit east-southeast from his current position. Making a quick decision, Alex set out toward the glitter.

There it was. The rear of one of the Range Rovers, a full ten minutes further. Upon reaching the rear of the Rover, Alex could see that the cargo area was full. He looked at his dive GPS, noted the discrepancy in the identified coordinates, and calculated the additional distance he was from the location of the Goose on the surface.

This is going to take longer than I planned. If I can angle my descent to these coordinates, it will take about thirty minutes from this Rover to the plane for each trip. The other Rovers are further up—I can just make them out. They may take about forty minutes from the second Rover and about fifty minutes from the third. Alex paused and thought, *Well, it's not going to get done on its own.*

Alex opened the rear of the Rover and began attaching the inflatables to the crates, one per crate. He thought it lucky that the crates were sealed in Visqueen—it would make them more portable without the concern of dumping their contents onto the sea floor. With the buoyancy bladders now inflated from the compressed air and attached to ten crates, Alex guided five crates with each hand along the calculated hypotenuse to the surface.

His math was good. Alex came out of the water just at the plane. Rene was standing on the ice, where he appeared to have been searching for Alex. He saw him and visibly gave a large sigh of relief. "Not where they were supposed to be?"

Alex replied, "No. Gonna take longer. Don't dare move the plane in all of this. If we damage the Goose, we're done for."

Rene pulled the crates, one by one, from Alex and placed them just into the plane's cargo area. "I'll move them further back during your next dive. Now that you've found them, what kind of return timing do you figure?"

"Each dive will take about an hour for the first Rover, then about an hour and twenty for the second, and about an hour and forty for the third one. All in all, I figure we have all of them by about midnight our time. It's gonna be close. I've got to keep moving."

"Can you do that? I mean, you never really told me the whole story, but I know you're not normal."

Alex gave him a quirky smile.

"Oh, you know what I mean!"

"I know. I can do this. But I do need your help with the cargo loading; I've got to keep at this. We're on an unforgiving time clock."

"Then quit jawing at me and go get me some more rocks."

Alex smiled, turned, and went back on his trajectory course, this time straight to the Rover.

The second and third trips went as the first. On what was to be the fourth and final trip from this Rover, Alex could now see two things. He could now see into the passenger area, where there were four dead men still sitting in the seats they'd died in, looking forward as if still driving.

He could also see that there had only been thirty-seven crates in the cargo area, but he knew there were supposed to be forty. *They must have put them in the passenger area since the cargo area was full.*

Alex left the remaining seven crates in the back of the Rover and kicked gently to the right side of the vehicle. He peered inside and beheld the gruesome sight of the dead men in their seats. He could now see their faces clearly. He looked to the floor area and saw two crates in the backseat floor area and the remaining crate in the front passenger floor area. *I bet this will be the case in the other two Rovers as well. That's just great.*

Ignoring as best he could the stiff bodies of the men whose feet were resting on the remaining crates, Alex pulled the three crates to the rear of the Rover. He connected the inflatables to the ten crates and began the final journey from this Rover back to the plane.

"That's forty. How's it going?"

Alex was a little slow to respond. "I found the dead crooks in the first Rover on this last trip. I know they got their just rewards after what they did to Evie's people when they stole this crap, but it still bothers me that I have to mess with them in their current state. Just another new experience I owe to the Skipper."

"How you doin'?"

"Could use a quick cup of coffee, if you have some made."

Seeming surprised, Rene responded, "I'll have a fresh pot ready for your next visit. The Goose is well appointed and the cupboards are full, thanks to the navy."

"Deal; be back this time in about an hour and twenty." With that, Alex submerged again to begin his search of the second Rover.

Having found the first, he had no trouble finding the second. It was right where Alex had expected it to be and sitting in the same orientation as the first. Alex went through the same process he had honed on the retrieval of the first Rover's cargo.

This time, though, something was different. Alex was becoming cold—very cold—and he could hardly wait for that cup of coffee Rene had promised. It had been about five hours since he'd started looking for the first Rover. More than that, fatigue seemed to be setting in, as well. This was a feeling Alex had not felt since before his encounter with the hammerheads and the experiences that had followed.

Alex began to worry that he might not be up to the task. Angela's and Tony's lives depended on his succeeding, and he told himself there was no alternative, but he was starting to get tired and cold, and he was nowhere near finished.

The second Rover was now emptied and the crates from it delivered to the plane. Rene was as good as his word and had a cup of fresh, hot coffee for Alex each time Alex returned to the surface. Alex nearly guzzled the hot coffee, and it felt good and warming, but the feeling did not last long. He was getting chilled to the bone. He was shivering steadily now, and he still had the third Rover to empty.

He thought of increasing the number of crates he brought back and maybe clean out the third Rover on three trips instead of four, but he'd nearly lost control of the crates on the last trip. If he lost the crates while bringing them to the surface, there wasn't much chance he would ever find them again in the open sea. They would be lost forever.

No, five per hand, ten total—he had to stick to the plan. But he was wearing out.

Upon Alex's first return from the third Rover, Rene surprised him with a hot cup of soup instead of coffee. It seemed to warm Alex a little deeper than the coffee had, but when Alex again submerged into the freezing depths of the Arctic Sea, the warmth rapidly dissipated and the bone-aching cold took over again.

He was now surfacing with the third batch from the third Rover. He was quaking so violently that he nearly cramped up and released the inflatables' cables. He got control of himself just in time, but the episode put him off course, and he surfaced one hundred yards from Rene and the flying boat.

When he was thirty feet from the plane, Rene was able to throw a line to Alex and pull him the rest of the way to the plane.

"You've got to call it quits, my friend. You're all in."

"Can't. Angela and Tony's lives are at stake. Can't stop till we got it all," was Alex's reply. His speech was so garbled that Rene did not understand a word, but he understood the tone and handed Alex another cup of hot soup.

"All right, then," Rene spouted as he accepted the empty soup cup from Alex, "if you're not going to get out of the water now, then get your lazy butt back down there and bring up those last ten crates. Stop screwing around, and get your butt in gear!"

Alex smiled and said, "You're a lousy meanie. You just don't have it in you—but thanks for the effort. I'm on it, boss."

Rene slowly shook his head as Alex submerged. He still hadn't been able to understand a word Alex said. Alex had been shaking so violently on this return that it was a surprise he was able to keep his regulator in his mouth. And what Rene did not tell his friend was that his trips were taking much longer than Alex thought. It was obvious that Alex had lost all concept of time. The last two trips should have taken an hour and forty minutes each. Each had taken well over two hours. Alex was moving barely faster than the dead men he'd described sitting in the Rovers at the bottom of the frigid sea. Even worse, Alex was in such bad shape that he didn't realize how slowly he was moving.

Alex found the third Rover in what felt like an eternity to him. He had made an error in direction and found the first Rover instead. He panicked, believing that the vehicle was empty, that the sea had turned against him and washed away the final ten crates—the ten crates he needed to save Angela and Tony.

Then he saw the glitter from the second Rover ahead and realized his mistake. He punched the first Rover on the fender and kicked to the second Rover, passing it and finally arriving at the third Rover and the remaining ten crates.

He had the inflatables in place and the ten crates were on their way to the surface when he began to convulse from the cold shivers racking his body. He nearly lost the inflatables. He did lose his e-reg—it fell from his mouth and began dropping to the sea floor.

Reacting with all the energy he had left, to save first his own life and subsequently the lives of Angela, Tony, and Mark, Alex kicked hard downward, and he found his e-reg resting on top of the third Rover's roof. Alex grabbed it with hands shaking so badly he could not get the e-reg back in his mouth on the first, second, or third tries.

Somehow he finally managed to get the e-reg back in his mouth. His body was shaking so much that Alex could hardly kick his fins evenly. He wrapped his arms around the outside of the inflatables' cables, clenching them to his chest, and placed both hands on his e-reg. With all the concentration he could muster, he held it in place, pressed desperately in his mouth by both hands.

He headed for the surface and robotically kicked and kicked his fins. He pushed hard, knowing he was about to give out. There was no concentration, no thinking, no sensation. He was just kicking and gripping for his life the e-reg clenched precariously between his teeth.

When Alex awoke, he was groggy and motionless. He saw Rene sitting in his pilot's seat and he could still feel what he thought was the movement of the ocean fighting against him, keeping him from surfacing just one last time. He could not speak.

"Relax, buddy," Rene spoke. "You're out of the water now. All of the cargo is out of the water and in the plane. We're in the air and on our way home."

Alex croaked, "How?"

Rene gently responded, "You bobbed up out of the water like a fishing bobber. You must have put the last of the compressed air into your BC vest, and you shot right up. I thought you were dead, but I threw a rope at you, hooked you with a lasso I added to the end, and pulled you over to the plane." Sounding exasperated, Rene added, "You would not let go of your regulator, which made it nearly impossible for me to get those inflatables from you, but I did, and you're here, and we're on our way home. So sleep; we'll talk later."

Rene touched down in Rum Bay just before eleven in the morning. When he touched the water and the plane jarred, Alex awoke. He had slept the entire trip, including the refueling stop Rene had been forced to make in Galveston.

"Where are we?"

"Ole buddy, we're home. You feeling alive at all?"

"Too soon to tell, but I understood your question, and I gotta think that's a good sign."

With a relieved smile on his face, Rene responded, "You're making sense for a change, too. That is a good sign."

"What time is it?"

"About a quarter to eleven in the morning. I think we're in time."

"We are. I gotta get to the house. They're supposed to be calling at noon."

"We'll be in the house before noon."

CHAPTER 12

P recisely at noon, Alex was picking up the phone. The call was cold and to the point; no discussion except for the coordinates for the exchange. Alex tried, but the caller hung up after speaking the information only once.

Immediately after the call, Alex started walking toward the rear door of his home. Standing there for a moment in his khaki-colored cargo pants and loose fitting island shirt, Alex looked out toward the flying boat. The Antilles, in view from his doorway, seemed to wait restlessly, tied firm at the far end of the extended dock. Her blue-and-yellow fuselage was scarred just above the waterline from scraping against the Alaskan ice that had tried to prevent their escape just twelve hours earlier. But floating gently on the warm azure water, she looked as if she had just begun to fight and was ready for more. She looked the way Alex felt—they both had endured Alaska and were now feeling their second wind.

"I'm not going with you, am I?" Rene stated.

"You know as well as I do it's a trap." Alex was calm, matter of fact.

"And where Angela and Tony are concerned, a trap is no deterrent, is it?" Rene didn't expect an answer, and he didn't get one. He only received an extremely calm look from Alex in return. "Call me when you get back. You can buy me a beer."

"You're on."

Rene loosened the line from the dock. The twin turbo props roared to life at Alex's first touch of the starter. "Good girl." The stop at

Galveston for fuel had given the Goose more than enough for a round trip, if needed, from the coordinates now set into the navigation unit.

Alex was truly feeling his second wind, but he still felt sluggish. He still had no memory of what Rene described as his final extraction from the Alaskan Sea. His thoughts lingered a bit on what may have been his near death. How was that possible? The question was more of an investigative question rather than one of doubt. It was a topic to be examined later; for now, he needed to focus.

Alex circled the coordinates before angling for his landing. He counted three speedboats surrounding a medium-sized yacht. As he landed, the three boats converged on his location, while the yacht held back. Each speedboat had two occupants: a driver and a second man aiming an automatic weapon at the Goose. Alex cut his engines as one of the three boats came close enough to talk.

"Stay in your seat until we tell you otherwise."

Alex sat still. The yacht now started moving toward the Goose. Moving its nose toward the rear of the Goose, the yacht stopped with its eighty-foot hull forming a nontouching hypotenuse as its foredeck extended just past the flying boat's tail section and the yacht's aft section, extending just past the right wing's extension. The next moves came from the speedboats moving to form a line of stepping stones between the side cargo door of the Goose and the side cargo door of the yacht.

The man in the speedboat closest to the Goose called to Alex to open the plane's cargo door. Alex moved carefully from the pilot's seat to the door and slid it open.

"Now," said the man doing all of the talking, "start off-loading, one crate at a time. Hand it to my partner here." The second man in the lead speedboat now stood in the middle of his boat. This boat was sitting in line with the Goose's fuselage. He took the first crate from Alex, turned to face the opposite side of the small boat, and handed it to one of the men in the second boat. The second and third boats were positioned perpendicular to the Goose, with the rear of the second boat positioned just to the right of the front of the third boat.

The man in the second boat took a few steps and handed the crate to the other man in his boat, who took two steps to the rear of the second boat. He then handed the crate over to the man who waited at the front of the third boat. This first man on the third boat then took a few steps and handed the crate to the second man on his boat, who went to the rear of the third boat and handed the crate to the waiting hands of men standing at the cargo door of the yacht.

With the three speedboats tied to one another, the lead boat tied to the Goose, and the rear boat tied to the yacht, they all stayed fairly stable throughout this process. Each crate went through all the hands until it had been passed from the Goose to the yacht. They off-loaded 120 crates in all.

"Do you have anything else for us?" the first man in the first boat asked Alex. He had obviously been counting and knew he had all of the 120 crates.

"That's it," responded Alex. "Now where do I go to find my wife? What message did your Skipper send me?"

The voice of the man in the speedboat was now very clear. As he spoke, Alex became aware that he was the man on the phone, the man with the helpful hotel clerk's voice. "The Skipper did send a message. The Skipper says in reply to your message to him, 'No, *you* are the dead one.'"

With that comment, the man lifted his gun and quickly fired three shots at Alex's heart. "Let's get out of here; we're done." They untied each of the boats, and the speedboats began clearing away from between the Goose and the yacht.

"Ouch!" Alex rubbed his chest. Knowing it was a trap, he had worn a Kevlar vest under his floral island shirt. "That hurts more than they tell you in the movies." He moved toward the open door and saw that the three speedboats were gone and the yacht was just starting to move away from the Goose. Alex dove headlong into the water and kicked hard for the yacht's under-hull. He had guessed correctly and was able to firmly grasp the sonar antenna under the front third of the yacht. Reaching into one of the pockets of his cargo pants, Alex retrieved his e-reg and placed it firmly into his mouth. Now able to breath, Alex reached into a second pocket of his cargo pants and pulled out a bungee cord. He wrapped it around the under-hull antenna and then wrapped the other end around his left hand. *I miss my BC vest,* he thought. *D-rings galore.*

Clinging firmly to the cord connecting him to the under-hull of the yacht, Alex started to realize how refreshing the warm ocean water felt. *Maybe this'll help me forget about feeling chilled to the bone last night.*

But as time passed and the warm ocean water rushed by him, with the yacht now at full speed, Alex realized it was more than just warming the memory of the cold from his bones. *I feel stronger. More than that, I feel healed. Makes sense to me now! I was changed by warm-water creatures in a warm-water setting. I'm guessing, if I didn't know it already, I'm a warm-water creature myself, through and through. The prolonged exposure to the cold water was killing me, while this prolonged exposure to the warm water is revitalizing me.* Knowing she couldn't hear him yet, Alex still formed the words, *Angela, I'm on my way. It won't be long now.*

Instead of being able to hear Alex, Angela was at that same moment being forced to listen to the Skipper. "I have just been informed that your beloved husband is not as smart as you and I thought he was. He willingly walked right into a trap. He underestimated my resolve. Now he is dead as a result of his mistake. True love is so blind."

"You're lying." Angela held her resolve.

"What is the benefit of me lying to you? Other than your physical gifts, which I may choose to partake of later, you have nothing I need."

"True love is not blind," Angela spouted out while working to buy time. "What would you know of true love, anyway?"

"Ah, I see your point. I knew love before. I was married once. A lovely girl with many of the same physical gifts you possess. Now that I think of it, the two of you look very much alike. This could prove more satisfying than I first thought. Nonetheless, she was the only woman for me. We had started a small import-export business, located near the docks in Malta. We were making ends meet and starting to make a bit more than we were spending. Our shipping business had the promise of a good, but small, future to it.

"On a dark and stormy night—I just love saying that line—I was approached by a man with an offer for extreme business growth. He wanted to partner with our small shipping business and arrange for us to handle the products he was shipping in from South America. We would accept the South American imports, repackage them, and export them to the States. His claim, and it has proven to be true, was that it would be worth millions of dollars to us.

"I liked the idea. I liked it a lot. But I knew my lovely wife would not accept the offer. She was as honest and forthright as she was beautiful. So, I needed a plan. For many nights I lay awake at night, resting in the bed next to her, working on the details of my plan.

"One weekend, we went camping on the Italian mainland. We had camped many times, and it was a very natural thing for us to do. But I chose this location based primarily on two things. We had never camped there before, and it possessed a beautiful landscape that included stark hills and ocean-carved cliffs.

"It was a beautiful location. When the time was right, I dragged my beautiful, now struggling, wife to the edge of a dramatic cliff and told her I could not let her stand in the way of my success. With that, I threw her over the cliff to the jagged rocks below. I am a cautious man, so I hiked down to the jagged rocks where she had landed.

"I am glad I did. The first fall had not killed her."

Angela interrupted with shock, "The first fall?"

"Yes, the first fall. I carried her broken body back to the top of the cliff and threw her over it again. She pleaded and cried, asking me why, but I ignored her. She was already dead to me. My decision had already been made. After the second, more successful, fall to those same jagged rocks, she was dead to everyone else, as well.

"I still had the rest of my plan to fulfill, so I picked up her broken, now assuredly dead, body and carried her the three miles to the nearest village, where I cried and explained how she must have accidently fallen while exploring in the darkness."

"You're a monster!" Angela was in shock.

"Possibly, but I knew at that point it was not true love. If it were true love, I might still be in that small shipping office with my wife to this day. So you see, true love *is* blind. He died for you, like a blind idiot."

"You're wrong about Alex, you warped, murderous creature. He's no idiot. You're the fool if you think this is over."

With that, calmly, the Skipper moved in close to Angela and began punching her repeatedly in the face, right then left then right again. After she fell unconscious, he said, "I don't want you dead yet. I want to try to relive a pleasant memory or two before I kill you."

CHAPTER 13

The yacht began slowing, and Alex could see the below the surface portion of an oil rig. *So this is where he hides; wise thinking, for a pirate.*

Alex stayed put while the yacht went still, directly next to the oil rig. He stayed there for half an hour. His fear was that now that the Skipper had what he wanted, Angela's life would be of no use to him any longer. Also, Alex had tried to communicate with Angela with no success. He was beginning to fear that either Angela was not being kept here or that he was too late.

I will not accept that I am too late. Alex began moving from beneath the yacht. It was near nightfall, and the dark could be his friend as he ventured onto the girding of the rig, still beneath the surface. Steadily he climbed until his head was just above the surface. He was still, listening for any sound. Hearing nothing but the gentle movement of the sea against the rig, Alex placed his e-reg back into a cargo pocket and continued his climb.

Nearing the main deck, now well hidden from sight, Alex heard movement. He turned his head to the left, just under the largest housing unit on the main deck. That's when he saw them. Moving closer, but saying nothing, Alex embraced his son and then Mark in silence.

It was Mark who first spoke. "We can talk if we keep it down. We have been over most of the rig, and this spot has the best protection from sight and sound."

"Later, Tony, I'll ask you what you were thinking when you decided to come out here."

"Dad, let me ask you: What were you thinking?"

Alex stared into his son's face for a moment and then replied, "Point made, son. Later I'll talk to you about how proud I am of you instead."

"If you two are done?" Mark spoke in a blurted whisper.

"Yeah, okay. What do you know about where they're keeping Angela?" Alex now spoke with regained focus.

Tony explained, "We know exactly where she is. She's not even locked in, but they keep a guard on her at all times." Mark and Tony continued to share with Alex the layout of the rig and Angela's precise location.

"Okay, here's what I want us to do. One of you waits here while the other one goes down to boats. Down there, I want you to cut the fuel lines of all but one of the speedboats. Make sure that one is fully fueled and ready to go. That boat will be your escape boat."

"What are you going to do?" asked Tony.

"I'm going to get your mom."

"I can go with you," Tony pleaded.

"We need three of us to make this work: one to get the boats ready, one to be his lookout and be ready to take Angela from me and get her down to the boat—"

Mark interrupted, "And one to cause a diversion to allow us to get away."

"Exactly," stated Alex.

"I understand." Tony paused and then added, "Mark, you are stronger than I am. You stay here and help Mom; with what she's been through, she may not be able to climb down on her own. I'll get the boats taken care of."

Mark looked at Tony and then to Alex, "Makes sense. Let's do it."

Alex bear-hugged Tony again and warmly shook Mark's hand, and then Tony and Alex set off while Mark stayed put. Tony began climbing down toward the area where the speedboats were tied. Alex started climbing toward his Angela.

The knowledge Mark and Tony had acquired while waiting for Alex was proving to be invaluable. The timing of the guard's steps, their pathways and rounds, had been measured so precisely that Alex didn't see a soul until he saw the single guard sitting lazily at the door that Alex knew Angela was behind.

Alex hadn't tried to connect with Angela since coming onto the rig, but now he did. *Angela? Can you hear me, my love?*

Alex! Yes, you feel so close! Angela's thoughts were so excited. *Where are you?*

Close; I need for you to call for your guard. Get him to come into your room.

All right. Angela started speaking out loud. "Guard, guard! I need help. I'm about to fall over."

"I don't care. You're already bruised up; a few more bruises won't bother the Skipper."

"If you don't help me now," Angela continued, "I'll tell your beloved Skipper you came in here and forced yourself on me. You and I both know he wouldn't like that. You know how he is with his possessions."

The guard looked troubled at that, "What do you want?" he said as he stood and entered the room, leaving the door open behind him.

"I don't want to fall over. I'm already sore enough."

Alex bolted down the short hall, into the room, and into the back of the guard, cupping his hand around the man's mouth and lower jaw. Then, he jerked his arm with such force that the man's neck gave out a bone-cracking sound that could not be confused with any other sound. Alex laid him to the floor as quietly as he could.

Alex began untying Angela, who had a look of shock on her face at the act that Alex had just committed on the guard. She had never seen Alex act with such malice and had never seen his face so detached from an act anywhere near that violent.

Noticing her expression, Alex said, "No time to talk now. We'll deal with this later. We've got to get you out of here."

"Tony? Mark?" Angela questioned.

"Waiting for you; ready to escape." Alex's tone was pleading for her to be quiet. Then he looked into her face for the first time during this meeting. He saw first her bruised and beaten face. He then saw her surprise at the way he had entered the room. Finally, he saw her reaction to his reaction to the condition of her face.

Angela whispered, "My love, I'm okay."

"You will be when we get you out of here and not until. Now, let's go. Can you walk?"

"I'll bet you a Diet Coke I can run if needed."

"That's my girl." And with that, they silently crept to where Alex knew, thanks to Tony and Mark, the guards would not be.

Alex delivered Angela safely to Mark, who then carefully guided her down the girding to the waiting speedboat and her son. Alex had explained the plan, and Angela had accepted it without question after seeing the continued look in his eyes and the overwhelming expression covering his entire face.

Alex went to the center of the main deck and started yelling. "I have come for my wife! Bring her to me, now!"

The Skipper slowly walked from the door of his private quarters, located one level above. He paused at the top of the metal stairs that connected his private level to the main deck. His neck turned slowly as he took in the sight.

Alex was at the end of the main deck furthest from the stairway. The Skipper's crew, about twenty of them, were on the same deck level as Alex, but they were on the stairway side of the rig.

Several of the crew had obviously been caught off guard by Alex's invitation. Many stood there without weapons. Alex quickly counted only three holstered handguns and one guy standing with a Remington single-barrel, pump-action shotgun. The shotgun was leveled in Alex's general direction.

Looking up to the Skipper, Alex said, "I will not repeat myself. I have come for my wife. Bring her to me."

Moving slowly down the stairs, the Skipper spoke calmly, hardly raising his voice,; it was unnerving, given that they were standing in the open air, on the main deck of an ocean-based oil rig, and he was still clearly heard. "Mister McFearson."

"The name is McPherson!"

Stopping midway down the stairway, the Skipper looked at Alex and asked, "Why do you keep correcting us? What is so important?"

"My name is important to me. My name is McPherson. I have explained that to you before: there is no *fear* in a McPherson."

"So you have." He continued down the stairs. "I won't play games with you. You know I have your wife. You know I made a deal to trade your wife for my diamonds. You know I tried to have you killed, and apparently failed at that attempt, fully ignoring our arrangement." Now reaching the main deck, taking only a few steps in Alex's direction, and standing just in front of his crew, the Skipper continued, "What makes you think I will deal with you now?"

Alex squared his shoulders and spoke directly to the Skipper, ignoring everyone else on the deck. "I think you would rather not die, and the only way you're going to escape death today is to bring my wife to me—right here, right now—and let us go our way."

The Skipper tilted his head slightly to the right, his dark eyes empty, with a shark-like grin still pasted to his face. "Not going to happen. You will finally die today. From my point of view, it is long overdue. As to the aspect of your wife, she will remain mine to do with as I wish, again and again, until I am bored with her cries of pain and pleas for release."

Still looking directly at the Skipper, Alex coldly breathed, "Guilty as charged; execution to be carried out at the earliest opportunity."

"Goodbye, mister …" the Skipper slowly enunciated his next words, "Mister McFearson."

Turning slowly around and starting to walk away from Alex to a point behind his crew, he spoke to his entire crew and to no one particular, "Take your time with him. Beat him to within an inch of his life. Take a break, and then beat him again. Make it last; make it painful; and then kill him and make it final." He growled out the last words, and then the Skipper walked away and started down the stairs that led to his yacht—the yacht loaded with the diamonds.

The twenty started spreading out around the deck. Alex accommodated them by moving forward, which allowed several of them to get behind him. "You guys have no idea, do you?"

With a murmur from a few of the crew, about four of them moved in quickly on Alex. Alex shed some of the punches, dodged some completely, and handed out a little punishment of his own when they came in close.

Alex's goal at this moment was a simple one; make enough noise and take enough time for Mark and Tony to get Angela and themselves away from the oil rig on the speedboat they had commandeered. So stalling, rather than winning, was Alex's first priority. Alex was quick. His immersion and rebaptism in the warm Caribbean Sea had returned Alex to full strength and full confidence.

When the group around Alex saw he was toying with them, they grew angry. No longer just on an assignment, now they were emotionally involved, and they started to lose control through frustration. Alex slipped a couple more punches, and then the four corners started at him at once. It was just as he had anticipated.

Alex half-turned to the right, in front of the man he was facing, and slammed his left triceps and elbow into the back of the man's head and neck. The rushing man continued forward, out of control, and crashed into the man who had been to Alex's rear. From his left, Alex saw the oncoming freight train of the third man, easily fifty pounds heavier and a few inches taller than Alex, coming at him with his hands above his head, ready to swing down with the baseball bat in his hands. Alex pivoted quickly toward and into the oncoming Goliath, getting there before the man's arm completed their swing downwards. Alex grabbed the man with both hands, gripped the shirt over the man's chest, and started pulling the man forward, increasing his already powerful forward motion. Alex then fell on his own back, placing his right foot firmly and quickly into the man's groin, and pushed up hard as the two fell to the ground. The man sailed over Alex in a speedy forward flip and collided with the man who had been to Alex's right—who hit himself in the face with the Remington military-grade shotgun he held close to his chest.

The result was quite satisfying to Alex. The flying Goliath had momentum working against him and was unable to stop. He plowed onto and through the fourth man, pommelling him while hitting himself in the head with the bat.

With the four on the floor, Alex shifted his attention. He could tell that the boat with Angela was gone and the yacht with the Skipper was ready to start pulling away from the rig. Alex snatched the Remington, ran to the edge of the rig just above the yacht, and leaped into the sea.

Quickly recovering from the jump, Alex made his way to the nearest part of the yacht, the rear port side where the short stationary ladder was attached. The climb was easy, and Alex was soon standing on the aft deck, as he listened and looked all around and then began his search for the Skipper.

The Skipper had first checked to see that the crates of raw diamonds were still in the cargo area under the foredeck. Feeling quite satisfied, he casually walked to his cabin suite located in the lower aft deck section. Pouring himself a celebratory drink, he then turned his music system on. The power of Mozart's Requiem was subdued only by the low volume setting.

Alex pushed the cabin door open slowly and walked in unnoticed. He stood there looking around the cabin at the ornate décor until the Skipper turned around and saw him.

"Well, well. Escaped, but left your wife behind. We are more alike than you may think. Revenge is the ultimate goal for you, as well."

"We are not at all alike. Revenge was not my ultimate goal, at least not until Angela was safe. Angela has been off the rig for some time now. That being said, and now that she is safe, I am in the mood for a large portion of revenge."

Alex lowered the Remington shotgun toward the lowest part of the side wall, just above the cabin's floor and pulled the trigger. The result was a hole punched through the side exterior wall, about ten inches in diameter.

The Skipper, responding to the damage to the boat, scoffed, "That's your revenge? The boat will sink, with you on it." Nearly laughing, he continued, "You are a joke. You cannot beat me with a move like that."

Alex calmly growled, "The hole in the wall was not my goal for revenge."

"Really? Then what is you plan?"

Alex muttered with a primal growl, "This is!" Alex threw down the gun, grabbed the Skipper around the back of his head, and head-butted him with such raw power that the Skipper was immediately dazed. "Now, what do they say about revenge? Something about it being served?"

Alex griped the Skipper, his right fist locked in the back collar of the Skipper's shirt and his left fist locked around the Skipper's belt at the rear of his waist. He stated, "This is me serving up some revenge."

Swiftly, Alex nearly threw the Skipper toward the cabin's side wall, where water was forcing its way in, never releasing his two-fisted grip, and jammed the Skipper's head into the hole. He felt the Skipper struggle for a few moments, and then the Skipper's body went limp.

Leaving the Skipper where he'd placed him, Alex walked quickly from the cabin and headed to the engine room. Looking around at the storage shelves, Alex pulled a can from the top shelf and returned to the Skipper's cabin. The water was now about two feet deep in the cabin, even though the influx of water was greatly decreased by the Skipper's predicament.

Alex positioned the can above the Skipper's head and began releasing the pressurized contents around the Skipper's neck. The leak stopped completely. "There now. Finally, value has been provided from your existence—you and a can of liquid steel." Alex threw the empty can at the Skipper's body and started walking from the cabin. "Game over," he said.

While the fight was going on, the Skipper's yacht crew, hearing the commotion, had taken a life boat and abandoned ship. Alex was alone on the yacht. Going to the bridge, Alex set a course on the computerized navigation unit for Rum Bay. He then went to the radio console and set the dial for a prearranged frequency.

"Admiral, are you monitoring this frequency?"

"Alex, good to hear from you boy! What's your status?"

"Angela, Tony, and Mark are safe and on their way home. I am piloting the Skipper's yacht with the stolen diamonds in her cargo area. Can you meet me in Rum Bay and take possession?"

"Of course. We'll be there when you arrive. What about the Skipper? Is he giving you any trouble?"

"He was not very cooperative at first, but now he is assisting in my return—not as a volunteer, but assisting nonetheless."

"I'm sure I'll understand that better later. We will expect to see you in three to four hours. I can't begin to tell to how I feel that you are all safe. The drinks are on me at our next gathering."

"You're on."

Then Alex changed the radio to the second planned frequency.

"Tony, Mark, do you read me?"

"Alex," Angela's voice nearly screamed through the radio, "Are you all right?"

"I'm fine; the Skipper's a bit worse for wear, though."

"Never mind him," Angela blurted abruptly. "Where are you?"

"On my way home. It'll take me a bit longer than you, but I'll be there."

"You'd better, mister, or you'll get yourself in trouble with me."

"Ah, you sweet talker. You know I love your kind of trouble. Be home soon."